D0334832

9030 00007 8589 7

One
Moonlit
Night

RACHEL HORE

One Moonlit Night

**SIMON &
SCHUSTER**

London · New York · Sydney · Toronto · New Delhi

First published in Great Britain by Simon & Schuster UK Ltd, 2022

1 3 5 7 9 10 8 6 4 2

Simon & Schuster UK Ltd
1st Floor
222 Gray's Inn Road
London WC1X 8HB

Simon & Schuster Australia, Sydney
Simon & Schuster India, New Delhi

www.simonandschuster.co.uk
www.simonandschuster.com.au
www.simonandschuster.co.in

A CIP catalogue record for this book
is available from the British Library

Hardback ISBN: 978-1-4711-8722-3
eBook ISBN: 978-1-4711-8724-7
Audio ISBN: 978-1-4711-8726-1

Typeset in Palatino by M Rules
Printed and bound by CPI Group (UK) Ltd, Croydon, CR0 4YY

MIX
Paper from
responsible sources
FSC® C171272

To the Harlow Twins, Phyllis and Anne,
who lived through this war.

London

Autumn 1977

Grace glanced at her watch. Had she been clear enough about the whereabouts of the tea shop? The woman was twenty minutes late and Grace had ordered tea to placate the waitress. What was an extra twenty minutes after thirty-six years, she mused as she poured milk into her cup. Perhaps her train was late or she'd got caught up in the tail end of the anti-racism protest dispersing from Trafalgar Square. She reassured herself with this notion.

The Earl Grey was fragrant and comforting. The plate of cakes looked shop-bought, but she selected a slice of Swiss roll, even now unable to resist sugar after a childhood without it. She and her sister still loved swapping opinions about their worst wartime dishes – ersatz gooseberry crumble had Grace's vote, but Sarah screwed up her face at the memory of tapioca. 'And we had to eat everything on our plate. My kids,' said Sarah, 'don't know they're born.'

Sarah had refused to come today. She was still angry, absolutely furious. Grace understood why, but she was more detached about it. It was funny how, despite their closeness, she and Sarah were such different people. Sarah was a housewife, mother of three and now grandmother to a one-year-old. Grace had remained determinedly single – 'a career girl', as everybody pigeonholed her, although she'd never been particularly ambitious, simply not interested in marriage and what she called 'that side of life'. She liked living on her own, knowing where everything was in her neat flat in Putney, and content in her work as a solicitor specializing in property law. Travel was her great thing. She'd learned Spanish and French at evening classes and spent most of her holidays abroad. She and her friend Milo had conducted their version of the hippy trail for three glorious weeks last autumn. India, Nepal and Thailand. Magical. The photograph albums were stacking up on the shelves. Greece, Spain, Australia, Kenya, the United States, the Soviet Union . . . said the labels. Grace had pen pals all over the world. She smiled as she remembered the travel brochure in her bag. South America was to be next. Somewhere they weren't having a revolution, she thought with a shiver, remembering a tricky episode in Egypt. She'd be forty soon and it would be wonderful to do something special with Milo to celebrate.

She dabbed up the crumbs from her Swiss roll, wiped her fingers on a paper napkin and gazed out of the window at the passers-by. Drat the woman. She hoped something wasn't wrong. When the letter had arrived, the one that had shocked them so much, Grace had been sent off balance, tipped back into the past, thoughts stirred up that she'd kept buried for years. She'd been amazed at how bravely her mother had accepted the news. It was a tragedy, as Sarah said, that their father wasn't around to deal with the fallout. Mother was so heroic. She always had been. Grace and Sarah adored her. She'd put up with so much, yet made a success of her life. After all, what child hadn't heard of Madeleine Anderson?

One

West Kensington, London

March 1941

There was a before and an afterwards. Later, Maddie would trace back to this moment the way her life changed.

A shaft of sunshine found its way through a rip in the blackout curtain. It played on Maddie Anderson's sleeping face, teasing her into awkward consciousness. She blinked and lay quiet, still caught on the coat-tails of her dream. In it her husband, Philip, had returned. He was searching blindly for her in the ruins of their home, shouting her name. She'd called back in anguish, but could not make her voice heard.

The dream faded. Maddie saw that she was in a narrow bed in a strange room with five-year-old Sarah's gently breathing body pressed hotly against hers. She sniffed. Her daughter's fine hair smelled of stale smoke. And now the awful memories tumbled in.

It hurt when she raised her head, but she was glad to see three-year-old Grace asleep on a mattress beside the bed. Grace had thrown off her blanket and lay curled in a ball, clutching her toy rabbit.

The rush of relief that the three of them were safe in Mrs Moulder's front bedroom was quickly succeeded by despair. Was last night's bomb damage as bad as she feared? Maddie had to see. Sliding out of bed, she gathered the folds of the unfamiliar flannel nightdress and went to push aside the curtain. Her gaze roved along the row of red brick-terraced houses opposite where neighbours were already out, boarding up broken windows, until she came to a smoking gap between the houses and caught her breath.

All that was left of Number 38, with its white-painted front door and low arched gate, was a cloud of dust and a heap of rubble spilt across Valentine Street. An open truck was parked nearby and in the pale spring sunshine two stalwart men in breeches and hard hats were shovelling debris into a wheelbarrow. Several onlookers idled about and as Maddie watched, a scrawny woman pointed a broom at what had been Maddie's stubby front garden with its pots of nodding daffodils, then darted forward. She tugged something out of the rubbish and brandished it in triumph. It appeared to be a doll. The woman was Norah Carrington from next door. Maddie inwardly groaned. The sight of that irritable busybody swinging one of her daughters' precious dolls by its leg was not to be borne. And then – she briefly closed her eyes – there was the matter of her missing handbag. She dropped the curtain and turned from the window. Never mind her headache and the ringing in her ears. She must *do* something.

She peered round the gloomy bedroom but saw only the pile of filthy rags they'd peeled off last night. Tears prickled. They had nothing, not even clothes to wear today. Just Rabbit, which Grace had been clutching when they were dragged from the air raid shelter. A small mercy, but it had soothed the anxious child to sleep after they'd reached the safety of Mrs Moulder's house at past three that morning.

Maddie stepped over Grace to reach the bedroom door and crept downstairs in her bare feet. Hesitating in the narrow hallway, she felt the eyes of sepia-tinted photographs of Moulder ancestors upon her and heard the sounds of Mrs Moulder preparing breakfast. When she pushed open the kitchen door the elderly lady looked up from spooning reddish gloop from a storage jar into a china jam pot and greeted her, concern in her brown eyes.

'My dear Mrs Anderson, you look dreadful. You should go back to bed.'

'No, no, I have to go out. May I borrow shoes and a coat? I don't mean to sound rude. It's simply ... they're clearing up already and I need to rescue my handbag.'

'Surely a cup of tea first.'

'No time. Mrs Moulder, would you keep an eye on the girls? They should sleep for ages, I think.'

'Of course I will, but let me find you some proper clothes.' Mrs Moulder wiped her hands on her apron and regarded

Maddie doubtfully. 'Though you're such a slender little thing, I don't know what will fit you.'

'Just the shoes and an old coat will do for now. Please.'

Mrs Moulder bustled into the hall and soon Maddie clopped out of the house in a flapping pair of court shoes, a paisley headscarf and Mr Moulder's shabby raincoat, whose only virtue was that it covered up the nightgown.

The site of last night's bomb was attracting a lot of interest and the handful of bystanders had swollen to a small crowd. The family next door on the other side to Norah Carrington was out in full force, the mother and three boys gathering broken roof tiles from their own front garden while the father engaged in lively argument with a pasty-faced official in a suit who was inspecting the damage to the party wall and making notes in a small black book. The crowd, seeing the normally neat Maddie Anderson approach in her odd attire, parted to let her through, several people murmuring their sympathy. She ignored them and pushed as close as she could to stare through the dust at the ruins of her home. A lump formed in her throat as she absorbed the awful extent of the devastation. The roof was gone and only the back of the house was still standing, stumps of floor joists and partition walls stretching uselessly into mid-air. A glimpse of the rose-sprigged wallpaper from the girls' nursery made Maddie's eyes swim. Everything else, the brick frontage, roof beams, tiles, floorboards, shards of furniture, lay in a heap as though smashed downwards by a giant's fist. A bathroom pipe dripped water over it all. If any of their possessions had survived the blast intact they would surely be coated in soggy brick dust and unrecognizable.

Maddie felt a large hand clamp her arm and a ripe male voice said, 'Stay back now, madam.'

'But it was my house,' she said, looking up at the burly workman's weathered face with pleading eyes.

'No good if the rest of it falls on you, eh?' He marshalled her to a safe distance then raised his voice to the crowd. 'Stay well away, so we can get on with the job.'

Everyone shuffled back a few inches. Someone asked Maddie, 'How are the little girls?', but she hardly heard for she had spotted a pathetic pile of objects lying on a sheet by the truck. She stepped toward it, then caught Norah Carrington's eye, and reached out her hand for the doll the woman held. 'I wasn't going to keep it, you know,' Norah whined as she relinquished it. She muttered something that sounded like, 'Some people,' as Maddie turned away without a word. Nosey Norah Carrington was the worst thing about living in Valentine Street. The woman had mistaken Maddie's natural reserve for frostiness from early on and never lost an opportunity to be offended by it.

The doll was one of Sarah's. Maddie couldn't see what lay on the pile, but when she called to the burly man he took the doll, went over and tied everything up in a grubby bundle, which he laid at her feet.

'This is it for the moment,' he said, sympathy in his eyes. 'Not much, but better than nothing.'

'Oh, but the air raid shelter!' Maddie said, grasping the bundle. 'I left my handbag there with our ration books in it and ... everything.'

'Tell you what, I'll have a look when I get the chance.'

'I'd be so grateful. We're staying at Number 21. Down there, with the privet hedge and the blue front door.' She should return. The girls might wake up and be frightened.

'Twenty-one,' he repeated. 'Before you go, have a word with his nibs here, eh?' The official in the suit was approaching, a self-important expression in his baleful eyes. 'He'll tell you what you're due. Get you sorted out.'

Twenty minutes later Maddie let herself into Mrs Moulder's to be told that the girls were still sleeping. She hung up the coat, kicked off the shoes and dumped the bundle by the kitchen sink. Then she joined Mrs Moulder at the kitchen table, where she sipped tea and nibbled on a piece of toast, not because she was hungry, but to stop the old lady fussing. Mrs Moulder questioned her about her plans for the day, but Maddie could not engage with what she said. Her mind, now stuffed with instructions about government forms and entitlements, wouldn't process anything more.

Instead her thoughts drifted over the events of the night before and her breath quickened with remembered fear. One moment the three of them been huddled in the tight dark space of the shelter that shook to the roar of the planes overhead, flinching at the crump of the bombs. Then there had come a strange silence followed by a terrific boom. The earth shuddered as if all the oxygen had been sucked out of the air then the whole world tumbled round them.

For ages after the blast they had clung together awaiting rescue, trapped in the suffocating blackness, the girls whimpering. And the old terror fell upon her. *Come on, Maddie.* She forced herself to fight it off, to breathe deeply, croaked shreds of nursery rhymes until her voice gave out. 'Jack and Jill' and 'Humpty Dumpty' – why were so many about falling and breaking one's head? Then, eventually, she heard men's voices and managed a hoarse shout, 'Here, we're in here!' Sobs of relief filled her throat, but she held them back. *Not in front of the children*. There came a scrabbling at the front of the shelter, a flicker of torchlight then the sense of something heavy being lifted. The door screeched open and a blessed draught of cool night air brushed her face . . .

'Mrs Anderson, you're shivering.' Mrs Moulder's quavering voice brought her back to the warm kitchen. 'Are you all right?'

'Yes, I think so.'

'You don't look yourself. I don't think you heard me. One of those volunteer ladies came when you were out. She brought some clothes for you and the girls.'

'How kind!'

'And I know you washed last night, but there's plenty of hot water this morning if you'd like to do your hair.'

Maddie fingered her sticky locks with distaste, then smiled at the old lady. 'Thank you. You're so nice and I'm being useless.'

'No, you're not. You've had a bad shock.' Mrs Moulder rose, with a determined expression on her face. 'Come along now. The bag of clothes is on the landing and I'll look out a clean towel.'

'Thank you so much.'

'No need to hurry over it. I can deal with the little ones when they wake up.'

Maddie washed her hair while bent over the bath, surprised at the amount of dirt that flowed down onto the chipped enamel. As she towelled her hair dry and raked the short sandy-coloured waves into their usual swept-back bob, her tragic face stared back from the mirror. Purple smudges under her brown eyes and a graze on her cheek spoke their story, but without her handbag she had no powder or lipstick to help her put a brave front on the day.

While she buttoned up a faded green dress and secured the belt at its tightest hole, Maddie's thoughts ran ahead. What should she do first today? According to the man in the suit there was a whole host of officials she must consult for emergency supplies, for compensation for loss of her home, the list went on. Her head ached harder at the thought of it all.

Suddenly, longing for Philip surged in. If only he were here she'd feel so much stronger. *But Philip has gone, so you'll have to manage by yourself. Buck up, Maddie Anderson.*

She frowned. Where would they live? Mrs Moulder was a brick, but they shouldn't impose on her for long. The old lady wasn't used to children, she had none of her own. Maddie had noticed the fragile vases and porcelain figurines that the widow kept on every surface. Grace, particularly, could be clumsy.

She slipped on a pair of low-heeled shoes. What a pleasure that they fitted. Pretty, too, with their bow trim. Funny how a nice pair of shoes made one feel better. She wondered who they'd belonged to and why they'd been given away. People could be so kind. Her eyes were filling again and she blinked furiously. She had to keep herself together for the girls.

She spread the damp towel over the rail then went to peep in at the children. Sarah was snoring gently, little Grace had turned onto her side now, clutching Rabbit's ear and sucking her thumb. Maddie smiled tenderly as she retreated, pulling the door to.

As she made her careful way downstairs in the unfamiliar shoes someone rapped on the front door and she saw, distorted by the cracked half-moon of glass, the helmeted head of the burly workman she had spoken to earlier.

'It's for me,' she called softly to Mrs Moulder and went to the door. The man on the step smiled sheepishly as he held out a beige leather handbag streaked with grime.

'Oh, thank goodness,' she cried in relief. She took it from him, flipped open the clasp and peered inside. Yes, her purse was there along with the family's identity cards, allowance and ration books, her engagement book. 'That's truly marvellous,' she told him. 'I'm so grateful.'

'And we found this in a broken desk.' He held out a damp manila packet the size of a slim library book. 'Maybe you can dry it out.'

'Thank you.' She took the package from him puzzled, for she'd never seen it before. Something was scrawled on it in Philip's handwriting, but the single word was barely legible for the ink had run. *Knyghton*, it said.

'Well, that's it.' The man touched the brim of his helmet in a gallant gesture. 'We'll be finishing up soon. Sorry for your trouble, but glad you're all safe.' He turned to go.

'Wait.' Maddie took out her purse, intending to give him some coins to thank him, but he shook his head.

'Even if I was allowed I wouldn't.'

She watched as he set off down the road again with his jaunty walk, thinking about the pity in his eyes, then went back inside.

A thin wail sounded overhead. Grace was awake. Maddie hastily set down the bag and package in the kitchen and hurried up the stairs. Grace was at the top, tottering sleepily, Rabbit in hand. Maddie opened her arms and Grace fell into them. In the bedroom they found Sarah sitting up in bed, rubbing her eyes and complaining that everything hurt.

As Maddie bustled about dressing her bewildered daughters in smocks and cardigans once worn by other little girls, she was astonished and thankful all over again that they'd survived their ordeal with life and limb intact. Grace would keep crying, though, and Sarah was unusually whiney. *They're exhausted*, she told herself. She struggled to keep her attention on the task in hand.

When she heard the truck drive off she went at once to the window. The scene of last night's disaster looked tidier, the street swept clean, everyone had gone. A woman pushing a pram past hardly gave the site a second glance. The ruins of their home had become simply another bombsite. Commonplace. Maddie didn't blame the young mother. If you thought too much about the tragedy each bombsite represented you'd go out of your mind.

'Let's go down and have breakfast,' she told the girls with a bright smile and held out her hands to them. She loved them too much to give in to her despair.

Two

In the kitchen, Mrs Moulder did her cheerful best with meagre resources, and the children were content to sit with her at the table as their mother paced about. They drank milk and ate bread with margarine and carrot jam while the old lady entertained them with a story from when she was a little girl and had stolen a piece of cake. The tale had a lame ending, but Sarah and Grace listened with rounded eyes. Sarah ate daintily as usual, but Grace smeared milk and jam around her mouth. Maddie, crossing to the sink in search of a cloth, noticed the knotted bundle of possessions that she'd brought home earlier. She felt curiously reluctant to face the reality of what it might contain. Still, she should give Sarah her doll.

She dragged the grubby bundle into the scullery, untied it and glanced inside. The doll was on top. When she picked it up its blue eyes blinked at her. Its name was Angela, but it no longer looked angelic, its dress being soggy and its pale hair caked with plaster. However, it was still in one piece. She'd clean it up before she surprised Sarah with it.

Putting the doll to one side, Maddie let the sheet fall open to reveal the rest of the contents and sank to her knees. As she'd feared, it looked like rubbish. She brushed the dirt from a torn box and raised the lid. A lump came into her throat. She'd last seen the box pristine, at the bottom of Philip's wardrobe. It contained his black polished dress shoes, which he'd forgotten to take with him or perhaps hadn't needed in the army. An old picture calendar with views of India lay underneath the box. It had hung on a nail above Philip's desk in a corner of the dining room. It reminded Maddie of the package the rescue worker had given her that he'd found in the desk drawer.

But what was this filthy object? A large wooden box with a hinged lid. *It can't be.* Maddie wiped off wet plaster with a corner of the sheet. *Oh joy, it is.* She knelt on the floor and lifted it onto her lap, running her fingers feverishly over a vicious dent in the top, then flipped up the fastening, raised the lid and smiled. Her art materials. They were all safely here, the tools of her livelihood, tidied away, thank goodness, because she'd been between projects. A stranger might think the stained tubes of paint, the inks, pens and brushes didn't amount to much, but to Maddie they meant everything, and in these straitened times would not have been easy to replace. She righted a fallen bottle then refastened the lid, set the box carefully to one side and turned her attention to the dwindling pile of objects on the sheet.

Apart from a milk saucepan, and a case of antique fish

knives, a wedding present from her father's cousin, never used in six years of marriage, that was it. All that had been rescued from the life that she and Philip had made together in the days when they'd been so happy and in love … No, she mustn't think about that now or she'd cry. Instead she clambered to her feet and fetched a damp sponge to clean up Angela.

'Oh, *Mummy*!' Sarah's delighted face when Maddie handed over the doll gave her hope that her darling girls would be all right. 'You've got Rabbit,' Sarah told Grace, whose face was crumpling into a frown, 'and I've got Angela, so it's fair.' Grace paused to think then gave a regal nod of agreement. 'When can we go home, Mummy?' Sarah asked.

Maddie exchanged glances with Mrs Moulder and drew a heavy sigh, realizing that the girls didn't understand their plight. But why should they? They'd been carried from the air raid shelter in darkness, wrapped in blankets. They would not have seen the ruins of their house.

'Oh, darling, we can't go home.' Maddie explained that a bomb had 'damaged' the house, but the important thing was that they were safe. 'We'll need to find somewhere new to live, but it will be all right.' The girls looked at her, aghast.

'You will all stay for a while,' Mrs Moulder hurried to assure them.

'You are kind,' Maddie murmured, then bit her lip to see the old lady's worried face.

'What about our things?' Sarah persisted. 'We must fetch our clothes. And I need my satchel for school.'

'You'll need new clothes. That's why you're wearing these

funny ones. And you're having a day off today,' Maddie said, promptly. Sarah looked crestfallen. 'School tomorrow, maybe.' No uniform. Another problem. She must start a list, she thought, looking round for her handbag. There it was on top of the mysterious package on the cabinet. She fetched it and wiped it clean, delved inside then sat tapping a pencil against her teeth before she wrote in her engagement book. *School uniform, forms, food, bank* … There was so much to do today. The longer term question of where and how they were to live would not go away, but for the moment she could not think beyond another night at Mrs Moulder's.

'Cooee, Maddie, dear,' the old lady called from the back door the following day. 'I want a bit of string from the top drawer of the white cabinet but my boots are muddy.'

'I'll get it.' Maddie, who'd been washing up after lunch while Grace had a nap, quickly dried her hands.

The drawer opened easily. It was full of useful bits and pieces tidily arranged – folded paper bags, light bulbs, pencil stubs.

'I can't see any string.'

The mysterious brown package lay unopened on top of the cabinet. She picked it up and again examined Philip's smudged handwriting on the front. *'Knyghton'.* The name stroked her memory with the softness of a feather.

'It's at the back, I think.' Mrs Moulder's voice broke in. 'A long piece, please, the pyracantha is falling off its trellis.'

Maddie pulled the drawer out further and saw several hanks of neatly coiled twine. Hastily, she took one out to Mrs

Moulder, then returned to the cabinet, nudging the drawer shut with her hip. The thick envelope peeled open easily. Her fingers closed round a small velvet-covered book, snugly packed, and edged it out. It was navy blue with a tassel on the spine. She ran her finger over its worn softness then opened it. It was an album of black-and-white photographs.

The picture at the front was tinted brown and was of an old timber-framed manor house, broad and comfortable-looking, overgrown with a creeper in flower. Sunlight played on the square-hatched windows and on the flagstones where a lean yellow Labrador dog lay asleep, its head between its paws.

She turned the page. Two small boys with grave faces sat on a lawn in front of the house with the same dog sitting between them, its ears cocked. One, she saw, had to be Philip. The next photograph was of a regal-looking lady seated in a wicker chair by a glasshouse crammed with plants, her hair hidden by a wide-brimmed hat. At her feet lay a trug of cut roses.

There were only a few more pictures in the album and they were all of the two boys, older now. In one, the last picture in the album, a girl with fair hair stood shyly in the background in front of a shed where a row of tall hollyhocks grew. She blended in with the plants and at first Maddie didn't notice her, but when she did she was struck by her watchful expression.

Knyghton. She picked up the envelope, deep in thought. She'd heard Philip mention it and knew it was the house in Norfolk where he'd lived when he was a schoolboy and his parents were still in India. But he'd said little about it and she'd surmised that although he'd spoken with affection of the house and his aunt and his dead grandmother, it was a period of painful memories for him and she hadn't asked questions. How she wished she had. Even looking through this little book felt like an intrusion, yet she had not been able to overcome her curiosity. Now that Philip was absent from their lives, missing in action for ten months since Dunkirk, she badly wanted to feel closer to him and here was as good a starting point as any. The regal lady was probably his grandmother, but who was the other boy, Philip's companion? And the girl who had wandered into the final photograph, where did she fit in?

The album did not slide back easily into the envelope and realizing something was preventing it, Maddie felt inside and withdrew a small crumpled packet. It was unsealed. She tipped it upside down and a tiny ornate silver key tumbled into her palm. There was no label, nothing written on the packet to identify its purpose. Thoughtfully, she returned the album to its packaging and tucked the packet containing the key in beside it. Later she took it upstairs and hid it among her few possessions out of the way of Grace's sticky fingers. And forgot about it.

Three

The question of where the little family should live did not go away. The billeting officer, who visited two days after the disaster, declared it best that they stay with Mrs Moulder for the time being. The old lady tried to be cheerful about this, but as the days crept by Maddie saw the strain that it put on her. She herself felt as though they were existing in limbo. After the first day Sarah had returned to school and Mrs Moulder had to entertain Grace while Maddie went out to queue for food, clothes and a new sketchbook. Her work was on hold for the moment. She wrote to her editor to inform him that they'd been bombed out and the illustrations for the new picture book might be late, not least because she had no paper. Thankfully he managed to send her some.

One afternoon, when they'd been at Mrs Moulder's for a week, Maddie took Grace to visit Denny Lewis, one of the few good friends she'd made in London. Denny had two daughters the same age as the Anderson girls and Grace and the younger girl, Polly, played in the Lewises' warm kitchen while the mothers talked and altered some old clothes that Denny had offered her.

'I wish we could have you to live here,' Denny said and bit off a thread, 'but ...'

'We couldn't possibly impose,' Maddie said quickly. Denny's husband, who was something high up in the War Office, was a good few years older than his wife and both women knew without saying that the arrangement would be a strain on all concerned.

'What about your godmother?'

'She's gone to her sister in Ealing. There's no room for us there. Anyway, I'm wondering whether we should move out of London again.'

As soon as Maddie said it, she realized this was what she longed to do. She and Philip had talked about her going to Norwich to live with her father and stepmother in the event of war, but not long afterwards her father had a stroke and needed his own room and a live-in nurse and suddenly there wasn't space for family. Now, Norwich too was a target for the Luftwaffe. She wouldn't feel safe. Somewhere more rural was the answer, but where?

'What about your husband's family?' Denny asked. 'Doesn't he have relatives? I know about his parents, but brothers or sisters?'

Philip's father had died in India shortly before the outbreak of war, his mother some years before that. 'He's an only child,' Maddie told her. 'But there's an Aunt Gussie. She sent us an old silver teapot as a wedding present.' She paused in her sewing, remembering how she'd written to tell her about Philip and been struck by the simplicity of the address: Knyghton, Monksfield, Norfolk. The reply to her letter had been in quavery handwriting, the tone understandably upset at the bad news. 'I've never met her. I've always had the feeling that he wanted to keep it that way.'

'Perhaps you should leave things as they are, then,' Denny said in a voice filled with foreboding. 'You don't know what you might be stirring up.'

'Heavens, Denny. That sounds sinister. I'm sure he was fond of her – he visited her in hospital ages back when she was ill.'

'Don't say I didn't warn you.' Denny said, stabbing her needle into a pincushion.

Maddie remembered Philip's photograph album. Knyghton looked old and beautiful, a rural haven, surely with plenty of spare bedrooms. Was Gussie the regal lady in the photograph or had that definitely been Philip's grandmother? It was hard to think clearly at the moment, but a plan began to form in her mind. By the following morning she'd decided. She would write to Philip's aunt and ask if there was room for three bombed-out waifs at Knyghton.

Four

Norwich

May 1934

Maddie was sure she had seen the stranger a few weeks before. She'd been standing dreamily at her bedroom window when he'd walked past the house. He'd glanced up and their eyes had met briefly. Later, he claimed not to remember this.

This Thursday afternoon it was quiet in the museum and Maddie had the gallery to herself. She sat on a folding stool with her sketchbook on her knee and studied the dog fox closely through the glass case. Its pelt was as bright as it must have been in life, though she noticed that the individual hairs were different shades of cream and grey, ginger and red, and together they imprisoned the light to a vibrant effect. The fox was long and lean, with a magnificent brush, its green glass eyes alert, and she wondered how the taxidermist had made it appear unaware that it was dead. She hoped this was because it had died cleanly, a quick bullet to the skull, perhaps, rather than after a terrifying pursuit by hounds. She held her pencil poised above the page for a moment, allowing a sense of the creature to enter her, then swiftly she began to sketch.

So absorbed was she in her work that it was a long while before she broke off, realizing that someone was watching her from a few feet away. She glanced up warily and there he was, a youngish man in a cream-coloured suit, pale-skinned, his hair and moustache only a shade darker than the fox's. His eyes with their long dark lashes held hers, then he smiled and cleared his throat.

'I didn't mean to disturb you. I was admiring your skill.' His voice sounded low and musical in the quietness of the room.

'Thank you,' Maddie said, angling the sketchbook away from his gaze, 'but I'm afraid I can't work with someone watching.' She waited for him to apologize and move on, but he did neither.

'Don't mind me. I promise not to look. I came to see the polar bear, if he's still here. The one wrestling the seal. I last visited when I was a boy and couldn't take my eyes off him.'

'The polar bear is in with the zoo animals.' She pointed with her pencil to the arch that divided the gallery in two.

'Of course.' He walked into the next room and Maddie returned to her work, but before she'd drawn even a line he called back, 'He's as magnificent as I remember him.'

Exasperated, she twiddled the pencil between her fingers, then tried again to draw, but found she couldn't go on. The fox still posed before her in its glass case, but her sense of its spirit had fled. It was replaced by an awareness of the man in the next room, the soft sounds of his footsteps on the wooden floor. She rose and went to stand beneath the arch, the sketchbook clasped to her breast. Being more interested in drawing familiar animals of the English countryside she rarely came to see the exotic exhibits, but when she looked past the young man she was struck anew by the size of the huge polar bear, rearing up on its hind legs, its hapless victim clutched in its vast claws.

'You must have found that terrifying as a little boy.'

He looked at her, a serious expression on his face. 'Yes, but I was filled with awe. I've never seen a live one, have you?'

'So far as I know, this is the only polar bear in Norfolk,' she said gravely and he laughed.

'Oh, and I remember this fellow.' He stepped across to study a moth-eaten tiger with gleaming eyes, its face contorted forever in its final snarl. 'My pa lives in India. I'm sure that he's brought down one or two of these in his time.'

'How horrid.' The words were out before Maddie could stop them.

He looked at her sharply. 'Do you think so?'

'Beautiful wild animals, shot for sport? Yes, I do.'

A troubled expression came into his face. Lor', she'd offended him now.

'Yet they live by killing.' He stared across the room, and Maddie was surprised to see despair in his eyes.

'But that's different. Tigers kill to eat. But I suppose if they start attacking people . . . that's a good reason to hunt them.'

'Yes, I'd agree. What about shooting for sport here in Norfolk? Deer and pheasants and so forth. Foxes, like your pal in the other room.' He was studying her now, as though her answer mattered.

'Foxes are pests, I suppose, and deer, as well, if there become too many of them. Still, I could never kill an animal. Unless I had to eat it, but even then . . .' Maddie thought of the poulterer's shop near the cathedral. She could never pass it without a pang of pity for the feathered geese and ducks hung up in the window above trays of quail and pigeon. There would be brightly coloured pheasants, partridges and woodcock later in the year. And yet she enjoyed eating their meat. She looked down at the floor and nudged a dust ball with her shoe.

'You're a city-dweller, I take it.' There was a dull note in his voice. 'I was brought up mostly in the country.' He gave a bitter laugh. 'Violent death is a way of life there.'

Her brow furrowed. He was probably right, but what an odd way of putting it.

'I suppose so. I've lived in Norwich all my life. But I do *know* about the countryside.'

'I'm sorry. You must think me rude. In fact, I largely agree with you. I don't approve of killing for sport. In fact, I detest it.'

She blinked at him in surprise, then asked, 'Where in Norfolk are you from?'

'I'm not, originally. I was born in Delhi, but my folks sent me back here for boarding school and I lived with relatives in the holidays. Have you heard of Monksfield?'

She shook her head.

'Nobody ever has. It's a village several miles inland from Sheringham. The family pile is called Knyghton, spelled like one of King Arthur's knights, but with a y instead of an i.'

Maddie knew Sheringham, of course, had often been to the beach there, a train ride away or sometimes, if her father was in the right mood, in his precious car, which he kept in the garage and generally preferred to polish than to risk scratching the paintwork in the narrow country lanes.

He glanced at his watch and said, 'I ought to leave you to your drawing and go to catch my train. I had a few minutes to spare, which is why I came. I've enjoyed talking to you, Miss . . .?'

'Fielding. Madeleine Fielding, though everyone calls me Maddie.'

'Maddie,' he repeated. 'It suits you. I don't know why, but I knew when I saw you that you wouldn't have an ordinary name. I'm Philip Anderson. Lieutenant Anderson, but only since last week.

'Congratulations.'

'Thank you. Good luck with your art. I hope we meet again.' He delivered the slightest of bows as he wished her goodbye and set off towards the exit.

The gallery seemed even quieter now he'd left, and darker, Maddie noticed, for the sun had moved round. It had been an amusing encounter, but she gauged he'd only been visiting

Norwich and that despite his polite wish, she wasn't likely to see him again.

She put Lieutenant Anderson to the back of her mind and returned to her seat, tucking away a loose strand of hair as she leaned forward to study the fox again, then after a moment began to draw. Over the next few days, though, she found her thoughts returning to the softly spoken officer with his unusual opinions and disturbing gaze.

A few weeks later, Maddie stared from the train window at a tranquil passing view of cows grazing lush grass by a stream fringed by willows. It was so lovely in the afternoon sunlight of early June that she longed to paint it. Her mind wandered to the luggage rack above her head where lay a leather satchel full of her illustrations. At the behest of Mr Lowe, her art school tutor, she'd sent a small drawing of a nest of harvest mice to an editor he knew at a London publisher, mentioning Lowe's name as a reference in the accompanying letter. She'd received a reply the very next week, requesting a meeting. Here she was, travelling to London on her own for the first time in her twenty-one years, her fingers tingling with nerves, her head full of hopes and dreams.

At Ipswich a smartly dressed lady entered the compartment. She sank gracefully onto the seat opposite and gave Maddie a shrewd up and down glance before elegantly lighting a cigarette and turning her attention to a magazine. *You'll do*, was the unspoken message and Maddie felt a thrill of pleasure. The tan coloured skirt and jacket she'd bought in Jarrold's set off her pale wavy hair and light brown eyes, and the shallow straw hat with its narrow curved brim was a real find. At Norwich station, before getting on the train, she'd slipped into the Ladies' and applied some lipstick. Her father disapproved of her wearing make-up. Even face powder he frowned upon. To him she was still a child. He'd hardly noticed that his quiet, motherless little girl had blossomed into a shy but determined young woman.

The smartly dressed lady abandoned her magazine on the seat when she left the train at Chelmsford. Maddie leaned over and picked it up and turned the pages, fascinated by a world that was foreign to her, of expensive designer dresses, society gossip and a most educational problem page. 'Is he the man for her?' was the question a heading posed. It was a letter from a girl whose boy minded that she had been engaged before.

Maddie read it avidly, dismayed by how naïve she was. Having no brothers or sisters or even cousins her own age, she'd had no one to learn from about such things. Her schoolfriends had been like herself, well-behaved, studious sorts, though one was getting married to a boy she'd met in the offices of the chocolate factory where she worked as a typist, the manager's nephew, no less. Maddie herself had never had a boyfriend, or even been to a proper dance. She'd once been followed about by a lad at a funfair and had had to hide from him by visiting the fortune teller's tent where she was told a lot of nonsense about overcoming darkness. At art school for several months last year she'd developed a silent, tortuous pash on a flamboyant willowy youth with intense dark eyes and long narrow hands, who teased her amiably, but in the same way that he treated everyone.

She sighed and closed the magazine. As she folded it into her handbag she caught sight of a man in military uniform passing along the corridor. His reddish moustache made her think of the young man in the museum. If it had been him, she thought, he hadn't noticed her. The idea of going to look for him didn't cross her mind. Her stepmother was very clear that one should never chase boys.

The train was passing through the outskirts of London now, between endless rows of sooty brick terraces, factories billowing out smoke, and the odd slender church spire, grey with dirt. It trundled through a station and Maddie was shocked by a noisy throng of black-clad men that filled the platform. Thank heavens it didn't stop.

'Mr Mosley's men,' remarked an old gentleman opposite to a portly matron next to Maddie who was counting stitches on her knitting. 'A bunch of thugs, if you ask me.'

'Disgraceful,' murmured the matron, who'd now lost her place and had to start again.

The next station was just as busy, but this time the train shuddered to a halt and at once the louts on the platform surged in through the doors at either end of the carriage and stormed along the corridor, laughing loudly and shouting to one another in their search for seats. The door to Maddie's compartment slid open. 'There's plenty of room in 'ere,' a stocky, bullet-headed man called behind in a rough voice, then turned to the passengers and added cheerfully, 'if everyone shoves up.' The old gentleman objected, but was ignored. The newcomers barged around him, claiming the empty seats. Maddie found herself jammed between the knitting matron and the window, but still they crammed in, standing room only, the strong smell of humanity and stale tobacco overwhelming, the heat mounting. 'Here, open the window, will you, Atkins?' called one.

The man who answered to Atkins pressed himself against Maddie's knees as he tried the window then shouted back, 'Can't, the bloody thing's stuck.'

'Language, young man,' the matron quavered.

Outside, urgent whistles sounded. Doors slammed and the train jolted into motion. Maddie tried to make herself as small as possible, shutting her eyes and clutching her handbag, but she began to tremble, her heart pounded and soon it was hard to breathe. It was the old panic mounting, the awful sense of the world closing in around her. *It will soon be over. One more station to the end of the line.* Beside her the matron was making genteel whimpering sounds. *We must be almost there now. Breathe, Maddie, breathe.* At last she felt the train slow, then its brakes squealed and it jolted to a halt. Maddie's eyes fluttered open to pressing darkness. Not the station. A tunnel. The men's voices filled her ears and the heat and smell of their bodies felt unbearable. She squeezed her eyes tight and concentrated on breathing.

Just as suddenly the train lurched off again, and soon with relief Maddie sensed the high echoing space of Liverpool Street Station. It screeched to a final halt, throwing her back in her seat. She was aware of the swarm of men surging along the corridor, then tramping along the platform beside the train, laughing and talking. The compartment emptied, but still she sat there, dazed, unable to move, eyes still tightly shut.

'Are you all right there, dear?' Beside her the matron was shifting about, stuffing her knitting into her bag. Maddie blinked at her and managed to nod. 'In all my born days,' the woman muttered to herself, then stood and departed in a waft of talcum powder. Someone else entered the compartment.

'Miss Fielding? Maddie?' Maddie's eyes flew open at the voice and met a familiar gaze. So it had been him she'd noticed earlier, the man she'd met at the museum, Lieutenant Anderson. He sat on the seat opposite, leaning towards her with his cap in his hands, his concerned face so close that she could see glints of green in his hazel eyes. Gradually, the world righted itself. 'Sorry,' she murmured, gathering her things. 'It was so ... overwhelming. Where are they going?'

'There's a big convention at Olympia, apparently. Blighters. Here, let me ...'

He rose and lifted down her satchel, which she insisted on taking from him, and they left the train together. As they strolled towards the ticket barrier they were aware of a commotion ahead as the crowds of Blackshirts pushed their way towards the underground.

'Where are you off to now, Maddie?' Philip Anderson said. 'It might be worth holding back until they've gone.'

'Green Park.'

His face lit up. 'So am I! Meeting a fellow at his club in Jermyn Street.'

She wondered what kind of club it was, but felt it unsophisticated to ask. Her father was a Freemason, which involved him going off to mysterious meetings in evening dress and carrying a tiny black suitcase, but she wasn't sure if this club was the same kind of thing.

'What about you?' he prompted, then grinned. 'Or is a deadly secret?'

'No, it's not a secret,' she said carefully as they joined the shuffling hordes at the barrier 'I'm showing someone my portfolio. St James's Street – do you know it?'

'Good for you. Of course I know it, it's only a step from the underground.' His face darkened. 'Damn, I suppose the Central Line will be pretty crowded. Perhaps the bus would be better. What d'you think?'

She shrugged, but liked the assumption that they would travel together. 'I don't mind trying the bus, if you know where the stop is,' she said. Their turn came at the barrier and she handed in her ticket with a rising sense of adventure.

Five minutes later they were sharing a front seat at the top of a bus. The bus was full but there were no Blackshirts, and with Philip beside her Maddie felt perfectly at ease, though she thought it quite unnecessary that he paid her fare. *London is so interesting*, she thought as she glanced into the office windows they passed and watched the people scurrying about below, each going about their business.

'There's St Paul's!' she exclaimed.

'You haven't seen it before?'

She shook her head and explained that she'd never visited London, had not otherwise been out of Norfolk. Except to

Cambridge once on an art school outing where she'd loved the soaring spires of King's College and the willows weeping into the river.

Philip pointed to the satchel in her lap. 'I'd love to see your pictures. Who is it you are showing them to?'

'My tutor knows an editor at Ackroyd and Briggs. They publish books for children and he thinks this man will be interested. I'm not very hopeful, but it's worth a try.'

She felt a tremor of anxiety as she let Philip take the soft leather bag from her and carefully unbuckle it. One by one he slid out the mounted drawings and lifted their tissue covers to examine them. 'I remember this old boy, of course,' he said, recognizing the fox she'd been sketching in the museum. 'You've got him perfectly. The colours are glorious.'

He professed to liking the other animals, too. A pair of deer in flight through a forest, rabbits feeding near their warren. She remembered how unafraid they'd been as she'd sat quietly nearby and sketched them.

'This is very different.' He'd found one of what her tutor called her Beatrix Potter paintings, though Maddie didn't believe the imaginary anthropomorphized animals were the same style as Miss Potter's at all.

'There are only a few of those, but my tutor thought I should show that I had range.'

'Very engaging,' Philip said, as he came to the last one. She took the portfolio from him and slipped everything back into place. 'You have talent, Maddie. Even an ignoramus like me can see that.'

'That's kind, but I'm sure you're only being polite.'

'I really do think so.' He was looking at her with frank admiration and she laughed as she rebuckled the satchel.

The bus conductor called up the staircase, 'Piccadilly next. Anyone for Piccadilly.'

'We're almost there,' Philip said, and Maddie felt desolate that they were soon to part.

After they'd regained the safety of the pavement he walked down with her past the Ritz Hotel and pointed out the building she wanted. She thanked him, and he hesitated, apparently sharing her reluctance to part, then said, 'I say, would you let me know how you get on? I should like to know.'

'Would you really?'

'Yes. Otherwise I'll be wondering. Here.' He took a small notebook from his breast pocket, scribbled in it, tore out the page and handed it to her. 'It's my address. Drop me a line. Promise you will.'

'Of course,' she said, touched by his earnestness. 'And thank you again. For rescuing me. Sometimes situations like that on the train overwhelm me. I'm supposed to have grown out of it, but I'm afraid that's not happened yet.'

'I'm supposed to have grown out of stuffing my hands in my jacket pockets and ruining the line of my suit,' he laughed.

'That is a bad habit,' she said mock-seriously, glad to be feeling so comfortable with him.

After they'd set off in their separate directions, each turned back at the same moment and saw the other looking. Maddie felt herself blush to have shown such obvious interest, but

Philip smiled and gave a mock salute so she waved the scrap of paper he'd given her in reply.

When she examined it as she walked down St James's she was surprised to see that the address was a London one. SW1, like Ackroyd & Briggs. What then had he been doing on the train from Norwich? She should have thought to ask.

Five

2 Featherstone Road, Norwich
8 June 1934

Dear Lieutenant Anderson

I promised to let you know how I fared in my interview yesterday, and I'm pleased to tell you that Mr Edwards, the editor at Ackroyd & Briggs, was extremely pleasant and admired my little pictures to the extent that he has commissioned me to undertake the illustrations for a children's book about British mammals! I am delighted, as you might imagine! I must take the opportunity to thank you properly for rescuing me on the train yesterday. You'll be glad to hear that my journey home today was uneventful!!! I stayed with my godmother last night in Bayswater. She took me to a wonderful Mozart concert and this morning I visited the National Gallery. The Stubbs horses are so glorious, I could stare at them for ever. I hope that you enjoyed the evening with your friend, and thank you again for your kindness.

Yours sincerely
Maddie Fielding

10 June 1934
13A Eccleston Square

Dear Miss Fielding

Congratulations upon your success! I look forward to visiting a bookshop in the not too distant future to buy a copy of this book about British mammals. I told my landlord, who has a nephew of seven, so that's two sales you've made already! I very much enjoyed dinner with my pal, thank you. I envy you your visit to the National Gallery. I never seem to make time for that sort of thing, but you inspire me to change. I wonder if you'd like to meet for lunch next time I'm in Norfolk on exercises, which should be in the next few weeks? I'll write nearer the time to find out if you are free.

Yours truly
Philip Anderson

'On exercises'. It was army duties then that took him to Norwich. No mystery there, Maddie reflected as she folded the letter away. There was still so much to find out about him, though, and already she longed for their next meeting.

*

The six months that followed were a period of great happiness for Maddie, but of great anxiety, too. She graduated from art school with distinction, knowing she'd secured the kind of work that filled her days with pleasure. She devoted far more time to her drawings for the book than the job was worth financially, but it was an opportunity to prove herself. If *Mammals of Great Britain* was successful more commissions from Mr Edwards might come her way.

And then there was Philip.

He wrote to her, as good as his word, ten days after his first letter, asking her to join him the following Friday for lunch at the Royal Hotel in Norwich. Maddie knew where that was, of course, near the castle, but she'd never been inside before. The Fieldings rarely ate out *en famille*, and when they did it tended to be at a reliable restaurant by the market where a well-cooked roast or a steak and kidney pudding with treacle sponge and ice cream to follow could be had for the three of them for less than five shillings. Her father was prudent with money, and he also hated anything 'fussy'.

The Royal couldn't be called fussy, but it was a level or two higher than the Market Café, with a proper wine list and fresh game in season. And Philip behaved as perfectly as any man of a young girl's dreams, helping her off with her jacket, making sure she had what she liked to eat and being very sweet. He was looking trim in his military uniform and Maddie enjoyed the curious glances of the other diners, while secretly wondering what it was he saw in her. *Oh, don't be silly, Maddie*, she told herself, but it didn't do any good.

She knew she wasn't conventionally pretty, not by comparison to her more popular schoolmates, but nor was she
plain, her large brown eyes and chin-length, naturally wavy
light brown hair being her best features. Everything about
her was neat and average, she always thought, from her
small straight nose to her slender figure. What she could
never see was that apparently she possessed a certain air.
According to the fellow art student she'd fallen in love
with, her resting expression made her look as though she'd
'landed from a faraway world'. At school she'd often been
told off for daydreaming, even when she hadn't been. It was
simply the way she'd been made, her slight smile the natural
set of her mouth.

Philip was watching her now with a smile of his own, as
though amused by her.

'What is it?' she asked, as she picked up her knife and
fork to eat the grilled sole, peas and new potatoes that they'd
both ordered.

'You look as though you have secrets,' he said, dipping a
potato into the sauce on the side of his plate.

'I assure you that I don't.'

Did she? She told him that her mother had died when
she was six, but that wasn't a secret, only a sad thing in her
background. He frowned in concern and murmured that
he was sorry. His own mother, he told her, had died a few
years ago.

'She'd been ill for some weeks and died in hospital in
Bombay,' he said when she enquired. 'The worst thing was
that I didn't get there in time.'

'Oh, Philip.' They sat eating quietly for a moment, each lost in their own thoughts.

'My father remarried,' Maddie said finally. 'I have a stepmother.'

'A wicked one?'

'No, nothing like that. Nor did she try to replace my mother, which I would have hated. She's ...' How should she describe Monica, who was aloof and self-contained, and had regarded the acquisition of a shy, but biddable thirteen-year-old stepdaughter as a purely practical endeavour, part of the deal of becoming Mrs Albert Fielding? Maddie said loyally, 'She's just Monica. We get along all right.'

'You call her by her first name?'

'She isn't my mother. We tried "Aunt Monica" for a while, but neither of us liked it.'

'Do you remember your mother?'

Maddie turned aside a piece of fish skin then looked up at him and was touched by his gentle expression. 'A general sense of her as a loving presence, yes. And sometimes if I smell a particular scent ... that brings her back. But otherwise, no. I only have a few photographs. My father ... he took it very hard when she died and didn't like to talk about her.'

'Had she been ill?'

'It was an accident in the street. She was running and fell into the path of a car.'

His eyes widened. 'What a dreadful thing to have happened,' he mumbled.

It hadn't been as straightforward as that. Maddie took a deep breath to say more, but at that moment the perky waitress arrived to bear away their plates and to take their orders for pudding and she lost courage.

'I'm sorry to have made you talk about it,' Philip said when the waitress had gone.

'Don't be. The worst thing is the feeling that there's a gap. Something missing. Do you understand?'

He nodded. 'I think I do.'

'Most of the time I don't dwell on it.'

Two dishes of plum tart arrived, and they gave it their full attention, the sharp-sweet taste of the fruit mingling deliciously with the smooth richness of the cream.

'There were plum trees at Knyghton,' Philip said between mouthfuls, 'and our cook made the most wonderful tarts. This is almost as good as hers.' His eyes shone.

'You mentioned Knyghton when we first met. It sounds an idyllic place,' Maddie prompted, reaching for the cream jug, and was surprised to see him frown.

'I suppose it was. Especially for a small boy who'd been cooped up at boarding school, but ... it wasn't home. It belongs to my father's family, but my father was a younger brother so the house wasn't his to inherit. My grandmother took care of me. Like you, I missed my mother, though at least mine was alive and wrote me letters from India.'

Maddie asked him about India. His father had been in the army there but was talking about coming back to England now that he'd retired. 'In another year or two.'

Philip had loved India as a young child, but the occasional visit there in the holidays after the Great War had unsettled him. He hadn't visited for several years, since attending his mother's funeral, though he hoped to through his work.

'How long have you been in the army? It's the Norfolks, isn't it? I recognize the badge.'

'I've been in nearly two years.'

'You're not based here, though, are you?'

'No, no, I'm here purely for training. There's a place out near the coast. Look, I'm afraid I haven't explained myself properly. I'm not a regular, just a Territorial. You must know what that is, we're part of the reserve. If there's another war we get called up first.'

'Oh, I see. Do you have a job in London?'

'Yes. I work for a tea merchant. It's a long way to come up here for exercises, but it's unusual to have had to do so more than once a month. The first time you and I met, in the museum, I was in Norwich for another reason. My Aunt Augusta – Gussie, we call her – was in hospital for a routine operation, then a convalescent home, and I was visiting. She's back at Knyghton now, though.'

'So you'll not be here again for a while.' Maddie sipped her wine, trying to appear nonchalant, but not feeling it.

'I didn't say that.' His smile warmed her. 'I appear to have found another reason to come.'

She met his eye with a steady gaze and laughed. 'The museum,' she said mischievously, 'is always worth another visit. I love Alfred Munnings' pictures of horses.'

'We've time, I think, before my train. Is there still an Egyptian mummy?'

'There is. And his cat!'

Two weeks passed after that blissful day, but Maddie didn't hear from Philip, though she watched for the postman every day. Then one Wednesday evening in early July the telephone rang. Monica went out to the hall to answer it and returned to say with surprise, 'It's for you, Maddie. A very polite young man, I must say.'

He could get away the following Sunday. Would she be free? He'd like to meet her father and stepmother. Would that be possible?

Maddie invited him to Sunday lunch then passed the next few days in a state of anxiety, but she needn't have worried. From the time Philip arrived in a well-cut suit, bearing a box of chocolates and a bottle of whisky, he charmed her father and stepmother. Over roast beef and apple pie he explained how he and Maddie had met, described his work in the City of London for a tea importer, saying modestly that his employer seemed pleased with him. He spoke knowledgeably to Maddie's step-mother about contract bridge, asked Mr Fielding about his collection of Caruso records and appeared to enjoy listening to one as he complimented Monica on her best Darjeeling tea in the drawing room after the meal.

'I think they approve of you,' she told him as the two of them ambled arm in arm round the local park.

'I hope they do, seeing as I admire their daughter.'

'No, don't be smarmy, you know I don't like it.'

'I'm not. I genuinely want them to approve of me.' His forehead wrinkled. 'Do you think I've overdone it?'

'Not really,' she laughed. And it was true. He knew how to talk to people as though he was interested in them. It was an enviable gift.

When he wrote to Mrs Fielding to thank her for her hospitality, Mr Fielding read the letter and said tersely, 'A good chap, your Lieutenant Anderson.'

High praise indeed from Maddie's reticent father.

One Saturday in the middle of July Maddie travelled to London. She and Philip visited the British Museum together and had tea afterwards in a pretty café whose walls were lined with paintings that looked like scenes out of happy dreams. She'd told her father that she would stay overnight with her godmother, but when the time came to say goodbye to Philip she hesitated.

'Do you have to go?' Philip's eyes were pleading. 'I thought I'd show you where I live.' She knew he had a room in a wealthy school chum's flat in Victoria.

'I didn't tell my godmother when I'd arrive exactly,' she said. Perhaps it wouldn't hurt to stop by. 'But I mustn't be long.'

'Of course,' he said, his face brightening with delight.

Eccleston Square was imposing, with high white-porticoed residences set around a large iron-railed garden. Maddie followed Philip up several flights of a broad staircase then he wrested open a front door into a spacious hallway with half a dozen doors off it, all left ajar. It smelled of stale smoke and was littered with the evidence of whirlwind male activity, an opera hat on a chair, a fallen waxed jacket, a pair of muddy boots slung in a corner under the baleful eye of a stag's head mounted on the wall.

'Dalloway?' Philip roared, shoving wide one door after another. Maddie waited shyly in the hall as he marched about.

'Good, we're alone,' Philip said cheerfully, returning to help Maddie off with her coat. 'Come and make yourself at home.'

He led her into a lofty drawing room with chandeliers, artfully draped curtains and a moulded plaster ceiling, and threw open a sash window. The sound of traffic rose from the street, but it was pleasantly distant, like the sound of the sea. Maddie gazed down with interest at the bird's-eye view of the garden square.

'A tennis court. Do you play much? I'm afraid I'm useless.'

'The court's so popular, it's difficult to get a look in. Something to drink, a sherry maybe?'

'A small one.' She turned back to the room, staring round at its high ceiling, the vast Knole sofa and a pair of roomy armchairs set about a stately fireplace with a huge painting of Venice above it in an ornate gilt frame. At the far end of the room stood a billiard table and the walls were lined with books and oil paintings of pastoral scenes. 'It's so grand,' she whispered, sitting down at one end of the sofa and feeling very lost and little.

'It's a cut above anything I could afford. Dalloway's been generous.' Philip handed her a glass and came to sit beside her, laying his arm along the high back of the sofa. 'I say, you're shivering. Are you cold?'

'A bit.' She didn't like to admit that she was nervous.

Maddie watched his deft movements with pleasure as he went about closing the window, fetching a travelling rug, which he tucked gently round her shoulders. He crouched by the grate to set his cigarette lighter to the gas fire, which lit with a *whoomph*, before returning to her side. The evening was drawing in around them. With the fire and the rug and the sherry warming her inside it began to feel wonderfully cosy. Philip's arm moved from the back of the sofa to pull her to him. She snuggled closer, he bent towards her and touched his lips to her hair, then her face, her mouth.

'Dear Maddie,' he sighed, but she stopped him with another kiss and they kissed and kissed until she felt dizzy with desire. Then gently he withdrew, smiling at her, and they sat warm and peacefully together talking about their hopes for the future, the blaze of the fire now the only light in the room. Philip spoke about his work at the tea importer, the opportunities to travel to visit the suppliers. India, Ceylon. 'It's so beautiful out there. The colours are so bright and the greenery so lush. You'd love it.'

'I'd be no good with the heat.'

'Oh, you get used to that. Monsoon season is the worst, I'll admit. The humidity knocks one out, but we could avoid going then.'

Maddie liked the way he assumed they'd be together, but he didn't seem to notice what he'd said. Instead he squeezed her hand. 'You'd love the wildlife. There are monkeys everywhere. And the birds are so colourful. And their song. Walking in a park there before dusk, everything's ten times more alive than it is here in drab old England.'

'It sounds wonderful.' She waited for him to say 'we' again, but he didn't.

'Of course, I love England,' he went on. 'It's my motherland, after all. I was brought up here, it's my blood and I'd defend it to the death, but sometimes I feel we live in black and white.'

'You haven't wanted to follow in your father's footsteps? The British Army in India, I mean?'

Philip shook his head. 'Once I thought I might, but not now. It's changing so quickly. The Indians don't want us there. My father's letters are full of it, the politicking, the rebellions. They want to run themselves and who can blame them. There's a chap at the office, he's all for Mr Gandhi. Empire's dead, he says. India will go the way of Australia and Canada, like it or not. There's no point in us dragging our feet. No, the future's in trade.'

Maddie was silent, not knowing much about the subject. She'd seen newsreels at the cinema, of course, the pictures of Mr Gandhi visiting Britain a few years ago, an odd fragile figure in his simple cotton dhoti next to his stiff besuited hosts. Clips of British ceremonies in Delhi or Bombay had a quaintness about them, like something from the Edwardian past.

It was all far away and had nothing to do with here and now in the semi-darkness, close to a man she was beginning to love. She felt his fingers interlace with hers and his warm breath against her face made her heart beat faster. 'Maddie,' he whispered, 'you don't have to answer now, but would you think about becoming my wife?'

She opened her mouth to express surprise when they

heard the sharp sound of the front door opening. Their heads snapped round as a hearty male voice cried, 'Hello?' and the room filled with harsh electric light. An untidy, portly man with cropped curly hair and a genial round face stood frozen by the open door. 'Dash it, I'm so sorry. I had no idea, old chap . . .'

'Maddie,' Philip said, disentangling himself, laughing, 'This is Bill Dalloway, my landlord. Dalloway, this is Maddie, my . . .'

'His fiancée,' said Maddie firmly and smiled at the flash of delight that crossed Philip's face.

Six

1935

Maddie and Philip were married the following March, in a beautiful light-filled church in Norwich's market square, where the family occasionally worshipped. Maddie's step-mother took charge of the arrangements. A simple white dress and Maddie's mother's veil for the bride, pale blue for Joyce from school, Maddie's bridesmaid, bouquets of spring flowers, lunch for two dozen at the Royal Hotel, Philip and his best man, Dalloway, both distinguished-looking in uniform, but nearly all the guests were for the bride, an elderly line of Fielding connections brightened by a sprinkling of Maddie's friends. At the reception, Dalloway read out a telegram from the groom's father in India and made appropriately censored jokes about past schoolboy capers and Philip's failings on the domestic front.

They spent their week's honeymoon in a misshapen

black-beamed cottage by a stream on the edge of an ancient Suffolk hamlet. Maddie sketched the family of ducklings that she encountered in the lane each morning when she went to the shop to buy fresh milk and bread for breakfast. Philip cut a blackthorn stick to clear brambles on the footpaths as they explored the surrounding countryside. Once they stopped entranced to watch hares leaping and boxing in a fallow field. At night Maddie sometimes lay awake in her sleeping husband's arms, troubled by the hoot of an owl or a vixen's anguished bark that pierced the pitch darkness. Although she'd never felt happier, the strangeness of married life was bemusing and the sense of a night-time world beyond the window underscored this feeling. Often, she woke first, at dawn, loving to lie warm and safe, listening to a deafening chorus of birdsong. Then Philip would stir and turn towards her with a 'Hello, you,' and they'd lie staring dreamily into one another's eyes before he drew her to him. *Never, never, have I felt so loved*, she thought.

They'd gone house-hunting in London together before the wedding and Maddie enjoyed furnishing the first-floor maisonette they rented in a respectable Victorian terrace in Earl's Court. She was clever at searching junk shops for pictures and unusual lamps, and successfully French-polished a careworn dining table and matching chairs, ran up curtains for the windows on a sewing machine and bagged a couple of colourful rugs in a closing-down sale at a Fulham warehouse. The marriage bed was new from Heal's, a wedding present from her father and stepmother, and Maddie's godmother supplied a canteen of silver cutlery to go with the Wedgwood dinner service paid for by Philip's father. Maddie often felt weary in these early days of her marriage, but she put this down to the newness of everything and fitting in her work amid the dashing around. *Mammals of Great Britain* was to be published in the autumn and illustrations for a collection of animal fables was her next commission. It was several months before she realized with a shock that she was expecting a baby.

Their daughter Sarah, named for Maddie's mother, was born on the January night in 1936 that King George V died, one soul slipping quietly out of the world as another rushed in with a furious wail, for she was a baby who rarely stopped crying, and there was nobody to help Maddie. Neither Monica nor Maddie's godmother were any use in that department, but after Mr and Mrs Fielding visited to pay homage to the newcomer, her father sent money for them to employ a daily woman. Unfortunately, the letter accompanying the cheque was poorly expressed and Philip inferred from it that Mr Fielding was criticizing his son-in-law for failing to keep his daughter in proper comfort. His response was to return the cheque and to work harder in the hopes of promotion, leaving Maddie to tear her hair out managing a baby that would not settle while her husband arrived home late, strained and exhausted, presumably expecting the comforts of a calm and pretty wife and a perfectly cooked supper and finding instead a tearful young mother, a grumbling infant and the remnants of a dried-up stew.

A sullen side of Philip that Maddie had rarely glimpsed

during their courtship began to show itself. Sometimes he'd sit in silence in the evenings, smoking and lost in his own thoughts. One night his face fell when a ruined steak and kidney pie was put before him and he pushed it around his plate without speaking.

'If only you hadn't come in so late,' Maddie cried plaintively. 'I had to have mine hours ago. I was so hungry.'

'It doesn't matter,' he murmured, stirring from his malaise. 'I'm sorry.' He began to eat quickly. When he finished he helped her with the dirty dishes then moved to the drawing room to read the evening paper while Maddie made him a cup of cocoa. A thin cry came from their bedroom and Maddie hastened away to pluck Sarah from her crib and walked about, unable to soothe her. Then Philip took the baby from her and she went to sink wearily down on the sofa. When he joined her a moment later, smug for having succeeded where she'd failed, they sat quietly together, she leaning against him while he stroked her hair until she fell into a drowsy state and before she knew it, it was bedtime. Settling into bed each night felt to her not a respite, but like hunkering down ready for battle. For each time Sarah woke Maddie would go to her, never knowing how long she'd need to sit shivering in the darkness, feeding her or rocking the cradle.

After the early weeks of new motherhood had passed, sometimes Philip would turn towards her and his attentions felt unwelcome, with her breasts swollen and the deepest parts of her still tender and strange. Insistent, he'd push his way into her, but when his passion was sated, he'd roll off whispering, 'I'm sorry, I'm a brute,' and once he wept, which frightened her. 'It's all right,' she whispered back, trying to comfort him. But she wondered to herself what had stirred him so deeply, some deep distress perhaps. There was so much about her husband that she didn't know. She'd never known his parents or visited Knyghton where he'd been brought up. In some respects he was a mystery to her.

By the following March, after chicken pox, bronchiolitis and intermittent teething, Sarah had turned into a lively, laughing cherub, ready to walk and into everything, and Philip won a longed-for promotion. 'We can look for somewhere bigger to live now,' he said, his eyes sparkling.

'I think we'll need it,' Maddie murmured, stroking her belly.

'You're not.' The sparkle vanished.

'I am. The doctor thinks November.'

His face softened in a smile. 'Well, I suppose it was likely to happen sometime.'

She felt nauseous this time, which she hadn't with Sarah, which convinced her that the baby was a boy. They started referring to it as William, after Philip's father, and when a girl was born were at a loss for a name. It was Maddie's godmother who laughingly suggested 'Grace' as a mark of God's unexpected gifts, and they both liked it so it stuck. Grace proved an easier baby than Sarah, but forceful, with a strong sense of herself and her place in the world, quite unlike her uncertain elder sister.

By this time they'd moved to a bigger house in West Kensington, where they at last had a garden. Maddie pushed a sturdy table under the window of the spare bedroom where she set out her paints and papers and worked in snatched moments. In a rare exchange of harsh words, she insisted to Philip that they employ a reliable girl to mind the children when Maddie had a deadline. The money Maddie earned would just about pay her wages. Philip couldn't understand what the point of her working was and hated the idea of a stranger bringing up his daughters. 'It's so I don't lose myself,' Maddie cried, with a tilt of her chin. 'Especially if you're not going to be here.'

For Philip's promotion meant trips abroad twice a year, visiting warehouses and plantations in Ceylon and Darjeeling for weeks at a time. He was happy and excited as he prepared for these, humming as he packed his cases, while Maddie watched, subdued, wondering how it was that she and the babies weren't enough to make him cheerful like this. She missed him when he was away, but she didn't worry about him, and got used to it, so that it was strange for a while when he returned and disrupted the even routine of the house. As rumours of war grew so did the demands on Philip's time. Weekends away training with the Territorials he felt it his duty to attend. His commitment also meant that once war was declared he was among the first to be called up.

In the early days after war broke out, Philip was away but didn't leave British shores. Maddie received regular letters in which he described drills and exercises and gave thumbnail portraits of fellow officers and asked anxiously after his daughters. Now and again, with little notice, he'd be granted a few days' leave and arrive home suddenly, the girls dancing round him in the hall with excitement. It was a strange period, the autumn of 1939, with an air of unreality. The country was officially at war, people carried gas masks and followed the blackout rules, but the dreaded air raids had not materialized and the garden shelter Philip had installed was as yet unused. After their plan to move home to Norwich had fallen through because of Maddie's father's illness, they put off thoughts of evacuation. Residential West Kensington was surely unlikely to be a target for the bombs. The Luftwaffe's first air attack came in Scotland, on ships in the Firth of Forth. The boys living next door to them in Valentine Street were sent off to the country, but soon returned, which confirmed Maddie in her decision to stay put.

One morning at the end of November 1939 Philip arrived home unexpectedly. He was to join the rest of his battalion in France and had been given forty-eight hours' leave to say goodbye. The memory of those two days was still precious to Maddie. It was like a return to the early part of their marriage, full of the joy of being together, their love deepened by the knowledge of the separation to come and fear of the dangers they each might face. Then Maddie and the girls waved as the train steamed out of Victoria station and that was the last time they'd seen him.

At the end of May Maddie held her breath as she listened to wireless reports about the brave flotilla of little boats rescuing the remnants of the British Expeditionary Force from Dunkirk and waited anxiously for news that Philip was safe. That news never came.

Seven

Norfolk

April 1941

'Steady there, Bonnie!' Flegg mumbled in his cracked voice as the trap hit a pothole in the country lane and the pony stumbled. The trap jolted then righted itself.

The little girls gasped and clutched at their mother.

'I don't like it,' Sarah moaned. 'I want to go home.'

'We'll be at Knyghton soon, darlings.' Maddie held them close. 'Won't we?' she asked the old man sitting up front.

'Not too far now,' Flegg growled, without turning.

They'd been the only ones to leave the train at the little station. Gussie's latest rambling letter had promised that someone would meet them on the platform, but Maddie had got the girls and their single suitcase down the steps to the road to find only an old trap waiting, the scruffy piebald pony between its shafts nibbling leaves from a beech hedge. The cragged old man in the driver's seat was puffing at a cigarette stub, but on seeing them he pinched it out, tucked it in his top pocket and clambered down to heft the case. 'This here's Bonnie and I'm Flegg.' The girls had stared in wide-eyed surprise at the pony and the grizzled old man, and to get them to climb up onto the back seat Maddie had to pretend the whole thing was a game. It was fortunate that Bonnie was lazy, there was little traffic and though the clouds looked ominous it wasn't actually raining.

Nevertheless, the journey through country lanes between fields greening with early growth and hedges creamy with blossom seemed endless. There were no road signs to tell Maddie where they were, but the pony was confident of her way and the driver needed to do little to guide her. They jogged along for half an hour or so, the only sounds the jingle of the harness and the rhythmic clop of Bonnie's hooves.

'Is this Monksfield?' Maddie asked the old man as they passed through a hamlet with a large green and a pond. He shook his head and pointed the whip ahead to where she could see a church tower rising above a cluster of trees in the distance, but before they reached it the pony wheeled a sharp left off the road and up a gravelly lane. Here, the hedgerow brushed the trap on either side as it swayed along, shedding leaves and white petals over its passengers' feet. Maddie hoped they wouldn't meet anything coming the other way, for there was nowhere to pull in.

After a minute or two the fields and hedges petered out

and woodland began, the gritty lane becoming bare earth and loam. The pony slowed to a walk beneath a shady broadleaf canopy through which green light filtered until suddenly the track widened into a grassy clearing. To the right a pair of mouldering gateposts grew out of the ground. Above the open gate a moss-covered sign with 'Knyghton' painted on it clung by a rusty nail to a gnarled oak trunk.

'Hold tight now,' the old man called as he goaded the pony into a sweeping arc before they plunged forward between the gateposts and into a wild garden beyond. Maddie's spirits rose as the trap wound along a narrow drive between lush banks of dark laurels and rhododendrons in bud. They rounded a bend and she gasped for, with all the magic of a fairytale, a timber-framed manor house lay before them, long and low, like a sleeping wild animal on a rough lawn where spring flowers tumbled, all creamy white and purple and saffron.

'Are we here?' Sarah perked up.

'Here, Mummy?' her sister echoed.

'Yes, we're here,' Maddie said, her eyes darting between the smoke issuing from one of the four chimneys to the lopsided lean of the black and white walls and the square-hatched windows, all as she remembered from the photographs in Philip's album.

The trap bumped onto flagstones and drew up before the wide doorstep of a dark oak front door, which was flanked by a pile of sandbags and a fire bucket. The old man lowered himself stiffly to the ground, knotted the pony's reins to a ring in the wall, then reached up to help Maddie and the girls down with gentle courtesy. Then he went to the front door, pulled an ancient bell rope and took off his cap. They all stood silently waiting, then came the tap of footsteps within and the rattle of the door being unbolted. It crept inwards and a woman's grim face under a mobcap poked out.

'Thu'r'n here,' the man said with a gesture.

'So I see. Don't stand there, old man. Bring 'em in.' The door opened wider.

Maddie felt the woman's eyes inspect her briskly, and her gaze softened only slightly when it shifted to the children as they passed inside. The entrance hall was gloomy, wood-panelled, its floor covered with worn rush matting. Several doors opened off the hallway and to the left a stout wooden staircase with carved posts turned in neat right-angled flights up to a galleried landing. In the wall above the first turn a tall narrow window of coloured glass provided the only daylight. The hall was chilly, the grate in a fireplace empty but for an old vase full of dried hydrangea heads, and Maddie's nose wrinkled at a smell of ancient damp.

She smiled at the woman. 'How do you do. I'm Maddie Anderson. This is Sarah and here's Grace.'

'Pleased to meet you, I'm sure. I'm Ruth Flegg. Cook and general whatnot. And my husband here does everything else.'

Maddie nodded, hearing the bitterness inherent in 'general whatnot'.

'Get their cases in, Flegg,' Mrs Flegg commanded.

'There's only the one, though it is quite large,' Maddie admitted. They watched him shamble back to the trap. 'We lost everything, you see.'

'The bomb got it.' Sarah's face was solemn.

'Reckon it did,' Mrs Flegg said cryptically as the old man returned. 'Take it upstairs, will you, Flegg.'

The old man hefted the case once more, and his boots creaked as he mounted the wooden stairs.

'I'll let Miss Gussie know you're here.'

She disappeared through a door near the back of the hall, leaving Maddie and the girls alone until Flegg lumbered downstairs again and mumbled cheerfully to the girls that he was off to put Bonnie in her paddock. Maddie thanked him as he departed, which elicited a nod and a crack of a smile.

'Grace, dear!' Her younger daughter, idling by a console table, was lifting the lid of a willow-patterned teapot that stood upon it. It clinked as it dropped back into its hole. Just then they heard a tapping sound and looked up to see a slight old lady enter the hall, leaning on a cane. Mrs Flegg hovered behind in close attendance.

'Welcome to Knyghton!' the lady said in a sweet treble voice. The expression on her pale heart-shaped face was serene. Maddie took in her narrow figure neatly encased in a thick brown woollen skirt and jacket over a high-necked ivory blouse with a ruffled collar that set off her loose bun of ashen hair. Her vague blue-eyed gaze travelled fondly over the children, then she smiled warmly at Maddie.

'Forgive me. I've left my spectacles in my room. You're Maddie and these are ...'

'Sarah and Grace,' Maddie said clearly. 'This is your Great-Aunt Gussie, girls.'

'Dear sweet things. Do you like doggies, my loves?'

'They're not used to dogs, are you, girls?' Maddie prompted.

The girls looked wary, but it was too late, because Gussie had called behind her and a pack of small dogs flowed into the hall round their mistress and began to sniff at the newcomers. The girls froze in fear. Maddie scooped Grace up into her arms and Sarah retreated to the staircase, but the dogs were small and gentle enough and bobbed about, tails wagging, and Grace soon begged to be set down.

'That's Phoebe, she's a Pekinese,' Gussie said, pointing with her cane. 'Queenie the fluffy white one there's a mixed biscuits, and Jane and Rochester are Jack Russells.'

'Why does he only have three legs?' Sarah was staring at Rochester.

'Because the other one got caught in a nasty snare.' Gussie's eyes grew rheumy and the dogs instantly swarmed round her, whining at her distress.

'Poor doggy,' Sarah whispered and put out her hand to him, but Gussie cried out and she whipped it away.

'Don't do that, dear, he might nip you.'

'You must watch that Phoebe, too,' remarked Mrs Flegg. 'If you've food in your hand, she'll snatch it quick as anything.'

The girls looked alarmed and edged over to their mother's side.

'Anyway,' Maddie said brightly. 'It's very good of you to have us. I hope you don't mind me asking, but breakfast was an awfully long time ago and the girls will be hungry. May I make them a snack?'

'Oh, bless them,' Gussie said, her eyes rounding. 'Is it lunchtime yet, Mrs Flegg?'

'Lunch will be ready at the usual time, Miss Gussie.' Mrs Flegg looked severely at her mistress. 'One o'clock sharp,' she told Maddie.

The hands on a grandfather clock ticking in the shadow of the stairs displayed twenty-five past twelve.

'Can you wait until then?' Gussie asked in her high girlish voice.

'I'm sure we can.'

'I'm hungry, Mummy,' Grace moaned, but Maddie shushed her.

'Show them their bedrooms, Miss Gussie,' Mrs Flegg ordered. 'Then maybe, Mrs Anderson, you'll lay the dining room table for five.' She turned away mumbling, 'I can't be expected to manage everything by myself with three new mouths to feed.'

'I'm so sorry to put you out,' Maddie said anxiously, but the cook merely sniffed and pushed her way through a faded green-baize-covered door at the back of the hall, leaving it swinging behind her.

Maddie took the girls' hands and they followed Gussie's stiff progress up the stairs with the dogs bounding ahead.

'Won't it be six, not five, if Mr and Mrs Flegg are eating with us?' Maddie thought to ask.

The old lady paused and beamed down at her. 'Oh, no, the Fleggs eat in the kitchen. It's Lyle who'll be in for lunch.'

'Who is Lyle?' Maddie asked, puzzled.

'Who's Lyle? My nephew, of course. Philip's cousin.'

'Oh,' Maddie said, her eyes widening. Had Philip told her about his cousin? She didn't think so. The photos in the album came into her mind, of Philip with the other boy in the garden. Perhaps that was Lyle. If so, why had he never been mentioned?

Flegg had left the suitcase against the wall at the top of the stairs and the girls dragged it between them as they followed Gussie along the narrow landing.

'This is to be yours, Maddie, next to mine and opposite Lyle's.' Gussie pushed open a door into a large light-filled bedroom. Maddie loved it instantly. She sniffed at a hint of lavender and went at once to the wide window that looked out onto a back lawn edged by trees. The walls were half-panelled, the upper parts papered with an intricate design of birds and berries and flowers. A curtained four-poster dominated the room and a kidney-shaped dressing table stood under the window. 'This was Mamma and Papa's room,' Gussie announced as she poked her cane at a bumblebee bumping itself against the glass. Maddie opened the window and shooed it out, then stood listening to the birdsong and the rustle of the trees. Despite the lukewarm welcome she felt herself fill up with pleasure.

'Dear me, little girl, no!' Gussie cried. Maddie swung round to see that Grace had climbed onto the bed and started to bounce.

'Come down right away,' she said, more sharply than usual, and Grace's face crumpled as she slid off the silky eiderdown.

'I'd have been whipped if we'd done that when we were young,' Gussie said. Her thin lips settled in a wrinkled moue and Maddie's heart sank.

'They're tired and hungry which makes them naughty,' she said gently, putting her arm round the cowed child. 'Perhaps we should see where they're going to sleep.'

'Ah, the nursery.' Gussie's face brightened.

She led them back to an end room at the other side of the stairs. It had barred windows on two sides and two dear little truckle beds. The girls' footsteps pattered on the wooden floor as, before Maddie could stop them, Grace rushed to mount a noble-looking rocking horse that posed mid-gallop before a window and Sarah to touch a shy finger to a doll's house on a table next to it. Fortunately Gussie merely watched fondly from the door with clasped hands.

'It's lovely to have children in the nursery again,' she breathed. 'Philip and Lyle shared it at the beginning, you know.'

'The beginning?'

'When Rose brought Philip home from India. Poor little boy. A terrible thing for a young child, to send him away to school like that.'

Maddie felt tears prickle but blinked them away. Gussie's simple insight into her husband's experience had stabbed her heart and found it undefended.

A few minutes later, Maddie and the girls carried out Mrs Flegg's instructions, setting out cutlery with yellow bone handles on a dark polished dining table, the girls chattering cheerfully as they laid down mats with pictures of hunting scenes. Maddie tried to order her thoughts. She loved the house already, its ancient feel, as though it was part of the woods that surrounded it, built perhaps with some of its oaks. However, she realized it would bring her face to face with a part of Philip that she'd never known, the secret part that had formed him, his childhood.

Already she had mixed feelings about coming here. Gussie had welcomed them, but Mrs Flegg clearly resented their arrival and since Gussie apparently left the running of the house to her this could prove a problem. Maddie had to win her over. Registering their ration books with local shop-keepers would be a priority. And there'd be plenty of ways in which Maddie might help. Once the girls were settled, of course. She smiled to see that Sarah and Grace were sitting in their places already. Sarah was telling Grace a fanciful story about a horse on one of the table mats. They'd loved their new nursery. That was a blessing. Maddie kissed them both on the tops of their heads and set off to find the kitchen to fill the water jug.

Out in the hall she heard distant voices and paused. One, too vigorous to be Flegg's, came from behind the baize door to the kitchen. There came the sound of hurried footsteps and she leaped back just in time as the door flew open and a man strode through.

'Sorry, I didn't know you were there!' He gazed at her in surprise and she stared back, speechless with shock and confusion at his likeness to her husband.

Lyle Anderson was tall and broad-shouldered, with unruly

tawny curls, a tanned face and a look of Philip about the eyes and mouth. He brought with him a scent of fresh earth and growing things. His scowling gaze suggested a less gentle, more purposeful version of her husband. She found him dangerously attractive.

Eight

'You must be Madeleine.' His voice was low and surly and he did not smile. His eyes narrowed.

'Yes, Maddie,' she said, standing straighter. 'And you, I imagine—'

'Lyle, Philip's cousin.' His hand was rough and warm against hers. 'Welcome to Knyghton. You must take us as you find us, I'm afraid. It will seem dull after the excitement of the big city.' Lyle dropped his cap onto a chair and hung his tweed jacket over a hook on the wall. His quick movements and physical presence brought the hall to life. Maddie couldn't stop staring at him. He was a taller, burlier version of her husband, and lacked Philip's grace, but the likeness was still strong. 'You're being well looked after, I take it?'

'Mr Flegg met our train and our rooms are lovely. I don't mind quiet. We're glad to be out of London frankly.'

'Ah, yes, your home. A bad job. I was sorry to hear about it.'

'We lost almost everything, but other people have it worse.

At least we survived. It's kind of you to have us and we'll try not to be a nuisance. This is such a beautiful house ...'

Maddie looked round the hall, taking in things she'd missed on their arrival, oil lamps on the walls, an old framed map of Norfolk.

She moved closer to examine it and Lyle pointed out Knyghton for her. 'It's the best place in the world. Especially for children. Where are yours?'

Maddie noticed the dining room door quiver and smiled as first Sarah's face appeared round it and then Grace's. She introduced them to 'Uncle' Lyle. 'We've been laying the table for lunch, haven't we, girls?' There were giggles and they vanished again.

'They look like miniature versions of you,' he said. His gaze was a tad forthright and she drew herself up, blushing.

'Do you think so? I always say they have a look of Philip.'

His face clouded. 'Of course, of course. Have you any news?' He spoke more gently.

She shook her head. 'Nothing at all.'

'He'll turn up, I imagine.' His voice was too bright. 'A bad penny, is Philip.'

She had to look away. If Philip had been taken prisoner by the Germans they'd have heard by now. Surely. Perhaps he'd escaped, though.

When she looked up, Lyle's expression was unreadable.

'All we can do is peg on,' she murmured. 'And hope.'

'Of course.'

The grandfather clock struck one, ending their conversation, for the house came suddenly to life. The baize door flew open and Mrs Flegg entered bearing a tray of bowls and a tureen. Gussie slowly descended the staircase, the dogs bobbing along beside her.

Maddie slipped along to the kitchen and filled the water jug. There was only a cold tap. A kettle on the stove was sighing softly, ready for the washing-up. She remembered the oil lamps in the hall. There was no electricity, it seemed. She turned at the sound of the door to see that Mrs Flegg had returned.

'You forgot the ladle,' the woman said severely and handed her one she took from a deep drawer before reloading her tray with a greyish loaf, a cube of cheese and a butter dish.

'I'm sorry,' Maddie said humbly, following her out. The woman had said nothing about ladles until now.

Lunch was largely a silent affair, Mrs Flegg serving a stew that was mostly potato with a side dish of cabbage, but the bread was fresh and there was more butter than Maddie had seen for a year. For pudding there were small portions of bottled raspberries and a thin custard. Grace followed Gussie's lead in dropping crusts for the dogs, earning Maddie's frown. Lyle ate quickly and in silence, then wiped his mouth with his napkin and pushed back his chair. 'I must ask you to excuse me. A man from the Committee is coming about grain yields,' he explained to Maddie. 'I'll see you at dinner.'

There was a sense that with his departure, life had left the room. Gussie was only a pale presence in comparison. However, she spoke more now that he'd gone.

'He works so hard and these officials are always bothering him.'

Maddie wondered whether Gussie had noticed that there was a war on. 'Knyghton has a farm, of course. I hadn't thought.'

'Are there cows?' Sarah piped up.

'Yes, dear, we've always had cows, but only a few Red Polls now. And some pigs. Otherwise it's wheat, oats, barley, beet, whatever they tell us,' Gussie grumbled. 'And we keep a few animals behind the house – goats, chickens, rabbits. Flegg looks after them.'

'Can we see them?' Sarah asked, her eyes shining.

'I don't see why not.' Gussie beamed at her.

'Now?' Grace said. She dropped her spoon in her dish and slid off her chair.

'You must fetch your coat,' Maddie said, 'but first ask Aunt Gussie if you may leave the table.' Grace dutifully chanted the request in her shrill voice.

'Of course, my sweet. You'll need to go through the kitchen garden.' Gussie waved a hand in the general direction. 'Mind your clothes or the goats will nibble them. Jessie is especially naughty. She's the biggest.'

The children had taken to the old lady, Maddie saw. Gussie was in some ways still a child herself, with her absorption in animals and her engagement with Grace, who reached down gingerly to stroke one of the Jack Russells.

'Goodbye, Jane, we'll be back soon. Auntie Gussie, do the dogs sleep on your bed at night?'

'Oh, no, dear, Mrs Flegg wouldn't hear of it. They have

their own baskets on the floor.' She looked anxiously towards the door as she said this and Maddie smiled to herself at the obvious white lie.

'Will you take something out to the kitchen first?' Maddie called as the girls rushed for the door and they turned back. Sarah solemnly bore her own pudding plate, but her sister seized the empty raspberry bowl and gave the inside a great lick. 'Oh, Grace!' Maddie closed her eyes briefly then started stacking dishes. 'Put on your outdoor things, dears, then wait. I'm just coming.'

'What will you do this afternoon, Maddie?' Gussie asked, picking up a stray teaspoon and putting it down again. Mrs Flegg appeared and began to wipe the table mats.

'Unpack, I think. Then perhaps I'll take the children for a walk.'

'I hope you'll excuse me then. I must retire to my room. There are always letters to write.'

Mrs Flegg rolled her eyes at Maddie, making her understand that Gussie would spend the afternoon sleeping. *And why shouldn't she at her age?* Maddie silently thought.

'Don't they girls have a nap?' Mrs Flegg asked with her hands on her hips.

'Usually Grace does,' Maddie said, 'but they're both much too excited today.'

'Of course they are,' Gussie smiled. 'By the way, there's a cupboardful of toys in the nursery.'

'Thank you. We'll explore.'

'The doll's house was mine when I was a girl. There were three of us, perhaps you know. George, Lyle's father, Philip's father, William, and me. I was the eldest and I'm the only one left.' There was a faraway look in her eyes.

The Pekinese put its paws up on her lap. 'Dear Phoebe,' Gussie cupped its fluffy face in her hands and bent to kiss its nose. 'They always *know*, animals, don't they?'

She rose, gathering Phoebe in her arms. The other dogs leaped to their feet and Maddie held the door open for the little procession to pass.

'Oh Christmas,' Mrs Flegg groaned. Out in the hall the girls in their eagerness had thrown all the coats on the floor and Grace was standing like a scarecrow with hers on upside down.

Outside, a shower of rain had left the world with a well-washed look. Following Gussie's vague directions, Maddie led the girls along a flagstone path from the back door, past some outhouses. Just before they reached a small cottage, they came to an arched doorway in a high flint wall and turned through it into the kitchen garden. There they found Mr Flegg on his knees sowing lettuces, the trademark cigarette stub clamped between his lips. When Maddie called to him and asked about the animals, he sat back on his heels wordlessly, and pointed with his trowel to a door in the far wall. She thanked him and set off towards it, the children skipping ahead between cucumber frames and beds of young plants. Opening the door, they stepped into a walled orchard. At one side, several goats were corralled in a large grassy pen while chickens pottered under the fruit trees near a ramshackle henhouse. The girls were suddenly shy, retreating as a hen came near. Grace, trying to pat a goat, shrieked with terror when it nibbled at her fingers, but Maddie calmed her and showed her how to feed it hay and explained that the chickens were merely curious about the shiny buttons on their shoes.

They were standing before a silent old dovecote, its ruined roof thick with moss, Maddie pointing out the holes where the doves would have flown in and out, when Flegg's growling voice behind her made her jump.

'That was her put him up, old Mrs Anderson.' The old man was clutching an empty pail.

'My husband's grandmother?'

'She could never get the birds to lay. So that were a waste. You must keep this door closed. I'm too old to be chasing chickens.'

He stumped off about his business, shutting the offending door. After a while Maddie and the girls retreated, too, Maddie closing it firmly behind them.

'Sorry,' she said as she passed the old man, bent over his seedlings and he grunted.

Did everyone resent them being here, she thought with a heavy heart. As they crossed the lawn and passed the line of outhouses, the sun striking the window of a long wooden shed woke a memory. It was the shed in the photograph album, surely, where the shadowy figure of the girl could just be seen, the boys sitting in the foreground. A cloud crossed the sun and the memory faded.

'Shall we see if we can find the cows?' she called to the girls. She knew better than to introduce the word 'walk', the very notion of which would exhaust them.

'Yes, cows,' they agreed and each put a hand in hers as she drew them round to the front of the house, up the drive and along a rutted lane as Gussie had instructed. The air was alive with birdsong and the distant cries of animals, and Maddie cheered up again. Very soon the trees gave out and ploughed fields divided by hedgerow began. They idled on a wide stone bridge over a stream lined with willows. Beyond, the path led past a pasture of glossy brown cows with their calves. The children climbed onto a gate and sat to watch them. A pair of young women in rubber boots and breeches, laughing and talking, ambled past carrying pails of water and Maddie returned their greeting. Further along the track she could see a group of farm buildings nestled in a dip around a muddy yard. Beyond that was a pond shaded by willows, where a huge chestnut horse with a fine arched neck stood in the shallows. Two others cropped grass nearby. She shaded her eyes but couldn't see Lyle anywhere.

The gentle scene was spoiled by the onset of a far-off rumble that grew to a roar. The girls climbed down from the gate and clung to her, whimpering in terror, as a squadron of planes swept overhead. 'It's all right, they're ours,' Maddie cried, crouching to hug their shivering bodies, but it was a while before they were calm enough to turn for home.

Home! she thought, mutinous, as she trudged back to the house, carrying Grace and with Sarah clutching her hand. Knyghton might be beautiful, but its inhabitants were grudging. They may well be safer here from air raids, but there were clearly other battles to fight.

Nine

That evening, after the girls had eaten tea, been bathed and put sleepy to bed, Grace cuddling Rabbit and Sarah her doll, Maddie helped Mrs Flegg lay out a cold supper. Then she joined Gussie in the drawing room for sherry as they waited for Lyle's return. The old lady had changed into a high-necked blue dress as if for a grand dinner. A fluffy white shawl round her shoulders did not hide a string of pearls gleaming at her breast.

It was dusk and the room lay in shadow. A fire leaping in the grate was the only point of light, and the blackout curtains were as yet undrawn. The dogs lay stretched out on the hearthrug, but for the Pekinese, who was tucked up next to her mistress in one of a pair of armchairs by the fire. Maddie held up her glass and studied the flickering light in its amber depths, feeling that she'd returned to another, older time, the only touch of modernity she'd noticed being a magazine lying on a pretty black lacquer coffee table painted with boughs of cherry blossom.

She was hungry.

'Does Lyle often work this late?'

'It's not unusual, these days. He complains of being short-handed.'

'But he has land girls, I think. At least, we saw some young women today.'

'Oh, yes. But it's not the same as having men. Is it, Phoebe dear?' Gussie smiled down at the dog and smoothed its long hair.

Maddie decided not to argue the point. 'It's very good of you to have us, you know. We'll try not to be a burden.'

'Oh, you won't be, dear. They're lovely children. So long as they don't tease the dogs.'

'I'll make sure they don't. And I'll help Mrs Flegg in any way I can. It's a big house to look after.'

'It is. Do you know, when I was a girl, we had four maids as well as a cook and a boot boy. My mother – that's her up there.' She gestured to a large portrait lost in the darkness above the fireplace and Maddie narrowed her eyes trying to see it. 'She had her own maid. Such a shame . . .' Her words trailed away and her hand felt for her necklace.

'What was a shame, Gussie?'

'Everything was different with the war.'

'The Great War, you mean?'

'Yes. George was killed.'

'He was your brother? The one who inherited Knyghton.'

'Yes, do you know, they sent his clothes home in a parcel. They were dark with dried blood. It was dreadful! How could they do that? We burned them in the garden. Had our own funeral for him.'

Maddie looked into the flames dancing in the grate and swallowed, thinking about Philip and how she would be unable to bear it if . . .

'Is that Lyle now?' Gussie said, straightening in her chair. The dogs sprang to their feet and Rochester limped across to the door, his ears cocked. From the hall came the sound of Lyle's voice, then his footsteps on the stairs. 'He's gone up to change.'

Maddie sought a new subject of conversation. 'You've always lived here at Knyghton?' she said.

'I was born in the bed that you'll sleep on,' she whispered triumphantly. 'And I've never spent a night away.'

'That's very unusual.' Gussie was sugary sweet, but also very strange, Maddie decided. Indeed, the whole household was strange. Philip's cousin in charge, living here with only this confused old lady for company. She wondered if Lyle had ever married and if he hadn't, why not. He would have had his pick of local girls, given his handsome looks and commanding air, which many women would find attractive. Then she'd be mistress of Knyghton. But not every girl would like this ancient mouldering house – or want to have a crazed old aunt living with them.

Just then, the door opened and a golden light filled the room. 'Good evening, ladies.' Lyle, hair combed and casually dressed, carried a lamp. He lifted it onto the drinks cabinet, where he adjusted the wick, so that the flame leaped then steadied. After drawing the heavy curtains, he poured himself a drink and came to stand before the fire. His jersey, Maddie noticed, had a hole at the elbow.

The lamplight leaped and intensified as she tipped her face to look up at Lyle, and her attention was caught by the portrait above him. She drew a sharp breath, seeing it fully at last. It was of a seated youngish woman in a long white dress, her dark hair caught up in a style that made it seem like a soft halo, framing her pale forehead and rosy cheeks. Dark eyes looked out shyly at the beholder. She wore a sparkling necklace and was cradling a light brown hare in her lap, its long ears laid flat across its back, its almond-shaped eyes as bright as its mistress's.

'Is that your grandmother?' Maddie whispered and Lyle followed her gaze.

'Yes, that's Gussie's mother, Eleanor.' He stood back to admire it. 'She died when I was eighteen. I didn't know her when she looked like that, though. She seemed rather formidable to me.'

'My father adored her,' Gussie sighed. 'Everybody did. She had this marvellous way about her. Calming. She would make everything better.' Gussie's eyes were large and sad.

'I love the gentle way she holds the hare.' Maddie said. 'Was it a pet?'

'I don't know.' Gussie looked thoughtful. 'It was painted before I was born. She had a way with all wild creatures, I can tell you that.'

'I imagine the hare to be a reference to the history of the house,' Lyle said. 'If you look outside above the front door you'll see what I mean.'

'I will, tomorrow.' It was too dark now.

Lyle tossed back the last of his sherry and Gussie said,

'Since supper's laid out in the other room, shouldn't we go and eat it?'

Lyle was friendlier this evening, Maddie thought, as they ate crumbs of cheese with more of the bread and a rather dull vegetable salad. There was bottled apple to follow with left-over custard. What cheered the meal was red wine, which Lyle poured from a dusty bottle into crystal glasses that threw patterns on the polished table in the lamplight.

At first the talk was of the farm. The official who'd visited earlier had made requests that would be difficult to meet, even if the weather proved favourable. A fallow field was to be cleared of stones and sown with peas. Lyle spoke of his work with great seriousness. He'd inherited Knyghton when a boy on the death of his father, George. The farm was then run by a manager until Lyle left school and had learned enough to take over. Now that more labourers were being called up, the strains were obvious. 'At least the Land Army girls aren't bad.' Lyle reached for his wine and sat back in his chair to drink it, suddenly looking tired.

'That's good to hear,' Maddie said.

She noticed again the hole in Lyle's jersey, and when he set his glass back on the table, she saw that his shirt cuff was frayed, too. There was no one who had the time or the inclination to do any mending, she supposed, and decided that she must find the right moment to offer. There were other things more pressing for her. She spoke into a silence.

'I need to take Sarah down to the school in the village tomorrow.' She'd written to the headmistress before they left

London and had been relieved to hear that there was space for her daughter. 'Is it easy to find?'

'Very,' Lyle said. 'It's at the far end of Monksfield opposite the church. The school bus passes the end of our lane at half past eight. Flegg will take you down in the trap to meet it if you don't want to have to walk on the first day.'

'I wouldn't want to bother him.'

'Oh, Flegg won't mind.'

'If you're sure.'

Mrs Flegg, when she came to clear the table, said that she'd tell him and Maddie thanked her.

'There's something else, Mrs Flegg. I need somewhere to work. A table with good light.'

'What work is it you do?' Lyle asked with a cagey look.

'I'm an illustrator.' Maddie briefly described her next project, a children's story by a well-known writer.

'Well, I never,' Mrs Flegg said, while Gussie stared at Maddie in surprise. Lyle looked thoughtful, then said, 'Maddie could use Philip's old bedroom, couldn't she, Gussie? There's a decent-sized desk in there and it's north-facing.'

'I suppose so,' Gussie said, looking vague.

Mrs Flegg crossed her arms. 'And who's going to look after your little one while Sarah's at school and you're working, Mrs Anderson? I'm sure I won't have the time.'

'Of course, I know that,' Maddie said quickly. 'I wondered if you knew of anyone, a young neighbour, perhaps, who'd like to earn some pocket money.'

But Mrs Flegg couldn't think of anyone.

After supper they repaired to the drawing room, where

they tried to listen to the news on the wireless, though it kept fading in and out.

'I must get the battery recharged,' Lyle said, thumping it.

'The news is never very cheerful anyway,' Maddie said. No one could deny that with defeats on every front a sense of desperation was setting in. She felt draggingly tired after a long and onerous day so she made her excuses and wished Lyle and Gussie goodnight.

As she climbed the stairs, the flickering candle flame made the shadows leap and dance. She went to the girls' room first, lifting the candle to illuminate their sleeping faces. How peaceful they looked. Sarah's hair fanned out on the pillow, like Millais' painting of Ophelia floating in the stream. Grace was curled on her side amid a tumble of blankets. Maddie fetched her sketchbook and sat down to draw their dear faces. Then she listened to the sound of their soft breaths and smiled to herself as she left, pulling the door to.

In her own room she slipped out of her clothes and into her nightdress, then shivered as she slid between chilly sheets. It might well be spring, but tomorrow she would see if there was a hot water bottle. She blew out the candle, stretched the hem of her nightdress over her toes and lay curled up in the darkness, listening to the sigh of the wind in the trees and the quizzical hoot of an owl. Her thoughts rambled over the day's events, the tearful farewells to Mrs Moulder, the exhaustion of the journey, the delights and disappointment of their arrival at Knyghton. But they were here, safe and sound in Philip's family home. Without Philip, it was true, and to a chilly welcome, but surely, Maddie thought stubbornly, they had a right to be here if they contributed to the life of the house. She loved Knyghton already. It felt like a place of refuge. Here the girls had a chance to be happy again and she could fashion some kind of life. She thought of the photograph album still in her case and the key tucked away with it. Perhaps here she would feel closer to Philip while she waited for news of what had happened to him.

Her last thoughts as she fell into sleep were of the portrait above the fireplace in the drawing room. Gussie's mother Eleanor, Philip and Lyle's grandmother. She had such a lovely face. It was possible to think of her as a kind of guardian angel, watching over the house, her diamond necklace sparkling.

Maddie slept deeply, waking only once, unsure what had disturbed her. A cry, she thought, but though she lay alert, it did not come again and she slipped back into slumber.

Ten

As it was Sarah's first day at school, Flegg offered to take Maddie and the girls all the way into the village in the trap. If Maddie didn't mind waiting an hour, he'd then bring her and Grace home again. He had errands to run. So did Maddie, so she gladly accepted.

In Monksfield Flegg tied Bonnie's reins to a ring sunk into the wall of the churchyard opposite the school, which was a Victorian redbrick building surmounted by a clock tower. Children milled about in the playground behind the iron railings, swinging their satchels, playing with balls and skipping ropes or simply sitting on the steps chattering as they waited to be summoned inside.

Sarah, in her navy tunic and white blouse, already looked one of them, but she hung back at the gates, clutching her mother's hand tightly. Then a dumpy young woman strode out of the building and rang a handbell. The children swarmed towards the doors, the teacher caught in the midst of them, braced against the flow like a rock in a fast-flowing stream.

Maddie tugged her daughters along in their wake and was directed by the teacher to the headmistress's room. She knocked and they were admitted to a gloomy office lined with books and group photographs of pupils long grown and gone.

'Mrs Anderson, I'm Miss Blackstone.' Maddie shook hands with the tall, cheerful headmistress. 'And this must be Sarah. And her little sister. How very charming. Do sit down.' Although her manner was kindly, Miss Blackstone's smile was unusually wide and revealed a set of artificial teeth. Sarah surveyed her with alarm from the safety of her mother's side, while Grace snuggled into Maddie's lap.

'It's very good of you to find a place for my daughter,' Maddie said.

'I have to say it was a surprise to receive your letter. It's been a long time since there were children at Knyghton. I hope you'll be happy here, Sarah. Some of the boys and girls find our rules strict, but we think they appreciate having boundaries. Some of these London evacuees need watching, Mrs Anderson. It's not their fault, it's the way they've been brought up.'

'I don't doubt it, but I'm sure Sarah will give you no trouble,' Maddie said nervously, aware of her daughter's tight grip on her arm.

'She's in Miss Dale's class. I'll take you there.'

Miss Dale turned out to be the teacher they'd met earlier. The high-ceilinged classroom where they interrupted her calling the register contained a couple of dozen old-fashioned desks in strict rows of six. The only one unoccupied stood by itself at the very front and was covered in chalk dust. Miss Dale's own high desk loomed over it.

The children briefly rose from their seats at the entry of their headmistress and parroted her 'Good morning,' back at her.

'This is Sarah Anderson, children,' Miss Dale said, sending Sarah to the vacant desk. The child looked back at her mother with a deeply unhappy expression, and Maddie's heart nearly broke. Sarah had loved her school in London. Maddie had therefore assumed that she'd like it here, but, as she glanced round, something about the rows of set faces told her otherwise. There were several boys not in uniform, hungry-looking, with pinched unhappy countenances. The posters on the walls enjoined the observer to *Keep mum – she's not so dumb* and to *Dig for Victory*. A dog-eared map of the world tacked to the wall by the blackboard was printed with such tiny lettering that it would hardly be inviting to young eyes.

'We'll leave you to it, Miss Dale.' Miss Blackstone ushered Maddie and Grace out, closing the door. 'I don't believe in soppy goodbyes,' she said briskly, seeing their crestfallen faces. 'Much better to let Sarah get on with it.'

Maddie bit her lip and Grace's grip tightened on her hand as Miss Blackstone led them back down the hall to the entrance. When they reached the heavy double doors, the headmistress paused, one hand on a brass doorknob. 'And how are you settling in at Knyghton?' she asked, an expression on her face disturbing in its shrewdness.

'We only arrived yesterday, but I'm sure we will settle in very well.' Already Maddie felt a rush of loyalty to Knyghton and its inhabitants.

'I'm glad to hear that.' Miss Blackstone waited, eyebrows raised, but since Maddie didn't add anything she pulled the door open and released them into the fresh spring air.

'I wanted to say goodbye to Sarah,' Grace whimpered as Maddie unfastened the gates.

'So did I, but I'm sure Miss Blackstone knows best.'

Across the road, they saw the empty trap, Bonnie champing patiently at her nosebag. 'We have some things to do while we wait for Mr Flegg to take us home,' Maddie explained to Grace. 'Let's look at the shops, shall we?'

Monksfield was a sizeable village with its own high street and a pub called the Knyghton Arms. Grace skipped along beside her mother quite happily. At the butcher's they joined a short queue of women with shopping baskets. Maddie registered for rations, enabling her to buy bacon, then did the same at the grocer's where she bought tinned meat. At the newsagent's two doors further on she stopped to study a notice board hanging in the window, then plucked a local paper from a stand and went in, a plan forming in her mind. The lad behind the counter looked at the newcomers suspiciously, but Maddie stared back boldly as she paid for the paper. 'How much is it to place an advertisement in your window?' she asked him.

'A penny a week,' he told her, then, at her request, rummaged below the counter, producing a scrap of card and a pencil stub. A moment's thought before she wrote: 'Responsible woman wanted to mind girl, 3 yrs, two mornings. Apply Mrs Madeleine Anderson, Knyghton, Monksfield.' It was annoying there not being a telephone in the house, she thought as she paid and watched the lad pin the card to the board inside the window.

Outside, she was pleased to glimpse a sign for a library, but before they could cross the road to investigate, she caught sight of the stocky figure of Flegg plodding towards them. He was carrying a cardboard box, which clinked loudly with bottles, and as he drew near she saw an old pair of garden shears sitting on the top.

'Would you like a bottle of beer?' he asked Grace with a twinkle in his eye and she nodded shyly. He was, Maddie noticed, happier to talk to children than adults.

'Well, you can't have one,' he said.

'I should think not.' Maddie smiled.

'You can have something else then.'

Good as his word, when they reached the trap he offered each of them a dry rusk from a paper bag. Grace sat next to her mother, happily crunching hers as Bonnie trotted them back along the street towards Knyghton. Maddie read the newspaper she had bought and trawled the list of classifieds, but there was no one asking for domestic work.

When they reached Knyghton, Gussie was sitting on a bench on the grass grooming her dogs. She waved at them cheerily. Maddie helped Grace down from the trap, and the little girl ran off to help. Gussie gave her a comb and showed her how to use it on Jane, the quietest of the four. Seeing her thus absorbed Maddie rescued her shopping bag from the step where Flegg had left it and, glancing at the front door, remembered to look for the hare Lyle had mentioned. There it was, a delicate carving up on the lintel, its legs stretched in flight. She moved closer, craning her neck. It was easy to understand why she hadn't noticed it before for the wood was old and weathered.

After checking that Grace was still happily occupied, Maddie walked round to the back door to give Mrs Flegg the food that she'd bought. A savoury smell drew her inside where she found Flegg already there, pouring a mug of tea from the pot, and his wife at the stove, browning some scraps of meat in a frying pan. Seeing Maddie, Flegg wordlessly fetched another mug from a cupboard.

'May I help in some way?' Maddie asked Mrs Flegg, laying her purchases on the rough wooden table.

Mrs Flegg inspected the bacon she'd bought then added it to her frying pan with a 'Next time don't let him pass off such fatty bits on you. You can wash them ones for me.' She nodded at a mound of muddy potatoes and carrots lying on the table. 'Then peel 'em and cut 'em up. Knife's in the drawer there and there's an apron behind the door. Pity you couldn't find an onion.'

'I didn't know you wanted one, I'm sorry.'

Flegg went outside with his tea and his newly sharpened garden shears, clearly set on some task or other. Maddie and Mrs Flegg were left working in uncomfortable silence. Maddie's hands were soon red and numb from the cold water as she scrubbed and peeled the vegetables. She wondered what tone to take with this taciturn woman who stood with her back to her scraping the seared meat into a waiting pot. Although Maddie fully intended to pull her weight in this new arrangement, her pride was stung by Mrs Flegg's rudeness. She would simply not humble herself.

Finally she settled on, 'I'm happy to shop for us all when I can, but I'll need a proper list.'

'Flegg takes me down to the village most days,' Mrs Flegg snapped, 'or he goes himself if I can trust him.' She spooned the lard off a bowl of dripping into the frying pan and pushed it about till it melted, then sprinkled flour and worked it in with short savage movements. Maddie pared the potatoes and took down a large saucepan from a shelf to put them in. Out of the window she could see Flegg hacking at an unruly hedge with his shears, a cigarette taped to his lower lip.

She ran water over the potatoes and fitted on the lid. 'Where shall I put this?'

Mrs Flegg jabbed a finger towards an empty ring on the stove and Maddie carried the pan to it, trying not to splash water.

'There. I'd better check that Grace is happy,' she said, wiping her hands on her apron. 'I'll come back and finish the carrots.'

'D'you know your herbs? There's rosemary and thyme outside the window.'

'I bring some back in a moment,' Maddie sang as she flew out of the back door.

The garden bench was empty. There was just fluffy dog hair blowing like thistledown in the wind. Then she heard voices, Gussie's, Grace's high tones and a bark, in the distance. She followed the sounds and glimpsed them together at the edge of the treeline, Gussie leaning on her stick laughing while Grace tossed a ball and the dogs chased it. Maddie smiled to herself and returned to the kitchen, stopping to gather the herbs that Mrs Flegg required, drawing a rosemary twig to her nose to breathe in its woody scent.

Back in the kitchen Mrs Flegg glanced suspiciously at the handful of leaves Maddie gave her, then nodded her thanks and began to shred rosemary into the gravy.

Maddie picked up the knife. 'Do you like carrots cut into rounds or sticks?'

Mrs Flegg turned and stared at her in amazement. 'As you like, I don't mind.'

Maddie sighed. She was getting nowhere with this woman. She hastily sliced them into discs then added them to the pot. The peel she scraped as directed into a bucket by the back door for the dogs and the rabbits.

'What are we having for pudding?'

'There's the last of last year's stewed plums in the pantry through there, before you reach the dairy, top shelf on the left.'

The pantry, a closet off the scullery, was lit by a scrap of window and smelled pleasantly of grain. Jars of fruit labelled in wobbly capitals stood in neat rows above bags of flour, oats and rice. Maddie stepped over a baited mousetrap and examined the jars, selecting one that was half full. After closing the door, she peeped briefly into the shadowy dairy beyond. Several covered jugs stood on the stone worktop next to a small butter churn and a bowl of brown eggs. They'd fallen on their feet coming to a farm, she thought. There would be milk, cream and butter. The odd chicken, she supposed, and the vegetables Flegg grew, game in season. The children would not go hungry.

When she returned to the kitchen, Mrs Flegg was bent to the hot oven, sliding her stewpot inside. She straightened and fastened her eye upon the jar in Maddie's hands. 'That's the one. Leave it on the side. There's plenty else to do now the lunch is on. Cleaning the bathroom, sweeping the floors, it's endless, Mrs Anderson.' For the first time that morning their eyes met.

'I'm sorry, Mrs Flegg,' Maddie said, trying to keep her voice level. 'I know that it's hard having more mouths to feed. I'll do my best to help, I promise, but . . .'

'You've got the girls to manage, I can see that.'

'I ought to have told you, I've advertised for someone to come to help with Grace. So I can do my work.'

'You have, have you?' Mrs Flegg banged a lid onto a saucepan. 'Well, you'll be lucky, I can tell you. We can't get another maid. Nelly went off to that ATS. She was a good girl. Sensible, too, didn't get the willies.'

'The willies?'

'In an old place like this it's easy to be spooked. The furniture creaks or a door slams in a draught, it's just that. All silly nonsense to say otherwise. You'll not be getting paint all over the place, will you?'

Maddie explained briefly how she worked and that she'd be using the spare bedroom. 'Don't worry, I'll be responsible for looking after it.'

'You'll not want a fire in April.'

'Of course not.'

'That's all right then. Still, I say you'll be lucky to get anyone for Grace.'

'I hope that you're wrong. I have a deadline to meet.'

'Well, I can't look after her.'

The back door opened and Grace came in, followed closely by Flegg. The little girl proudly showed her mother two eggs that she held. 'Oh, darling, you are clever,' Maddie said as she went to take them from her daughter.

'The hens make them in their tummies,' the child said in wonder and everyone smiled at the thought.

Maddie took Grace upstairs intending to make the children's beds and tidy the nursery. She opened the door of the toy cupboard.

'Look, Grace, a train set.'

The child ran over as Maddie dragged out a cardboard box.

'Trees and people!' Grace exclaimed as together they picked out its contents. She helped Maddie fit the wooden rails together in a figure of eight across the nursery floor and assembled the trains. The wood was dark with age and the engines old-fashioned ones with odd-shaped funnels. Probably Lyle and Philip had played with them once, but Maddie saw that they'd belonged to an even older generation for *VR* was painted on one of the engines and the wooden stationmaster and passengers wore Victorian clothes.

Once Grace was lost in her own world, arranging the figurines, the trees and a group of little houses, talking to the passengers and making whistling noises, Maddie made the beds, folded clothes, then rooted about in the cupboard to see what else she could find. Maybe something to remind her of Philip.

She sat on Sarah's bed to sort through a box of books, school stories with brightly illustrated spines, and some wooden jigsaw puzzles. Maybe he'd played with these. Philip had only been seven when he'd arrived at Knyghton, she remembered him telling her that, and she felt a lump in her throat, imagining the small boy in school uniform who'd sailed across the sea to be left in a strange house in a cold climate without his mother. Had that made him vulnerable? Undoubtedly.

The bedroom door creaked open and Maddie looked up to see Gussie's curious face peeping round. 'May I come in?'

'Of course!'

'Oh, you've found my brothers' trains.' She sat down in a rattan chair to watch Grace, who smiled at her briefly then continued with her game.

'Grace, you will be careful, they're quite old.' Maddie put down the books.

'Don't worry, dear. I'm delighted that they're being played with again. It's been a long time since we've had children in the house. That's what I told Lyle when you wrote to me. "They must come. Philip's children have the right to be here. And it would be lovely to hear young voices again."'

So Lyle hadn't wanted them here? Perhaps Maddie shouldn't be surprised.

'Lyle hasn't ever married himself?' she asked tentatively. He'd be the same age as Philip, thirty-three, she supposed.

'No. I wish he would or what will happen to Knyghton if there are no heirs? There is a girl I thought he'd choose ... Susie Welbourne. The families have always been close, I don't know why he hasn't, but if I say anything he bites my head off. Poor Lyle. He never has any time for himself. I think he wanted to enlist, you know, but he couldn't because of the farm.'

'He should be glad of that excuse,' Maddie said in a bitter voice.

'Oh, sorry, I didn't think. Maddie, dear, don't give up hope.'

'I try not to, but it's hard.' She glanced at Grace, but the little girl was occupied with her game and didn't appear to be listening.

Gussie sighed. 'Philip was such a dear child. I remember so clearly the day he arrived at Knyghton with his mother. Very loyal to her husband, Rose was. Wouldn't stay here with Philip. Simply dropped him at his school and went back to India. That was the year that the last war broke out, 1914. My brother George and his wife Daphne agreed to have him during school holidays. Everyone felt sorry for him, but we also thought he'd be a companion for Lyle. Perhaps it would have been better if he'd attended the village school as well, but instead he was sent away to board. It was the school Rose's brother had attended and I think her father paid the fees. William just went along with it.'

'George was killed in the war, did you say?' It wasn't easy keeping up with Gussie.

'That's right. George was in the army reserves and called up immediately war started. We had a manager for the farm back in those days so there wasn't a problem about him going. He was killed in the Battle of the Somme. Oh, it was terrible. They sent back his uniform, you know ...'

'Yes, you told me about that yesterday,' Maddie said gently, glancing at Grace again.

It struck her that Philip must very quickly have found himself in a house of grief. And George was Lyle's father, it must have been terrible for Lyle.

'What about Philip's parents?' she thought to ask. 'Did they remain in India during the war?'

'Yes, they didn't dare risk the journey home. Not with the Germans sinking passenger ships. So Philip didn't see them at all for four years. He didn't appear upset, but then he always was a quiet boy. Children are like that sometimes, and you don't necessarily know what's going on underneath.'

There was something sinister about Gussie's tone and again, Maddie glanced anxiously at her daughter. Grace was still talking to herself, and Maddie watched her play with the wooden passengers. Then she distinctly heard the child say, 'No, my daddy's gone away, so I'm going on a train to find him.'

Oh, Grace, she thought. Though she badly wanted to know what else Gussie had to say, she was keen that her daughter shouldn't hear of any more sadness.

She glanced at her watch, stood up and said, 'I ought to go down to help Mrs Flegg finish getting lunch.'

Lyle was late back so they started lunch without him. When he did arrive he seemed harassed. Something about the tractor having broken down again and not yet finding the right part to fix it. He ate quickly, in silence, and went out again without drinking his tea.

Grace kept rubbing her eyes and didn't eat much so after lunch Maddie put her to bed. She snuggled down without complaint and quickly fell into a doze. Maddie tiptoed away and went to explore the bedroom Lyle had suggested she use as her studio. The one next door to his, at the front of the house, he'd said. Opposite Gussie's.

She pushed open the door and stood in the doorway, struck by dismay. The room lay in darkness and the furniture was shrouded with dust sheets. She stepped across to the window, pulled back the curtains and turned to survey the situation. There were layers of dust everywhere, the room would need a good clean. She twitched a dust sheet from a table to find that it was actually a desk inlaid with leather, its surface worn, but still smooth. If she pushed it nearer the window and protected it with newspaper it would, as Lyle had surmised, make a good worktop.

The desk was heavier than she'd imagined and creaked when it moved, but she shuffled it into place then, looking round, identified the muffled shape of a high-backed chair in a corner. This she rescued from its covering, coughing at the dust. The chair had a comfortable upholstered seat and it fitted easily under the desk. Maddie sat down and looked dreamily out of the window at the front drive and the swaying trees. It was a beautiful view and she'd be able to see who came and went from the house while she was working. She looked round at the room again, the double bed, a large wardrobe and various other bits of shrouded furniture whose nature could only be guessed at. Mrs Flegg would surely be pleased if Maddie gave it a spring clean. Then it would be perfect for her needs. She started by throwing open the windows and gathering up dust sheets before fetching a broom and some dusters from downstairs.

The job finished, she went to find her box of paints and pencils and the precious sheaf of special paper that her editor had secured for her. Fearing little hands meddling, she opened the wardrobe, intending to store the paper inside. What she saw inside caused her to stand stock still, her mission forgotten.

A young man's school uniform hung from the rail, a striped blazer, shirts, trousers. A straw boater lay on a shelf next to a neatly folded navy and maroon scarf. Maddie had seen a badge bearing Philip's school crest that he'd worn pinned to his lapel on the rare occasions when he'd met up with Dalloway or other school chums after they were married. She fingered the blazer, turning it towards her, seeing that it bore the same crest. She released it from its hanger and held it to her face, breathing in its woollen scent. Why these items struck her so poignantly she could only guess. Whether it was because she'd held back for so long, damming up her feelings to get through the days, being brave for the girls, but suddenly tears were rolling down her face and she could not stop them. She sank to the floor with the blazer crushed to her chest and sobbed and sobbed.

It was there, drawn by the sound, that Grace found her. 'Mumma?' she said in a small voice. Seeing the child in the doorway clutching her rabbit with an expression of alarm on her sleep-crumpled face, Maddie opened her arms. Grace ran and clung to her and her small warm body comforted her in a way that nothing else could.

Later the two of them stood hand in hand at the end of the lane to meet the school bus, which was bringing Sarah home. The small careful figure that climbed down the high steps, jumping from the last, her satchel slapping on her back, wore a sombre look, but she ran smiling to her mother and sister. Maddie thanked the driver and took Sarah's hand.

Sarah answered Maddie's questions softly as they walked back to Knyghton. Yes, she could do the lessons, no, she didn't play with anyone at lunchtime, but had found a quiet seat in the school hall to eat her sandwiches along with several other children who couldn't go home for lunch. Then she'd read a book until the bell went for lessons.

She'd brought home a picture that she'd drawn during the afternoon. When she showed it to Maddie as they sat over milk and rusks in the kitchen, Maddie felt a stab of sadness. Stick figures lay on their backs, limbs waving in the air next to a ruined house. 'That one's you, Mummy, this is Grace and this is me.'

'And who's this?' she asked about a supine figure to one side.

'I don't know,' came the reply. Eventually she muttered, 'It's Daddy. He's died.'

A moment of silence. Maddie swallowed the lump rising in her throat. 'Oh, Sarah. We don't know that. We have to hope that he's alive somewhere and hasn't been able to let anybody know.'

Sarah gave her a long stare, then with a sudden sharp movement brushed the picture to the floor and lowered her forehead to the table. Grace swung herself down from the chair, picked up the paper and gave it to her mother, then climbed back into her seat and drank the rest of her milk, apparently unperturbed.

Maddie put her arm around Sarah's quivering shoulders. She thought that she'd brought her daughters to safety, yet she could not protect them from their misery.

Eleven

Several days passed, days in which Maddie, at least, felt more
at home. Each morning she took Sarah down to meet the bus
and Sarah went off more or less happily. Each afternoon,
Maddie was there with Grace to collect her. Her daughter
was always composed as she walked up the lane with them,
but Maddie detected a change in her from the happy, spirited
child she'd known in London. Sarah had become more serious, quieter. Was it simply that she was growing up or was
there something actually wrong?

On Friday Maddie sent a note in with Sarah to give to
Miss Dale, saying she'd like to speak to her at the end of the
day. Since there had been no response to her advertisement
for a childminder, Maddie entreated Mrs Flegg to look after
Grace, promising in return to purchase some boot polish and
candles. It was a blustery day and she held onto her hat as she
walked down the lane to catch the bus to Monksfield.

The main street was deserted. After buying the provisions

and checking that her card was still up in the newsagent's window – it was – Maddie still had half an hour to kill before the end of the school day. She crossed the road to visit the library, but it was closed, with an apologetic note pinned to the door. Seeing the round tower of the church rising above the trees she decided to investigate.

Gusts of wind assailed her as she lifted the latch of the lychgate and entered the churchyard. A gravel path led to the south porch of the simple flint church with pointed arched windows. Daffodils pushed up through the straggling grass between the graves and the air smelled of earth and green sap. The caws of rooks came from the swaying trees all around and Maddie's spirits rose.

Inside the whitewashed porch she dutifully secured the wire bird screen behind her and consulted a noticeboard on the wall. Her eye passed over a list of services, the name of the rector, and details of a jumble sale to be held in aid of war orphans. Then she twisted the iron ring in the heavy oak door until something lifted with a loud clunk and the door swung inwards.

It was the stillness of old churches that she loved, she reflected, as she stood in the gloom. The silence was rich, as if the air was filled with all the words of prayer and comfort that had been spoken here, the traces of music that had played and hymns sung. She breathed in the smell of old wood and candle wax, so familiar. Her childhood had been full of churches, for Norwich had many, and she'd loved the soaring gothic beauty of its cathedral.

This church was humble, with only a dozen rows of pews

on either side of a central aisle and a white-clad communion table at the far end beneath a triptych of stained glass, but it bore the marks of love by generations of worshippers. Maddie wandered about, glancing at the memorial plaques, running her finger over a pew end with a blunted carved face and thinking how restful it was.

'Have you seen our angels?' a voice came.

'Oh!' She turned to see a studious old man with a shining bald pate and wisps of silver hair above a clerical collar who had emerged from behind a curtain at the back of the church. 'No, I haven't,' she said and glanced up, following the line of his pointing finger.

High above, where each pair of rafters met the spine of the roof, a small carved angel nestled. Each was different, one with folded wings, another playing a lute. Like the grotesques on the pew ends, however, their faces had been damaged.

'What happened to them?' she asked.

'The Puritans didn't appreciate them as much as we do, I'm afraid. I'm the rector here, Alwyn Clairmont.' He held out his hand.

She remembered his name from the noticeboard in the porch. 'Maddie Anderson.' Mr Clairmont's hand as she shook it felt rough and calloused. Not just a man of prayer, she thought, but one who worked with his hands. His eyes twinkled behind his spectacles, but she saw signs of suffering in the furrowed brow.

'Anderson? You'll be the new lady at Knyghton then. Miss Blackstone told me your daughter has started at the school. Welcome.'

'Thank you. I hope I'm not trespassing here.'

'Of course not. The church is for everyone. I was sorry to hear about the loss of your husband, though. It's quite recent, I gather?'

Maddie stared at him. 'He's missing. I don't know what the headmistress told you, but I still have hope.' Almost a year had passed. Once more she wondered if she was wrong to cling to that hope.

'My apologies. I misunderstood. That still must be very hard for you.'

'It is,' she said, warming to him. 'There's nothing I can do about it. I simply have to carry on as normal for the children's sake and wait.'

Her voice cracked on 'wait' and he was silent as she recovered herself. 'My dear,' he said eventually. 'If ever I can help ... the power of prayer, you know ...'

She nodded, her heart too full to say anything further.

The rector offered her his handkerchief and when she shook her head, mopped his brow with it.

'I hope to see you in the pews on Sundays. My wife takes Sunday school in the hall. How old are your children?'

'Five and three. They're both girls.'

'There is a class for the young ones. Plenty of colouring in, I believe.'

'I'll have to see. Does anyone usually attend from Knyghton?'

'Miss Anderson came at Easter and she'll turn out at Christmas. Otherwise Monksfield doesn't see much of the family, which is a shame given that Knyghton is one of our manor houses and their forebears were valued patrons of the church.'

'I see that some of the plaques here are to Andersons.'

'Yes, and the bodies of past Andersons fill the top left corner of the churchyard. Do you have time to look?'

'Not really, I'm afraid,' Maddie said. She consulted her watch. 'School comes out in a few minutes.'

'Is it that time already? Then I'll point out the area where the graves are and you may visit in your own good time.'

'Thank you.'

On their way out through the porch the rector stopped at a small round window of painted glass that Maddie hadn't noticed on her entrance. 'Now this might interest you because of a link with Knyghton.'

She looked closely. 'More hares!' It was a clever design, three leaping creatures forming an endless circle. Each hare's ears were shared by the other hares at the circle's centre so that only three ears were shown.

'It's an optical illusion,' he said.

'Does it have a meaning?'

'No one's quite sure. The device is very old and found all over the world, though most examples in Britain are in Devon where they're known as Tinner's Rabbits.'

'Why tinner's?' Maddie frowned.

'A reference to local tin-mining, I suppose. I've researched it and printed a booklet about my findings, in fact.' He spoke modestly. 'No one knows precisely what this motif means, but hares are universally an important symbol of fertility and new life. You may see the association with Christianity.'

'Of course. Easter. You spoke of Knyghton. There's the relief of a hare over the front door there.' Maddie told him. 'And have you seen the painting in the drawing room?'

'I know about both of those. Perhaps they're a reference to this window. Or the other way round. Let me fetch you one of my booklets.' He disappeared briefly back into the church and returned with a pamphlet, which he gave her, brushing away her thanks. 'Think of it as a gift of welcome to the parish.'

'You're very kind,' she said. And now, through the wire bird screen, she could see that across the road the children were coming out of school. 'I must go now.'

'Of course.' The rector let her out. 'The Anderson graves are up there.' He pointed past the church tower to a far corner of the graveyard that was overhung by ancient yew trees.

'Thank you. And for this.' She slipped the pamphlet into her handbag and said goodbye. He'd been very kind, she thought as she hurried down the path. Maybe she would talk to him about Philip sometime, although Flegg could hardly be expected to turn out on Sundays to take them to church if he didn't attend divine worship himself.

Sarah was among the last of the children to trail out of school, but her eyes brightened when she saw her mother and she ran over and put her arms round her.

'Will you be all right waiting here, sweetheart, while I speak to Miss Dale?'

Sarah nodded solemnly and Maddie left her sitting on a bench in the playground, watching the school bus pull away.

Miss Dale was cleaning sums from the blackboard when Maddie entered the classroom. She looked up with a watchful expression.

'Mrs Anderson.' She put down her cloth and dusted her hands.

'I've come about Sarah, of course. How is she settling in?'

'All right, I think. She's very silent.'

'That's what's worrying me.'

'I take it that she's not normally?'

'No. She loved school in London. Was always chattering about her day and eager to go every morning.'

'I see.' Miss Dale crossed her arms and looked defensive. 'It's not easy for me. There have been several new children in the class this year and they take time to fit in.'

Maddie felt a rush of impatience but mastered it. 'I wasn't being critical, just wondering how to help her.'

Miss Dale nodded, then bit her lip before saying, 'I'd have a word with her if I were you about being friendly to the other children.'

Maddie's eyes widened in surprise, but before she could reply Miss Dale rushed on. 'She needs to learn to put up with a little teasing. All children do. Sticks and stones won't break my bones. It's a life lesson.'

'What are they teasing her about?' Maddie asked in dismay.

'Oh, just silly things.' Miss Dale looked embarrassed. 'Apparently there hasn't been a child from Knyghton for many years. The village seems unhealthily interested in the place.'

'I'm not sure that I understand. Are you saying it's because we're living at Knyghton?'

'Isn't it daft? Now, you're not to worry, Mrs Anderson. I'm sure that Sarah will find her niche here. She's a clever child, I can see that already.'

'But what is it about Knyghton?' Maddie persisted.

'I don't really know because I don't come from this area, but some people think the house is cursed.'

'Cursed?' Maddie echoed. 'What sort of curse?'

Miss Dale picked up the blackboard cloth again. 'I told you it was daft. Don't take too much notice. It's probably old wives' tales. Sarah will settle down.'

It was with a troubled mind that Maddie left Miss Dale and went out to the playground. Sarah was playing with a young ginger cat, whisking her hair ribbon for it to bat with its paw, and had such a rapturous expression on her face that Maddie's fears were temporarily allayed. 'Look, Mummy, can we have a cat?'

'I don't think so, darling. Aunt Gussie's dogs might chase it.' The joy left Sarah's face like a light being turned off and Maddie's spirits fell. 'Come on, it's time to go.'

Sarah left the cat reluctantly. Maddie retied the ribbon in her daughter's hair and they went out to wait for a bus home.

As they walked up the lane to Knyghton together, Maddie asked Sarah if the other children at school were kind. Sarah was quiet for a moment, then said, 'Freda gave me a sweet today. It was her last one.'

'That was nice of her.' Maddie had no idea who Freda was, but she immediately achieved a saintlike status in her imagination.

'It was to say sorry.'

Freda's imaginary halo vanished.

'Sorry for what, darling?'

'For calling Aunt Gussie a witch. They say Knyghton's got a ghost and a witch lives there. Aunt Gussie's not a witch, is she?'

'Of course she isn't.' Maddie was outraged at the idea. Gussie dressed in an old-fashioned way and it was strange for an elderly lady to have a face as innocent as a little girl's, but she was completely harmless. 'You must tell the other children that it's rubbish.'

Sarah nodded. She shrugged her satchel into a more comfortable position on her back and said, conversationally, 'Witches have cats, don't they? I think we should have a cat.'

'You'll have to make do with the dogs, I'm afraid.'

That night after the girls had been put to bed Maddie had her first proper conversation with Lyle. Tonight's supper had been potato cheese with last year's bottled gooseberries, rather sour, to follow. The children refused to eat the fruit, so Maddie fetched them some bread. She had helped Mrs Flegg fill a zinc bath with specially heated water. The girls had begged to use the huge roll-top bathtub with clawed feet in the chilly bathroom, then submitted willingly enough to the easier and thriftier alternative in the kitchen.

'I met your rector today,' Maddie said conversationally as she and Lyle sat in the drawing room later, Gussie having retired to her room. 'He seems a kindly man.'

'Old Clairmont?' Lyle was squinting at a hinge on his

aunt's spectacles that he was fixing. 'He's well liked in the village. A bit of an antiquarian, from what I gather.'

'That's what I thought. Wait.' She fetched the booklet the rector had given her from the hall.

He finished mending the spectacles then flicked through the book with interest before returning it to her. 'I should like to read it sometime. I've often wondered about the connection of hares to Knyghton.' He looked up at the portrait of his grandmother.

'Do you remember her?'

'Yes, of course. She was an important figure in my life.'

'She was rather beautiful.'

'She was. The story goes that when she met my grandfather it was love at first sight for her and she wouldn't have anyone but him. However, she was a wealthy landowner's daughter and naïvely expected life at Knyghton to be easier than it turned out.'

'What was your grandfather like?'

'He died when I was very young, but I gather he was quite a character. One of the first to have a car in Monksfield and drove about the winding lanes like a lunatic. Worse, he was also careless with money. But my grandmother adored him. Everyone did.'

'And Gussie was their eldest child?'

'Yes. Gussie always idolized her mother. They were very close. Less so to her father.'

Gussie must have been a shy, home-loving child. Maddie could imagine her needing special encouragement, but perhaps her mother had mollycoddled her. Maddie remembered what

Sarah had said, about the children in her class calling Gussie a witch. She could hardly repeat this to Lyle. Instead she said carefully, 'I went to see Sarah's teacher today. It seems the other children are teasing her for living at Knyghton. Stupid, isn't it?'

Lyle's face darkened and Maddie wished she hadn't mentioned the matter. 'Children can be silly. I suppose it's a sort of envy. I was tormented, too, when I went to the school. I expect it will pass.' His expression softened. 'I'm sorry if Sarah is unhappy. She seems a nice kid. I'm sure she'll make friends.'

'I hope so,' Maddie sighed.

'A drink?' he asked.

'No, don't worry.' She prised off her shoes and tucked her legs under her on the sofa. Lyle went and poured himself some whisky then slouched in his chair with his legs stretched out, staring into the dying fire.

'It's strange that we've never met until now,' Maddie observed. 'I'm afraid Philip and I had to have a small wedding. Hardly room for anyone on his side.'

'There's no need to defend him, Maddie,' Lyle said, giving her a sharp look. 'We've not seen much of each other for years.' His eyes narrowed.

'I didn't know.' She waited for him to say more, but he didn't so she said tentatively. 'Knyghton meant a lot to him, I think.' She told him about the photo album that he'd kept by him in his desk drawer. 'I've brought it with me if you'd like to see it.'

'Maybe sometime, but don't trouble yourself. We got on well enough when we were boys, but our lives became very different and we drifted apart.'

'That's a shame if you were cousins.' The pictures in the album suggested that they'd indeed been close, playing together in the sunny garden. 'You went to different schools, I gather.'

'Yes. Maybe if Philip had gone to the day school in Norwich as I did after Monksfield we'd have had more in common, but his parents sent him away to board. I helped with the farm work in the holidays, but Philip often bunked off and no one seemed bothered.'

'That must have annoyed you,' Maddie said. Lyle toyed with his empty glass, still staring into the flames. He had an unhappy air about him, she thought. Bitter, as though life had disappointed him. What was it? The loss of his parents? Disappointment in love? The strains of wartime? Any of those would make their mark on a man, and Lyle must have suffered all of them.

Philip, too, had endured loss. She wondered again what he had been like as a boy, something she could never really know.

'Lyle, forgive me if I'm stirring up difficult memories, but I'd love to hear more about my husband. What was he like as a boy?' In the seven years since she and Philip had first met, the last two of which she'd hardly seen him, she couldn't say she'd really come to understand him.

'What do you want to know?' he sighed and she sensed his reluctance.

'Well, the kind of boy he was. Things he liked doing.'

'He was, on the surface, like any other boy of his class.' He shrugged. 'A good throwing arm, an average swimmer.

He had enthusiasms. Found an old coin in the potato field once, and started a collection that he sold for ten pounds after he lost interest. Could shoot a bottle off a wall at twenty paces. Makes me think he'd survive out there in France.'

Lyle had told her very little about what mattered.

'What about his parents. Did he show that he missed them?'

'I suppose so. His mother, Aunt Rose, must have found it difficult to leave him, but he hardly spoke about it. We always knew when a letter arrived from her, though. He'd cheer up like anything. He kept them in a box under a loose floorboard in his bedroom. I know because I caught him stashing one away there once.' He gave a grim smile. 'Don't be shocked, Maddie, but I had a look myself when he was out, to see what else he kept in there, but he'd moved it. I don't think he trusted me, even then.'

Even then. Maddie's mind stirred. What had gone wrong between them? Should she be more wary of Lyle?

She supposed many people would think she was unrealistic, clinging to the belief that Philip was still alive. His commanding officer had been able to tell her nothing about when he'd last been seen. There had simply been no trace of him. There was nothing she could do but hope for news.

She would plod on, do her best to keep life normal for the girls, help Mrs Flegg where she could, do the work she was paid for and, while she waited, keep thoughts of Philip in her heart.

Twelve

Several days later the morning post brought a letter with a local postmark addressed to Maddie in a careful hand. She picked it off the mat, turned it over thoughtfully, then slit it open. The letter inside was headed 2 *Grove Cottages, The Green, Carshall*.

The note read, *Dear Mrs Anderson,*

I saw your card in Chapman's window and I would like to apply for the post. I am used to the work as I have often looked after my neighbours' children. I should explain that until recently I was a nurse, but I became nervously exhausted and have been discharged. I am much better now, however, and would enjoy looking after your daughter.

I can supply references if required and look forward to hearing from you.

Yours sincerely,
Christine Sutton (Mrs)

A response at last! Maddie took the letter along to the kitchen where Mrs Flegg was washing up after breakfast. 'Where's Carshall?' she asked her.

'It's the village going that way,' Mrs Flegg said with a nod. 'They've a green there and a pond with swans.'

'I think we passed through it on the way from the station. You haven't heard of a Mrs Christine Sutton there, have you?'

Mrs Flegg came across, drying her hands. 'Let me see. Grove Cottages. I know the line of houses on the green, but I don't remember any Suttons.'

Maddie reread the letter and wondered about Christine's nervous exhaustion, but it was the only application she'd had and she was itching to get on with her work.

After she'd seen Sarah onto the school bus, she sat in the nursery while Grace played with the train set and wrote a reply inviting Mrs Sutton to interview.

Mrs Sutton arrived on her bicycle two days later, a plain-featured, neatly dressed woman in her thirties with a helmet of short brown straight hair, a snub nose and watchful pale blue eyes. In the hallway she glanced warily at the pack of dogs that came to investigate, but they took one sniff of her and retired to the drawing room.

'It's kind of you to see me,' she told Maddie in a breathy voice. She was well spoken but had a worried look, Maddie thought. She fetched her the glass of water she asked for and showed her into the dining room where they sat down at the table.

'Where's your little girl?' Mrs Sutton asked. 'I'm looking forward to meeting her.'

'Grace is with her great-aunt in the next room. I wanted to speak to you alone first.'

'Of course. I brought my references.' Mrs Sutton unfolded two letters and pushed them across the table.

Maddie read them quickly, then said, 'They're very complimentary. Perhaps you'd tell me a bit about yourself, Mrs Sutton.'

The interview proceeded. Christine Sutton had looked after her ailing mother until the latter's death a few years ago. She'd then married a travelling salesman, but he'd left at the start of the war and she didn't know where he was. It was most upsetting. No, there hadn't been children. She would have liked to have had her own, but instead she enjoyed looking after other people's. She'd turned to nursing after war broke out, thinking she'd be useful, but found the work too onerous and the matron had been a terrible bully. She'd become ill with her nerves and returned home. Now that she was well again she badly needed some diversion.

'I want something to take me out of myself, Mrs Anderson. When I saw your card in the window, I felt a sort of rightness about it. Sometimes things are meant, don't you agree?'

Maddie studied the woman's plaintive face and thought of Philip. 'I don't know,' she replied. Were bad things also 'meant'? Life was an uncertain muddle in her experience.

'Two mornings a week would suit me very well,' Mrs Sutton continued, her pale eyes pleading. 'I shouldn't take on too much. Still have to rest, you see.' She had a composed air that would calm a child, Maddie thought.

'Grace is not a difficult child, Mrs Sutton, but she's very imaginative. I need someone who understands that.'

'She sounds a dear.' Mrs Sutton prattled away about the children she'd looked after before the war. Kathleen and Peggy, whom she'd helped with reading and hand-writing, and Victor, whose scatty mother hadn't known how to manage him but she, Christine, had brought him into line.

'You didn't ever strike him, did you?' Maddie asked anx-iously. 'I have never struck my girls.'

'I respect your views, Mrs Anderson. I'm sure Grace and I will get on very well without resorting to that.'

Somewhat reassured, Maddie asked a few more questions about Mrs Sutton's child-rearing practices and read the references again thoroughly. Kathleen and Peggy's mother wrote that Mrs Sutton had been punctual and kind. Victor's mother had only dispensed with her services because she'd sent the boy to live with cousins. The mysterious missing husband was peculiar, but otherwise all seemed to be in order.

She took the woman through to the drawing room and introduced her to Grace and Gussie. Mrs Sutton spoke to Grace in a friendly fashion, asking whether she liked the 'little doggies' and Grace nodded solemnly and explained that Phoebe sometimes stole food, and that Rochester only had three legs because 'a nasty trap had hurted him'.

Gussie, however, regarded the visitor with suspicion. 'Mrs Sutton has come to meet Grace,' Maddie explained. Gussie nodded, but the expression did not leave her face. *Dear me,*

Maddie thought, *sometimes it is as though a cloud descended*. Was it age or had Gussie always been like that?

After a few minutes Maddie and Grace took Mrs Sutton upstairs to show her the nursery. The woman seemed very interested in her surroundings, glancing about at everything. In the nursery she went at once to the doll's house with an exclamation of delight. Maddie unlatched the front and Mrs Sutton lifted Grace, who was too young to be allowed to play with its delicate contents, so that she could see the rooms and the little figures. Watching them together, Maddie made her decision. She couldn't say that she warmed to Mrs Sutton exactly, but she would be up to the job and Grace appeared to like her.

Downstairs once more Maddie saw the longing in Mrs Sutton's eyes as they watched Grace run back to the drawing room. 'I would be much obliged,' she told the woman, 'if you would take the job.'

'I'd be glad to.' Christine Sutton's face lit up with satisfaction. They discussed hours and payment and agreed that she should start the following week. Monday and Wednesday mornings with some flexibility if required.

Maddie watched the woman's upright figure cycle away with a feeling of relief. On Monday she could begin work on her illustrations.

When Maddie returned to Grace and Gussie she carefully explained to Grace that 'Nanny Sutton' would be coming to look after her. Grace frowned. 'But I want you to look after me, Mummy.'

'I'll still be here, only making my pictures.'

'I want to make pictures.'

'And so you shall, my love.'

'That woman,' Gussie cut in. 'Who is she?'

'I told you, Gussie. She's coming here twice a week to help me with Grace.'

'Is that wise, to ask a stranger?'

'I did explain,' Maddie said gently.

'Did you? What's her name again?'

'Christine Sutton.' Really, Gussie was very distracted today.

'I hope you know what you're doing. She looks a miserable sort to me.'

'I don't think she's had an easy time recently,' Maddie said. 'She cheered up at the idea of looking after Grace. I'm sure we'll all get on very well.'

Mrs Sutton arrived punctually at nine on Monday morning, hung up her navy coat and tied on a pinafore as though she meant business. 'It's a lovely day,' she told Grace, who stood by watching, clasping Rabbit. 'Will you show me the garden?'

'Why don't you take Nanny Sutton out of the back to see the animals?' Maddie said.

Grace's eyes lit up. 'A goat ate Sarah's hanky,' she told Christine Sutton and took her hand to lead the way.

Maddie gratefully escaped upstairs to her workroom, closed the door behind her and leaned against it with a sigh of relief. The night before she'd laid out pencils and paper and now she had a whole three hours to herself.

Her latest commission involved illustrating the text of a charming story for young children about a community of woodland animals. She'd finally visited the library, chatted to Clara Mace, the friendly librarian, and managed to borrow two useful illustrated natural history books. This morning she needed to look over some rough drawings in her sketchbook and plan the layouts according to the text she'd been given and her editor's detailed instructions. She was quickly absorbed.

By the end of the morning, Maddie had planned twelve double-page spreads – twenty-four pages – positioned the lines of text and drafted the composition of one of her illustrations. At noon, she almost skipped downstairs, light with the sense of achievement.

There she found Mrs Sutton in the hall buttoning her coat and Grace still clutching Rabbit, her thumb in her mouth.

'We've had a very busy morning,' the woman said brightly. 'Haven't we, Grace?'

Grace shrugged and came and buried her face in her mother's skirt. Maddie ruffled the child's soft hair. 'Thank you, Mrs Sutton.'

'Do call me Christine. I expect she's tired.' The woman's forehead creased in a frown. 'We went for quite a ramble. I'll see you on Wednesday, Grace!'

'Was everything all right with Nanny Sutton?' she asked Grace when the woman had gone. Grace merely nodded and ran upstairs to play with the trains. Maddie watched her anxiously the rest of the day, but Grace seemed as normal so she stopped worrying. Christine Sutton, it seemed, was going to be a success.

*

That evening, Maddie went to bed early, taking the rector's hare pamphlet with her. The light of her candle danced on the page as she read, and she liked the cosy feeling it gave her. The rector wrote in a formal, old-fashioned style, but vividly, too. He began by explaining the origins of the hare as a mythological animal in many parts of the world, then took a Christian angle of it as a symbol of new life. His mention of the hares at Knyghton and the window in the church porch did not add anything to Maddie's knowledge. *But I must lend the booklet to Lyle as I promised*, she told herself as she blew out the candle.

Lately Maddie had slept without interruption, but tonight she was wrenched from a dream about hares by a terrible cry. She sat up, fully alert in the darkness, her heart beating wildly. There it came again. Not one of the children, thank heavens, but a man's voice, long drawn-out and anguished, then tailing off. Lyle. She slid out of bed, tiptoed to the door and listened. At that moment, one of the dogs started barking in the next room and then came Gussie's sleepy tones quietening it.

Softly, Maddie opened the door and crept out into the pitch darkness of the landing, feeling her way along the opposite wall to the door of Lyle's room. There she waited, alive to any sound, but there was nothing more. After a minute or two she padded back to bed, where she pulled the bedclothes over her ears and settled down to sleep. But sleep she could not. She was wide awake now and anxious thoughts whirled in her head, of Lyle and what nightmares were troubling him.

After a while, her thoughts turned to other areas of worry – Sarah, still no happier at school, then on, inevitably, to Philip. What had happened? Where could he be? Over the last year she'd imagined all sorts of possibilities. That he was a prisoner in some German Oflag, or he'd become separated from his company and lost his memory and was wandering somewhere. Tonight a cruel voice began to whisper in her mind, *he's dead, he's dead,* and she tried her best to shut it out. She must keep hoping for her own sake as well as that of her children.

It was both comforting and alarming that there were so many reminders of him at Knyghton, a place that was strange to her. She remembered her conversation with Lyle and imagined how lonely Philip's childhood here must have been, how precious to him the letters from his mother that he'd hidden away.

She gave up trying to sleep. She had to look for it – the place where he'd kept that correspondence. *Wait until morning.* She could not. It was stupid, she knew, but that didn't stop her. She rose once more, lit her candle, shrugged on her dressing gown then tiptoed out onto the landing. The flame guttered in a draught, causing shadows to leap up the walls. She passed Lyle's door, where all was silent, and clasped the door handle to her workroom, Philip's old bedroom. The door creaked as it swished open. She froze, but no dog barked.

No one had bothered to put up the blackout in here, and the room lay dappled by the glimmer that presaged dawn. Maddie stepped inside, leaving the door ajar, and made her

way over to the bed. Which side? If Lyle had seen Philip
from the doorway it must be the nearer one. Tentatively she
tested the floorboards through the rug with her toe. None
were loose. She padded round to the far side, but it was the
same story. She sat on the mattress and thought. Either the
floorboard had been nailed down since or . . . the bed might
be in a different position. She prowled about the room,
but just as she was giving up hope she felt under the near
side of the bed with her foot and drew a quick breath as a
board wobbled.

Now she was on her knees, scrabbling with her fingernails.
At one end of the floorboard her forefinger found a gap. She
pinched the board and tugged at it. It groaned, then moved
suddenly and a waft of cold air hit her. She reached for the
candle and held it so that its light fell into the hole. She saw
dust balls, fragments of plaster, a metallic gleam from what,
when she fished it out, turned out to be a tiny toy soldier.
Maddie sat back on her heels examining it, thinking that her
husband must have hidden it here. Was there nothing else?
Her legs were prickling with pins and needles so she shifted
herself onto hands and knees before reaching her hand into
the gap and feeling about. There was a clink as her wedding
ring hit something hard. It felt cold to her fingers as they skittered over its surface and her heart leaped with excitement.
Her hand closed around the corner of a rectangular box of
light metal not much bigger than a tea caddy. She edged the
tin towards her and its contents rustled. Then she grasped it
with both hands, lifted it from its hiding place and set it on
the floor. Using a corner of her dressing gown she wiped off

the dirt, then sat cross-legged with it on her lap and lifted the candle.

The flame flickered above the surface of the tin to show an illustration of an English country scene in the snow and the words, 'Christmas Biscuit Assortment'. The lid stuck at first when she tried to open it, so she turned the box round, trying its different sides until one gave and she lifted the lid with a clatter that sounded loud in the silence. From across the corridor a dog gave a loud whine. Again Maddie froze. There was no further sound so she pressed the lid back down. She replaced the floorboard with care and crept out of the room holding the box, and returned to the dark safety of her room. She went to open the curtains. Outside, light gleamed pink and gold now above the trees and the birds were in full song at the new day.

Maddie blew out the candle and climbed back into bed, pleased to find it still warm. Stretching her legs out comfortably, she drew the tin onto her lap and wondered, for the first time, if she had any right to look at the contents. If Philip had hidden it the box was obviously private. And yet under the circumstances ... *We must have hope.*

In the end she could not resist. She needed to know more about her husband, to feel close to him, and if the box contained what Lyle had said – letters from his parents in India – perhaps these were not so very private.

I'm sorry, Philip, if you do mind. The lid lifted more easily this time, and she set it aside and stared down at the piles of neatly stacked envelopes inside. She smiled and her eyes briefly prickled with tears. Philip had always been tidy. She

wondered if he had learned it from school, then remembered
that his old landlord Dalloway certainly hadn't. She reached
for an envelope at random and angled it towards the thin
daylight. A carmine stamp, the address written in a looping
feminine hand. She slid thumb and finger inside and withdrew the letter. It was written on pale blue paper that crackled
as she unfolded it and was dated 28th October, 1917, a glance
at the postmark revealed. Philip would have been, what, ten
years old.

My darling Philip, his mother had written.

*Your last letter arrived safely today and was received with
much joy. I hope my letters have been reaching you as you
didn't say, but I have written to you every week. I'm so glad
that school has been better this term and you're in one of the
rugby teams. I wish we could be there to watch you play. Do
your best, my darling, and we'll be proud of you. You don't
say if that matter about the missing money was ever cleared
up. I hope so as it sounded most unfair of your housemaster
to assume that it was you. Chin up! As I said in my last
letter (did it arrive safely?), these things are sent to try us. We
become stronger because of them. If you are honest and stand
your ground then right will prevail. My poor boy, I wish I
could be with you to comfort you, but as long as this wretched
war lasts we know that it is impossible.*

*I imagine that it's becoming colder in England now. I
miss those lovely autumn days with the changing colours of
the leaves. Here in Delhi it's pleasantly warm and I've been
amusing myself by organizing a picnic in Lodhi Gardens last*

weekend for the officers' wives to keep the spirits up. Your father is well, I think. I had a letter from him only yesterday and I know he would want me to send his love.

All my love to you, my darling boy,
Your adoring mother

Maddie read the letter through again, a tender lump in her throat. That Philip's mother missed her young son was in no doubt, and surely he would have understood that, but the anguish for both of them in their separation must have been terrible to bear, especially in wartime when Mrs Anderson had to manage alone while her husband was away. She returned the letter to its envelope and started flicking through the piles, noting the dates on the postmarks. The earliest she found were from 1914, when Philip would have been seven. The very first was piteous indeed.

My darling,
I hope by now that you've settled well into your new school and are so busy that you don't have time to think of your mother. Be a brave little man, my sweet, and remember what Daddy told you, that big boys don't cry and that you must play the game to the best of your ability and we will be proud of you. So proud, my dear big boy. I'm sorry if it looked as though I left without saying goodbye, but I couldn't bear it, and I saw you out of the window of the cab, didn't I, and waved to you. You didn't wave back, so I hope that you did see me. I stayed a few nights with my friend Mabel Godrick in London

and tomorrow I get on the boat at Southampton and sail all the way back to Daddy. I'll send you a picture postcard from Port Said as I know you liked the camels. Remember to ask your grandmother if you need money or anything else as it will be much quicker than writing to me. Please send me a letter as soon as you can, though it will be some weeks before I receive it, no doubt.

With my best love,
Mummy

'*I left without saying goodbye*'. What an awful thing for poor Philip. And it sounds as though he didn't see her when she waved, or else ... no, that was terrible, that he was too shocked or surprised to wave back, that he'd never expected her to leave like that. What a betrayal.

Though the room was growing lighter, Maddie was beginning to feel weary. She arranged the bundle of letters back in the tin, then hid it under the bed, tucking it up against the bedside cabinet so that it couldn't easily be seen. Quite why she had this instinct she didn't know, but she felt a very strong desire not to show the contents to anyone yet, especially Lyle. It was like a secret between her and Philip.

She snuggled down, pulled the blankets around her and drifted off to sleep. She dreamed of a small boy with a tuft of red hair, pale skin and freckles, dressed in knickerbockers and a grey jersey. He was sitting on the edge of her bed swinging his heels and the lost expression in his eyes made her want to reach out and pull him to her, but he did not see her and, drowning in sleep, she could not move to help him.

When she woke it was to the distant sound of the girls' voices. She lay unrefreshed, staring up at a jagged crack in the ceiling, and wondered how the dream had been so real.

Thirteen

France

May 1940

Philip woke to a sense of something heavy being lifted from him and an immediate awareness of unbearable pain. He gasped, blinking against the sudden light. A woman's voice sounded close to his ear, *Mon Dieu! Monsieur, ouai, monsieur!* He let out a groan. *Papa, viens!* the woman called. He opened his eyes, saw the comfortable bulk of her against the twilit sky. Her hands fumbled at his collar and her breaths came quickly.

Another figure joined her, a man, this time, smelling of tobacco, *Dear God, how he longed for a cigarette.*

Vas vite. The man's voice was gravelly. Together they worked quickly. When they peeled the cloth from his shoulder, he shouted in agony. *Shhh,* the woman said, *'nous voulons vous aider.* We help.'

It was coming back to him now in hot waves of shock. The angry mouth of the machine gun, the cries of his fellow soldiers as they jerked, twisted and fell. Then came a bolt of pain worse than any he had known, he fell into blackness and when he next surfaced someone heavy was lying across him and something warm and wet was dripping in his eyes. Harsh German voices rent the air. He heard the scrape and scuffle of boots as the soldiers moved near him. Then the sound of someone retching, only to be cut off by the awful whump of metal entering flesh. Somebody kicked his leg, but he managed not to cry out. All his effort went into playing dead, though he could not dull the pulse of the blood pounding through his veins. A rough hand seized his hair, tugged at it painfully, but then a harsh *Kommen Sie!* split the air. The hand released him and the tramp of boots and the guttural voices retreated. Soon, but for the cawing of crows there was silence. He'd survived. But how long for?

He'd begun to feel cold, very cold, and his shoulder hurt like blazes, but he had no strength to shift the dead man who pinned him down and soon he gave way to the pain and passed out again. Until now the French woman and her father had come.

The woman laid a blanket out beside him, and he moaned as she and the old man shifted him onto it then he was lifted into the air, bumping about as they picked their way between the bodies. The air smelled of gunpowder and something rank and metallic. Philip gazed up at the darkening sky, watched a solitary plane swoop low and his eyes widened in fear. Luftwaffe, he thought, and braced himself for gunfire as his bearers halted. But then it gained height, flew on and was gone.

'*Allons-y,*' the woman said, and something he didn't understand and they struggled on. Then he found himself being hefted onto a rocking wooden surface. A handcart.

'Wait,' he said, and raised his head. For the first time he saw the full extent of the dreadful scene. A score of bodies lying in the field, some thrown together in a macabre embrace, others twisted and far-flung. His murdered comrades. A sob tore from his throat. He lay back, feeling tears spilling over his face, washing blood into his eyes.

Was that all of them? Yes, they'd been down to twenty-two or three, he thought, when they'd run out of ammunition and surrendered to the Germans who'd besieged them all day in the lonely farmhouse. The Kommandant, tall, tense, angry, with eyes full of cold hatred, had ordered them to be rounded up and divested of their weapons. When instructed to march they'd fallen reluctantly into line on the dusty lane, expecting to be taken to join other prisoners ready to be transported onward to some camp, in Germany if they were very unlucky. But instead he'd made them turn off into a meadow behind a barn, and there the wide mouth of the machine gun had been waiting. And now it appeared that Philip was the only one left alive. The only witness. He had not known the Kommandant's name, but he'd never forget his face, the curled upper lip as he'd given the order to fire.

The cart juddered into motion and bumped over a rutted lane with the woman walking beside him. Once, they stopped for her to wipe his face and tuck the blanket more tightly round his throat. She spoke reassurance, but Philip's attention wandered. Despite the blanket he began to shiver again. It was cold, so cold. How long the journey lasted he didn't know for he drifted into unconsciousness. When he came to he was lying on a bed in a dark room before a muttering fire and the woman was mopping his forehead with a damp flannel. His surroundings swam in and out of focus. There was a sharp chemical smell and the pain from his bandaged shoulder was exquisite. He raised his head as sickness threatened and the woman cradled him, offering a bowl, then gave him sips of water from a cup. Her murmurs of comfort lulled him and he slept again. When he woke next daylight filtered through the curtains and she was checking the bandage on his wound. Apart from the pain he felt better, if not much. At least he no longer felt sick and the room had stopped going round. She asked his name in a soft whisper. *Philip*, he replied in a rasping voice not his own.

She was Adele, the man was her father, this much he understood. She was in her thirties, he reckoned as he watched her rise to feed the fire, strong and thickset, with a kind, squarish face and eyes as dark and shining as a blackbird's. From her words and urgent, mimed gestures he gauged that a doctor had visited the night before and removed two bullets from his shoulder.

At a crack of gunfire nearby she was up and stepping to peep through the curtains, returning with an expression full of fear. *'Les soldats, ils viennent.'* Her hands fluttered helplessly. He must be moved. Somehow, with her help, he stumbled to his feet and she bundled him through the kitchen out into a yard and shut him into an empty low roofed henhouse that still stank of its previous inhabitants. Here he lay in the darkness, straw tickling his nose, his every nerve twitching, his hearing acute.

They'd been just in time. Marching footsteps, German voices, loud blows on the farmhouse door, Adele's imploring response, muffled sounds of disturbance, impatient boots scraping the stony yard. Shouts, doors slamming, close, closer. Then a strip of daylight widened as the chicken house door fell open. Philip held his breath, tensed for the inevitable, but it never came. The shouts and footsteps grew fainter. At last they were gone. He waited in his hiding place, petrified, for what felt like hours, the fingers of a cold breeze ruffling his hair. Then he smelled smoke, heard the crackle of flame and stirred at last. When he crept out he saw the farmhouse was on fire.

He glanced around and, seeing no one, stumbled over to the nearest window, clutched the sill and peered into the kitchen. Cupboard doors stood open, a chair lay on its back. He frowned, leaned against the wall briefly to recover his strength, then began to work his way round to the front of the house, keeping a watch out for soldiers and pausing at every window to look for Adele.

They'd left the front door wide and he gasped with shock to see her body lying in the ruins of the hallway ringed with flame. She'd been stabbed to the heart. *Why?* he asked himself, struck by guilt. *It was because of me.* Someone had betrayed them, but who, the doctor? Surely not, the man had tended him. He turned, hearing cries, and saw an old man shambling towards him over a ploughed field, carrying a hoe on his shoulder, his arm flung wide in despair. It was the farmer, Adele's father, who must just have seen the smoke. Philip watched him approach, full of pity, then hobbled to meet him. The man read his face, threw down his hoe and walked slowly past him to the door. Here he stood looking down at his daughter's body. Suddenly he fell to his knees as though hit and began to sob. After a while he clambered to his feet and stood for a moment, his cap in his hands, staring into the flames. Then, as Philip cried out 'no!' the old man walked purposefully into the house. A great burning beam fell on him then he was swallowed up by the fire.

Philip coughed at the smoke and sobbed, then turned wildly, uncertain what to do. Others would be drawn to the scene of the disaster. He must leave, but where should he go? He was shuddering, with cold or fever or shock – or all of these – and his legs were giving out. There was no point in trying to go far, he hadn't the strength, and if the wound became infected he'd stand little chance. What to do? He swayed with sudden dizziness, put out a hand to stop himself from falling, and immediately snatched it back. The door frame was burning hot. All he could do was to find somewhere nearby out of sight.

Nursing his hand, Philip crept away from the choking smoke to a barn with a hayloft and a stout ladder up to it, though there was little hay to conceal him. After the effort of the climb he lay curled up tenderly to recoup his strength. Then he dragged himself by the strange yellow light of the fire to a far corner of the loft where he hid beneath some sacking. If the flames leaped across to this barn he'd be done for, but he didn't have the stamina to strike out further. This was the best he could do.

Whether anyone came, he couldn't tell. All he heard for some time was the distant roar of flame and the crash of falling debris. After that, a crackle and a creaking as the fire died down, then silence. As the day wore on he slept fitfully without dreaming. At twilight, he woke coughing and his eyes prickled. A pall of smoke hung on the air, but when he crawled down the ladder he saw with relief that the barn was intact. Outside a fresh breeze soothed his raw throat. He glanced about, but saw no one. The house was a roofless shell, where bright embers glowed. He did not go near, fearing the sight of the bodies. Instead he drew water from a well in the yard and drank and splashed water on his face, doing his best to keep the bandage dry. He was hungry, very hungry, and blood was seeping through his clothes from his shoulder. The dressing should be changed, but there was nothing he could do. He must wait until darkness fell then move on. He walked out onto the field and gazed about. Far off, the tower of a church nestled in the folds of the landscape, a peaceful scene. If he headed in that direction he might find help. And if he were captured? He'd have to take the risk.

Hours later when he reached the church he found the doors locked. He slid down in a heap. He'd never known such despair. He'd stumbled several miles without seeing any house to call at or barn to rest in, had plunged into under-growth to evade a passing lorryful of German soldiers and

now this. He lay on the doorstep, half dozing in the moonlight, his mind empty of thought, his body aching.

It was here at dawn that the priest found him. He'd not been
friendly, but he did well enough by his calling, inviting Philip
into the church and down through a trapdoor in the vestry
into an airless crypt. He'd fetched him a pallet and blankets,
bread and cheese and a flask of coffee. It was cold, smelly
and damp down among the dead of centuries, but it was the
darkness of the undercroft that oppressed Philip the most.

A woman, the priest's housekeeper maybe, came and
washed and dressed his wound by the light of an oil lamp.
Her hands were gentle but her gaze was full of fear. All these
people helping him, risking their lives. Tears came to his eyes
as he thanked her. She left him with a stub of church candle
and some matches. He lay fearfully watching the shadows
leap up the walls before the flame fizzled out leaving the
darkness complete. He slept fitfully.

He felt more than heard the heavy wheels out in the
street. German voices, the doors of the church crashing open,
impatient footsteps overhead. He lay still, hardly daring to
breathe. Cruel laughter. The sound of something smashing
on the flagstones, then retreating footsteps, vehicles revving
and after that only the distant creak of a door swinging in
a breeze. When the priest found him half an hour later it
was to bring him food and to tell him in heavily accented
English that he could stay until he felt stronger but then
must move on.

'I don't know where to go,' Philip said simply. 'How far is
the sea – La Manche, which way?'

The man shook his head. 'The news is very bad,' he said. He explained that the British forces had been overcome. Many had been rescued in British boats from Dunkirk, but others taken prisoner or worse. It was then that Philip told him how he and his companions had been mown down in cold blood and he was the only one who'd escaped. '*Sacré Dieu*,' the man whispered, his eyes gleaming in the gloom. 'Then it's true. We thought these things were rumours, exaggeration. How naïve we've been.'

He'd seen the flames of the farmhouse, but dared not go to see, nor had any of his parishioners. 'They're not from our village, God rest their souls.' He thought for a moment, his head in his hands, then said, 'You may stay today, but I must find you somewhere else. Don't go to the coast. Too many Germans.'

Philip thanked him, but his mind was in a whirl. If he could not go to the coast then what should he do? He'd wanted to join up with the rest of his battalion, but the priest had put him in doubt that there was a battalion to find. He would never give himself up. What had been done in that field might happen again. Not all Germans were bad, he knew that must be true, but after what had happened to his comrades and the murder of Adele he would never trust them.

He rationed the new candle this time when the priest left him, lighting it only in order to eat or to move around, restoring the blood to his cramped limbs, and blowing it out to sleep or simply lie and think. He was used to the place now and the idea of ghosts didn't bother him. It was the living he feared more. Once he was woken by footsteps and women's voices above his head, another time by organ practice. The rest of the time he was left in peace.

Peace. No, peace eluded him. His mind went over and over the events after his capture. The calculating expression in the Kommandant's eyes as he and his comrades were disarmed. Philip's cold fear when he saw the machine gun, the raw shock as it stuttered into life, cutting his comrades to pieces. These scenes would not leave him. They did not make sense. *That's enough,* he told himself, cradling his scorched hand in the gloom to comfort himself. But then there rose in his mind a picture of Adele lying dead and her father stepping into the flames. *I should have done something. But what?*

He tried to think of home, of Maddie and the girls, but they were all so far away he couldn't begin to imagine them. Violence and death filled his mind and he couldn't stop shaking. It was cold down here, a deadly cold that penetrated his bones. Damp, too, and breathing was becoming difficult. The pain from his shoulder had spread across his chest.

When the priest came next, Philip did not know it for he'd fallen into a delirium. When he woke finally he was somewhere else entirely, lying on a bed in a narrow room. Sunshine from a delicate fanlight high on the wall was playing on his face.

Fourteen

Norfolk

1941

Something was still stopping Maddie showing Philip's letters to Lyle. It was partly that she wasn't sure Philip would have wanted her to and partly that she simply preferred to keep the matter to herself, not to share her husband with anyone else. Her heart was too full.

Several days elapsed and one morning Mrs Flegg discovered that Lyle had forgotten his flask and mid-morning snack, so Maddie volunteered to take them down to him. It was a good opportunity to have a closer look at the farm. She persuaded Grace to accompany her by asking Gussie if they could take one of the dogs. The old lady agreed and suggested they take Jane, the female Jack Russell, although the list of instructions included not letting her off the lead as she might get in with the cattle and be trampled.

'Me take her, Mummy,' Grace insisted and Maddie conceded reluctantly for Jane, though small, was wilful. The dog, excited by the smells of the countryside, dragged the child on a zigzag path between the trees, sniffing at every leaf, her stump of a tail wagging, but Grace held on gamely, laughing. Thus they made their chaotic way past the woods towards the farm less than half a mile away. Maddie carried the bag of provisions, and assisted her daughter's hopeless efforts to control the dog. It was good to see Grace's joyful freedom with Jane. On a bright fresh day like this, the hedgerows snowy with hawthorn blossom and the world washed clean by a shower, it was easy for Maddie to feel glad that they'd come to Knyghton.

In the distance the farm buildings looked like a set of child's bricks, a cow byre, a pair of wooden barns, a stable, a simple flint farmhouse and another long low brick building, all arranged in a rough rectangle around a gated yard. But as they came closer the stink of silage became apparent and Maddie saw the buildings were shabby, the thatch was thin on the barns and the yard was rutted with muddy puddles.

As she opened the gate one of the cheerful young women she'd glimpsed before, her fair hair tucked under a scarf, appeared from behind a shed carrying a pitchfork. 'May I help you?' she asked. 'My, that's a dear little dog,' she told Grace, 'but who's taking who for a walk?'

'It's not my dog,' Grace said. She had no fear of speaking to adults. 'It's Great-Aunt Gussie's.'

'Is it now? Then you must be Mrs Anderson.' She turned to Maddie, with a smile. 'I'm Mary Lark, one of the land girls. Are you looking for the guvnor?'

She pointed to the long low flint building. 'He'll be in the office, but I think he's with someone at the moment.' Maddie thanked her and led Grace, who in turn led the dog, round the puddles to the door, and raised her hand to knock. She paused. The door was ajar and she heard a low angry voice from inside. It was Lyle's.

'For God's sake, Roger. Don't bully me about it. The Andersons owe you nothing and that's the last of it.'

'If that's the way you want to look at it,' came a harsh masculine voice. Impatient footsteps made Maddie draw back just before the door flew open and a middle-aged man in a tweed jacket emerged, his handsome face with high cheekbones blotched red with anger. He checked himself long enough to nod to her, then marched off in muddy riding boots to where an ancient truck waited. A moment later the engine roared and Maddie and Grace watched it bounce away along a potholed lane that meandered off into the distance.

'Who was that, Mummy? He did look cross.'

'I don't know. Let's find Uncle Lyle, shall we?'

Lyle's voice snarled, 'Yes?' in answer to Maddie's knock and they gingerly entered a small, untidy, low-ceilinged office lined with shelves filled with ledgers, cardboard boxes and various odd-looking bits of farming equipment. Lyle sat behind a large careworn desk in front of a bookcase, his head in his hands. He was apparently examining the closely typed document before him. The air crackled with tension.

'I'm busy,' he growled without looking up. 'If it's about that blinking tractor, they can't come till Monday.'

'It isn't. We're sorry to interrupt.'

His head jerked up and at the sight of Maddie with Grace and the little dog standing in a row before him his expression softened into a smile. 'My, what a surprise.'

'Don't get up. We're not staying. We simply wanted to deliver these.' Maddie delved in the bag for the flask and the greaseproof paper package and placed them on the desk.

He stared at the items as though they were alien. 'Oh, thank you.'

'We'll see you at lunchtime.' She turned to go. 'Come on, Grace—'

'No, wait,' Lyle said roughly.

She turned back, trying to look aloof, her eyebrows raised.

'I'm grateful to you, Maddie. I'd show you both round if . . .'

'Another time, I'd love that,' she said gently. 'You seem a bit . . . put upon.'

Lyle leaned back in his wooden chair and clasped his hands behind his head. 'I don't know what you heard just now,' he said bitterly, 'but you may have gathered that there are difficulties making ends meet here. It's the case with many farmers, frankly, but don't say anything to Gussie, will you? She's easily upset by this sort of thing.'

'The farm's in financial trouble?' Maddie said, trying to understand.

'Pretty bad, though I hope we'll pull through. I'd just be obliged ...'

'I assure you I've no reason to say a thing to anybody,' she murmured.

'Thank you.' He looked relieved. 'That was Roger Welbourne, by the way. He owns the neighbouring farm. Our families go back a long way here. He wants to buy some of my land and I don't want to sell. It's more complicated than that, but that's the nub of it.'

'I'm sorry to hear.' Welbourne. Maddie had heard that name before. Hadn't Gussie mentioned Lyle being involved with a Susie Welbourne? Roger's daughter, perhaps.

She and Grace said goodbye and set off for home. As they trudged back up the lane, past the field of grazing cows, she hardly heard Grace's chatter. Two things had struck her. One was that if the future of the farm was in question then so, presumably was life at Knyghton. Hundreds of years of Andersons and now this. The second was the glimpse she'd had of Lyle's anger. She wouldn't like to get the wrong side of him in an argument, she thought, and must be careful about trusting him.

Gradually, Maddie's new working life fell into a rhythm. Two mornings a week Christine Sutton cycled up the drive at the stroke of nine, hung up her coat and took charge of Grace. All appeared to be going well. Grace looked forward to Christine's visits as the woman often brought little treats for her, a tiny doll for the doll's house that had belonged to her mother, some biscuits she'd baked.

Happy to leave them together, Maddie retired to her workroom and spent the morning in dreaming reflection as she made pencil sketches for her illustrations. She found she was working quickly, the ideas flowing in this tranquil room where she felt close to Philip. Beyond the window a spreading horse chestnut tree produced candles of dark pink blossom. By the time the petals fell she had twenty rough drawings and four worked up in detail.

She arranged for Christine, who seemed delighted, to spend a whole Friday with Grace so that she could travel to London to show them to her editor. *Is your journey really necessary?* asked a poster at the library. Since she felt nervous about consigning her precious work to the mail, then yes. With luck she'd be able to meet up with her friend Denny as well.

The trip would involve an early start, but she'd tamed Mrs Flegg sufficiently to beg her to get the girls up and break-fasted and Sarah off to school. 'Flegg will take her down to the bus,' Mrs Flegg said. 'Don't you worry now.' Gradually the woman had become less frosty and a brief conversation in the kitchen one day after Maddie had cleaned out some of the cupboards explained her earlier surliness.

'Your help is much appreciated, Mrs Anderson. I thought that when you'd come we'd be left to do all the work, see. Mr Philip didn't ever bring you to see us so we didn't know what kind of lady he'd married.'

Maddie wasn't sure what to say to that. Philip had indeed never invited his fiancée to Knyghton, but it felt disloyal to him to tell Mrs Flegg that she would have liked to come.

Instead she said softly, 'It's a pleasure to help, Mrs Flegg. I can see all there is to do and I'm keen to pull my weight.'

Flegg, too, showed her frequent kindnesses. He'd taken to the girls, particularly Grace, and they to him. It was the sort of friendship that sometimes develops between the very young and the old, Maddie thought, as though they recognized a childlike quality in him. He would amuse them by folding his big handkerchief in a certain way to make it look like a rabbit or a cat. He liked to whittle and once he presented Grace with a pair of wrestling dolls made out of old clothes pegs. Maddie was perfectly happy to leave the girls in the care of the Fleggs. They got on well with Gussie, also, but it was no use expecting Gussie to look after their welfare. She was simply too frail and distracted to bandage grazed knees or smooth over disagreements.

The train was crowded with troops in uniform and it was strange returning to London even though Maddie had only been away a month. In most respects it was exactly the same, the sandbags piled against walls, the ugly gaps where build-ings had been, the grey faces of passers-by, the way her eyes prickled and grit filled her throat, but it was as though she was experiencing it all at a remove. She was a visitor, she told her-self as she stepped over a pothole in the street where Ackroyd & Briggs had their office. She no longer belonged.

Mr Edwards, her editor, was a slight, scholarly man with smoothed back salt-and-pepper hair and an ethereal aura, who sat behind a desk surrounded by piles of papers and over-looked by shelves of books of all kinds. He turned the pages of

Maddie's drawings with a keen look in his pale green eyes and an expression so serious that Maddie feared he wasn't pleased.

'Hmm,' he said when he came to the last one and finally he unhooked his spectacles, looked up at her and beamed. 'These are marvellous. Exactly what I was hoping for. The vignette composition is perfect and the animals so vivid and appealing. Sammy Squirrel himself . . .' He paused and turned back to the first of the drawings that she'd worked up in detail. 'He's a fine fellow. Exactly the right degree of cheekiness.' A wistful look came into his eyes. 'He reminds me of my own boy.'

Maddie asked tentatively after Joe Edwards and was relieved to hear that they'd heard recently that he was safe. The young man was a naval officer somewhere on the high seas.

'I'm so glad you like the illustrations.' She felt the tautness leave her shoulders. 'The squirrel is based on some sketches I made once of a young market-seller in Kensington. He was small, but extremely perky and self-assured!' She knew in her heart that her work was good, but she'd not allowed herself to believe it until she had Mr Edwards's approbation. 'It helps that Maud Brampton has written such a good story. I read it to my own girls and they loved it. They like my squirrel, too.'

'That's most encouraging. Now we ought to discuss colours. What sort of palette were you proposing? We're expecting full colour for this project. I just hope we can source enough of the right paper. It's a terrible struggle, as you may know. Never mind booking space at the printer.'

'Are the government still being mean with paper?'

'Ridiculously so. With reading so popular and the boost books give to public morale you'd think they'd support publishers, but instead one's going cap in hand to the authorities all the time. I gather that there's a move afoot to agree standard designs that will save paper, but I don't want to make *Sammy Squirrel's Holiday* look cramped and cheap. Indeed, I will fight against it.'

'I hope you win,' Maddie said anxiously. The normally mild Mr Edwards looked quite fierce!

When they finished their discussion he took down several new picture books from his shelves to give to the girls. 'This one about a runaway barrage balloon is jumping off the shelves,' he said. 'We've been forced to reprint.' He sighed. 'That may sound grudging, but the long wait for more stock is infuriating.'

Maddie thanked him for the books and slipped them into her portfolio.

When he showed her out he asked gently, 'Now, there's no news of your husband, I suppose?'

'No.'

He nodded, an expression of sympathy on his face. 'It must be very hard. I rarely hear from my boy. You're left to read about disasters in the papers and to pray your loved one wasn't involved.'

'It's impossible not to worry, isn't it?'

'It's a hackneyed thing to say, but it's useful to keep oneself occupied. It's much worse for my wife, being tied to the house all day. She's an invalid and Joe was our only child. All her hope is invested in him.'

'I'll keep him in my thoughts,' Maddie said. He said that he would do the same concerning Philip and shook her hand warmly before she left.

All this sadness is unbearable, she thought, as she hurried to the underground station, being late to meet Denny for a bite of lunch. Yet with her precious file of drawings snug under her arm she felt thankful. Like Mr Edwards she had a task in which to lose herself.

When Denny looked up as Maddie entered the tea shop she slipped a handmade marker into her library book and rose from her seat with a look of relief.

'I'm so sorry,' Maddie murmured as they embraced.

'Don't be. It's impossible to be on time anywhere any more,' Denny moaned as Maddie sat down opposite at the small round table. 'Charles now sleeps at the office three days a week. It's maddening waiting for buses to take him things that he's forgotten. It would be easier to cycle, but my tyres need new inner tubes. Oh, Maddie, I shouldn't complain. At least I know where Charles is. But you ...'

'It's all right, I'm tough, you know. We each have our own troubles and you're perfectly free to talk about yours.'

The waitress came. They ordered tea and sandwiches and talked non-stop between bites, exchanging news. Denny was a poor letter writer so there was plenty of catching up. Her domestic life sounded extremely full, so that she hardly had time to do any shifts at the local first aid post that she'd chosen as war work. 'Everything's grim, isn't it?' she finished. 'If only the BBC had something cheerful to say occasionally.

Now tell me more about the girls. I'm glad that they enjoy being in the country.'

'They do. We're all still getting used to it, to be honest. Knyghton is a little ... behind the times.'

Denny enjoyed Maddie's ensuing descriptions of life at Knyghton and soon Maddie found herself confiding more seriously the oddness of it all. 'They're Philip's family and I feel I'm learning about aspects of his life that I never knew before. It's hardly healthy for me to wallow in his past, and yet I can't stop myself. Do you think I'm wrong to keep hoping that he's still alive somewhere out there?'

'I understand why.' Denny's forehead furrowed with concern.

'And yet what else can I do at present but stay at Knyghton? I can't move the girls again, they're only now becoming used to a new place. Anyway, where would we go? The worst of the bombing might be over here, but it might start up again.'

Denny looked understandably anxious so Maddie quickly added, 'Though I sincerely hope not.'

'Perhaps things will become clearer,' Denny offered. 'After all, you haven't been there very long.'

'I suppose you're right.' She bit her lip and reminded herself that the important thing was that her daughters were safe.

The girls were still up on Maddie's return that evening, and Grace was tearful because she had lost Rabbit. An extensive search had taken place after tea, but the toy had not been found. Grace could remember having it in the drawing room after lunch, and Mrs Flegg's theory was that one of the dogs had taken it and hidden it somewhere in the garden, though Gussie hotly denied this. Maddie persuaded her daughters upstairs to bed and located an ancient teddy bear in the nursery cupboard as a replacement, but it smelled musty and Grace cast it on the floor in a rage. Sarah sat quietly turning the pages of one of Mr Edwards's books while Maddie soothed her little sister, who eventually cried herself to sleep.

The following day was a Saturday, a normal working day for the Anderson household, but with no school for Sarah. After breakfast Maddie decided to turn the hunt for Rabbit into a game. Each of her daughters was allocated a series of places to look in the house and garden, but with strict instructions not to trespass in rooms that were closed up, such as the front sitting room and spare bedrooms, nor to go anywhere outside that would discommode Flegg. Maddie sat with Gussie in the drawing room. Gussie handed out sherbet lemons from a secret stash whenever a child reported back.

'We've looked everywhere,' Sarah said finally after an hour of this, curling up on the hearthrug with the dogs.

'Everywhere,' Grace echoed indistinctly through a sherbet lemon.

'You can't have done,' Gussie said reasonably, 'or you'd have found him.'

Maddie thought hard about where the dogs' favourite places were outside. The kitchen garden with its vegetable patch and the animals was out of bounds, but Gussie often walked them round the perimeter of the lawn and Maddie had once seen Rochester bury a bone in the rose bed. 'The white roses near the bird table,' she suggested.

'We'll both go,' said Sarah, and she took her sister's hand.

'Poor Flora,' Gussie said, watching them go. 'She's very fond of that rabbit.'

'Do you mean Grace, Gussie?' Maddie said gently, wondering who Flora was.

Gussie stared at her calmly, then said. 'Grace, that's what I said.'

'Perhaps I didn't hear you properly.'

The girls ran back in, out of breath.

'We can't think of anywhere else to look,' Sarah said. 'We've exhausted all possibilities.'

Maddie smothered a laugh at the child's precocity. Sarah couldn't bear to be laughed at.

'That's probably a good thing,' Gussie said vaguely, 'as I've run out of sherbet lemons.'

'But my rabbit, where's my rabbit?' Grace wailed, and climbed into her mother's lap and buried her face in Maddie's neck.

'I expect he'll turn up,' she sighed, but several days passed and there was no sign of the toy.

The days were growing longer and on Monday, after the girls had gone to bed, Maddie went for a walk. She carried a small sketchbook and a pencil in case something of interest caught her eye, but mostly she enjoyed the solitude. It was one of those golden evenings when the air was clear and limpid. She walked through the farmyard, past the carthorses standing patiently under the trees and onwards, then glanced through a gap in the hedge to the green cornfield beyond.

She stopped dead, her eyes widening. Two brown hares, one sitting, one crouched, ready for flight, stared back at her, unblinking, a stone's throw away. Time paused as each party took measure of the other, Maddie enchanted by their long leanness, the hardly perceptible twitch of their ears. Her fingers itched to draw the line of the crouched hare's spine, to capture the pent-up energy of the animal. Slowly, slowly, she reached into her pocket for her sketchbook. Her fingers closed round it and she drew it out, but then something must have spooked the hares for they were off, first one, then the other, stretching their powerful bodies in lengthy, zigzagging bounds across the field until they were lost in the dazzle of the lowering sun. Her shoulders sagged in disappointment.

'I'm sorry,' came a gruff voice behind her. 'That must have been me.'

She whipped round to see Lyle.

'Never mind. They were beautiful, though,' she said wistfully. 'I hoped to draw them.' She made to return the sketchbook to her pocket, but Lyle put out his hand.

'Let me see.' It was like a command.

'No.' Her book was private, as writing a diary was to other people.

'Oh, come on. I'd like to see your drawings.'

'Sorry.' She grinned to take the edge off her refusal.

'It's full of secrets, is it?'

'They're not very good, I'd be embarrassed.' It was only

partly a lie. The sketches the book contained were hastily done, notes to herself. 'I'll show you the children's book illustrations that I'm working on back at the house, if you like.' So far, only the girls had shown much interest in her work. She didn't mind, not really, did not care for adult approval apart from her editor's. But now here was Lyle, pressing her, and it felt intrusive.

'I'll have to make do with that,' he said, smiling, as she tucked the book back into her pocket. Hurt by this dismissiveness, she didn't feel bad for not showing it to him.

'What is it you're growing here?' she asked, to change the subject.

'Wheat. Look.' He leaned down and plucked a stray ear to show her the pattern that the seeds made then went on to say, 'The hares lie in forms in the field, shallow dips in the earth made by the shapes of their bodies. They're difficult to see until they shoot off from under your feet.'

Maddie knew this from her reading and observation, but nodded politely. 'They're not pests, are they, like rabbits?'

'Not like rabbits, no. Actually, they're rather marvellous. I was reading the booklet you lent me. I'd not appreciated their magical significance before. The Chinese have their moon hare. And they're a symbol of fertility the world over.'

'I've read it, too, remember!' Again, she smiled to soften the chastisement.

'Of course you have.' He laughed.

'You can tell me about your work, if you like. I know nothing about farming.'

'If you show me your children's book illustrations, I'd be

glad to do so in exchange. I must have seemed rude just now, I'm sorry. Will you walk back with me or are you going on?'

In the distance the sun was sinking and across the flat landscape the shadows of hedges and trees were lengthening. The air had lost its warmth. 'I'll come back with you,' she said, and with a final glance at the field she fell into step beside him.

'What had you been doing out at the farm so late?'

'Checking some paperwork. There's a large bill to pay and I need to negotiate with the bank when I go to market tomorrow.' He sighed. 'I caught sight of you walking when I locked the office. You looked so trouble-laden and sad that I decided to catch up with you, to see if you were all right.'

'That's kind. But I assure you I wasn't sad. I was enjoying the peace and thinking.'

'Then, once more, I'm sorry.'

'Honestly, it's all right.' There was an edginess between them. Neither seemed able to say the right thing to the other. They crossed the farmyard and Maddie asked, 'Has the farm always been part of Knyghton?'

'As far back as we know. It's in the blood. All the land as far as you can see to the west belongs to us.' As they left the farm behind them, Lyle began to describe his work. She tried to make sense of the facts and figures of acreages and yields, but it was the sound of his voice she listened to most, and although she sensed the weight of expectation upon him in this war, it was also his enthusiasm that struck her, the way he spoke about working with the earth, the daily battle to bring riches out of the ground.

'Does anyone live in the farmhouse?' Maddie asked, remembering the flint cottage at one side of the farmyard.

'My estate manager, usually, but he took the king's shilling, so the land girls have borrowed the place. Robert, our horseman, lives nearby, but it's essential that there's someone on the premises to keep an eye on things. Especially during calving.'

They were approaching Knyghton now and darkness was gathering in the hollows of the thickets and under the trees. 'The house is so beautifully tucked away, isn't it?' Maddie mused as the path took them into the garden. She was coming to feel that the place was home.

'That's what I love about it,' Lyle grinned.

They entered via the scullery, where they prised off their muddy footwear. In the hall, she hung up her jacket and watched Lyle light a lamp. 'Come on,' he said. 'You were going to show me those pictures.'

'Oh. Wouldn't it be better in daylight?'

'I'm hardly here. Seize the moment, I say.'

She followed him up the stairs, the lamp casting its glow all around.

In Philip's old bedroom, Lyle seemed unexpectedly ill-at-ease, holding the lamp aloft to search out the dark corners. 'It's odd to see it as it was again.'

He set the lamp on the table and Maddie pulled the blackout curtains across the window, shutting out the last mauve hues of daylight. Then she drew the folder of pictures on the table towards her, explaining about the book as she turned the pages over for him to examine. She'd painted the first illustration and was pleased with it. The natural colours of tree and leaf and fur appeared infused with light so that they glowed on the paper.

'They're very charming,' Lyle said eventually. 'I'm sure children will love them,' and she felt that his keen eyes studied her with new interest, as though she'd revealed something worthwhile about herself. For some reason this disturbed her. With the darkness closing in around them she felt suddenly alert to the closeness of him next to her at the desk, his salty scent, the sigh of his breath and the shuffle of his clothes as he reached to pick up one of the pages. Her skin prickled with awareness of him. She used the need to close a slight gap in the curtains as an excuse to step away then replaced the drawings into the folder.

'No one's used this room since Philip left,' Lyle said, walking about, opening a door of the wardrobe briefly, straightening a picture on the wall. 'It seems right that you're here.' He examined a small print propped on the mantelpiece of a fair-haired Jesus blessing woodland animals and frowned. 'I'm sure this was mine. A christening present.'

'I don't expect Philip would fight you over it. When did he leave Knyghton? For good, I mean.' Maddie asked.

'After he left school – the same year as me, 1926 – he went up to university in London. I believe he intended to live here in the holidays.'

That must be why he'd left some of his clothes and the letters in their hiding place.

'But he didn't? You surely saw him now and then.'

'Yes, of course. He visited for short periods. He was very fond of Gussie, you see.'

'And of you?'

'Was he ever fond of me?' Lyle gave a chuckle, but didn't answer. Then he turned serious. 'When he first arrived we rubbed along pretty well. You know what boys are like – but perhaps you don't, having daughters. We did things together in the holidays – kicked a ball around, climbed trees, dared each other to do stupid things.'

'What kind of stupid things?' she said, smiling.

'Dropping conkers on the vicar, who was sitting under our tree having tea with Gussie and Grandmother. And I made Philip climb up onto the roof once – a workman left a ladder. There was a heck of a row about that. We both had hobbies. He collected coins, I told you. I liked natural history. He gave me a jolly good weasel skull once. We'd search for ammonites on the beach. I must still have those in a box somewhere.'

'I found his letters,' Maddie burst out and seeing Lyle's surprised face felt ashamed that she hadn't told him before. 'They were under the floorboard there.' Her eyes went to the spot. 'Where you said.'

His eyes narrowed. 'You've read them?'

'A few. Was that wrong? I don't know.'

'I can't think why it should be. Maddie, do you believe he's still alive?'

'Yes. Yes, I do ... A lot of the time anyway.'

There was silence in the room. Lyle stared sightlessly and she wondered what he was thinking about. Then he said suddenly, 'Were the letters just as I said?'

'Yes. Mostly from his mother, Rose, one or two from his father. He must have felt very alone. Especially being away at school,' she added hastily in case he thought she meant he hadn't been cared for at Knyghton.

'I'm sure my mother would have done her best.' Lyle sounded defensive. 'I know she wrote to him.'

But Philip hadn't kept any letters from his aunt Daphne in that box.

'Did he write back to her?'

'I don't know. She told me I had to be especially kind to him, I do remember that. I let him borrow my bicycle for a whole summer because he didn't have one at the time. I felt sorry for him being away from his parents, but I never knew what to say to him about that. Then my father was killed. That's when everything changed.' Lyle was moving restlessly around the room, now. 'It was as though a great dark pall fell across everything. My mother became a shadow, wrapped up in her grief, then after the war she met this cad Sugden.'

'She married again?'

'Yes. Cedric Sugden. Heard of him, no? He wrote adventure novels. The most awful codswallop, but people seemed to like them. So she went off with him to the south of France, if you please, leaving me here. Gussie tried to help me, but you know Gussie. I think she was frightened of saying the wrong thing and of course George had been her brother and she had her own sadness to deal with.'

'And later . . .?' Maddie prompted.

'By the time we were eleven or twelve, a year or two after the war ended, we were drifting apart, Philip and I. He didn't fit in with my friends. Mine was a good school, don't get me wrong, but nothing like Philip's. We were an ordinary lot, but he acquired real polish. When he came back for the holidays I teased him for his accent. That used to drive him wild, so he'd be speaking like the rest of us by the time he returned to school, and then he'd get ragged there for sounding "common".' Lyle gave a low, carefree laugh that Maddie had never heard before.

'He was at prep school first, then went to Upton, didn't he?'

'Yes. Aunt Rose's brother was an old Uptonian. Philip went at thirteen. Didn't he tell you all that?'

'Only the outlines. He liked the school, I think.'

'Never complained when it was time to go back.' Lyle hesitated then said, 'Were there any later letters there? From after the war, I mean?'

'One or two. I haven't investigated properly yet.'

He looked thoughtful, then nodded curtly. 'I'd be interested to know if there are. Well, I've things to do.' All the friendliness had gone, as though at the flick of a switch. 'Thank you for showing me your work.'

After he'd hurried off Maddie tidied her desk and went slowly downstairs. Was it her or was there was something bothering him, she thought, something he didn't want to talk about. If so, for the life of her she couldn't imagine what it might be.

Fifteen

'Rabbit! Oh, Rabbit,' Grace cried out with joy.

Christine Sutton had found the missing toy and brought it in with her when she arrived on Wednesday morning.

'It was under a bush near the front gate,' she announced, her normally pale cheeks flushed with triumph. 'I saw the blue and pink of his ear and I thought, *I know what that is!*'

'We didn't think to search there,' Maddie said, puzzled. 'Did we, girls?'

It had rained since the toy had gone missing on Friday, but Rabbit wasn't wet, only a little grubby, so Christine and Grace followed Maddie down to the kitchen where Maddie wiped it with a damp cloth before returning it to its anxious owner.

'Reckon it must have been a fox what took him,' Mrs Flegg said from her place by the stove.

'No, a fox would have chewed him,' her husband said.

'Naughty fox,' Grace said in horror, and examined the toy.

'I think it's all right, darling. Nothing's chewed it. Now say thank you to Nanny Sutton for finding it.'

Grace looked up solemnly at Christine. 'Thank you, Nanny Sutton,' she chanted. Suddenly she ran to her and hugged her.

Christine blushed with delight at this show of affection. 'That's all right, my angel. I know how much you love your little rabbit.'

All's well that ends well, Maddie thought with a sigh. Still, what had happened to Rabbit was a mystery to add to all the others.

Whether Sarah's schoolmates had got used to her presence or Miss Dale had clamped down on the teasing, Maddie was relieved to notice that her elder daughter seemed a little happier at school. One tranquil Thursday afternoon, Maddie and Grace accompanied Flegg into the village in the trap, the plan being to meet Sarah out of school. As a treat they would have tea in the chintzy teashop near the post office, while the old man conducted various errands.

Flegg tied the long-suffering pony to the usual ring in the wall of the churchyard and shambled off with his shopping bag. They were early, so Maddie saw an opportunity to seek out the Anderson family graves, as the rector had recommended. 'Shall we walk round the churchyard, Grace, love? It's pretty with the wild flowers and we can look for stone angels.'

Being in a remarkably cheerful mood, Grace agreed and Maddie transformed the steep walk up to the far corner of the churchyard into a game of spotting carved cherubs on the gravestones that they passed. The patch at the top where the Andersons were buried was poorly maintained, as though the sexton's mower hadn't made it that far. Clumps of nettles grew by the wall there and a great yew tree cast its shadow over an ancient family tomb, whose crumbling surface was yellow with lichen, its iron rail surround rusty and twisted. Grace danced about between the gravestones, singing to herself, while Maddie tried to read the inscription. Only the name 'Anderson' was clear enough to make out. She found a smooth pebble on the ground near the wall and placed it on the tomb. She'd read in one of her art books that it was a mark of remembrance in some cultures.

'There's an angel on this one, Mummy.' Grace summoned her to an ornate gravestone near the wall.

'It is a beautiful one,' Maddie agreed. The creature appeared to be leaning over the top of the stone and had great folded wings like an eagle's. The inscription below was still remarkably clear. *James Anderson* and below, *Eleanor Anderson, wife of the above.* 'It must be the grave of your great-grandparents,' she told Grace, remembering the lady with the hare in the portrait, but the little girl had already skipped off to inspect a cluster of poppies. This Eleanor was surely Gussie's mother. The date of death was given as 1926.

Maddie ambled among the graves looking for other familiar names. No George, of course, his grave, if he had one, would be among those serried ranks of white round-topped gravestones in France. Perhaps there was a memorial to him in the church that she'd missed? She moved on, and though other Anderson names meant nothing to her, each inscription spoke a story of this family she'd married into. She stood for a while before an account of two small Victorian girls who'd died within days of each other in 1867. Some infection must have swept them away. She squeezed her eyes shut at the thought of their parents' grief.

The church clock struck the half hour and she looked round for Grace. 'Time we went,' she called out, but there was no sign of the child. 'Grace?' she called, and felt a sudden panic. A rustle of branches and Grace appeared from behind a bush growing near the wall. Maddie breathed again. How silly. The atmosphere of the place had got to her. She stepped across and put out her hand. 'Come on! Sarah will be coming out.' As they turned to go, Maddie glanced at a simple grave-stone standing apart from the others and stopped short. It was the name on it that caught her eye. 'Flora.' She spoke the name softly. Someone had mentioned the name Flora recently. Gussie, she thought.

The stone was soft and creamy, the inscription already wearing away, and a creeper grew across the surname. She bent and scraped it aside and frowned, for she couldn't make it out. Not 'Anderson' anyway, although it was near the cluster of Anderson graves. What was it doing out here on its own? The dates, too were barely legible. She traced the incisions with her finger. 1908 to 1925, she thought. Flora had died young. Sixteen or seventeen.

'Come on, Mummy,' Grace was tugging at her sleeve, so she straightened, took the little girl's hand and they hastened down the path in time to see the children surging out into the playground. And there was Sarah, trailing behind alone – Maddie's heart gave a pang – but the child's face lit up when she saw her mother and sister and she ran.

Sixteen

Gussie was sorting through a tin full of buttons in the drawing room early the following afternoon while Maddie unravelled a ragged old navy jumper of Lyle's, intending to knit a cardigan for Sarah. Grace was asleep upstairs. The door to the garden stood open, quivering in the warm breeze, and the rhododendrons at the edge of the treeline were blossoming a deep crimson.

'These were from an old silk coat of my mother's,' Gussie said, holding up a set of large pale blue buttons with scalloped edges. 'I remember when she had it made for George's wedding. Oh, and look.' She dropped the coat buttons back in the box and picked out a small ivory button in the shape of an elephant. 'I loved this, it was from a cloth purse dear Rose sent from India for my birthday. Ginger, a setter we once had, chewed the purse, the naughty boy, but I rescued the button.'

'They tell quite a history, buttons,' Maddie said, tossing a ball of wool onto her pile. 'What are you searching for?'

'I'm not searching for anything,' Gussie said, puzzled. 'I simply like looking at them all and remembering the stories behind them.'

'Well, I'm going to want buttons for this cardigan. Have you got a set I can have? Here's the pattern.' She passed the booklet across and Gussie studied it with interest.

'It's five if you want one for the neck,' she said, returning it. 'Let's see.' She dug around in the box and came up with a card of small round shimmering buttons. 'Look, mother-of-pearl.'

'Oh, they're beautiful,' Maddie gasped, taking the card from her. 'Are you sure I may have them?'

'I don't see why not. I remember seeing them on a blouse, but I don't recall whose it was.'

'You're very kind. There are six, but I can sew one inside as a spare. Oh, it'll look so pretty on Sarah.'

'Now who did wear that blouse?' Gussie wondered. She was, as so often, lost in her own world, a world of the past, as far as Maddie could make out, when her parents were alive and she grew up in happiness with her brothers. What had happened to keep her in that world?

'Knyghton must have changed a great deal in your lifetime,' Maddie said, sitting back in her seat, balls of wool nesting like eggs in her lap.

'Oh indeed. It was a perfect place to grow up.' The perpetual expression of innocent bewilderment left Gussie's face when she talked about her youth. It was possible to imagine how she must have been – a demure little girl, whose mother kept her close.

Maddie smoothed the knitting pattern open on the sofa beside her and peered at it. 'Tell me what it was like when you were little,' she urged. She reached for a soft bag at her feet and drew out a pair of knitting needles.

'What do you want to know?' Again, that expression of puzzlement.

'Was the house the same? It must have taken a great deal of work to look after and you told me you had more servants, but with three children how did your mother manage everything?'

'She just did. I don't remember how. One of the maids, Dorry, used to help her with her hair and clothes. Mother loved her because she had such a sweet nature, and she stayed for many years until she became ill and had to retire and then she had Tilly for a few years. As for we children, we had Nanny Platten when we were little. She was very strict and didn't like spiders, which was a problem for her working at Knyghton.'

Maddie smiled, for Knyghton was home to many spiders. All those servants, though, she thought as she tied a piece of wool to a needle. And now they only had the Fleggs. Times had changed.

'When I was old enough,' Gussie continued, 'I was sent to the rectory for lessons. The rector's wife taught their two girls and my father paid for her to teach me, too. Our old horseman Dick Rix, Robert's father, drove me there every morning. George and William went to the village school. I was stupid at my lessons so after I turned fourteen I stayed at home and helped mother. She said I was delicate, but I wasn't. I was simply a home bird. I know I would have hated school.'

Maddie felt sad that Gussie thought of herself as stupid.

She wondered why her mother hadn't encouraged her more, for it seemed that Gussie had never had the opportunity to flower, to live her own life beyond the secure walls of Knyghton.

'After my father died in 1910, George became master of Knyghton, but in many ways things were much the same. His wife Daphne was a gentle person and she never minded my mother's presence, or if she did she never showed it. William married Rose, of course, and went to India. I missed him dreadfully. It was with the war and George's death that everything started to fall apart. My mother was heartbroken. Never got over it. Daphne did, though. She went off and married that man Sugden. Left Lyle behind because Sugden didn't want him and anyway, Lyle needed to be at Knyghton. It was his, after all. Then Mother passed away in 1926. After that it was just Lyle and Philip and me, and then Philip moved to London.

'So much sadness,' Maddie murmured, frowning at the knitting pattern.

'Yes. But I'm so pleased that you're here now. And the little girls. It's like old times. You'll laugh, but sometimes I think I hear children in the house. Not yours, other ones, from long ago.'

'It's a very old house. Perhaps it's the wind or the creak of old beams.'

'Perhaps,' Gussie said, but her face wore that unhappy look again. 'Nobody believes me when I say things like that. But I know what I hear.'

Maddie finished casting on a line of stitches and made

sure they were even. She thought of Philip's album. 'I have some photographs taken at Knyghton which I'd love to show you, though perhaps you have copies. They're of Philip and Lyle.'

'Taken here? Oh, fetch them, do,' Gussie commanded, so Maddie set her knitting aside and went upstairs.

When she returned with the album, Gussie moved to the sofa so that they could look at the book together. Close up Gussie smelled of lavender. Maddie opened the album at the first page and Gussie fumbled back the flypaper with her liver-spotted fingers and sighed in delight.

'Oh, I remember that dog. Yellow, Lyle called him. He was given him as a puppy and he followed Lyle everywhere.'

Gussie turned the pages eagerly. 'Oh, here's Mother. This would have been after Father died because she always wore black.'

Maddie glanced up at the portrait of the younger Eleanor on the wall. 'Did she become more stern as she grew older?'

'A little, perhaps.' Gussie remarked. 'She certainly expected people to do as they were told. That's why she liked Tilly when she arrived. Tilly knew exactly how Mother wanted her hair and she never scorched her clothes like poor Dorry did. It's a pity she didn't stay with us longer.'

'Tilly was the new lady's maid,' Maddie said, trying to catch up.

'That's what I said, didn't I?' Gussie snapped and Maddie flinched and quickly turned to the last page of the album.

'Drenched in summer sunlight,' Gussie sighed. 'That's how I remember my childhood at Knyghton.'

'And who's this?' Maddie said, pointing to the shy figure of the girl by the hollyhocks.

Gussie looked more closely, then frowned. 'I'm sure I couldn't say. It's too blurred.' She closed the album with a sharp movement and passed it back to Maddie and the bewildered look returned to her eyes. She reached down to lift Phoebe into her lap where the little dog snuggled down and licked her hand. She stroked it for a moment and gradually a tranquil expression replaced the distress.

Whatever had disturbed Gussie she didn't explain. Was it the blurred figure that had accidentally crept into a photograph, Maddie wondered. Who was she?

Seventeen

That night at the sound of a loud cry, Maddie woke and sat bolt upright. She'd left the window open and a breeze stirred the blackout so that for a moment she thought the sound had come from outside, but then it came again. Lyle. She threw back the bedclothes and felt her way to the door, reaching for her dressing gown. Out in the corridor she stood by Lyle's door, listening. The cry came again, followed by a long low moan, then he shouted something.

She knocked lightly. There was no reply so she turned the handle and pushed. Was it locked? She pushed harder and this time it sprang open.

'Lyle?' she whispered. His curtains stood open and a blanket of moonlight lay across the room. She saw the shape of him, curled up in the bed, the pillows awry. He moaned again, an agonizing sound. 'Lyle,' she said anxiously. She stepped over to the bed, reached and touched his shoulder.

Suddenly he rolled over. Maddie caught the gleam of

his eyes, open but unseeing, as he staggered to his feet and lunged at her. She fell back, with a scream, and it was enough to wake him. 'Good God, what the hell . . .?' He stood blinking down at her where she lay sprawled on the floor, then snatched up his top sheet and covered himself. At that moment Gussie's dogs began to bark.

'I . . .' she began.

'Shhh.' They both froze, listening as a door creaked along the corridor and the barks loudened briefly. 'Damn,' Lyle whispered.

Maddie heard Gussie's soft voice quaver, 'Hello?' Slow footsteps neared, passed Lyle's door, stopped and they heard another door groan open. 'Are you all right, Maddie dear?' she heard Gussie say. Maddie held her breath. After a long moment and a rustle outside Lyle's door, the footsteps retreated. Gussie's door closed, the dogs' barks subsided and the house sank into silence once more.

Maddie pushed herself to her feet and retied the belt of her dressing gown, aware of Lyle staring at her from the bed. His bare shoulders gleamed silver in the moonlight and she fixed her eyes on his angry face.

'It's not my fault,' she whispered fiercely. 'I heard you shouting. I thought something was wrong.'

'A bad dream. You gave me a shock creeping up on me like that.'

'I did knock.'

'I didn't hear.'

'That's because you were shouting.'

They glared at each other.

'You might at least be grateful. Now Gussie probably thinks . . . well, I don't know.'

'That we're having an affair?'

'Don't laugh. It's rotten and it's not funny.'

Maddie made to go, had reached the door when Lyle said, more gently, 'Wait. I should explain. Sometimes I have nightmares. There's nothing wrong with me, I've had them for years. I'm sorry if I disturbed you.'

She turned. 'It's not your fault that you disturbed me, but it is that you are so angry with me.'

'I know. It was a shock to be dragged awake and finding you there, that's all. Please forgive me.'

She nodded. 'What on earth do I say to Gussie in the morning? I won't be able to look her in the eye.'

'Tell her the truth,' Lyle said. 'She knows I have nightmares.' A smile played around his lips.

'What?'

'It'll be more fun if you say nothing, though.'

'Don't be ridiculous,' she said, and returned to her bedroom.

As she lay in her bed waiting for sleep to overtake her she thought that it was the first time she'd felt a rush of real sympathy for Lyle. What did he dream about and why? She should have asked him, but the moment had gone.

The next day, when she and the girls came down to breakfast, he'd already left for the farm. By the time she saw him alone in the evening, he acted the same as ever – as if the events of the previous night had never happened.

Eighteen

For several weeks Maddie's nights were unbroken. If Lyle had bad dreams and cried out then she didn't hear him. The dull May gave way to an unsettled June and any news of the war continued to be disheartening. Often Maddie found thinking about it unbearable and it was always a relief when Christine Sutton appeared on her funny old bicycle and took charge of Grace so that she could retreat to the peace of Philip's old bedroom and continue with her commission.

The detailed drawing for all the illustrations was done and she'd experimented with the colours until she was certain what to use. Each picture had to be executed quickly and deftly, lighter colours first, and there was little possibility of correcting mistakes. She made a mess of one and had to start again from scratch, but otherwise she worked confidently, caught up in the pleasure of it.

One Monday morning towards the end of June, the sky suddenly darkened. Heavy showers rattled on the gravel forecourt and turned the gutters into miniature waterfalls. Christine had taken Grace out for a walk, but they'd been wearing waterproofs so Maddie wasn't worried. She pinned back the curtains to admit as much light she possible, reached for a fresh drawing, dipped a thick brush into water and loaded it with pale green from the box of colours. She carefully painted a patch of grass at the bottom of the roundel. While it dried, she returned to an earlier illustration, a side view of a loping rabbit, and dabbed at its amber eye to give it a white point of light, grimacing at the delicacy of the brushwork, before doing the same to the black buttons of its scarlet waistcoat. She selected a pen for the finer work to its face so that its anxious expression came to life. Its pose was inspired by the leaping hare above Knyghton's front door, and she was pleased by how it turned out.

She washed the brushes carefully, wondering what to attempt next. While she pondered she heard a child's tuneful voice from downstairs – Grace and Christine must have returned – and struck by its unearthliness, was visited by a sudden impulse. Reaching for a fresh sheet of paper, she selected a pencil and began to sketch a face. She had no sense of purpose in her drawing, just that a vision of a girl had appeared in her mind and she felt the urge to get it down. A high, wide forehead with delicate winged eyebrows, hair springing back in waves from an oval face, a determined chin. Large almond-shaped eyes and a neat nose above small moulded lips, slightly open to reveal even teeth. The face was an intelligent one, its expression serious. Maddie shaded the line of a cheekbone and sat back to see what she'd done.

It was the head of a girl on the brink of womanhood, fresh-faced, her cheeks downy, her eyes full of life and hope for the future. Maddie was pleased with it. But where had the image come from? She was used to the random ways that ideas came to her, so after a moment she shrugged and carefully laid the sketch in a folder. A moment later footsteps pattered in the corridor and the door handle rattled. She glanced at her watch. It was twelve noon already and the little face that appeared round the door was grumpy. 'Grace, what's the matter?'

Grace did not reply.

It was with concern that Maddie hurried downstairs and wrenched the front door open. Outside, Christine stood astride her bicycle with one foot on a pedal. She was busy retying her rain hat while staring across the garden. Following the direction of her gaze, Maddie was surprised to see two figures standing together at the edge of the treeline. One was Lyle, smoking a cigarette with sharp angry movements, as he conversed with the other, a young woman in breeches and rubber boots whose arms were tightly folded. Their terse voices, one high, the other low, drifted on the breeze, but Maddie couldn't hear what they said. The woman was probably one of Lyle's other land girls, Maddie thought, but there was something intimate about the way they stood together, her hand on his arm. Never mind, it wasn't her business. She looked away, remembering her concern about Grace.

'Mrs Sutton?' Christine turned her head and Maddie was taken aback by her desolate expression so instead of demanding what had upset Grace she approached the matter more tentatively. 'I ... wanted to say thank you for looking after Grace. How was she this morning? Did you get awfully wet?'

Christine blinked then snapped back into her usual cheerfulness. 'Not very wet. We were in the woods, under the shelter of the trees. It was a nature ramble. We were looking for flowers, but Grace and I disagreed over a rather nasty ants nest.'

Maddie smiled. 'She likes creepy crawlies.'

'Yes, but these were red ants. They sting, don't they?'

'Mummy?' Grace had appeared in the doorway and cast Christine an unfriendly look, her mouth turned down. 'Nanny took my stick away.'

'She was trying to poke the ants with it,' Christine explained. 'Nearly had my eye out, too.'

'Oh, Grace,' Maddie sighed, feeling caught between them. Grace turned and stomped indoors. 'Come and say goodbye,' Maddie called, but there was silence. 'Grace?'

'I'm so sorry ...' she said. Christine looked utterly cast down.

At that moment Maddie's attention was caught by the scene across the garden. Lyle broke away suddenly, walked off into the trees and was quickly lost to sight. The young woman paused, gazing after him, then she shot Maddie a scornful look, tossed her head and followed in his wake.

'Wasn't that Mr Anderson?' Christine asked Maddie.

'Yes.'

'Who was it with him?'

'I don't know. Why?'

'No particular reason.' Christine's face had taken on a thoughtful look and her hands tightened on the handlebars.

'Don't worry about Grace,' Maddie continued, wondering what was going through the woman's mind. 'She can be quite stubborn sometimes.'

Christine's brow furrowed. 'I'm sure I didn't mean to upset her.'

'I'll have a talk with her. Please don't worry.'

Maddie wished her goodbye and waited until the wobbling bike with its raincoated figure was taken by the bend of the drive. She couldn't make Christine Sutton out, she thought as she returned to the house to seek out Grace. Surely the woman had been right to challenge the child's behaviour, yet she'd seemed worried that Grace wouldn't forgive her for it. It was most unsettling.

Maddie found her daughter sitting hunched up on the bottom stair holding Rabbit, her thumb in her mouth. She looked at her mother with accusing eyes. With a rush of love Maddie went to sit down next to her. Grace leaned against her. She was obviously tired.

'Darling, you mustn't be rude to Nanny Sutton.'

Grace removed her thumb long enough to say, 'She shouted and took my stick. I wasn't going to hurt the ants.'

'I'm sure she was trying to keep you safe from them. You've upset her, I think.'

Grace said nothing so Maddie hugged her and decided to drop the matter.

If Lyle had noticed Maddie watching him that morning, he made no mention of the fact when he came in at lunchtime. Instead he was self-absorbed and ate quickly, without saying much, then rose from the table, growling that he'd better get back to work.

'Is something wrong, Lyle?' Gussie commented. 'You're as cross as two sticks.'

'We're getting the peas in and two of the girls are off sick,' he threw over his shoulder as he left.

Maddie watched him go, certain his mood had something to do with the mysterious argument she'd witnessed earlier, but she had no chance to find out. She hardly saw him that evening either for he came in late for supper and retired early to bed. During the night, she heard him cry out, but this time she pulled the bedclothes over her head to block out the sound.

Two mornings later, Christine arrived as usual and Maddie was relieved that Grace went off with her companionably enough to the nursery, Monday's quarrel apparently forgotten.

She shut herself away in Philip's old room and managed to complete another illustration. While setting it aside to dry she noticed Christine and Grace walking away up the drive. *Good*, she thought, *it's a lovely day for an outing.*

She glanced down at the folder and her attention was caught by the drawing of the girl she'd imagined two days before. She slid it out and brooded over it. Something settled in her mind. Another vision. She turned to a fresh sheet of paper and started to sketch again, trying not to think too much, simply going with the movement of her hand. The page wasn't big enough so she pushed it away, reached for a larger one and began again.

When she'd finished she found that she'd drawn a

full-length figure of the girl. The hair was shorter than in Monday's picture, and neater, cut in a fringe above her high brow. She was tall, Maddie realized, slim, with narrow wrists, her ankles slender. She was wearing low-heeled shoes and a drop-waist print cotton frock. She held a book in her hands, cradled to her chest. Her expression was serious and there were shadows under her eyes. Maddie's pencil hovered above the book she'd sketched. What was it? Suddenly the answer dropped like a pebble into a pool. It was poetry. She printed the title in gold on the spine: *Golden Treasury of Songs and Lyrics*. Who was this girl? She was a little older than in the earlier portrait, but not much. Though the freshness of youth was still upon her, the hairstyle and the studious pose gave her a quieter, more sophisticated air. Perhaps something had happened to her to bring about a change.

Maddie reached for her paint box, paused, then without conscious thought, dipped a brush into water, and mixed a colour on her palette. She began to paint. The girl's hair was a soft honey brown, her eyes a blueish grey with dark rings around the irises. The mouth was sweet, but firm, a natural red, the skin lightly freckled. That she was a beauty was in no doubt; that she didn't know she was, very probable.

After she'd finished Maddie stared at the painting for a while, wondering who this young woman was, whether Maddie had seen her before somewhere and squirrelled her away in her memory. Her thoughts were interrupted by the chime of the clock in the hall. Then she heard footsteps on the gravel and looked out to see Mrs Sutton and Grace returning from their walk. Grace was clutching a pink-striped paper bag.

She pushed the picture aside and hurried downstairs where she was glad to find that her younger daughter was her usual sunny self. The paper bag turned out to contain coconut ice and Christine Sutton's crestfallen mood had cleared like the mist from the morning grass.

'I've a list of shopping as long as your arm, and Flegg's woke up liverish.' Mrs Flegg, frying bread for breakfast in the smoky kitchen the following day, looked enquiringly at Maddie, who was chivvying Sarah to eat up and ready herself for school. 'I'd go meself, Mrs Anderson, but I've the beds to strip before the laundry van comes.'

'I expect I can go if Gussie will keep an eye on Grace.' Surely Gussie could manage that for once.

Gussie agreed, so after seeing Sarah off and clearing up the kitchen Maddie left Grace playing Snap with her in the drawing room and borrowed Mrs Flegg's ancient bicycle, which had a large front basket for parcels.

Riding through the fresh air to Monksfield she felt a guilty sense of freedom, which was quickly dispersed by having to queue at the butcher's then again at the grocer's. In the draper's shop, however, she was served straight away by a neat old lady who sold her navy thread to mend Sarah's school tunic. She was preparing to leave, thinking she might have time to visit the library, when the bell above the door tinkled and a young woman walked in. Slender, with a crop of wavy fair hair and a determined expression, it took Maddie a moment to realize that, though a trim skirt and blouse had replaced the breeches of yesterday, this was the woman she'd seen in the garden arguing with Lyle.

Their eyes met and a look of puzzlement leaped into the other woman's face.

'Are you . . . excuse me . . . but are you Maddie Anderson?' The woman was well spoken, her voice charming with its slight huskiness and Maddie smiled politely.

'Yes, that's right.' Another woman came into the shop and they shuffled aside to let her reach the counter.

'I'm Susie Welbourne, a friend of Lyle's.'

'You're neighbours of ours, aren't you?' Maddie replied. So it was Susie she'd seen with Lyle. Their closeness made sense now.

'Our families go back a long way together. They probably met at the Norman Conquest.' She gave a light laugh. 'Or before. I rather see us as Anglo-Saxon farming stock.'

Maddie smiled politely. 'I've met your father, I think, down at our farm.' Susie must be the daughter of Roger, the angry man she'd encountered at the farm office. Lyle had been arguing with Susie yesterday. Maybe he was at war with the whole Welbourne family.

The old lady and her customer were talking loudly across the counter. Something about a shortage of brass buttons.

'Anyway,' Susie went on. 'I glimpsed you yesterday with your little girl. So sweet. Lyle was being stubborn about something, the dear man, or I'd have asked to be introduced. How are you finding life here? I'm so sorry to hear about your loss. It must be awful.'

'My husband has been *missing* for over a year now.' Maddie felt a cold prickle of resentment at the way the people of Monksfield assumed that Philip was dead.

'Missing. Sorry, that's not what I heard.' Susie Welbourne looked flustered and Maddie relented.

'You undoubtedly know that we were bombed out?' Susie nodded. 'Knyghton's been a lifeline for us. Lyle, Miss Anderson, opening their home. The girls were so frightened in London, but now ...'

'Lyle told me your eldest isn't getting on well at the school.'

'Did he?' Again, she felt annoyance. This woman had a way of wrong-footing her. 'Maybe at the beginning, but it's always difficult starting somewhere new.'

'People here have got a bee in their bonnet about Knyghton after *what happened*, that's all. Even though it was a long time ago.'

'What do you mean?' Maddie watched as a look of horror crossed the other woman's face.

'You don't know? Me and my big mouth. Forget I said anything.'

Maddie opened the door to allow the previous customer to leave, then hovered uncertainly as Susie Welbourne went to the counter and spoke to the old lady. 'I need a packet of bodkins. Large enough to mend sacking.'

'That's kind of you to wait.' Susie said as she opened her purse to pay.

Outside they sized one another up.

'I wanted to know what you meant by "what happened",' Maddie said.

'I think you should ask Lyle about it.'

They stood aside to allow an old man with a stick to hobble past. Maddie felt annoyance build inside.

'You're one of Knyghton's land girls, aren't you, Miss Welbourne? Are you allowed to call him Lyle when you're working?'

'I am a land girl, yes, but on my father's farm. I don't think Lyle and I would work well together, oh dear me, no.' She gave another of her little laughs. 'Well, good luck with your shopping, Mrs Anderson. Monksfield's not too bad for everyday needs, is it? Personally I like to shop in Norwich when I need something stylish. Jarrold's is my favourite store. Toodle-oo.' She fluttered her fingers in farewell and Maddie, warm with fury, watched her lithe figure slink off down the street.

Everything about Susie Welbourne irked her. That she looked elegant in country tweeds and brogue shoes, her casual tactlessness, the way she spoke about Lyle as though they were intimates, the fact that she had hinted at some unpleasant past event, but wouldn't explain what it was. Maddie sighed and forlornly crossed the street with her parcels to where she'd left the bicycle. The thought of the library cheered her as she took several books out of the basket and stowed the parcels there instead, fitting the oilskin cover back over the top to secure them.

The library building, a notice at the front entrance said, had once been the village gaol. It was a tiny eighteenth-century building, its two rooms crammed with books. Maddie loved the cheerful higgledy-piggledy air of it, and enjoyed chatting to Clara, who Maddie had learned had been in charge since her brother, the usual librarian, had joined the RAF as a wireless operator.

'Morning, Mrs Anderson.'

'Hello, Clara.' While Clara added Maddie's books to the returns shelf beside the counter, Maddie noticed the title of a small slim volume there that had fallen on its side. It was a history of Monksfield and she asked if she could borrow it.

'Of course. The rector has just brought it back.'

'And did the rector like it?'

'He did say that it had been most useful.'

'I'll definitely take it then.'

The hands of the clock on the wall overhead were creeping towards half past eleven. Gussie shouldn't be saddled with Grace too long, so Maddie went and ran an eye over the fiction shelves, adding a couple of fat novels to the Monksfield history waiting on the counter. After exchanging a few further pleasantries with Clara, Maddie rode back to Knyghton, a more onerous journey with her heavy basket and the worries she carried beside.

Somehow she must get to the bottom of the secret that the tiresome Susie Welbourne had alluded to. If the villagers' children were holding something against Sarah because she was staying at Knyghton, then her daughter's happiness was clearly at stake.

Nineteen

'I met a friend of yours in the village this morning,' Maddie told Lyle at lunchtime.

He'd been silent and distracted, but now he frowned. 'Who do you mean?'

'She recognized me from yesterday in the garden,' she continued. 'Susie Welbourne. It was she who approached me. In the draper's.'

'The draper's,' he remarked, 'is obviously a hive of dangerous gossip. What did Miss Welbourne want?'

'To let me know how much better she knew you than I did, I think,' Maddie said, grinning as she forked up a bit of potato. 'Eat your food, Little Ears,' she said, seeing that Grace was listening.

'I didn't know you were still friendly with Susie, Lyle,' Gussie said.

'We're on good enough terms,' her nephew remarked. 'Can't we talk about something other than my private life? I saw you bought a newspaper, Maddie. Full of the usual doom and gloom, is it?'

'Not in front of *l'enfant*,' Maddie whispered fiercely. It was her turn to be annoyed. She had not been able to protect her children from the bombs in London, but she was doing her best not to speak of the war here.

'Then it seems there's little we're allowed to talk about today.'

'You can read the paper yourself after lunch, unless you have to rush off.'

Whether it was mention of Susie Welbourne or something else that had made Lyle cross she was not about to find out. They conducted the rest of the meal in relative silence while Grace and Gussie talked to the dogs, who had long learned to crowd round Grace at table as another ready source of dropped crumbs. Lyle finished his pudding and hurried off with a mumbled, 'See you later.'

The laundry van had visited during the morning and after the lunchtime washing-up, Maddie assisted Mrs Flegg by spreading fresh linen on all the beds while Grace played in the nursery. Gussie's bed was first, as the old lady was waiting to have a nap. It was like a young girl's room still in many ways, Maddie thought, as she counted out pillowcases from the bundle of clean laundry. Several dolls sat stiffly staring at her from a top shelf, and on another, a set of dancing china figurines in harlequin costumes pirouetted and bowed. Dog hairs on the blankets told their story, she noticed, smiling as she made the bed. Then she righted a sampler stitched by a twelve-year-old Gussie that hung askew on the wall and moved on to Lyle's room.

It was the first time Maddie had seen it since his nightmare had drawn her there and she was glad to have a legitimate excuse to enter. The room lay in shadow and felt airless, so she pulled the curtains back fully and opened a window to let in the breeze, supposing that Mrs Flegg had been too busy to do these things earlier when she'd stripped the bed.

The pillows and blankets lay in a tumble on the rug and while she shook out the folds of a fresh-scented sheet an airborne corner caught a photograph on the bedside table and sent it clattering to the floor. She bent to pick it up, hoping she'd not damaged it, and was sorry to see a crack snaked across the glass.

It didn't hide the face in the photograph and looking at it more closely her heart stilled. She knew that face. It was the same one that had come into her mind while she worked and which she'd idly drawn. She sat down on the unmade bed and stared at it. It was only a snapshot, a little blurred, showing the girl from the waist up, her face brightly smiling. She held a bunch of sweetpeas before her like a bride's bouquet and her arms were bare in a summer dress. Who was she?

Perhaps, Maddie thought suddenly, she'd unwittingly glimpsed this photograph on the night she'd woken Lyle from his nightmare, and the image had lodged itself in her mind. She certainly didn't remember noticing it and anyway there had been insufficient light. How strange. She stood the photo carefully back in its place, then carried on making the bed, her thoughts awhirl. After she'd straightened the candlewick bedspread and folded a fresh towel over a rail on the wash-stand she closed the window and took one final look round the room. Apart from some discarded clothes draped on a chair it was clean and tidy. It was the photograph that still troubled her. She glanced at it again and realized something about the young woman's pose. The tilt of the chin was the same as that of the girl in the background of the final photo in Philip's album. The girl in that other snap was much younger, but there was no mistaking the way she tipped her face and raised her eyes to the camera. Surely they were one and the same person. Who was she and why did Lyle keep a photograph of her by his bed?

Maddie was still thinking about this when she closed Lyle's door and stared sightlessly at the remaining items of fresh laundry on the landing floor. Along the corridor she could hear Grace's little voice through the half-open door of the nursery as she played. She sounded content, so Maddie picked out a set of linen for her own room and was about to enter when she heard Grace say sharply, 'No, don't, that's bad. Mummy will be cross,' Still clasping the sheets she tiptoed over to the door of the nursery and listened. 'Naughty, that's naughty,' the child continued.

Curious, Maddie pushed the door open an inch and peeped in. Grace was sitting, legs splayed, on the floor with the pieces of a metal farm set scattered before her. She'd built a higgledy-piggledy sty for the pigs and a ring of fencing for the sheep and cows. 'I won't let you play with me,' Grace said loudly. Her head was raised and she appeared to be addressing an empty space. Sunlight shimmered on the wall beyond.

'Gracie?' Maddie whispered and the child looked round. 'Who are you talking to, dear?'

'Sebby,' Maddie thought Grace said. 'He's my friend, but sometimes he's naughty.' She started rearranging some ducks and geese around a tiny silver-coloured pond.

Maddie's heartbeat quickened. 'Sebby? Grace, there isn't anyone.'

Grace's expression turned mutinous and she did not answer.

'There isn't anyone, is there?' Maddie repeated, unsure.

Grace shook her head. After a moment she drew her legs together in a sharp movement that knocked pieces of the metal farm flying. Then she reached for her rabbit and slotted her thumb into her mouth. Maddie put down the sheets and went to embrace her. Who on earth, she wondered, was Sebby?

Twenty

Maddie almost bumped into Lyle when he arrived home that evening. She was coming out of the nursery with an armful of dirty clothes and he was on his way to his bedroom. Since he might notice it, she confessed right away to breaking the glass of the photograph.

'I'm so sorry. If I can pay to have it mended—'

'No, I'll do it myself when I've a moment,' was his abrupt response, then in softer tones he said, 'Thank you for telling me.' His eyes searched her face for a moment too long.

'Who is she, the girl in the photograph?' she could not help saying. 'I apologize for being a busybody, but I've a particular reason for asking.'

For a second Lyle was silent, then he sighed. 'Her name was Flora.'

'Flora?' She was astonished. That was the name she'd seen on the lonely gravestone. Was she the same Flora? And the girl pictured with the hollyhocks whom she'd linked to Lyle's photograph, was that her, too? And was it her image she had drawn and painted?

'Yes. Why are you surprised, may I ask?'

'I'd like to show you something later.' She needed time to think. 'You'll want to change for supper and I'm still busy putting the girls to bed.'

'All right.' He went on his way. Maddie stared after him, feeling troubled.

'It's this,' she said later. She and Lyle were standing in the fading light of Philip's old bedroom looking down at the pair of pictures of the young woman on Maddie's desk. Lyle's hand hovered between them and his face was ashen.

'It's uncanny,' he whispered. 'You've captured her completely. But how and why?' His voice was rough and she flinched. 'What has Philip said to you, Maddie?'

'Philip?' She gazed at him with wide eyes. 'I don't know what you mean.'

'Look, if you're accusing me of something—'

'I'm not. '

'Then why have you drawn her?'

'I don't know,' she whispered. 'I felt compelled to do so, that's all. The image of her filled my mind. No one's told me anything about her or who she was, least of all Philip. I don't even remember seeing the photograph by your bed before today.'

'You must have done. There's no other way—'

'Wait.' She left the room and returned a moment later with Philip's little photograph album, which she handed to him.

'I've never shown you this before, but it was found in the ruins of Philip's desk after the bomb.'

Lyle stood leafing through the book, angling it towards the light. 'I'd no idea he had this. My mother Daphne must have taken some. She was the photographer.' The expressions on his mobile face changed in reaction to the different pictures. 'This one with Grandmama, I've seen before. Ah, and this handsome dog, it's Yellow, I'm sure.'

'That's what Gussie said. But go on. It's the last photograph in the album that's important.'

When he came to the last page, he stared at the picture with narrowed eyes.

'The girl in the background, see.'

'Yes, I do see.' His voice was gruff. 'I wonder who on earth took that? Susie, perhaps.'

'Is that her, Lyle? Flora.'

He nodded slowly then closed the book, weighing it in his hands as he stared out of the window, his thoughts far away. Outside, threatening clouds were gathering and wind stirred the trees. Blackbirds called urgently to one another.

'What is it?' Maddie whispered, but he did not answer. 'Lyle, what's wrong?'

His eyes locked with hers and his lips parted as though he'd speak, but then he seemed to think the better of it, because he thrust the book into her hands and strode out of the room without a word or a backward look, leaving her staring after him, devastated.

*

What was it that troubled people in this house, Maddie asked herself as she lay on crisp fresh sheets that night. Knyghton had lost its heart somehow, if it had had one, and the empty space had been filled with ghosts. Not that she believed in ghosts, but she could not deny that there were times that the house had an oppressive atmosphere, and much of that was to do with Lyle. Now that she'd latched on to a clue – Flora – it seemed that he did not wish to explain anything to Maddie. Yet he'd been concerned that Philip had done so first. Surely Flora wasn't that important or Philip would have told Maddie about her. It was all most puzzling.

'Christine,' Maddie said on Monday morning. 'How do you think Grace is?' She had taken a break from her work and come downstairs where she'd met Christine in the hall carrying a glass of water.

'Grace? She's not unwell, is she? She's playing very happily in the nursery, Mrs Anderson. I'm just going back up there. She's not upset with me again, is she? She wanted to get out some old tin soldiers, but I thought they weren't appropriate for a girl so we're investigating the doll's house instead.' She looked anxious. 'I hope old Miss Anderson won't mind. Some of the little things in it are quite delicate. I've only left her for a minute.'

'I'm sure Miss Anderson won't mind if Grace is careful.' Maddie didn't want Grace or Sarah playing with the soldiers either, but not because they were girls. She was trying to protect them from the war and fears of what might have happened to their father. 'But generally, I mean,' she persisted. 'Do you think she's happy?'

Christine drew herself up. 'Mrs Anderson, if you think I'm doing anything wrong ...'

'No, of course not you're not,' Maddie stressed. 'It's only ... I think she has an imaginary friend. He's called Sebby. It makes me think I should find another child locally for her to play with.'

'I can assure you that nothing untoward has happened while I've been with her. We're very companionable. Though she does sometimes tell fibs. Do you know she says the goats talk to her? What a funny little girl.'

'She has a strong imagination,' Maddie said hesitantly, 'but I wouldn't say that she was lying, exactly.'

'But I was brought up to tell the truth.' Christine's brow furrowed and Maddie gave an inward sigh. The woman was perfectly safe and clearly very fond of Grace, but she was far too keen that Grace should like her in return and also nervous that Maddie was being critical of her child-care methods.

'I'm sure that Grace is all right,' she said, regretting having raised the question.

She followed Christine back upstairs, and returned to her illustrations. She was coming to the end of them now and was torn between satisfaction at a job well done and the reluctance to finish a project and let it go.

As she picked up her paintbrush she thought of Grace and smiled. She knew she was right in one thing, which was that Grace had a lively imagination. Sarah was different, good with numbers and curious about how things worked. One day, when this war was over, Maddie would see that they had the best schooling possible. She wasn't sure how she'd do this without Philip's support . . . No, she was getting ahead of herself. She would manage, and trust that he'd come home.

That evening Maddie sat in the drawing room alone with Gussie, the dogs ranged around the fire that Gussie still liked lit in the cool of the summer evenings. Lyle had gone out straight after supper to a Home Guard exercise and wasn't expected back until late. Maddie had brought out the history of Monksfield, and was reading bits out to Gussie to prompt her into conversation.

'Knyghton was mentioned in the Domesday Book, it says here, Gussie . . . It was rebuilt in 1610 after a devastating fire.'

'There have always been Andersons at Knyghton,' Gussie said vaguely.

'This is interesting,' Maddie said, turning a page. 'A Tobias Anderson bought a hundred acres of land in 1861 from – Percival Welbourne. How curious. I've met two Welbournes recently. Susie and her father.'

Gussie's expression turned shrewd. 'I still think Lyle might marry Susie.'

Maddie felt a stab of irritation at the thought of sharing Knyghton with the awful Susie. 'When I saw her and Lyle together the other day, they didn't look very loving. Oh, I shouldn't have said that, it's none of my business.'

'Our families were close friends, but there was a falling-out during the war.' The last war, Maddie understood Gussie to mean. 'Susie's father put in a claim on the farmland, you see, while George was away.'

Maddie frowned in surprise. 'By what right did he do that? This book says the Welbournes sold it to the Andersons.'

'My great-grandmother was a Welbourne. I don't know what the arrangement was exactly, but my great-grandfather acquired her and the land together. However, her cousin said he had been the rightful heir and the argument has never gone away.'

'So Susie is part of the rival Welbourne line.'

Gussie picked a thread from her dress. 'Yes, and her father still wants the land back, even if he has to pay Lyle for it. If Lyle married Susie it would solve everything.'

'But he won't? Why not? She seems keen.'

'I don't know.' Gussie's face hardened, then her eye fell on the sleeping dogs and softened. 'Dear little things. They're all exhausted from their walk today.'

Maddie smiled to herself. More likely they were sluggish because Gussie kept slipping them scraps from her plate, but she wasn't going to interfere. Gussie's dogs were like her own children. Perhaps they were the only creatures in the world that truly loved her, for Gussie seemed to have no friends. Her whole existence was bound up in Knyghton and its routines.

'And you, Gussie, would you like Lyle to marry her?' she teased.

'Look at Jane, she's so sweet when she lies on her back. Little fox legs, she has, so delicate.'

'Gussie?'

Gussie raised her eyes and looked at Maddie directly. 'All I mind about is Knyghton,' she said in a voice of such fierceness that Maddie recoiled. 'It belongs to us, the Andersons, and I will live here until I'm carried out in a box. Lyle should marry and have sons. I don't care for Susie, don't trust her at all ... but if that's what it takes to keep Knyghton in the family ...'

Her face took on a frightened look and Maddie's heart went out to her. If Lyle married and had sons, the Anderson line might be secure, but suppose the new wife – Susie or someone else – didn't want an old lady like Gussie and her dogs about the place? What then? It was indeed a conundrum.

As Maddie closed the *History of Monksfield* another thought struck her. Susie's father, whom Lyle had been arguing with when she'd walked into his office that day. Lyle had begged her not to tell Gussie, but it seemed as though Gussie had guessed already that Knyghton was in trouble. Just not how much trouble probably.

Gussie turned in early with a glass of milk that Maddie warmed for her on the dying range. She watched the dogs hopping and bouncing after the old lady, as she walked stiffly up the stairs like an ancient chatelaine of a tumbling castle. Maddie returned to the drawing room where she poked the embers into life and sat staring into the fire thinking as the darkness spread its skirts around her. If Philip was alive, where might he be tonight? She whispered his name and wondered. If she really focused her mind perhaps he might hear her and be comforted. When Lyle came in and found her she was almost asleep. He banked the fire and bade her go up to bed. She went obediently.

Twenty-one

A letter arrived for Maddie the following morning that made her heart sink, for she recognized the thick black handwriting. From its several postmarks and the crossings out she deduced that it had been sent in May to her old address, but despite the arrangements she'd made for post to be forwarded, it had taken several weeks to reach her. Alone in her bedroom she opened it, read it quickly, then sank onto the bed with a little cry. She stared at the floor unseeing, unable to process the letter's contents.

After a moment she forced herself to read it again. It was from a colonel in Philip's regiment who had known Philip personally and had written to her previously after he'd first gone missing.

My dear Mrs Anderson
We have no news specifically of your husband, but grave rumours have reached us about the fate of some of his platoon

who are also missing. Details have come recently via the Red Cross of disquieting German activity in the Dunkirk region during the retreat of our forces there last May. It appears that there may have been isolated examples of summary executions of British prisoners of war by rogue German officers in breach of the Geneva Convention. It is impossible at present to investigate the truth of these reports, but our Red Cross source indicates that the remnants of Philip's platoon surrendered to a German unit in Pas-de-Calais and their fate is now unknown. I regret that I'm able to offer no further information, but from your last letter I discern that you wanted me to pass on any scrap of knowledge I could.

My thoughts are with you and your daughters in these desperate times.

She could no longer read for tears crowding her eyes. Colonel Bradley had not spelled it out, but it was clear that he believed the possibility that Philip and some of his comrades had been murdered in cold blood. And yet ... Maddie squeezed her eyes shut, causing the tears to run down her cheeks. Nothing was known for sure. It might be that they were prisoners somewhere. *All of them? Really?* a voice in her head replied. A sneering voice, a voice that told her she was stupid, naïve. At some point she would have to face the possibility that Philip was dead, his grave an unmarked pit in a field. The tears flowed faster and she began to sob. After a while she managed to compose herself, splashing her face with cold water in the bathroom before going downstairs to see to Grace.

Somehow she got through the hours without anyone

noticing. Mrs Flegg was snappish about some misery of her own and Lyle didn't return to the house for lunch. Only Gussie glanced at her curiously, but Grace was there too so Maddie couldn't confide in her.

Lyle returned while she was putting the girls to bed and she came downstairs to find Gussie helping Mrs Flegg lay the table for supper, so she went into the drawing room and sat brooding by herself until Lyle came to join her and poured her some sherry.

'How was your day?' she asked and her voice came out strangely so that he looked at her curiously.

'Particularly frustrating,' he said, then, 'Are you all right?'

She shook her head and immediately he came and sat down by her, bringing with him a scent of earth and of a particular brand of tobacco that reminded her sharply of Philip. Tears threatened once more.

'Has something happened?' Lyle's voice was urgent.

Maddie withdrew the letter from her pocket and handed it to him. He read it quickly, then looked up, his eyes full of anger. He rose and began to pace the room. She stared down at her sherry.

Finally, he came to sit down again. The anger had gone and a look of misery had taken its place. 'I ... I don't know what to say to you. It's horrible, desperately awful. To think – no – damn it, Maddie.'

'They don't know anything for certain ...' she said, her bottom lip jutting like a mutinous child's.

Their eyes locked, she challenging him to deny her this

faint comfort. Lyle broke the gaze first. He turned to the log basket and with slow, careful movements began to lay sticks on the fire. She watched him, her hands twisting in her lap, her throat aquiver.

Finally he sat back in the chair, brushing dirt from his knees, a reassuring presence, yet there was a thrum of tension in the room. She pressed her palms on her knees to stop them shaking. He reached across the space and gathered her hands in his.

'Maddie,' he said, and she felt the warmth of his breath. 'We must face the fact that Philip might not come back. God knows, we've had our differences, he and I, but I loved him.'

'No,' she said. 'I'm not ready. I can't . . . The children. Sarah already thinks he's dead and I'm sure that's mostly why she's unhappy.'

'The girls will be all right. If it helps to know, Gussie and I . . . we'd be happy to have you here as long as you want to be.'

'You're very kind, but I know that things are stretched. With the farm, I mean.'

'We'll manage somehow.' Lyle frowned at his own thoughts. 'We have to.'

'I wish I could help.'

'Unless you suddenly inherit a large sum of money, I don't see how you can.' Maddie must have looked devastated, because he added, 'I'm sorry, that was tactless of me.'

'Even if Philip is . . .' She checked herself. 'You know we're not wealthy.'

'No, it was a stupid thing for me to say.'

'What of the Welbournes?' she said.

'What of them?' His tone was abrupt.

'Gussie mentioned Susie recently, that's all. She was telling me about some family history, the Welbournes' claim on the farm.' The library book was still lying on a side table and she handed it to him. He flicked through the pages, stopping occasionally to read something that caught his eye, then tossed it back down with a frown.

'The Welbournes have no legal right to Knyghton or its lands,' he said, 'but Susie's father likes to think they do, as did her grandfather before him. Susie's an only child. She and I have known each other all our lives and we think the whole thing is nonsense.'

'Gussie thinks you should marry her,' Maddie said lightly. 'To continue the Anderson line and save the farm.'

'Gussie, as we know, lives in Cloud Cuckoo Land. Anyway, there's no guarantee that Welbourne would pay Knyghton's debts simply because I married his daughter. He's hard-nosed, that man.'

'But your children might inherit both farms.'

'Is that a basis for a good marriage? This conversation is ridiculous.'

It was as well that Mrs Flegg put her head round the door at that moment to call them for supper.

The next few days after receiving the letter were dark ones for Maddie, but darker still were the nights, when she tossed and turned, her dreams full of terror, cries of pain and mirthless laughter. Often she'd wake in the depths of the night and lie with her mind working, going over and over the likely events that Philip's colonel had outlined in his letter. A picture kept forming of a line of a score of exhausted men stumbling along a dusty lane. She could hear the crunch of their boots, the sough of their breaths. The sun blazed down and from overhead came the exultant song of a lark. They did not know where they were going as the dust became grass and she could sense Philip's sudden fear, the dryness of his mouth. Then the shouted order of an angry voice, stuttering gunfire and pain, an agonizing pain. After that no more.

It wasn't a dream, exactly, but it came to her in that dream-like state between waking and sleeping and she wondered if she'd made it up or whether it was true. Each time after it faded she lay clutching her pillow for comfort and tried to reason with herself.

Accept it, he's dead.

No, it's not true.

It is, everyone thinks so except you.

Was it being here – in this place where she felt a strong sense of Philip – that stopped her accepting the truth?

Twenty-two

The furniture in the winter sitting room at the front of the house was swathed in dust sheets. Like the spare bedrooms upstairs it had been shut up for several years, Lyle had told Maddie, to save on cleaning and fires. This sitting room housed the family's collection of books so Maddie was keen to explore. Although Christine had arrived and it was a working morning she was tired and out of sorts and on impulse she opened the door and went in. She stood breathing in the now familiar smell of Knyghton, a mixture of lavender polish, damp wood and ashes.

Lifting the sheet of a glass-fronted bookcase, she was disappointed to see rows of old volumes with dry-sounding titles about crops and animal husbandry. The collected sermons of one Very Reverend Ebenezer Toogood and *A Countryman's Tales* on the next shelf down were light relief in comparison. Maddie dropped the sheet and moved to the second bookcase where she was gratified to see copies of some of her favourite classic novels. She opened the doors and took out *The Moonstone*, flicking through to admire the illustrations, then turned to *Wuthering Heights*. These were books which as a very young woman she'd read curled up on her bed, a bag of humbugs by her side. She looked round the room at the shrouded shapes of armchairs, the carved wood mantelpiece. This must be cosier in winter than the large airy drawing room. Perhaps Mrs Flegg wouldn't mind if she used it in winter if she dusted it herself and collected wood for the fire.

She returned *Wuthering Heights* to its place and bent to examine the titles on the next shelf down. Reaching to touch the beautifully tooled spine of a *Complete Works of Shakespeare* her eye was caught by a smaller volume next to it. Her heart skipped a beat. The title gleamed in gold leaf on the navy-coloured spine. *The Golden Treasury of Songs and Lyrics*. The title of the book that Flora held in Maddie's drawing of her. Her father had a copy and when Maddie pulled this one out it sat snugly in her hand in the same familiar way. She opened it at random. A coloured postcard slid out and fluttered to the floor. She bent down and picked it up, keeping her thumb in the place in the book. It was pretty, the postcard, a painting of two young women dressed in long flowing garments plucking lilies in a lush garden. She turned it over. Her eyes widened. It was addressed to 'Flora Simpson, Knyghton, Monksfield, Norfolk' and as she read the message her sense of disturbance grew. *'Dear F, I found this card in a curio shop at half term and thought of you. It goes with your poems, n'est-ce pas? Hope all's well at Knyghton. Write soon if you can. P.'*

'P.' Though neat, careful schoolboy italics, it was definitely Philip's handwriting. Maddie stared at it for a moment or two, then turned her attention to the book she still held. She flipped it open at the place marked by the card and her eye fell on lines she knew well, 'There is a garden in her face/ Where roses and white lilies blow.' It was, she knew, a poem about feminine beauty, but a beauty that is inaccessible. The lady concerned will not let any man near her unless she chooses. It had always been a favourite of hers.

Sliding the postcard back into its place she flicked the pages, rereading poems to long-dead Celias and Antheas and Julias, smiling to herself as she remembered how she'd once yearned to find one to a fair Madeleine. She'd never talked to Philip about poetry, it struck her, but here was evidence that he had done so with the mysterious Flora. A stab of jealousy pierced her, then she castigated herself. The card was only a schoolboy missive. There was no date on it and the postmark was smudged so she could only guess at how old he was when he'd written it. *Still, Flora.* Lyle kept a photograph of her close and Philip had talked poetry with her. Maddie closed the book thoughtfully and put it back on the shelf.

It was strange, but she no longer felt alone in the room. Someone, she was sure, was watching her. She stepped across to the mantelpiece and ran her fingers over the dusty edge, with its carvings of fruit and flowers, then reached up to raise a corner of a sheet to see what picture hung overhead.

'Oh!' The sheet slipped to the floor with a silken sigh to reveal a large mirror, old and tarnished. Maddie found herself staring at the reflection of her own frightened face. Above her image something billowed out like smoke. She gasped and turned to the room, her heart pounding, to realize that it was only a cloud of dust displaced by the falling sheet. She blinked as some settled on her face and brushed it away, then stood for a moment, sensing a charge in the air. Reflected light from the mirror danced on the ceiling. A scrabble then a movement outside the window. A bird, she told herself, seeing its shadow sweep across the rug and she exhaled, allowing her fists to unclench. The room fell tranquil once more. Maddie could not bear to look into the mirror again so she ignored the fallen dust sheet and fled out into the hall. To meet the accusing eyes of Mrs Flegg.

'What were you doing in there, Mrs Anderson?' Mrs Flegg was arranging a handful of creamy roses in a vase, their sweet fragrance filling the hall.

'Looking for something to read.'

'Not found anything?' She glanced at Maddie's empty hands.

'Nothing I was in the mood for. Mrs Flegg ... who was Flora?'

'Ouch!' Mrs Flegg flinched at a thorn, then licked a bead of blood from her finger. For a moment she said nothing, then she sighed. 'You don't want to be worrying about her now,' she said finally. She dropped the last rose stem into the vase and gathered up some fallen petals.

'I'm not worrying, exactly.'

'It's all behind us now and we've more important things to do. Doing our bit for victory, like that Mr Churchill says.'

'Of course, I know that.'

'So if you don't mind, I'll be getting on. Lunch won't cook itself.' Mrs Flegg's voice faded as she swept through the baize door to the kitchen and was gone.

Maddie sighed as she clambered upstairs to continue her work. There was no sound from the nursery – Grace and Christine must be out somewhere on one of their walks, so she settled herself at her desk and selected a paintbrush. But as she picked out the details of a mouse's waistcoat she felt deeply unsettled. Something was being kept from her and Mrs Flegg had implied that she shouldn't try to find out what. Even if she decided on someone else to ask, she felt that she shouldn't, that it would be disloyal to the family. Was that a sigh she heard behind her? Her hand stilled on the brush. *Really*, Maddie told herself, *if you treat every noise in this old house as sinister you'll drive yourself mad.*

'Is that our tea?' Sarah asked, wandering into the kitchen late that afternoon.

Maddie was pricking eggs with a pin. 'Yes, darling. Boiled eggs with soldiers. We're very lucky that the chickens have been so busy.' She spooned the eggs one by one into a saucepan of simmering water then glanced at her daughter. 'Oh good, you've changed out of your uniform. Now where's your sister?'

'In the garden with Flegg.'

'Mr Flegg, to you. Will you tell her tea's nearly ready, please?'

Sarah nodded and skipped out through the scullery while Maddie, collecting cutlery from a drawer, watched through the window as she ran across the lawn towards the kitchen garden. Maddie picked a tiny slug off a Webb lettuce and washed the earth from the fresh green leaves, then cut some bread before rescuing the eggs. Wiping her hands on her apron she went to the larder for something to bulk out the simple meal. The scraps of yesterday's pie made with last year's blackcurrants? Maybe if she added some precious honey to the custard, the girls wouldn't find the pie so acid. For a moment Maddie paused, overwhelmed with longing for the sweet fruit tarts of her childhood. It was such a pity the girls had to miss so much. *Don't be silly, not having their father, that was the very worst thing,* she berated herself, and felt a lump in her throat. She was doing her best to give Sarah and Grace what they needed, but could do nothing about that. Trying to protect them from news about the war, which was going so badly for Britain, the sense of dread that the grown-ups felt all the time, was as much as she could do.

'Mummy?' Sarah appeared at her side. She was panting.

'Did you find Grace?'

'Yes, she's up near the chickens, but she's talking to Sebby and won't come.'

Maddie frowned. 'Didn't you tell her tea's ready?'

'Yes, but she just gave me a funny look. Like this.' Sarah's features arranged themselves into a gormless stare.

'That is indeed a funny look.' Maddie returned to the kitchen and popped the pie into the bottom oven to warm, then hung up her apron. She marched out to the garden, Sarah trotting close behind. It was warm and the air was still. Maddie heard Grace's little voice as soon as they entered the walled garden and there she was, sitting on a low wall near the chicken run, but with her back to the hens, chatting away cheerily to ... thin air.

She didn't appear to see them, so Maddie gestured to Sarah to be quiet and together they crept round the edge of the garden to hear what Grace was saying, but as they neared her the little girl glimpsed their movement. A strand of hair fell across her eyes and she brushed it away as she stood up in a way that somehow reminded Maddie of Philip and came to greet them, wordlessly putting her hand in her mother's, looking up at her with a smile.

Back in the kitchen Maddie gave the girls their tea, still worried. Poor Grace must be lonely at Knyghton when Sarah was at school. They were awfully isolated here. Perhaps she should try harder to meet other mothers with young children. It was another reason she missed Denny. Perhaps the Sunday school was worth investigating.

It was harder than Maddie imagined to persuade someone to drive the three of them to church, but Monksfield was too far to expect a three-year-old to walk and the buses were particularly unreliable on Sundays. The Lord's Day was simply another working day for Lyle, who had the hay to mow. In the end it was Flegg who agreed. *I ought to learn to drive the trap myself,* Maddie thought, as he handed up the girls but she was nervous of horses, even gentle ones like Bonnie, and worried that they would all end up in a ditch. Flegg dropped them at the lychgate and promised to be back later. Maddie took the girls by their hands and hurried them up the path to the church, hoping that no one would mind that the children's best dresses were so skimpy because they'd grown.

They were late and the rector was reading the Bidding Prayer as Maddie opened the door of the church. Heads turned at their entrance, but a smiling motherly woman in tweeds stepped forward, handed Maddie a hymnbook and showed them into a pew at the back just as an asthmatic organ started up. Everyone stood to sing 'Oh, God our help in ages past', except Grace, who sat with her thumb in her mouth. Maddie glanced round at the congregation, mostly women, children and a few older men. Well, that was all right, it was the women and the children whom she'd come to meet. There were faces she recognized from her occasional appearances at the school gate. Perhaps they'd be more friendly on Sundays at church.

When the hymn was over, the rector announced that the children should follow his wife out to Sunday school. Sarah took Grace by the hand and joined the throng being marshalled by Mrs Clairmont, the woman in tweeds, like a more comforting version of the Pied Piper. It was only to the church hall they were going, Maddie knew, but this didn't stop a pang of unease. She hoped they'd be all right in a new place. Surely Sarah would look after her sister. Maddie settled back in the pew and tried to concentrate on the familiar old words of the service.

Afterwards, as everyone filed out, the rector smiled as he shook her hand. 'I'm glad you made it.'

'I'm sorry it took so long,' she said. 'And thank you again for your little book about hares. It's been most interesting.'

In the church hall she admired the girls' colourings of Noah's Ark then queued for a cup of tea, which she stood sipping by herself, feeling self-conscious as the other women formed close-knit groups. She smiled in satisfaction as Sarah chatted to a shy-looking girl with pale skin and straight black hair while a little boy with the same colouring bonded with Grace over some metal cars from a toy box. After a minute or two a woman who by her looks was the children's mother detached herself from a conversation with Mrs Clairmont and came to introduce herself to Maddie.

'I am Anna Wyhowska,' she said in a quiet voice. She was slim and gentle with a short curtain of dark hair and a face as serene as a Renaissance Madonna's and Maddie warmed to her instantly.

'Wyhowska,' she repeated slowly.

'Yes, it is Polish. Please, call me Anna, it is easier.'

'I'm Maddie. Maddie Anderson,' Maddie said smiling.

'I know. Mrs Clairmont told me. She said I should come and speak to you. It's my first time, too. We are Catholics, but we have just come to live with the Clairmonts and it's easier for us to attend this church. Also, Nadya's schoolfriends are here.'

Maddie nodded. Nadya. She remembered Sarah talking about a new girl.

At the sight of his mother, the little boy ran to wrap his arms round her legs. 'This is Milo,' Anna said, stroking his hair. The boy gave Maddie a solemn stare.

'Hello, Milo.'

He smiled then looked quickly away. After a moment he

returned to Grace's side and gestured to her to pass him a toy lorry.

'He does not speak yet,' Anna murmured. 'It's not been easy since his father was killed ... He was a pilot.' Maddie saw the pain in her eyes.

'I'm so sorry,' Maddie murmured in dismay.

'I think that's why Mrs Clairmont thought ... we would have something in common between us.'

'My husband is missing,' Maddie said, more sharply than she intended. 'We don't know yet what has happened to him.'

'Of course. I understand.' The expression in Anna's eyes was so tender that Maddie was ashamed of her rudeness.

'Nadya is in Sarah's class at school, I think,' she said, eager to change the subject.

'Yes, we came here recently from London.'

Anna explained that her husband's business interests had brought him to England a few years ago. She had met him during one of his return visits to Krakow and after a whirl-wind romance, married him and moved to London. 'I do not know how things are with my family in Poland,' she said gravely and briefly hid her face. 'There is no way to get news.'

'And you live with the Clairmonts?' Maddie followed her gaze to see the rector's wife smiling across at them as she conversed with a portly man whom Maddie had last seen in an air raid warden's uniform on a bicycle.

'They are very kind,' Anna went on. She dropped her voice. 'They have no children of their own, a great sadness for them, so they are like a nice auntie and uncle for Nadya and Milo.'

They watched Grace and Milo playing together, Grace
chattering as they raced their cars down the slope from
the flat roof of a wooden model garage. 'They get on well,'
Maddie said. 'It's been lonely for Grace at Knyghton without
other children.'

'It's the same for Milo,' Anna said sadly. 'Some of the
mothers, they don't mean to be unkind but ... Milo is ...
sometimes he ... they find him ...'

'Unusual?' Maddie tried.

'Yes.' Anna sounded grateful.

'He seems a sweet little boy.'

Anna nodded enthusiastically. 'He is, oh, he is. And
very loving.'

Maddie felt a rush of pity for this woman, struggling
with grief and loneliness in a land far from home, and was
drawn to her. 'Is it too far for you to come out to our home
one day? It's a mile out of Monksfield towards Carshall, but
there is a bus.'

At this point that Mrs Clairmont chose to join them, saying
heartily, 'I'm so glad that you two have met. My husband told
me about you, Mrs Anderson. You're always welcome to bring
your girls to the rectory, you know. My husband says it had
strong connections to Knyghton in the past.'

'What is Knyghton, please?' Anna asked.

Maddie explained and Mrs Clairmont said cheerfully, 'It
begins with a K.' She spelled it out.

'Knyghton,' Anna said slowly and Maddie saw realization dawn in her face. 'You know, that is funny, but in my
bedroom there is a cupboard in the wall and inside, well, I

found some papers there in a box. I haven't looked properly, it's not my business, but there's a notebook with 'Knyghton' written on the front.'

'Is there no end to the mess of books and papers in our house?' Mrs Clairmont sighed. 'The last incumbent was as bad as Alwyn, you know. He was ill when he left, poor man, and the place hadn't been cleared out properly when we moved in. We shall have to have a look, shan't we?'

Milo was tugging insistently at his mother's skirt now, and Maddie with a jolt remembered Flegg, who must be waiting outside for them.

'I'd love to know what you find,' Maddie said.

'Why don't we ask Maddie to bring Grace over tomorrow or Tuesday?' Mrs Clairmont suggested.

'Oh, that would be wonderful.' Anna's eyes were wide with yearning.

'Tuesday would be better.' Tomorrow was sacrosanct, a working morning. On Tuesday Maddie was sure Mrs Flegg would forgive her absence from chores if she brought back some shopping with her.

The rambling Victorian rectory was set back from the main street. After Maddie and Grace stepped off the bus on Tuesday morning and queued for bread, bacon and bones for the dogs it took Maddie a while to find its entrance, off a leafy lane that ran between its grounds and the churchyard. They stopped a moment by the mouldering five-bar gate to admire a fluffy black-and-white cat sitting on the flint wall washing itself before trudging along the gravel drive

towards the house. It was quiet apart from the cries of rooks
and the warning chuk chuk of a blackbird from the tangled
shrubbery.

The narrow pointed windows felt like watching eyes as
they approached, but benign ones rather than threatening,
and as they rounded a pile of sandbags at the front of the
house the sun came out, bathing the grey stone walls in
golden light. While they waited in the porch to be admitted,
Grace bent to trace the patterns on the floor tiles with Rabbit's
paw. 'Stand up, dear, best behaviour,' Maddie whispered as
the shabby front door rattled open and a skinny old lady in
a pinafore looked out, her wrinkled face brightening at the
sight of the child.

'Come you in, my angels,' she said in a birdlike voice and
they hung up their gasmasks and followed her along a gloomy
hallway with many doors off and into a cosy kitchen at the
back. There Anna and Milo were seated at a stout wooden
table over an open colouring book and a scatter of wax crayons.

'How lovely to see you.' Anna rose at their entrance, while
Milo peeped shyly at Grace through his long dark lashes.

'We're very pleased to be here,' Maddie said and prodded
Grace. 'Say hello to Mrs We . . .'

'Call me Auntie Anna,' Anna said, laughing.

'Hello, Auntie Anna,' the child said dutifully, then, more
confidently, 'What are you doing, Milo?' and ran to clamber
onto the chair next to her new friend, who pushed the colouring book between them so that Grace could start working
on the picture opposite. Maddie couldn't help noticing with a
pang that while Grace already held her crayon properly, and

chattered while she scribbled, Milo gripped his clumsily in his fist and watched Grace with silent admiration.

The skinny cook brought the women mugs of tea then set to work on a stack of muddy vegetables at a huge stone sink, busking hymns to herself as she scraped and chopped. The atmosphere was so peaceful after the tensions of Knyghton that Maddie quickly relaxed. Mrs Clairmont, it appeared, had gone shopping and the rector was visiting a sick parishioner so she and Anna had plenty of time to talk while keeping an eye on the children.

They shared their experiences of the school. Nadya, as well as Sarah, felt on the sidelines, but they acknowledged that Miss Dale had a difficult hand with several evacuees in the class who were not settling well. Anna's daughter had attended a small girls' school in London and was finding it difficult to adjust to the rough and tumble of boys. Anna herself was trying to make friends, but although other Monksfield women were pleasant, it was hard work, and she didn't always understand their country accent. 'And I think some don't like it that I live here at the rectory, that maybe I tell things about them to the Clairmonts, I don't know.'

'People are funny,' Maddie agreed heartily and explained that the villagers were suspicious of the Andersons of Knyghton. 'My brother-in-law doesn't care what anyone thinks and my husband's aunt is eccentric. The school-children say ...' Maddie glanced at Grace, but seeing her absorbed, whispered, 'They say that Gussie is a witch. Nonsense, of course, she's a harmless old lady, but sometimes they tease Sarah about it and it upsets her.'

'Children can be unkind.' Anna said vaguely and frowned, causing Maddie a twinge of anxiety. Had Anna heard those silly accusations, and, if so, had she believed them? Her heart sank.

'You must tell me more about Knyghton,' Anna said, looking directly at her, 'Is it very old?' and Maddie realized that her fears were unfounded.

'It's my husband's family home.' She explained to Anna about the simplicity of life at the manor house and how it centred round the farm. 'It is very old, it feels old, the atmosphere, it's as if the walls holds memories of all the generations that have lived there.'

'I think I understand. This house feels like that too.'

'Knyghton is much older than the rectory. There has been a house on the site for a thousand years or more. Sometimes,' Maddie added, with a swift glance at Grace, 'I sense things there that I can't explain.' She thought about the pictures of the girl that she had drawn. She couldn't tell an outsider about that, it would make her sound mad. 'But that doesn't mean anything bad. There are no witches or anything like that. In fact' – it came to her reluctantly, but once she'd thought it she knew it was true – 'I rather love the house. And it helps me feel close to my husband being there. Some of his things are there and I work in his old bedroom. I even found some letters from his parents that he'd hidden. I never met them, but now I feel that I know them a little.'

Anna nodded, but one hand fiddled with a locket at her collarbone and her thoughts seemed far away. In Poland, maybe, with her own family.

'Would you tell me a little about your husband,' Maddie asked, then bit her lip. 'I mean, if you'd like to.'

Anna gave a sad smile. She hesitated, then reached up and unfastened her locket, opened it and passed it to Maddie, who found herself gazing at the face of a good-looking young man in RAF uniform, the sharp planes of his clean-shaven cheeks and his deepset dark eyes replicated in his little son sitting opposite, quietly colouring a friendly-looking tiger. Anna stroked his hair.

'He joined up as soon as war broke out. He'd learned to fly in Poland, you see, and loved it. And of course, it was the only thing he could do to help our country. His Spitfire was shot down last August.'

'The Battle of Britain?' Maddie breathed and Anna nodded as she reclaimed the locket. 'He must have been a very brave man.' And now she and Anna had to be courageous, but it was a different kind of courage, not about heroic acts and physical endurance, but courage all the same. Anna was on her own in a foreign country, keeping strong for her children day after day. Thank heavens that the Clairmonts were so kind.

It was at this moment that there came the firm sound of the front door shutting and they looked up as the rector entered the room with an aura of bonhomie, greeting the children with an expression of pretend surprise and a trick with a disappearing coin. For the first time, Maddie heard little Milo laugh, while Grace stared in stolid disbelief at the reappearance of the sixpence in the rector's ear. The performance revealed a childlike side of the man which Maddie had not glimpsed before.

Mrs Clairmont arrived a moment later with a bulging shopping bag, efficiently returning dropped crayons to the table as she greeted everyone. She instructed the cook to make everyone more tea and sat down next to Grace. She was full of news from the village. An elderly lady she'd bumped into had found her lost cat. The butcher had kept some lamb chops for them. She'd greeted Susie Welbourne and thought she looked pale.

'Everybody looks pale at the moment,' Mr Clairmont observed. 'There's a war on.'

'Have you spoken to Maddie about those books yet?' his wife said, switching the subject and glancing from her husband to Anna. She took a sip of the tea placed before her.

'No ...' Anna said nervously and looked to the rector for support.

'The ones you found from Knyghton?' Maddie said swiftly. 'I meant to ask.'

Mr Clairmont cleared his throat and appeared embarrassed. 'They're mostly old school exercise books from years ago, but there is what appears to be a journal among them.' He clasped his hands together on the table as though about to say a prayer. 'I've looked through it and ... It seems to have been written by a member of your husband's family, Maddie. Her name is Flora.'

'Flora?' Maddie said uncertainly.

'You know who she was?'

'I've heard the name, that's all. And there's a gravestone in the churchyard to a Flora.'

'Who was this Flora, Maddie?' Anna wanted to know.

'I . . . don't know exactly. Just that . . . she must have lived at Knyghton and if she is the Flora buried in the graveyard then she died young.' Maddie glanced at the Clairmonts in turn. Mrs Clairmont was intent on helping Milo choose a crayon and only her husband met her eye.

'It is something of a mystery,' he said grudgingly. 'When Anna gave me this journal I read a little then telephoned Mr Jackson, my churchwarden, a man of encyclopaedic knowledge as far as Monksfield church is concerned. Flora Simpson died, it seems, in unexplained circumstances.'

'Remember there are children present, Alwyn,' Mrs Clairmont whispered and put a finger to her lips.

A warm, dangerous shot of adrenaline coursed through Maddie's limbs, but the rector went on. 'I'm sure Mr Anderson can tell you more about the matter. The journal is in my study. I've sealed it up in an envelope and I'd be glad if you would give it to your brother-in-law. As the head of the Anderson family I believe the journal is private and his by right.'

Maddie frowned at this excessive propriety, but said, 'Of course. But what is in it, if I may ask?'

'That's for Mr Anderson to choose to share with you.'

'I see.' What could the rector be hiding?

'I'll fetch it,' he said, pushing back his chair. He returned a moment later bearing a package tied up in knotted bits of string. 'Lyle Anderson, Esq.' it said on the front in the rector's sturdy black handwriting and 'Private and confidential', underlined.

It lay on the table after the rector left to attend a meeting and Mrs Clairmont rose to investigate the lamb chops for lunch. It wasn't easy for Maddie and Anna to talk naturally with her listening, and Maddie was distracted by the sight of the package. Before long she slid it into her shopping bag, made her apologies and left with Grace to catch the bus back to Knyghton.

All the way home she tried her best to concentrate on Grace's chattering. The little girl wanted to know why Milo didn't speak to her. 'I don't know,' Maddie replied and she wished she had found out, but she hadn't liked to quiz Anna about such a delicate matter on early acquaintance. It was enough to have talked about their husbands and that Anna had said Milo had already been marked out by other mothers in the village as odd. Yet Grace, with the innocence and generosity of a very young child, had not minded that he didn't speak, she simply sounded curious. Well, if Grace accepted him, then so would Maddie. The irony was not lost on her that her daughter was swapping one silent friend for another!

They arrived home shortly after midday and Maddie went straight to the kitchen to deliver the shopping. On the way upstairs to help Grace find something to play with, Maddie set the package on the console table in the hall on top of some other post. When she came down again a few minutes later to lay the table, having left Grace assembling a jigsaw puzzle, she lingered with one hand on the banister, staring at the table, the fair face of the girl Flora floating in her mind.

Flora, whoever she was, had died tragically, Maddie knew now, and from the postcard she'd found in the poetry book she'd learned of Philip's connection to her. How had Flora died, and why would no one speak of the matter? She badly wanted to reclaim the journal before Lyle arrived home, to open it in the secrecy of her bedroom and devour its contents. Her heart fluttered and her hands shook as she took a step towards the table. What harm would it do? She reached out and picked up the package, turned it over and saw how simple it would be to ease off the string and slip it back on afterwards. A lump came into her throat. The rector had been so kind to her. He'd trusted her to deliver the packet to Lyle without opening it. How would she look him in the eye? She laid it down again and stared at it, unhappily.

Just then, she heard Lyle's voice and Mrs Flegg's reply. He was home early for lunch. Maddie stepped back from the table as the baize door swung open and he strode in. Their eyes met, hers guilty, his surprised.

'Hello, has something happened? You look . . . I don't know.'

She blinked. 'I didn't mean to look anything. Mr Clairmont gave me something for you.' She gestured towards the package, glad now that she hadn't given in to temptation, then started towards the dining room. 'I must lay the table or Mrs F. will have my guts for garters.'

She left him turning the package over. As she was slowly setting out the table mats she heard a muttered 'Good Lord' and squeezed her eyes closed, half expecting Lyle to enter and confront her. But he did not come. Instead there was silence, then a moment later she heard his tread, slow and heavy, as he climbed the stairs.

He was late down to lunch and when he came his face was drawn and he said little. Gussie hardly noticed, but her eager questions about Maddie and Grace's morning activities and her own girlhood memories about her schooling at the rectory thankfully covered Lyle's silence.

The evening was fair and when Maddie walked in the garden after supper was cleared away she came across Lyle sitting on a bench by one of the sheds, smoking, head bowed in thought. At her approach he looked up and smiled and gestured for her to sit with him, which she did tentatively, unable to discern his mood.

'You know what was in the package, I suppose?' Whatever she'd expected, it wasn't this direct approach. Again she was glad that she hadn't opened it. She could at least deal with him honestly.

'I only know that it's Flora's journal. Anna, who I've told you about, found it in her room and gave it to Mr Clairmont. He didn't let me look at it. How would it have got there, to the rectory, I mean?'

'There was a period when Flora lived there.' Lyle's voice was dull. 'I can't remember how long for.'

'Did that mean she was here at Knyghton usually? Who was she, Lyle?'

Beside her he made a restless movement, then threw the cigarette butt onto the earth. They watched it glow and burn out before he answered.

'She lived here for a while, yes.' He sighed, studying his calloused fingers as though looking for answers. 'Flora

Simpson was the daughter of my grandmother's maid Tilly. A remarkably pretty maid, I gather, though I don't remember her as she married and left Knyghton when I was very young. Flora came to live here at Knyghton when she was eleven, shortly after Tilly died. For some reason Flora's father couldn't or wouldn't look after her and my grandmother, being a kind woman, stepped into the breach. I think there was some idea originally that Flora would be trained up for service when she was old enough.'

He was silent for a moment, deep in thought. 'When was this?' Maddie prompted. It was so sad to think that Flora's father sent her away. The child must have been devastated.

'What? It was a couple of years after the war that Flora came to us, 1920, I think, certainly after my mother Daphne had bolted with bloody Sugden. Flora lived with the Fleggs in their cottage and sometimes helped in the house. She already attended Monksfield school, but I don't recall her being there when I was.'

He sat back and stretched out his legs, settling in to his story.

'At first I didn't take much notice of her. She was simply a shy, slightly annoying, girl who hung around the place. Philip was away a good deal of the time, of course, and I'd started school in Norwich, so we didn't actually see much of her. She would have been lonely out here, though I suppose she had friends at school. I don't remember any of them visiting. When you showed me that photograph album, you remember the picture of her in the background? That says it all. Like a ghost, she was, quietly watching us, but if either of us lads spoke to her she'd turn and vanish.'

Like a ghost. Maddie felt a breeze lift her hair and the back of her neck prickle. She hunched her shoulders and pulled her cardigan tighter. Lyle lit another cigarette and inhaled deeply before continuing.

'It was the summer after Philip and I turned sixteen that it all began to change. It was Philip who realized first that she was growing up, but then he hadn't seen her for several months so he noticed the difference. I was used to her. She'd just left school, but Grandmother had been visited by her teacher who must have been persuasive about continuing her education because the result was that she was due to start at the High School in Sheringham in September.

'Philip was smitten by her that summer, though when I teased him about it, he denied it. I often caught them together. Philip said they were simply talking about literature. She liked poetry, he said, and he lent her some books from the shelves in the sitting room. You can imagine how this went down with a practical sort like me. I teased him like blazes. I couldn't deny, though, that she looked different. She'd shot up in height and her sleeves ended above her wrists. I heard Mrs Flegg complain once about the rate she was growing out of her clothes.'

Maddie recalled the tall willowy figure that she'd drawn. It wasn't difficult to imagine the response of two adolescent boys to the quiet girl turning into a pretty young woman in their midst. 'Girls are often ahead of boys at that age. I suppose you and Philip were gawky and spotty.'

'Philip certainly was.' Lyle grinned and Maddie caught a glimpse of the playful boy behind the moody man. 'No, Flora wasn't interested in us that way. Not initially, anyway.'

The slight emphasis on 'initially' stopped Maddie's smile. High in one of the great sweet chestnuts that edged the lawn a bird began to sing, full-throated, its song pouring over them in a golden flood. 'A thrush,' Lyle whispered. The garden was settling down for the night, petals closing, the light leaving the trees, the sky blushing mauve. The breeze quickened. It was as though a spell was falling over them and they sat in silence for a moment.

'Are you cold?' he asked, glancing at his watch.

'A little.'

'I ought to get going. A blasted night exercise and there's setting up to do.'

'Oh, I didn't know you were going out,' Maddie said in disappointment, then, in a rush, 'The journal. Is there any possibility that I can ...?'

'You want to read it?' His voice, which had been warm, turned to dull iron. 'I haven't had a chance to look at it properly myself yet.' He rose and stretched, then said lightly. 'You'll have to excuse me or I really will be late.'

After he left Maddie wandered round the darkening garden for a few minutes, thinking of how it might have been all those years ago. By the long black shape of the shed the pale shafts of hollyhocks still bloomed. The thrush that still sang somewhere out of sight might be descended from other birds that had sung in those trees. Knyghton itself was the same, its water came from the same well, the same oil lamps probably lit its rooms. The world beyond it might have changed in ways that threatened Knyghton's future, but for now it seemed to her that a single thread tied the present to the past.

Light glowed from the drawing-room window. Gussie, forever locked in the world of the past, had not attended to the blackout. Maddie hurried inside to close the curtains.

Twenty-three

France

June 1940

The sound of soft footsteps, a light knock and the door at the far end of the narrow room opened. Philip raised his head to see a young woman enter bearing a small round tray. *'Votre déjeuner.'* She pushed the door wider then touched a finger to her lips.

'Merci. Mais, combien de temps ...' His voice cracked from disuse. 'How long ...?'

She held up three fingers.

'Three days?' he whispered, surprised. *'Jours?'*

'Non, non. Trois semaines.' Her voice was low and musical.

'Three *weeks*?' He struggled to sit up but felt weak, then a sharp pain in his shoulder set his teeth on edge.

'Attendez.' The girl helped to prop him up with pillows. Her

gentle touch, the scent of her were familiar. There had been an older woman, too, who'd helped turn him in the bed, he remembered, but mostly it had been the girl.

She set the tray on his lap and gestured that he should eat. The salty smell rising from the broth made his mouth water and he closed his eyes to savour it, though when he took a mouthful it turned out to be little more than root vegetables. Still, he was glad to find that he was hungry and he dipped hunks of bread into it and tried not to wolf them down. The girl watched him from the chair, amusement in her face.

'This is good,' he said through a mouthful. '*Très bon.*' And she nodded.

'*Vous avez faim, n'est-ce pas?*'

He finished the bread and spooned up the rest of the broth, welcoming the warmth of it sliding down his throat. When he set down the empty bowl, he felt drowsy. She took the tray from him and left him to sleep. When he next woke the pallor of the fanlight told him it was evening. He rose with difficulty to use the covered bucket in the corner, then poured water into a bowl on the washstand to rinse his hands and face. He was just sinking back under the covers when he heard the girl's gentle knock.

Supper was bread and broth again, but this time with a few gobbets of fatty meat floating in it. He ate more slowly, while she watched from the chair, that amused smile on her face.

They exchanged names. Hers was Yvette. She pronounced Philip the French way, Philippe. The room was an attic in her mother's house. He learned that he hadn't come far from the church where he'd hidden. The house was in the same village. It was the post office, in fact. Yvette's mother was the postmistress and Yvette helped behind the counter.

All this would, Philip thought, explain the sounds he heard, the occasional roar of heavy vehicles, the drumming of rain close above his head, French voices chattering far below and a bell that clanged annoyingly each time the street door opened. Despite his gratitude to these people who'd taken him in he felt frustrated that he was stuck here. On the other hand, a public post office was a good place to hide in plain sight. No one would question the fact of people coming and going here. No sign of his existence had aroused suspicion. But once he was well enough, he needed to move on. He was putting people's lives in danger and he longed to get home.

He spent the days building up his strength, performing simple exercises to restore muscle lost during his illness, though he had to be careful with his shoulder. The weather turned hot and the attic room with its single window warmed up unbearably. All the time he was ravenous. The women did their best, but he felt ashamed to be taking their food and he dared not ask for more. A week passed and another. He still felt under par, but he was ready to go. When he confided this to Yvette she nodded sadly and later that evening, the priest who'd hidden him puffed his way up the stairs and sank onto the chair, fanning himself. 'You look better,' he said, waving away Philip's thanks. 'I will try to advise you.' From the folds of his cassock he brought out a map, which he spread out on the bed. Together they hunched over it, the priest pointing out the village. Calais, Philip saw, was tantalizingly close. And from there, on a clear day, he'd be able to see the cliffs of Dover, only twenty miles away.

'*Non, non,*' the priest insisted. 'You cannot go there.' Once again he spelled out to Philip that there were no boats to take him across the Channel. The Germans had taken control. The ports and beaches were heavily guarded. Philip felt shock and despair. The British were completely routed. A whole army. France had surrendered. Now England stood alone.

The Nazis had swept into Paris several weeks ago, the priest told him. The French government had betrayed their own nation by allowing the northern half to be occupied by Germany, while they retreated to Vichy, in the south, where they were doing their weaselling best not to annoy Hitler. The priest grew so agitated as he delivered his account that he spat on the floor in a most ungodly fashion. No, no, the best way for Philip to reach home was to travel south to the Mediterranean and find a ship. Or maybe to seek safe transit through a neutral country, Switzerland, Portugal or Spain.

'South?' Philip could hardly believe his ears. Why should he have to take such a long, dangerous and roundabout journey when he was so close to England here. He felt weak with horror at the thought of the difficulties. Suppose he was asked for his papers on a train? He had none. Nor did he speak much French. No, he must try the north coast first. Surely there would be some sympathetic fisherman who would smuggle him out at night. Or he'd borrow a boat and row it across the Channel himself. 'I must try, don't you see?'

he told the priest, who rolled his eyes and spread his hands in exasperation at Philip's stubbornness.

It was hard leaving Yvette and her mother. After his terrible experiences Philip had found respite lying in their attic room, for all its discomforts and the constant worry that he'd be discovered. Yvette looked miserable when he said goodbye, but her mother was clearly relieved. They'd procured old clothes for him, a torch, made him packets of sandwiches. They'd dyed his reddish hair brown, shaved his moustache and coached him to look less like an upright British officer and more like a worn-down French peasant. He must sling his haversack, like so, not wear it on his back. He should slouch, not stand so straight and wear his beret like this, not like that. Then, one moonlit night they let him out of the back door. Waving goodbye, he set off down the lane, the priest's map in his coat pocket. He was glad to stretch his legs. He met no one on the road till first light, when he greeted an old man digging up potatoes in a field. *'Salut.'* The man glowered back without speaking, leaning on his spade, and Philip was glad when the next bend took him from sight.

Nearing Calais, he spent more time hiding in hedges than walking, for German vehicles passed by frequently. The town, when he reached it, was busy and it was easy to lose himself in the crowd, but scouting round the harbour in the early evening he saw that he had no chance of escape that way. Nazi patrols were everywhere. Even if he found some unattended rowing dinghy amid the naval vessels and the fishing boats bobbing against the tide it would be impossible to cast off without being picked out by the searchlights. When he realized he was attracting the interest of a nearby sentry he turned reluctantly away and ambled back into the town.

It was growing dark now and he had nowhere to sleep so he left Calais and took the road to the west that skirted the coast. *'Bonsoir. Anglais?'* an old woman feeding her chickens called to him when he rested on grass outside her cottage, and he spent the night on her hearthrug. She must have regretted her kindness, however, because she woke him at dawn and sent him off with a hunk of fresh bread in his pocket and fear in her eyes. *'Allez! Allez!'*, she whispered, pushing him out and shutting the door.

Refreshed by his sleep and the bread and encountering no German troops on the road, Philip ventured with high hopes into each of the little fishing villages on his way. Time after time he was disappointed to see that the enemy had already been and departed, for although he could see fishing vessels out at sea the harbours were filled with sunken craft. At one hamlet he trudged over the sand towards a line of dinghies pulled up on the beach only to find that their hulls had been bashed in. This sorry state of affairs was repeated again and again. Once, when he approached a pair of fishermen mending their nets on a jetty, they shook their heads and motioned him away. *'Les Allemagnes,'* one said with a shrug and pointed two fingers to his temple in imitation of a revolver.

'Un petit bateau?' Philip beseeched.

The man shook his head, saying *'Désolé,'* and the other wouldn't even meet his eye. The Nazis had done their work well.

He walked on. He was almost at Caen, a big port that would be as dangerous as Calais, so he hid in woodland, where he sat on a fallen tree to eat the rest of his food and smoke a cigarette. He wasn't sure what to do now. He wasn't prepared to give up easily with the thought of England so close, but his hope of finding a means of crossing the Channel burned less brightly. Turning south to seek another way home was still unimaginable, too difficult. He extinguished his cigarette and carefully returned the stub to the packet. He was running out of supplies fast. The priest had given him a few francs, but they wouldn't last long. He would have to find help somewhere soon.

Philip slung his haversack on his shoulder and climbed back to the road, thinking he'd pass through Caen and see how things were on the other side. He'd stopped to check his route when two Germans on bicycles rounded the corner ahead. Seeing his map they dismounted and questioned him, then escorted him back the way they'd come. They were friendly enough – one even gave him some chocolate – but they marched him to a makeshift barracks on the edge of the city and left him with a group of other prisoners herded together in a dirty yard. After several hours of waiting, orders were given for them to move. Philip was briefly visited by a sense of foreboding as he fell in behind the long column of weary men, but this felt more orderly than the last time he'd been captured and they were soon trudging back the way that he'd come. Soldiers cycled up and down the line of prisoners, shouting to keep up the pace. Well, I've blown my chance, he thought to himself. How far he'd have to march he didn't know, on to Germany he supposed. Part of him, strangely, was relieved that he no longer had to struggle. Like a hunted animal, he could give up the fight. That image reminded him of Maddie all those years ago in the museum in Norwich. Thinking of her he felt strength and determination surge in.

They marched for the rest of the day, stopping occasionally for short rests or to pick up other groups en route. In the villages they passed, the inhabitants watched with pity in their faces. Some darted forward with gifts of food or cigarettes for the prisoners.

As the day wore towards evening they came to a hamlet where a publican handed Philip a glass of beer. His pace slowed as he gulped it down and as he stepped out of the line to return the glass he heard a girl's voice whisper, '*Allez, dépéchez-vous*', and to his astonishment a slim warm hand seized his. He caught a glimpse of her shining brown eyes and slight figure as she dragged him behind a wall. There they crouched till the column had moved on, his disappearance apparently unnoticed. '*Allons-y.*' He followed the girl down a winding lane through trees to a house a few hundred yards away. There he was introduced to an elderly couple, her grandparents, given syrupy coffee and a nip of Calvados before they dispatched him with instructions to reach a farmhouse several miles further inland. It was, he understood, the home of the girl's uncle, the old people's middle son who was married to a Dutch woman, and the whole family hated the Germans for their cruelty. This was why they wanted to help English evaders like Philip. At the farmhouse he was touched to be warmly welcomed. He remained there for the best part of a month, hiding in a hayloft while the sounds and scents of harvest rose all around.

There was time to think here, far too much time. Philip knew that he must wait, that he was in others' hands. He wished now that he'd listened to the priest and not tried the north coast, but set off south instead. He cursed himself for wasting precious time. He thought of Maddie, the anguish she must be going through, not knowing if he were alive or dead, but he could think of no way of letting her know. Sometimes in the evenings the farmer and his wife admitted him to their homely kitchen and they'd listen illicitly to the BBC on a home-built receiver. He was comforted by the familiar, cheerful English voices, but the news was never good. He learned how British Spitfires were battling the Luftwaffe in the skies above Kent and Sussex. The fear of invasion must be terrible, he told his hosts, and was dismayed by the woman's tears. She, too, had no news of her family in Occupied Holland.

Then one day late in August the farmer called to him softly in the barn. He'd heard from a contact and it was time for Philip to move on. His destination was Rouen, the next city inland towards Paris. He was going south.

Twenty-four

Norfolk

August 1941

On the first afternoon of the harvest at Knyghton Maddie took Grace down to the farm to watch the great machine cut and bale the corn, though not for long, for the air was full of dust and Grace complained of it prickling her eyes. They were walking back to the house when Maddie glimpsed the purposeful figure of Susie Welbourne in her overalls whizzing over the bumps in the lane towards them on her bicycle.

'It's quite a sight, the binder, isn't it?' Susie called, braking as she came near. 'I've come to help.' She wore a scarf tucked round her head with a few fair curls pulled out rather fetchingly in front.

'Lyle will be glad to see you,' Maddie replied. 'It's been

awfully tense the last few days with him worrying about the weather, when to start. I never realized it was such a difficult decision.'

'Of course. It's the culmination of so much hard work.' Susie smiled at Grace. 'What did you think, young one? She's not old enough to ride on top yet, is she?' she asked Maddie, who shook her head.

'It hurts my ears and my eyes,' Grace said.

'She's sad about the animals, too,' Maddie whispered. They'd seen mice, rabbits and birds fleeing the carnage.

'I'm sure they'll be all right,' Susie said brightly to the little girl. Maddie pressed her lips together. She'd heard tales of small creatures being marooned in the middle of harvested fields and shot for sport, though she'd seen no evidence of this casual brutality here. Of course, she knew they had to hunt rabbits, which did awful damage to the crops. She thought of her illustrations of animals dressed as people and guessed that she'd never be cut out for farming. The likes of Susie and Lyle had no time for sentimentality.

'It'll be all hands on deck round here for the next few days,' Susie said, staring over Maddie's shoulder at the distant farm-yard. 'I'm surprised Lyle hasn't got you involved.'

'He knows I'd not be much use,' Maddie laughed. 'Making tea is about my limit, and I can't even do that easily without someone to watch Grace.'

Susie's lips curved in a supercilious smile. 'Ah, speak of the devil and he appears.'

Maddie turned and together they watched Lyle close the farmyard gate and walk towards them.

'I don't suppose,' Susie murmured, 'there's any word of your husband?'

Maddie's heart was pierced by the woman's tactlessness. She gave a quick shake of her head and hoped that Grace hadn't heard mention of her father, but Grace was kneeling in the grass playing some private game with a handful of pebbles. Was the woman warning her off Lyle by reminding her that she was married? If so it was cruel and entirely unnecessary.

As they waited for Lyle, Grace tired of her game. She came and tugged at Maddie's hand. 'Can we go now, Mummy?'

'In a moment. We must say hello to Uncle Lyle. You're very grubby, dear.' She bent to brush at Grace's hands and knees with a handkerchief while the little girl whimpered.

When she glanced up Lyle was approaching.

'Sorry to be late.' Susie called, 'I couldn't get away earlier.'

'It's good of you to come at all.' He did not smile. 'Your father hasn't started yet?'

'He says he'll risk waiting a couple more days, so he'll be along.'

Lyle nodded, hands on hips as he surveyed the skies. 'The weather's set to hold.'

Maddie knew that the farmers helped each other in turn, the labourers moving from harvest to harvest until every bit was in. Despite his dispute with Susie's father they had to assist each other to survive.

He turned to Maddie. 'You won't let Grace near the machine, will you?' he said curtly. 'Robert wouldn't see her from his perch.'

'I'm not daft,' Maddie said, annoyed by his tone. 'We're on our way home, anyway.' She took Grace's hand, then remembered. 'Grace is worried about what happens to the field animals, aren't you, darling? Their homes are destroyed, you see.'

Lyle's expression softened. He sank down to speak to her, his eyes crinkling into a smile. 'Don't worry, Grace, they all run away and find new homes.'

Grace stared at him, round-eyed, sifting the truth of his words. Finally she nodded and looked up at her mother. 'Like we found a new home.'

'Exactly,' Maddie said solemnly.

As they started back to the house she pondered on the plight of refugees everywhere and of how the grand schemes of the powerful few ruined the lives of the helpless many.

Twenty-five

Maddie hardly saw Lyle during the long days of harvest. He was up very early and out late, arriving back exhausted at nightfall to eat a lonely supper, certainly too tired for civilized conversation. In the evenings after the girls were in bed she went out for a walk with her sketchbook and one or other of the dogs. Sometimes she sat with Gussie to keep her company.

One evening while she tackled a pile of mending she mentioned Gussie's mother, Eleanor, whose portrait gazed down from the wall. 'The Lady and the Hare,' Maddie said. 'Pictures often have a title and that's what I'd call that one.'

Gussie's eyes lit up. 'The Lady and the Hare. I like that. I miss her so much. Sometimes, when I was little, she'd let me brush her hair, but I could never do it right, like Dorry. Dorry was my mother's maid, did I tell you?'

'You told me about Dorry, yes.' Maddie said patiently,

threading a needle. 'She was your mother's maid when you were little. Then, after Dorry left, before the Great War, Tilly came. But she didn't stay long because she left to get married and had Flora. Have I got that right?'

'Yes.' Gussie gave her a puzzled stare and Maddie worried that she'd been rude, but then Gussie's tendency to repeat herself was annoying.

She understood the narrative now. Gussie loved to talk about the distant past of her childhood when (according to her) she'd been her mother's favourite child, the beloved girl that Eleanor had kept by her, indulging her, dressing her in pretty clothes, until first George and then Philip's father William were born and Gussie had had to share the attention. She also gauged that it was the loss of her mother that was the great tragedy of Gussie's life, not the deaths of her father or brothers or whatever mysterious thing had happened to Flora.

Gussie rarely spoke about James, her father, so Maddie asked about him now. 'Do you have a photograph of him? I should love to see what Philip and Lyle's grandfather looked like.'

Gussie's face clouded. 'There must be one somewhere, I don't know.'

'Did you tell me once that he died in 1910?'

'Yes, that's right,' Gussie said dreamily, then patted the sofa next to her. Phoebe the Pekinese jumped up, licked her mistress's face, then settled in her lap with a sigh.

'And that's when your brother George took over the farm.' Gussie nodded. And George had joined up to fight in 1914 and was killed two years later. *How awful.* No wonder memories of the distant past appealed to Gussie more.

'What was he like, your father?' she prompted as she darned a hole in one of Grace's smocks, but Gussie was picking burrs out of Phoebe's hair and did not seem to hear.

Then a moment later the old lady said carelessly, 'I believe there's a box of photographs in the attic. You can look for it tomorrow, if you're interested. I'd like to see the ones of Mother again.'

Maddie felt a prickling sensation that this was somehow important. 'I am interested,' she said soberly. 'Because of Philip. I didn't know much about where he came from when we married.'

'And now it's too late.' Maddie's head whipped up in shock at Gussie's words, but the old lady was staring sightlessly into the distance, slowly stroking the dog. 'We don't know what we have until it's gone.'

So Gussie believed that Philip was dead. Was she, Maddie, the only one still hoping? She sat in numb silence for a while, then shook herself and reached for one of Lyle's shirts, which had frayed cuffs, but outside the sky was darkening to mauve with streaks of red and it was difficult for Maddie to see her handiwork. She rose to light the lamps just as Lyle himself strode past the window on his way to the back door. She called out a greeting, glad that he was home. How tired he'd looked, she thought. It wasn't just physical exhaustion, it was as though the weight of the world lay upon his shoulders.

She wondered what it was that made him so unhappy.

She imagined that the demands of the wartime administration on farmers would be burden enough, and he must also
be worried about the threat to Knyghton. She couldn't help
wondering if there was anything more personal and private.
Something stirred in her at the thought, a sort of tenderness.
Despite his moodiness she was fond of him and felt he'd had
a raw deal in life.

When Lyle entered the drawing room a few minutes later
she poured him a drink, made him sit down and went to fetch
his supper on a tray. Gussie and the dogs watched him with
keen interest. He ate his stew as quickly as its heat allowed
and without speaking, and once he'd finished the semolina
pudding, he laid the tray aside and at last gave Maddie a
shadowy smile. 'Thank you. I needed that.'

Maddie couldn't help liking the amused way he looked at
her through narrowed, dark-lashed eyes.

That night she dreamed vividly of Philip. He was calling her
out of a swirling fog. She woke in the small hours to find tears
staining her pillow and feeling a dull ache inside. She lay
awake in the soft darkness listening to the ordinary sounds
of the house, the scurry of a mouse behind the wall and the
rustle of falling plaster, the whimper of a sleeping dog in the
next room. Outside, an owl hooted mournfully. A fox barked.
These were the sounds that Philip would have heard when
he lived here and they comforted her.

She was just falling back into sleep when there came a
sudden chilling cry. Her eyes flew open. It came again. Lyle.
The cry subsided into a moan. He was having one of his

nightmares. A dog began to bark and was hushed. Maddie lay tense, hearing floorboards creak across the way, then the groan of Lyle's bedstead before the house subsided into quietness again. She imagined him lying there awake as she was, waiting for sleep to come.

Despite her bad night Maddie woke early, a breeze from the open window agitating the curtains so that stripes of sunshine reflected from the mirror on the chest of drawers and blinded her. Clumsy with tiredness, she swung her feet to the floor to feel for her slippers, then rose, lifted her dressing gown from the back of the door and padded down the gloomy staircase. In the sunny kitchen Mrs Flegg poured her a cup of tea and as she sipped it and watched Flegg shuffle outside to fill the coal scuttle from the bunker, Lyle entered, nodding a greeting. He was dressed already but there were purple bruises under his eyes.

Mrs Flegg instantly began bustling about frying eggs, while Maddie sliced bread and Lyle paced about the kitchen with a mug of tea. His breakfast set before him, Maddie sat to keep him company while he ate quickly in silence. When he'd finished, he immediately took his plate to the sink, and pulled on his boots.

'I hope your day goes well,' Maddie said conversationally and watched him pause in the doorway.

'Thanks.' He patted his pockets for his cigarettes, lit one and inhaled deeply. 'I read bits of that journal before I went to bed.'

She met his gaze in surprise. 'And . . .?'

'You can fetch it from my room if you want to see. Don't think you'll make much of it though.'

With that he went on his way, the back door slamming behind him.

Frowning, Maddie watched him pass the kitchen window, his handsome face purposeful and grim. Then she poured herself more tea and took it upstairs. All was silence from the nursery – so she tiptoed along the landing to avoid alerting the dogs and opened the door to Lyle's room.

In the semi-darkness she breathed in the masculine scent of him as she crossed to the window to draw back the curtains. Outside, at the movement, a flock of starlings flew up twittering from a bush. She smiled and turned to view the room, the bedclothes thrown aside, water splashed over the washstand, yesterday's shirt scrumpled on the floor.

The journal was open, splayed face down on the floor by the bed. Maddie picked it up and glanced at the page. '*I am scared by him.*' The dramatic words danced before her eyes. She closed the book, tucked it under her arm and reached to smooth the tumbled bedclothes. And stayed her hand. Mrs Flegg on her morning rounds might wonder what Maddie had been doing here. Lyle might conceivably open his own curtains, but he'd never make his own bed or pick up his dirty shirt!

Safely back in her room she closed the door softly behind her. Not a moment too soon, for she heard Gussie's voice and the click of claws on the landing, then the scrapes and bumps of their slow progress down the stairs.

Clambering back into bed, she took a sip of tea and laid

the notebook on her lap, stroking the rough card cover, dog-eared and curling with age. Most thrilling of all was that 'Flora Simpson, private', was printed on the front in sweeping black capitals. She turned to the first page, eyed the date, '2nd August, 1924', and started to read.

'I've resolved to start a diary to help me record my thoughts and to reflect on the books that I've read.' Immediately under that Flora had written *'Jane Eyre* by Charlotte Brontë' and underlined it. Much of the ensuing review was a rambling retelling of the story that went on for several pages. *'I am scared by him.'* Only at the very end did it say, *'I loved this novel and found it most affecting, but I don't think I would ever like to marry a man like Rochester because he hid things from Jane very unkindly.'* Maddie smiled grimly at this youthful judgement, took another sip of tea and turned the page to see Flora's opinion of Mary Shelley's *Frankenstein*. *'Very frightening and unfair of Dr Frankenstein, but his family didn't deserve to die. I liked the scenes in the icy Arctic – they were MAGNIFICENT.'* Then Maddie's heart leaped as she read her husband's name. *'Philip says that the Shelleys went climbing in snowstorms in the Swiss Alps and that's where she found her inspiration.'*

She turned the page thoughtfully, remembering that *Frankenstein* had been a favourite novel of Philip's, and wished now that she'd read it, too, and could have discussed it with him. Another regret. She blinked and read on. Flora had written about *The Moonstone* by Wilkie Collins, *The Golden Treasury, Great Expectations*, and it was already the beginning of September. Maddie scanned the reviews, astonished that Flora read so quickly, but noticing, too, an improvement in what she wrote, a deepening of maturity. Often she'd come across Philip's name, *'Philip said'*, or *'Philip thought'*, as though he had directed her reading and discussed the books with her. Again she felt regret wash over her that she'd missed this experience with him herself.

She flicked the pages more quickly now, noting only the titles of the books and scanning the neat handwriting for mention of her husband's name. There was only one, which referred to a letter she'd received from him in September of that year in which he'd suggested that she read the book concerned – Kipling's *Kim* – to get a taste of Philip's early childhood in India. Flora, too, had found it *'ripping'*. Maddie silently vowed to read it when she could lay hands on a copy.

The reviews petered out to be followed by blank pages. Maddie sighed with disappointment as she laid the notebook aside. It contained no hint of what had happened to Flora or exactly why this book had ended up at the rectory. No wonder Lyle had so readily allowed her to borrow it. All it had done was to deepen her understanding of the young girl's mind and something of her personality. Flora and Philip had clearly been close at this stage in their youth, but as friends. Had this changed later? Lyle had hinted that it had. She wondered what had happened to Flora's letters to Philip, for they hadn't been in the tin underneath the floorboard. Would Philip have brought them with him to London after their marriage? A flash of jealousy. *Surely not.* They belonged to his youthful past, not to his marriage. They'd never discussed previous romantic entanglements. She wondered if that was unusual for couples. *I was so innocent when I met him*, she thought miserably. *I had nothing much to confess except a pash on a fellow art student. And Philip never asked me so I never asked him.* If he had kept the letters with him, they were certainly gone now, lost in the ruins of 38 Valentine Street.

At that moment her thoughts were interrupted by a shuffling noise as the door opened and Grace entered the room wrapped in a bedspread and with a circlet on her hair that looked suspiciously like Gussie's embroidery frame. 'I'm a princess today,' she announced, tilting her chin proudly, 'and I want toast and milk for my breakfast.'

'All right, Princess Grace,' Maddie smiled. 'Let me put on my shoes.' As she climbed out of bed she accidentally knocked Flora's notebook to the floor. When she picked it up the back cover fell open. The final page, she saw with surprise, was covered with writing. She hadn't noticed it before.

'Come on, servant,' Grace commanded, so Maddie smoothed the covers, left Flora's notebook in the drawer of the bedside table and followed the little girl downstairs.

Late in the afternoon she retrieved it and while the girls played in the garden, she sat on the bench where lazy bees visited the hollyhocks, flipped the notebook upside down, turned to the back page and started to read. The entries were written in the same hand as the reviews, but the flowing italics with their dashing strokes, hastily scrawled, suggested an older Flora.

'I'm frightened.' Maddie frowned, and read on.

The rectory is to be my home for now, but I feel lost and alone, not safe at all. They say it's my fault, that I'm the cause of the trouble, but it's not true. No one takes my side. Only Flegg believes me, but he can't do anything against them, poor old Flegg. I don't know what's going to happen to me, where I'm to live, if I'm going to return to school. Oh, help me, help me …

I feel a little calmer today. Mr Stainer the rector called me into his study after breakfast and explained that it's all for the best that I'm here. I will still attend school if I want to after all. Mr Stainer was only being kind, but he and Mrs Stainer treat me like a child. I know far more about life than they think I do.

The next entry was more steadily written:

I've been here a week now and I feel a great deal better. I think I shall be happy here. I hadn't realized how anxious I'd become and what a strange place Knyghton is. So much unhappiness. I wish I could see Philip, but not if it means Lyle is there too. I don't know what I feel about Lyle. I thought it was love, but now I'm not sure. But do I love Philip instead? I don't know. They're so alike in some ways but so different too. Perhaps it's that family thing. They've bad blood, Mrs Stainer said the other day, but then she apologized because "Jesus would not have said something like that about anyone." She's very worried about offending Jesus, is Mrs Stainer. It must be very wearing for her. She does look tired and her hair is always falling in her eyes. I've decided I will never marry a vicar because everyone expects the wife to organize so many things and listen to everybody's problems. Mrs Stainer has no time to herself and now she has a crazy seventeen-year-old girl to look after. (That's me.)

There was only one more entry:

It's the harvest supper tonight up at Knyghton and Mrs Anderson has told Mr Stainer that I can go!!! I really want to, but I'm nervous all the same. What shall I wear? Should I speak to Lyle and Philip if I see them? Oh, I wish

The entry finished mid-sentence. Flora had been interrupted. Perhaps by the rector's wife, Mrs Stainer, Maddie thought, to discuss what Flora should wear. If she'd been brought to the rectory at short notice she might not have had many clothes with her. Yet it sounded as though the move was meant to be permanent, at least in the short term.

Anna had found the notebook in her bedroom at the rectory. It would be reasonable, then, to suppose that Anna's room had once been Flora's. Anna had pointed out its window at the front of the house as Maddie had left the other day. She said it looked out across the garden to a line of trees that hid the road, a lovely view. The room would be bright in the morning sun. It was not as though Flora had been exiled or imprisoned, and the Clairmonts' predecessors in the rectory sounded sympathetic people. She wondered if they'd had children themselves, grown up by then and gone, and were perhaps glad to have a young person living with them again.

Poor Flora, though. One feels things so intensely at seventeen. Maddie recalled the pain of the secret crush on her fellow student. She sighed and looked down at the notebook again, flicking through the rest of the pages in case she'd missed something. They were blank and she was puzzled. Why had Flora stopped writing? Could it have been . . .? As there were no dates, it was difficult to tell how soon afterwards the girl had met her tragic death.

Maddie closed the notebook and brushed at a bee that was exploring the flower print on her skirt. She rose and wandered indoors. She was trying to visualize the date of death on Flora's gravestone that she'd seen in the church-yard some months before, but she couldn't. It hadn't seemed important then, but now that the girl's story involved Philip and Lyle it did.

The attic at Knyghton wasn't a proper room, but a long low loft space accessed through a hatch in the ceiling of a serv-ants' bedroom at the far end of the landing. While Mrs Flegg was giving the girls tea Maddie borrowed overalls, climbed a pair of steps and with some difficulty pushed back the trapdoor. Swinging herself up, she sat on the edge of the hatch and peered into the gloom, feeling her old familiar fear of dark tight spaces. Streaks of light pouring through tiny gaps between the roof tiles showed that the rafters had been boarded over to support the various oilskin-shrouded boxes and small bits of furniture abandoned there as well as a bucket or two against leaks and an old wasps' nest. Well, if she wanted those photographs, she'd have to grit her teeth.

She manoeuvred herself onto her knees and crawled about in the grime, peeping beneath tarpaulins, until with relief she spotted a small grubby weekend case lying under a box of books. A thin ray of light fell upon a handwritten label: *'Knyghton photographs.'* She edged the case out and tried to open it, but although one of the catches sprang up, the other stuck. It was heavy, but she managed to lug it down the stepladder. Quite why precious photographs had been left in such a vulnerable and inaccessible place she couldn't imagine.

Later, in the drawing room, with Gussie fluttering anxiously nearby, Maddie set the case on newspaper on the floor, wiped off the grime with a damp cloth and jiggled at the second fastening with a kitchen knife until it flew open. Then she levered up the lid and pushed aside a linen cloth to reveal a pile of photographs, a large black-framed portrait of a middle-aged lady on the top. She was dressed in a late Victorian gown. Maddie recognized her at once, and glanced up at the younger version of Eleanor Anderson cradling her hare above the mantelpiece.

'My mother was so beautiful,' Gussie sighed as she took the photograph from Maddie.

'She was,' Maddie said truthfully, leaning to see. Eleanor Anderson had possessed the kind of beauty that deepens with age, yet there was something about the photograph that troubled her. A tightness about the mouth, a timidity in the eyes. This woman had not been happy or completely fulfilled. Maddie didn't say so to Gussie, who was still gazing at the photograph with adoration in her eyes.

Maddie stared down at the case and the neat stack of pictures, then picked out another and turned it over, realizing the frame was identical to that of Eleanor's photograph. The imposing-looking bearded man in this portrait must be Gussie's father, Eleanor's husband James. Powerfully built with twinkling eyes and the weathered face of a farmer, his waistcoat tightly buttoned under a black jacket, his presence suggested that he was every inch a country gentleman. Gussie still held her mother's picture, but she glanced at her father's and Maddie noticed her expression change, a sadness come across her face. Gussie, she saw, had not felt as adoringly about her father.

'He was a handsome man,' Maddie ventured, brushing dust off Mr Anderson's face. 'Lyle looks a little like him, don't you think?'

Gussie gave a nod. 'Mother often said so. My father was a very charming man. He knew how to get people to do things for him. Everybody was in awe of him.' She sighed and handed back the photograph, but her gaze was dreamy now.

There was something Gussie wasn't saying, Maddie thought. She bent and started to sift through the rest of the contents of the case. She found plates of early photographs, Gussie's grandparents, aunts, uncles and cousins, many of whom the old lady could not identify. A small album contained a picture of George's wedding to Daphne, Daphne a palely pretty girl in a lace wedding dress in a garden that wasn't Knyghton. A studio portrait of Philip's mother Rose showed a radiant young woman in a sleeveless evening gown. 'That was taken when they became engaged,' Gussie said. Maddie examined the photograph carefully. Rose, of course, had died before Maddie could meet her. *Sarah has the look of her,* she thought, the retroussé nose and small oval face.

They'd been through the whole case now. There was only one frame left in the bottom. Gussie picked it out. 'Oh, I remember this,' she said, showing it to Maddie, who examined it with interest. It was of the Anderson family of Knyghton and their servants grouped in front of the house, everyone in their best clothes, the women in hats. 'We'd just come back from church,' Gussie said. 'It was my parents' fortieth anniversary. They had a party. Now, what year would that have been? Let me see ... 1907, I think.'

'Is this you?' She pointed to the shy-looking woman buttoned into a wasp-waisted dress, standing next to Eleanor.

'Yes, I was thirty-seven. Don't I look uncomfortable. My stays were laced too tightly.' Gussie's finger moved over the photograph. 'Mother, Father, George and Daphne, William and Rose. Mrs Woodcock, our cook.' Three young women in neat frocks and hats stood together on the back row. 'Bessie, Molly, oh, and this is Tilly, my mother's maid.' Maddie peered at the one indicated by Gussie's quavering finger. Bessie and Molly, the other two, were round-faced and comfortable-looking, but Tilly was a waif, stick thin with a pretty, heart-shaped face. Huge hungry eyes looked shyly up at the camera from under a straw hat dressed with ribbon.

'Tilly was an orphan. Mother took her on at sixteen after Dorry left as a favour to the old rector, Mr Stainer, and became very fond of her.'

'Weren't you jealous?'

'Jealous? Oh, no. Tilly kept herself to herself, barely said a word to anyone. Stayed for years. And then suddenly Mr Simpson, the blacksmith in Carshall, was courting her and, well, she . . .' Gussie stopped briefly as though to take breath. 'She had to get married. Quite a nuisance for my mother.'

'I see.' *So Tilly had become pregnant while still unmarried.* 'But she stayed in touch after Flora was born.'

'Sometimes she wrote asking for money. I saw the letters. Mother always sent her some.'

'And when Tilly died, her daughter came to Knyghton?'

A shadow passed across Gussie's face. 'Mother invited Flora to live here. They didn't have other children. Simpson looked after Flora at first with the help of his mother, but when she died a few years later he turned to drink and he couldn't look after Flora. Mother's idea was to train her up, but she was quick at her lessons and the school told Mother that she was too clever for domestic service.'

'And what happened to Flora exactly. How did she die?'

'It was an accident,' Gussie whispered, fiddling with her necklace. 'A terrible accident. Up in the fields after the harvest. They brought her here afterwards. Called the doctor, but they couldn't save her. Poor Flora.'

'Did she fall?'

'Fall? She might have done, I don't know, I didn't see. Philip shot her. He didn't mean to, but they said he did.'

Maddie felt as though she'd been struck.

'Philip? He . . . he killed Flora?' Whatever she'd expected it wasn't that. For moment she felt faint and the room spun round.

*

'Maddie?' She felt Gussie's hand on her arm and her eyes met Gussie's baby-blue ones, guileless but full of concern. 'I'm sorry, I've shocked you. Are you all right?'

'I . . . I think so. But Philip . . . wouldn't do a thing like that.'

'Some people said it was out of jealousy. They both wanted Flora, you see. Lyle and Philip.'

'But . . . did anyone actually see him do it?' She could barely get the words out.

'One of the farm labourers said that he did, but when they questioned him he said he wasn't sure. There were bullets flying around everywhere. They were shooting the field animals, you see. I knew they would so I hadn't wanted to go. The poor creatures, it's cruel.' Gussie's voice quavered with emotion.

The old lady reached for the picture in Maddie's hand and laid it back in the case, then began to pile the other photographs on top in a flustered, haphazard fashion.

'Let me do it, Gussie,' Maddie pleaded.

Gussie stepped away, muttering an excuse. She tucked Phoebe the Pekinese under her arm then hobbled from the room. The other dogs followed, whining mournfully, obviously sensing that their mistress was unhappy.

Maddie repacked the suitcase neatly with slow, heavy movements, then sat down, relieved to be alone to brood.

Why had Philip never told her about this terrible event? It would have overshadowed his young life. She was too stunned to take it in yet, but it seemed that she didn't know the man she had married. And that hurt. If only he was here to ask. She was left to deal with this alone. She linked her fingers together so that the nails dug into her palms. The pain offered relief from mental torment and she squeezed more tightly until they left deep livid marks.

She was still curled up on the sofa in the gloom when Lyle found her half an hour later, bringing scents of the outside with him – earth and straw and growing things – that brought her back to herself. She watched as he drew the curtains and lit the lamps.

'Have you finished the job?' she asked, stretching.

'Not quite. It was simply too dark to tackle the upper field.' He went to the drinks tray and poured some brandy. 'Anything for you?'

'Why not.' The amber liquid glowed softly in the lamplight and as she sipped it she felt some of her sadness slip away and her strength return. 'I suppose I must fetch your supper.'

'I'll have it in the kitchen if it's easier.' He smiled and she uncoiled herself and went to heat up the ham and pea soup Mrs Flegg had left.

A moment later he joined her with the brandy decanter and peered hopefully over her shoulder as she stirred the broth, so that she felt the warmth of his presence. She cut slices of bread for him then sat drinking brandy and watched him eat – 'it's mostly potato, to be honest, but at least it's salty and filling' – then when he'd finished she rose and fetched the dish of sponge pudding and custard from the oven.

It was calming to perform these mundane tasks, but all the time Maddie felt tears prickle for she was thinking about

Philip. After she served Lyle she licked a blob of custard from her finger and the honeyed sweetness comforted her.

Lyle had appeared not to notice her distress. His drawn face, the lines around his heavy-lidded eyes spoke of exhaustion. He scraped his bowl clean, knocked back the rest of his brandy, then rubbed his face and blinked tiredly. 'Thank you,' he murmured and she smiled briefly. It was the wrong moment to ask him about what she'd learned that evening. He was too weary and the matter might anger him. She began to clear the table, and felt his eyes on her as she returned the heel of the loaf to the bread bin and ran water over the plates in the sink.

'I think I'll turn in,' he said and pushed back his chair. 'Another early start tomorrow.'

'Very sensible.' Their eyes locked for a moment, then slowly, hesitantly he came to her. She very gently touched his cheek. 'You look so weary,' she said in a motherly fashion.

'I'll live,' he said. 'Thank you for my supper.'

'You ought to thank Mrs F., not me.'

'For serving it up and keeping me company. Nobody else does when it's late like this. It can be very lonely.'

'I think we both know about loneliness.' Her voice cracked at 'loneliness' and she had to turn away and busy herself rinsing cutlery.

She heard him draw breath and the air in the room seemed to thicken. *You fool,* she told herself, *you shouldn't allow this.* She dried her hands on a cloth and said gently but firmly, 'Go on, Lyle, off to bed. Tiredness causes accidents. I'm sure there's a government poster about that. There is about everything else.'

He laughed and the atmosphere lightened. He took his glass and the brandy bottle and said goodnight.

Maddie stayed a while in the kitchen clearing up until the lamp sputtered out with a stink of smoke and she stood in the darkness and thought about Philip.

Twenty-six

France

Late August 1940

'Rouen is not far,' the farmer explained, and he sketched a map of the route on a scrap of paper that Philip folded and tucked into his sock. He understood that he would be all right if he reached the Seine and followed its twists and turns south to the town. 'There's a particular hotel in the street behind the cathedral. You must go there and ask for a man called Lucien Martin. I'm told that he will help you.'

Philip thanked his hosts profusely and set out early that evening. Summer was waning and the fields were bleak and bare. There were few places to hide and it was easy to lose his way once it grew dark, for the moon was veiled with fast-moving cloud setting the road before him racing with shadows. Towards dawn it began to rain and he hid in a tumbledown shed that he had glimpsed at the far end of a muddy field and managed to catch a few hours sleep.

He was woken by a dog whining close by and froze in fear, his heart thudding, then heard a man call out, '*Tais toi*', but the dog snuffled at the gap under the door, which opened outward after a moment and a weathered face peered in at him huddled on sacking on the floor.

'*Tiens!*' The man held the dog back and Philip saw with horror that he carried an axe. Still, he had no choice but to trust him so he scrambled to his feet and introduced himself in French. In the half light he saw the man frown. 'Where are you going?' the man asked. When Philip explained, the man invited him outside and gave fresh directions. He should try to join the main road as soon as he could. There were so many refugees on it that he wouldn't be noticed if he kept his head down. And travel in the daytime. He'd look more suspicious at night.

He gave Philip a slug from a water bottle and a lump of pie from his bag then walked with him to the next junction, where they parted with an '*Adieu!*' *A dieu* – God go with you. It sounded better than 'Good luck'. On reaching the main road to Rouen Philip saw that the man was right about the refugees. Cars crawled past packed with people and luggage. Rags and scraps of humanity trudged along the road edge. Some carried possessions on their backs or babies in their arms or pushed perambulators or barrows piled high with their chattels. Others had nothing except the clothes on their backs and a desperate expression in their eyes. He wondered where they might ultimately be going, but following the woodman's advice he joined the line, meeting no one's gaze in case they tried to engage him in conversation. Soon, in the distance the three towers of Rouen cathedral, wreathed in early morning mist, drew him on. By lunchtime, the pie long gone and his belly growling with hunger, Philip crossed the Seine in an unsupervised ferryboat and entered the outskirts of the town.

It was a shock to him how many German troops there were, guarding the bridges, on sentry duty outside public buildings, loitering in little groups in the streets, their suspicious eyes raking the crowds. He hunched his shoulders and shuffled on, trying not to hurry, but his heart was pounding in his ears and the towers seemed to get no nearer. Finally he reached the great square where he couldn't help gawping at the gothic splendour of the cathedral looming above. Which way? He dared not slow his pace or consult the scrap of paper with the map and must trust to memory. Sure that the street he wanted led off the opposite side of the square he negotiated the crowds, stopping only to buy apples from a street seller to stave off his hunger, but the one he bit into was sour and hard to swallow.

Any road signs had been taken down, but he noticed a blue shop door that the farmer had mentioned and turned down a narrow street next to it that was cast in darkness from the overhanging buildings. It was a relief to leave the crowds behind, but he dared not let down his guard. Taking the first road to the left he began to look for the hotel he needed. There were several, but his was identified by the rusted sign of a cockerel above a green louvre door. Glancing in both directions, but seeing no German soldiers, he pressed the bell. An interminable wait, then footsteps and the door creaked open. A stocky man with a lugubrious expression looked out with suspicion. 'Monsieur Martin?' Philip asked quietly. The man's eyes shifted, checking that Philip had come alone, then he gave a small, but decisive nod. Philip spoke a password he'd been given and after a second's hesitation was admitted into a dark cold hallway with a tiled floor down which he followed M. Martin's shambling figure through a sitting room into an untidy windowless office lit by a dim ceiling light.

M. Martin was courteous, but he was clearly unhappy about Philip's arrival. The Germans were in and out of everything, he said. A friend of his was picked up only yesterday for consorting with English evaders. Someone had betrayed him. He feared for his friend – here M. Martin drew his finger across his own throat in a savage and unmistakable gesture. No one knew which of their neighbours to trust these days, but Philip's farmer was related to M. Martin's cousin and that was good enough for now. Philip could not stay here, though, it was simply too dangerous. M. Martin would feed him and give him a bed for the night, but he must leave the next morning, get out of Rouen, head for Paris. There would be people there who could help. The American Embassy, maybe. America wasn't in the war yet. He turned up his palms and shrugged.

Although Philip thanked him, his spirits plummeted. He didn't know what he'd hoped for, but something more encouraging.

The next morning at dawn he took to the streets again. At

least he had bread and cheese in his bag, a few francs in his pocket and new instructions in his head. But it was eighty miles or so to Paris, with danger at every turn. If he wasn't imprisoned by the Nazis for being English, M. Martin had warned him, he might, like many a young Frenchman, find himself carted off across the German border to work in a munitions factory or a coal mine. With these gloomy thoughts in his head Philip located the road that led eventually to Paris and soon left Rouen behind him. Each step south, he told himself, should feel like a step nearer safety, but it didn't feel like that at all. Instead it felt like a step deeper into danger and further and further away from home. Some men, he was sure, might have given themselves up, unable to take the strain, but not he. The call of country and family was too strong in him for that. Part of him also felt that this was some kind of reckoning and he must show himself worthy.

Twenty-seven

Norfolk

August 1941

Sarah woke early one morning complaining of toothache. Mrs Flegg gave her a clove to tuck inside her cheek and numb the pain, but the child spat it out and became tearful so Maddie cycled down to the post office to telephone her old dentist in Norwich. To her relief his receptionist gave Sarah an appointment for the following morning. 'Mr Salter may have time to give you and the little one a quick look over while you're here.' Maddie thanked her and replaced the receiver thoughtfully. They would do something nice afterwards to make up for the dentist, but they ought to visit her father and Monica. And there was something else she wanted to fit in if there was time, to research some information at the archive of the local newspaper. Yes, they would make a day of it. She shook more coins out of her purse and picked up the receiver again. There were two more calls to make.

Her stepmother, Monica, for once had sounded pleased to hear from her and she brooded on this as she cycled back to Knyghton. She hadn't seen her father and stepmother for months and felt bad about it, but there had been no particular excuse to go to Norwich until now and, anyway, the last visit had felt pointless. Her father had not recognized her.

Monica, it seemed, was living her life as she always had, meeting friends for tennis or bridge. This time Maddie would have the girls with her. Monica wasn't at ease with children. Still, the visit had to be made. Children had to learn respect for their elders.

As for the final appointment she'd made just now, she'd have to ask Lyle first when the inquest into Flora's death had occurred or she'd simply waste time searching for the report in the newspaper archive. She'd enquire in some roundabout way or he might be angry. He'd already made it perfectly plain that he didn't like talking about Flora.

A day away from routine should be something to look forward to, Maddie reflected, as they waited on a bench on the station platform the following morning. The train to Norwich was late, however, and all three of them were tired after another broken night with Sarah's toothache. Maddie felt a sense of dread about the whole outing. Only Flegg, who'd driven them to the station in the trap, had appeared cheerful, slipping the girls threepence each after he lifted them down onto the station forecourt and dismissing Maddie's thanks.

It was sad, she'd thought, as they waved goodbye, that he and his wife had no children of their own. Only Flora, who'd lived in their cottage for a while. She remembered how warmly the girl had written of him in her journal. Flegg must have been heartbroken about what happened.

'Don't,' she admonished Grace, who was swinging her legs wildly, and the girl looked up, hurt by her mother's angry tone. 'It's annoying to grown-ups,' Maddie said more gently and forced a smile. In the distance a whistle sounded and Sarah rose from her pain-filled torpor to cry, 'It's coming, Mummy.'

Dear old Norwich. A group of chattering young women in ATS uniform on a day out drifted ahead of them out of the station and there were piles of sandbags everywhere. The sky shone blue behind the delicate spire of the cathedral and the familiar bulk of the castle lay ahead up the hill. Maddie held the girls' hands tightly and Grace skipped along, while Sarah's steps dragged. 'I don't want to go,' she whispered when Maddie bent to ask her the matter. 'What if it hurts?'

'It's to stop the hurt,' Maddie said quite reasonably, 'but you might have to be brave first.' Remembering her own childhood suffering at the hands of a dentist, her sense of dread grew. She wouldn't lie to her daughter, but if she could suffer the pain for her she would.

In the end the experience was tolerable for Sarah. A new tooth coming through had not yet dislodged the infant one, causing the gum to become infected. Mr Salter whipped the old one out easily and the receptionist gave both girls a boiled sweet from a jar she kept below her desk. By the time they'd caught the bus up to Featherstone Road the tears had dried on Sarah's cheeks and she was showing off the bloody gap in her lower jaw to a round-eyed Grace.

A distant church clock was chiming midday as Maddie assembled her little party beneath the porch of her childhood home. She wiped a smudge from Grace's nose with the corner of her handkerchief, told Sarah to buck up, and rang the bell. It was Monica herself who admitted them, elegant in a lemon-coloured twinset and greeting them with a welcoming smile. 'Come through to the kitchen,' she said. 'I'm just preparing your father's lunch.'

Her stepmother looked tired, Maddie thought, as she watched Monica arrange cutlery on a tray and ladle vegetable soup into a bowl. 'I'll take it up to him, if you like,' Maddie offered.

'Can I come and see Granddad?' Sarah piped up.

'And me,' added Grace.

Monica glanced at the girls, looking a little alarmed. 'I don't think that's suitable. The nurse will be down any moment, Maddie. You can see your father a little later when he's been tidied up after lunch.'

The nurse who entered shortly afterwards was a large-boned older woman, wearing a nunlike blue headdress and clasping her hands together as though in prayer. She reappeared in the kitchen during after-lunch washing up to say that Maddie's father was sleepy, but that Maddie could go and see him if she wanted.

'Thank you.' Maddie hung up her tea towel and took each of her daughters' hands. 'He is their granddad,' she said firmly to Monica, seeing her frown of dismay. 'I'm sure he'd want to see them.'

'Be very quiet,' she whispered to the girls as they clambered the stairs ahead of her. The seventh step still creaked and she cringed as each of them trod on it. On the landing everything was different. The air smelled strongly of something chemical. She opened the door of her old bedroom. It now looked rather like a hospital room with a special railed bed and an invalid's paraphernalia. She glanced about, but there was no sign of anything that had once been hers. Last time she'd visited her old Arthur Rackham fairy prints were still on the walls, but now these had gone.

Her father lay in a doze on the bed, his breath rattling in his throat. Seeing an expression of alarm cross Sarah's face Maddie's heart plunged. Perhaps she shouldn't have brought the girls here after all. Well, it was too late now. She lifted a wooden chair across and Sarah perched on it, while she herself sat in the nurse's easy chair with Grace plumped on her lap.

'He looks very peaceful, doesn't he?' she said, wanting to reassure.

'He hasn't got any teeth,' Grace noted. Sarah pointed to a water glass on a table with a set of dentures in it. They both stared at it, fascinated.

He must have heard the girls' high voices for his breathing lightened and after a moment his eyes fluttered open. They clouded with confusion, then he focused on Maddie's face. To her relief delighted recognition sprang into his eyes. Then he spoke. 'Sarah,' he said.

Sarah flinched, then seeing Maddie's encouraging look bent nearer to him. His gaze transferred to her small face and at once he frowned. Maddie realized with dismay that the Sarah he'd called to wasn't his granddaughter, but Maddie's mother. He'd seen Maddie and thought that she was his dead wife. Now his eyes were on Maddie again and she said softly. 'Daddy, it's Maddie.'

'Maddie, dear.' He smiled and her heart melted. This was her father as he'd never looked at her before, with eyes full of fondness.

She put out her hand and touched his, where it lay on the sheet and he clasped it. 'This is your granddaughter Sarah,' she told him, 'and her sister Grace.' She continued to speak to him gently, telling him about the girls and Knyghton and what they'd been doing. All the time he was quiet, but his attention wandered and her heart twisted as she realized that he was weaker than ever.

After he drifted back into sleep, she encouraged the girls to whisper their goodbyes before they returned slowly downstairs.

The nurse was alone at the kitchen table crocheting a red square for a blanket, but she looked up at their entrance. 'Thank you,' Maddie said to her. 'My father looks well looked after,' and the woman smiled graciously.

Grace tugged at Maddie's skirt. 'What is wrong with Granddad?' she asked.

'Oh, my darling, he's very ill. His brain is not working as well as it should. But you mustn't worry, he's not in pain or anything.'

'Will he die?' Sarah wanted to know. The nurse bent closer over her work, but Maddie swallowed and said, 'He may live for a long time yet, but we can't be certain. All we can do is make sure that he's comfortable.'

The girls seemed satisfied by these answers, but Maddie briefly felt the prick of tears. They went and found Monica sitting on the sofa in the chilly drawing room, smoking a cigarette in a holder and turning the pages of a magazine. She pushed it aside when they entered, and by the way she glanced at the little gold wristwatch she wore Maddie sensed that it was time for them to leave.

'It's my bridge afternoon,' Monica said, rising, 'I did say on the telephone.'

'Of course you did.'

'It's wonderful that you came. You girls are getting so big now.'

'We've growed,' Grace said solemnly and Monica managed to crack a smile.

Out in the hallway, Maddie said in a low voice, 'My father seems very peaceful. I'm glad that Sarah and Grace could see him.'

'I suppose you know what you're doing,' Monica replied icily. 'It's not for me to say anything different, only, when I was a child we were kept away from that sort of thing.'

'I wasn't allowed to attend my own mother's funeral,' Maddie said, in a husky voice. 'There was never the chance to say goodbye to her. And with Philip ...' She breathed in sharply and found she could not go on.

'Oh, my dear.' Monica's gaze softened. Her carefully

constructed exterior had melted and the heart of her showed through. For a moment they stared at one another, then Maddie stepped forward, put her arm round Monica's neck and pressed her warm cheek to her stepmother's powdery one. Monica was bearing the brunt of her older husband's illness. Who was Maddie to criticize her? Monica stiffened, but then Maddie felt her relax and for a while they stood there together in close embrace.

After the front door closed behind them, Maddie pulled on her gloves, looked up at her old bedroom window and struggled to regain her composure. When she turned, Grace was stripping leaves from the privet hedge while Sarah lolled against the front gate, grimacing as she prodded the gap in her row of teeth with her finger. Maddie felt a rush of love for them both and grinned.

'Come along, look smart now,' she said, sweeping them out onto the sunny pavement. 'There's one more thing Mummy has to do and then I promise we'll have tea in Lyons and buy some sweets before we get back on the train.'

'What's the one more thing?' Sarah asked suspiciously.

'We're going to a special building to look at some old newspapers,' Maddie replied. 'And don't look at me like that, please. Goodness, here's our bus already. Aren't we lucky?'

The old clerk at the newspaper archive had already brought several heavy files up from safe storage in the cellar, and laid them side by side on a long oak table. Lyle had not been able to recall clearly when Maddie had asked him the night before, but he thought that there had been an opening inquest a few days after Flora's death followed by a full inquest a couple of months later, which gave her a rough idea of the dates she'd to look for. No, he had not attended either proceedings and nor had Philip. He was short with Maddie and since she did not volunteer why she wanted to know, he ended the conversation abruptly by stomping off to bed. They'd finished bringing in Knyghton's harvest, but the day had been an arduous one and tomorrow he was to help the Welbournes against the threat of poor weather rolling in.

The little girls sat dutifully on hard chairs and Sarah read to Grace from a book Maddie had tucked into her bag. Maddie, sitting at the long table, drew the first of the large volumes of newspapers towards her, opened it and leafed through until she came one dated the end of August 1925, the day after Flora's death. It took her a little while to accommodate herself to the layout and the tiny print, but the event was reported halfway down a page of local news: 'Young woman dead in firearms incident,' ran the headline, and her eyes widened as she read the three bland sentences that followed that mentioned a shooting party at Knyghton Farm after the harvest, the words 'possible tragic accident' and that a coroner's inquest would open on Friday. Maddie made a note of the date of the article in her engagement book then leafed quickly through the following day's newspaper, her eye falling on a heading 'Young woman named in farm shooting'. 'Schoolgirl Miss Flora Simpson, 17', the piece said.

Forward again, but there was nothing more on the matter until the Saturday edition, when the opening and immediate adjournment of the inquest the day before was reported. Thank heavens, the date to which it was adjourned was given: 'Monday 9th November'. Quickly she checked the dates covered by the other volumes on the table. Early November 1925 wasn't among them.

'I'll only be a moment, darlings.' She went out into the corridor and knocked on the door of the office opposite.

While the clerk wearily descended to the cellar to unearth the volume required, Maddie gave the girls some plain rusks she'd brought.

'No food or drink to be consumed on the premises,' the old man muttered as he placed another dusty volume on the table.

'I'm so sorry,' Maddie said meekly. 'Girls, put them back in the packet,' but as soon as he'd shuffled out, she handed them out again. 'No crumbs, for goodness' sake,' she whispered. After all, the children weren't touching the newspapers and she had to keep them occupied somehow.

Maddie tucked a lock of hair behind her ear and turned to the new volume of newspapers. She quickly found the edition for Tuesday 10 November, the day after the reopening of the inquest, and turned the first page with feverish fingers. On the second page she glimpsed a headline and her heart missed a beat. 'Schoolgirl gun death possible unlawful killing.' She blinked, then leaned closer to read the long column of small print, passing quickly over the preliminaries before coming to the bit she wanted.

'... The shooting party, who were exterminating vermin following the harvest, comprised a dozen farm labourers and villagers as well as Mr Lyle Anderson, age 17, of Knyghton and his cousin Mr Philip Anderson, also 17. Various statements were read out. Both Mr Lyle Anderson and Mr Philip Anderson denied firing the fatal shot and it has proved impossible to discover which gun was responsible. It was alleged that both young men had been drinking and witnesses state that they'd been acting in a rowdy fashion. Nobody noticed the deceased's presence at the scene until she ran suddenly into the field shouting loudly. She was killed by a single bullet to the head. A police investigation has concluded that there are grounds of motivation for a charge of manslaughter to be made against Mr Philip Anderson. The case continues tomorrow.'

Maddie raised her head and stared sightlessly at the window, trying to accommodate what she'd read. 'Unlawful killing', 'grounds of motivation'. Why had the police settled on Philip rather than Lyle? And what had Flora been doing, rushing onto the field like that? She read the article quickly again and made a note of where she'd found it, then it was with her heart in her mouth that she turned the pages once more. On the front page of the next day's edition the following headline met her eye: 'Open verdict for death of schoolgirl.' Hurriedly she scanned the short article. One particular phrase stood out and she read it twice: '. . . insufficient evidence that Mr Philip Anderson had fired the fatal shot'.

'Oh, Philip, my love,' she whispered and sat back with eyes closed. She imagined his relief on learning the verdict, that he wasn't to be tried, then brought her hands to her face. Perhaps he hadn't been relieved, for the truth hadn't come out, whatever that truth was. She knew the simple facts of the case now, such as they were, how Flora had rushed onto the scene and been killed. Surely that could have been an accident, but even then, it was someone's fault. Flora's possibly, but the report of the inquest suggested that the fault was Lyle and Philip's, that they'd both been drunk, and also there had been animosity between them. What had they been quarrelling about and how had this affected their behaviour? None of the other witnesses, it seemed, had been sure.

'Can we go now, Mummy?' Sarah's plaintive voice cut through Maddie's thoughts.

She looked round and had to smile. The biscuits were all gone and while Grace wore the evidence of them round her mouth, Sarah held a pile of carefully collected crumbs in her palm.

'Yes, it's time to get some tea,' Maddie said, as she closed the volume and added it to the pile. Thank heavens for her daughters, who could pull her out of her darkest mood.

Twenty-eight

France

September 1940

It was a fine afternoon when Philip reached the outskirts of
Paris, his feet aching and blistered. It had taken him four days
from Rouen, walking most of the way on back roads, for his
experiences in the town had rattled him and he wanted to
minimize the risk of being challenged by a German patrol.
Maybe in Paris he could obtain fake papers and risk getting
on a train south.

He'd slept in outbuildings on the first two nights, but the
previous evening he'd dawdled till closing time at a village
bar and the proprietor had looked at him hard, then invited
him up to his apartment above the bar. After a good supper
there, recouping his strength and listening to the proprietor
speak of his fears for his parents in Belgium, Philip slept in an

armchair. The man wanted him to stay longer – he sensed his loneliness – but something about him made Philip uncomfortable and he left early the following morning. He felt bad at giving him a false account of where he was headed.

He'd walked quickly, but with a shambling gait, trying to look like a peasant, but by the time the sun was at its highest the only people he'd seen were working on the land. Occasionally he passed small farms, but he did not dare to knock on doors. At lunchtime everywhere was deserted and he had no trouble in stealing a bicycle left against a barn in a farmyard. On this he reached the outskirts of Paris late in the afternoon where he hid the bicycle behind some tumbledown garages, thinking he'd be less obvious if he proceeded on foot. But where he should go next he didn't quite know. He had no contacts and no idea where the American Embassy was. For a while he wandered about looking into the windows of small shops and plucking up courage to ask directions, but who could he trust among the passing strangers?

In the end he ventured into an empty bar in a rundown area and brought out the last of his money, guessing it would buy him toast, the cheapest item on the menu, but when he approached the counter and greeted the middle-aged *patronne* the woman looked at him with what he thought, at that moment of desperation, to be the kindest eyes he'd ever seen. And all of a sudden he found himself confessing his plight to her in stumbling French. At once, she bustled out from behind the counter, showed him to a secluded table and brought him a beer, followed by a piping hot plate of egg and chips, waving away his protestation of penury.

Other customers came in, local men, and Madame chatted with them cheerfully in a French too fast to follow. They glanced at Philip without interest and he tried to eat slowly, savouring the food and enjoying the moment of peace and warmth, wondering how long he'd be allowed to sit here and where he might spend the night. He was downing the dregs of another beer when the last customer left and Madame came to sit down opposite him. He tried to offer her the rest of his money towards the meal but she pushed the coins away with a *'Non, non.'*

'You may stay here tonight,' she said gently, and when he thanked her she patted his arm in a maternal fashion, then went to put up the shutters. He slept on a lumpy sofa in her shabby sitting room and left the next morning with a breakfast of warm rolls and coffee inside him, a few extra francs in his pocket and, best of all, a tattered map of the city with the American Embassy marked. He could not thank the woman enough as she waved him off, wishing him luck. Feeling more confident, he went to retrieve his stolen bicycle whistling to himself, but it had vanished. Someone must have seen him hide it, he thought, looking about. Paris, it seemed, was full of eyes and few of them friendly.

When he reached the Avenue Gabriel later that morning he identified the grand embassy building easily enough. A pair of German guards were milling outside the high wrought-iron railings and as he approached he realized that they were checking the papers of any who sought to enter. He would be detained straight away if he tried. His spirits sank. All he could do was to amble past, wondering what to do next.

For the next hour he walked the nearby streets, then bought a newspaper, which gave him the excuse to rest on a bench in a small park and smoke a cigarette without attracting the attention of soldiers ambling past, talking and laughing. Then, having no further plan, he walked back towards the Avenue Gabriel to see if his luck had changed.

It had. This time there was no sign of the soldiers. Perhaps they weren't official sentries. Still there was every possibility that they would be back. Taking his chance, Philip slipped in through the gates and entered the building. The receptionist on duty, a shortish balding American man, was welcoming and he was shown into an office where a handsome dark-haired woman greeted him in a no-nonsense fashion.

'I'm British, not American,' he confessed, 'but I'm begging you to help me.'

She cross-questioned him for some minutes, then hesitated, thinking, before opening a drawer in her desk. Bringing out a wad of French notes she counted some out and pushed them across to him. He'd be able to buy a train ticket to Marseilles and food for a few days, at least! Gratitude flooded through him, but what she said next filled him with horror. 'Listen, Englishman, you must beat it. Get out of Paris. They're arresting foreigners.'

He half rose, then paused. 'Can you let the authorities in London know that I'm safe? My family ... they'll be wondering.'

She shook her head sorrowfully. 'It's impossible. We believe our lines are tapped. And if we're found to be helping you ...' She turned up her palms in a desperate gesture.

'I understand.'

She stepped to the window and looked out. 'It's clear. You should go.'

He thanked her warmly and quickly left. As he walked away down the street, the wad of notes a comforting lump in the inside pocket of his jacket, he noticed a different pair of Nazi soldiers stride across the street towards the Embassy. When he turned the corner he glanced back and saw they'd taken up position outside its gates. He'd made it just in time.

'*Garçon. Excusez-moi!*'

Hearing the unmistakable arrogant tones of an upper-class British officer, Philip, who was sitting outside a café in the Latin Quarter trying to make his cup of coffee last, glanced across to the next table to see a fair-haired young man paying his bill. The man's beret was tipped at a stylish angle above his perfect profile, but his pale sensitive face was unshaven and his eyes red-rimmed. He noticed Philip looking and their eyes locked. Philip allowed his eyebrows to rise and gave the slightest of nods in the cool sign of recognition bred by upbringing and education. The man gave a quick glance about, then picked up his haversack. As he passed Philip's table, Philip whispered, '*Monsieur! Un moment.*'

The man paused, then drew out the chair opposite Philip and sat down. Philip checked, but the tables within listening distance were empty. There were no soldiers about. He offered a cigarette to his new acquaintance, who lit it with a monogrammed silver lighter and a debonair gesture. They swapped names and stories. Flight Lieutenant Simon

Winthorpe's plane had come down near Calais a few weeks before. He'd been in Paris for several days but was leaving for Marseilles that evening. Philip would be wise to do similar if he could get fake papers. Winthorpe did not volunteer details of his plans, but there was something rash about his manner, in addition to his obvious Englishness, that made Philip think he would be a dangerous companion.

Philip darted a quick look about. 'Do you know of somewhere safe in Paris?' he whispered. 'I've nowhere to stay.'

'There's nowhere truly safe, I should tell you that now.' Winthorpe's eyes narrowed as he flicked ash from his cigarette. Then he leaned forward and mentioned a particular street a few blocks away and pointed it out on Philip's map. 'There's an art gallery at the junction there.' Philip squinted at a tiny alley on the map. 'Ask for Monsieur Rambert. He and his wife are the owners. She's half American and let's just say I'm not the first British airman they've helped.'

Philip memorized the instructions then thanked him as he put the map away. His heart beat faster as a pair of German soldiers swaggered past them along the street, but they were deep in conversation and hardly glanced at the customers sitting in the late afternoon sunshine.

'I must leave,' Winthorpe whispered, once they'd gone. He stubbed out his cigarette and once more gathered up his bag.

'Wait! I'd be much obliged … I think you'll get home before me … will you let the top brass know that you saw me fit and well? And my wife, Maddie. Her address is 38 Valentine Street, West Kensington.'

'Of course I will do that,' Winthorpe promised with a charming smile.

'Thank you. And ... good luck.'

'Break a leg,' Winthorpe said casually, and set off, his upright figure and marching stride marking him as every inch an Englishman. Watching him, Philip wondered if Winthorpe would ever make it safely home.

He left some coins for his coffee and walked off in the direction Winthorpe had shown him to look for the art gallery in the Rue de Colbert. There he indeed found the Ramberts, a well-heeled middle-aged couple who listened to his account with concern and to his relief agreed to help him. They let him stay in a cluttered back bedroom for a week, long enough for a well-placed friend of theirs to furnish him with forged papers. They also showed him a map published in a newspaper that displayed the boundary between occupied and unoccupied zones in the new France – a black line that slashed the nation in two. The north and west coasts of the occupied part were also fenced off. Anyone would need special permission to go there. Once again it was underlined that the only way for Philip to return to England was to go south. And so it was as 'Bernard Lavisse', a demobbed French soldier, that Philip, after thanking the Ramberts profusely, took the Métro to the Gare de Lyon and booked a seat on a train to Marseilles.

Twenty-nine

Norfolk

August 1941

'This letter was on the doormat.'

Maddie had found Lyle in the kitchen garden as the evening was turning to twilight. He'd gone out there after supper to check on the hens – Flegg said a fox had been trying to get in and they needed new netting for the enclosure – but half an hour later he hadn't returned. She left the house to give him the letter and glimpsed the orange glow of his cigarette beyond the arch. He was sitting on a low wall, apparently deep in thought, but greeted her with a smile.

'Thank you.' He took the letter from her, perused the handwriting on the front, frowned, then slid it unopened into his jacket pocket.

'May I join you?'

'Of course.'

Maddie sat down next to him, hugging herself against the coolness of the evening. 'I have to talk to you,' she said.

'About what?' He sounded suspicious.

'I visited the newspaper archive in Norwich this afternoon. I wanted to read about the inquest.'

'So that's why you were asking. You might have said.'

'I thought you'd be angry.'

'Why, Maddie? Why did you think that?'

'You sound angry now.'

'I'm not angry. Put out, perhaps. You've got a bee in your bonnet about what happened. It was years and years ago, Maddie. Done and dusted. Forget it.'

'I can't. Not if my husband was involved.'

Lyle sighed. 'And what did you find out? As I told you, neither of us attended the inquest. We were told we didn't have to. Frankly, I wanted to put the whole thing behind us. It was a tragedy, but that's all it was. Nothing criminal.'

'But you still didn't know exactly what happened.'

'Not for certain. I went over and over it, but it's hazy. One moment I saw Flora out of the corner of my eye, running towards us. The next, she fell.'

'Why was she running?'

'She was soft-hearted, Flora was. I suppose she found the shooting of small animals repulsive. Even when they were vermin.'

'Mice and rabbits and hares?'

'And rats. There were lots of rats. They get into the barns and ruin the grain.'

'You've made your point.'

'You don't approve either. Bloody hell, this is a farm, Maddie. It's what happens. We farmers can't afford to be sentimental.' Lyle finished his cigarette and ground the stub under the sole of his shoe.

'And that was the reason she was distressed?'

'I don't know, but I've always assumed it.'

'And Philip, why did the police focus on Philip?'

'I simply don't know, Maddie. Philip would never have done anything to harm Flora. He was too fond of her for that.'

What made her heart duck and dive? She laid her hands on the wall and the rough warmth of the brick steadied her. When she looked up next, Lyle was watching her thoughtfully.

'So you see, there's nothing for you to concern yourself with.'

There is, she wanted to say. *Why does Flora seem to haunt me so that I draw her and feel her presence. What is she trying to tell me?*

Instead she licked her dry lips and nodded slowly. Lyle sounded so rational, so sensible compared to her.

He smiled. 'You're cold, you should go in. I promised Gussie I'd play cards later. Will you join us? It's jollier with three.'

'Would you mind if I said no? It's been a tiring day and we've the harvest supper to prepare tomorrow. I think I'll turn in early.'

'If you will.'

Maddie went ahead of him towards the house, but when

she reached the kitchen door and glanced back she saw him standing framed by the arch to the kitchen garden, reading the letter she'd given him in the dying light. His face was in shadow so she couldn't see his expression, but as she watched he folded the letter away and lit another cigarette.

Later, as she put on her pyjamas, Maddie caught sight of herself in the wardrobe mirror. The candlelight softened her skin and made her eyes shine, but it also emphasized the hollows under her eyes. She stared at herself for a moment, thinking how much she'd changed since Philip had gone. Sorrow and worry had left its marks. She was no longer the shy gentle girl that he'd married. She'd thought that coming to Knyghton would be an escape from the war, that it would be a place where she and the girls could feel safe while they waited for Philip to come home. They'd escaped the worst of the bombs, it was true, though they could hear them fall on Norwich and the coastal towns, but there were other ways now in which they were in danger and if the dangers were hidden, they were no less menacing. She brushed her hair, the sound as soft as sighs in the quiet of the room, the rhythm of it calming, and thought of Tilly the maid brushing her mistress, Eleanor's, hair here, many years ago. Poor Tilly, what must have it been like for her to feel the child moving in her belly and to fear for her future?

The secrets that hung over Knyghton affected them all, but here was the closest she could feel to Philip and there were frequent moments when she felt she belonged. The purity of the light coming through the window when she worked, the view of the drive with all its coming and goings, these were all a part of her now. The people, too, poor confused Gussie and her dogs, Lyle's unhappy brooding presence as he trudged about doing his duty by Knyghton and his forebears, the good honest Fleggs keeping everything going because they, too, had put down their roots in Knyghton and would guard its secrets to the end.

As she laid the hairbrush on the dressing table Maddie smiled at her own sentimentality. The Fleggs had their own lives apart from the Andersons. What did she know of what they thought about their employers, or of their private joys and sorrows? As little as she knew of her stepmother Monica, she thought, remembering today's visit, or of Christine Sutton's lonely life.

There may be unease about the Andersons of Knyghton in the village, but Maddie and the girls were Andersons by blood or marriage and the villagers were getting used to them. She was friendly with the rector and his wife and with Anna, their lodger. The librarian always chatted to her when she exchanged her books and even the grocer's dour wife cheered up on seeing Grace.

She set a glass of water by the bed and climbed under the bedclothes, delighting in the cool softness of linen sheets. But after she blew out the candle and lay back in the darkness she heard Lyle's laughter from somewhere downstairs and remembering their conversation that evening, the doubts began to flood in.

Thirty

It was a scanty, wartime version of a harvest supper, an early evening affair in Knyghton's hay barn, where everyone brought their own food and the several farmers involved supplied beer. Maddie, who'd been helping Mrs Flegg prepare roast chicken, bread rolls and potato salad, took the girls with her when she walked down with the heavy basket. Lyle, Susie and two of Lyle's own land girls were already there. They had cleared the space, erected trestle tables and now Lyle was up a ladder looping bunting round a beam. Robert, the old horseman, was tuning his fiddle ready for the dancing. Maddie knew that several dozen labourers were expected, as well as extras like herself.

'The ARP warden's been along,' Lyle confided to Maddie as he descended the ladder with a twinkle in his eye. 'He's not happy. Last year's effort became a wee bit rowdy. We've had to promise him faithfully that it will finish before dark, then to make sure everyone goes straight home in an orderly fashion.'

'Tha' "straight" part's a good 'un,' Robert mumbled above his fiddle. 'After all tha' beer.'

Everyone was gathering now. Maddie found herself sitting next to Susie, with the little girls together on her other side on the high bench and staring shyly around at the noisy throng, the men sunburned, the women all in pretty dresses. They were the only children. Lyle joined them opposite, sharing round chunks of the roast chicken and exchanging merry conversation with the land girls on each side of him, who ate hungrily, but being nice well-brought-up types, went carefully with the beer. He was doing his best to be a good host, Maddie noted, but thinking of his mood the evening before she wondered if it was an act.

Susie, next to her, was her usual talkative self, her lively face framed by the scarlet scarf tied in her fair hair.

'You should have come in normal times,' she said, her eyes bright. 'We'd have a splendid do. A big ham and fresh white bread and butter, fruit tarts and cake and dancing late into the night. Lyle's good to do this, of course ... He's never liked it since ... that awful year.'

Maddie glanced over at Lyle. He was laughing at some story one of the labourers was telling. She asked Susie in a low voice, 'Were you there when it happened?'

Susie shook her head. 'No, thank God. And there was no harvest supper that evening.'

'I should think not.'

'Everyone was devastated. The Anderson boys, it changed them both. Of course, you wouldn't have known what Philip was like before, would you?'

Her tone was taunting, and suddenly Maddie didn't want to hear any more. Seeking diversion, she looked round the table. 'I thought your father might be here.'

'Maybe later. He's not feeling sociable. I must say, the grub's pretty decent, considering.' Susie turned her attention to eating. Every now and then she shot Lyle quick glances, but he hardly looked back at her and Maddie wondered if they'd fallen out again.

Instead, at one point, his eyes locked with Maddie's and she read such misery in his face that she had difficulty swallowing her food. Something was badly wrong and she did not know what it could be. So much had piled on top of him recently, problems with the farm, whatever his relationship was with Susie, her own probing of his past. Susie was now chatting to a thin, studious young man from the Welbournes' farm, who sat across the table and looked out of place among the lusty locals, but who hung onto Susie's every word.

The meal was over, though the beer was still being passed round, and the old horseman rose and began to play. Grace was burrowing sleepily into Maddie's lap. It was time to take the girls home to bed. Sarah wanted to stay, but Maddie insisted. They walked slowly back with the basket of empty dishes, the sound of voices and the merry tones of the violin following them all the way, fainter and fainter still. Then there was only the tranquil birdsong of the garden of Knyghton and then the silence of the house.

Why, Maddie thought as she left the girls with Gussie in the drawing room and took the basket to the kitchen, *did it feel like the calm before a storm?*

Thirty-one

One Sunday later in August there was a different celebration of the harvest – a service at Monksfield church. Lyle surprised Maddie by agreeing to attend and drove them in the trap along with a basket containing a plaited loaf made by Mrs Flegg with Knyghton wheat, as was the tradition.

The small church was full of people and the girls' eyes were large with wonder to see the displays of fruit, flowers and stooks of wheat that decorated every available space. Posies of wild flowers adorned the pew ends. Maddie went up with the girls before the service to present the loaf, which the rector's wife laid in pride of place at the altar. As they returned to their pew Maddie spotted Anna sitting with Nadya and Milo two rows in front and they exchanged smiles. Back in the pew, she bent to hear Sarah whisper: 'Who is all the food for?'

'People who are poor, I expect,' she replied vaguely.

The organ music ceased. 'Are we poor?' Sarah said into the sudden silence.

People's heads snapped round and Maddie's face burned. 'Shh, Sarah, goodness, no. Whatever makes you think that?'

At her mother's sharp tone, Sarah looked down at her shoes, and didn't answer. Lyle, next to them, was trying not to laugh. Now the rector was announcing the first hymn and everyone scrambled to their feet. 'We plough the fields and scatter ...' Maddie heard Lyle's fine tenor voice for the first time, met his eye and smiled, and for a moment a bolt of something passed between them and forgetting the moment's embarrassment she felt suddenly happy. For the first time in her life the service really meant something for she'd witnessed the ripening of the grain, the hopes and fears about the weather, had known the relief when the harvest was brought safely in.

After the hymn ended, the rector spoke. 'We'd like to thank everyone for these wonderful gifts. They show how generous we can be even at a time when we have little to share.' And he named a couple of local charities that would be distributing the food and Maddie was pleased to have an answer to Sarah's first question. The second one still troubled her, though. *Are we poor?* It was the rush of shame she'd felt at the very idea that they could be poor that shocked Maddie most. It was true that with a widow's pension on top of her tiny earnings she had very little money, but they were not in need at Knyghton. Though how long they would continue to be welcome there she did not know. Then what? Her thoughts trailed on during the sermon, and before long the congregation was rising to its feet again to sing and she realized she hadn't heard a word.

After the service they filed out into the churchyard. 'Maddie, it is good to see you!' Maddie turned to see Anna, clutching her son's hand as people flowed round them. Grace jumped up and down in excitement, while Milo gazed solemnly at her. Sarah and Nadya smiled shyly at one another.

'Is that Mr Anderson with you?' Anna whispered.

'It is.'

Lyle was exchanging niceties with the rector, but when he joined them she introduced him to Anna.

'Maddie often speaks about you,' he said, politely shaking her hand. 'And this young man is . . .'

'Milo.'

Lyle put out his hand. 'Hello, Milo.'

'Shake Mr Anderson's hand, Milo,' Anna cajoled, but the boy would not.

'I'm sorry.' Anna's gaze was direct, appealing.

'Don't be,' Lyle said sincerely. 'I'm a complete stranger to him.'

'I want him to learn good manners.' She pressed the boy to her tenderly and he looked up at Lyle with wide solemn eyes. Lyle smiled down at him and Maddie was struck by his gentleness.

They said their goodbyes. 'You must all come to Knyghton,' Lyle said.

'Yes, Grace would love to play with Milo, wouldn't you, Grace?'

Grace nodded.

'And Nadya and Sarah get on so well,' Anna added.

Out on the street, Lyle handed the girls up into the back of the trap, but when it was Maddie's turn she hesitated. 'I can manage.' But he gripped her hand and she was aware of its warm roughness and when he loosened his grip she felt its loss.

That evening she sat between the girls on Sarah's bed to read from a book of fairytales that she'd found in the toy cupboard, taking care to miss out Red Riding Hood for fear of nightmares. Cinderella was a favourite because of the illustration of the pumpkin which Cinders' fairy godmother had turned into the most imaginative-looking coach, driven by a mouse in a tricorn hat and pulled by prancing rat horses. 'Was Cinders poor?' she asked Sarah, thinking about what she'd said in church and Sarah nodded. 'But she has somewhere to live and food to eat,' Maddie countered.

'They treat her like their slave and don't give her any money and she only has rags to wear and she's not allowed to do anything except what they tell her to.'

'That's all true. She's not free, is she?' Maddie sighed. She closed the book and put her arms round the girls, wondering whether you needed to have money to exercise your freedom. 'What made you think we're poor?' she went on, determined to get to the bottom of Sarah's concern.

'I don't know.'

'I told her,' Grace said sleepily. 'Nanny Sutton said it.'

Maddie felt a prickle of unease. 'Nanny Sutton said that we were poor?'

'She said we are poor girls.'

'Did she now,' Maddie said thoughtfully, 'but did she mean you had no money – that kind of poor, or was it that she felt sorry for you?'

'I don't know.' Grace sounded cross. 'She was telling a man.'

'A man? Who?' Maddie's skin prickled. 'Someone who came here?'

Discerning Maddie's anxiety, Grace would say no more. Instead she curled up with her rabbit and pretended to be asleep.

'We aren't poor, darlings, we are safe here at Knyghton and have enough of everything,' Maddie whispered to them. 'You're not to worry. Think of the lovely things we have, all the blessings.'

But as she tucked them up in their beds, she could not dispel her unease. What did Christine mean when she'd said that they were 'poor girls' and who was the man she'd been talking to in such a disloyal fashion?

In the end, she tackled Christine about it the following morning, having sent Grace to ask Gussie whether they could borrow one of the dogs for a walk.

'Could I clear up a mystery?' Maddie asked and told her what Grace had said. 'It's only because the girls seemed disturbed by it. Who was the visitor you were talking to and what did you mean?'

Christine's face reddened. 'Goodness,' she said, 'I didn't mean to offend anybody. A gentleman friend of mine called by as he was up this way.' Maddie's eyebrows shot up. 'I don't remember exactly what we said,' Christine went on, 'but Grace must have misheard me.'

This seemed a reasonable explanation, but there was something that was too smooth about Christine's reply. And it was plain Christine had a follower. Well, why shouldn't she?

'I see,' was all Maddie said. 'I hope you don't mind, but I'd prefer it if your friend didn't come to the house. We don't know him, you see.'

'He didn't mean any harm, Mrs Anderson.' Christine looked alarmed.

'Of course not. But still . . . I'd prefer it if he didn't.'

'All right, I'll tell him,' she said, sullen.

As Maddie slowly mounted the stairs to begin work, she realized something uncomfortable, something she'd known for ages, but had never admitted to herself before. It was that she didn't like Christine Sutton very much.

She knew her to be safe and reliable with Grace and had overlooked other considerations because those were surely the important things about a minder for her child, besides which Christine had been the only person to reply to her advertisement. She'd supplied good references, and she'd been so generous to Grace, bringing her little gifts. And apart from the episode with the ants' nest early on, Grace appeared to like Christine. But perhaps, safe and reliable and generous were not enough. Christine had spoken insensitively about the matter of Grace's invisible friend. She did not appear to appreciate the three-year-old's whimsical side, thinking it 'odd'. And now, worst of all, Maddie suspected Christine of lying to her when she denied referring to Sarah and Grace as 'poor little girls'.

Maddie sat down at her desk, thinking miserably about it all. She supposed she'd have to do something, but what? Perhaps she should tell Christine she couldn't afford to pay her any more – there was certainly some truth in that – but then she herself wouldn't be able to work at all. She'd have to monitor the situation, she decided eventually as she sharpened a pencil, brushing the shavings into the waste paper basket. Then she opened her sketchbook and began to draw freehand, the first thing that came into her head. It was a man's face at three-quarters view, square-jawed with deepset eyes looking off into the distance and a lock of hair falling across his forehead. The tragic expression was exaggerated, she thought as she perused it, but otherwise it was a fair evocation of Lyle.

Thirty-two

Late that morning Maddie had put the finishing touches to the last of her animal pictures and was sitting happily looking over them all. She felt pleased with her work and full of hope that her editor would like them, too. She was wondering what he might commission her to do next when a squeaking noise outside made her look up. Their postwoman, the vampish Miss Quayle, sailed up the drive on her bicycle and a moment later Maddie heard the sonorous clang of the doorbell. As no one else went to answer it, she pushed back her chair and hurried downstairs.

'I'm afraid it's for you, Mrs Anderson,' Miss Quayle declared in her husky voice, holding out an orange envelope in her long-nailed fingers. 'Not good news, I'm sorry to say. I was there when it came through, and I said to the postmistress, that poor Mrs Anderson has had her share of bad news.'

Maddie stared fearfully at the telegram, hardly caring that the nature of its contents was probably all round Monksfield by now, then snatched it from Miss Quayle's talons and shut the door. *Philip. It had to be about Philip. Suppose . . .* She tore it open, read the contents quickly and let out a long sigh. *Not Philip.* But something else dreadful. Her father was dead. She stood very still, absorbing the shock. It was hardly unexpected but now that it had happened, she felt numb. Slowly, carefully, she returned upstairs, went to her room and lay down on her bed, her eyes open but unseeing, hugging the pillow for comfort. No thoughts of any kind crossed her mind, but after a few minutes she sat up again and reread her stepmother's message. She'd better go and telephone her straight away.

The funeral, organized efficiently by Monica for three days' time, was a modest affair. The girls were not invited, so it was only Maddie and Monica who followed the coffin down the aisle of the church where Maddie and Philip had been married, then sat together with heads bowed in the front pew as the vicar spoke of the dead man's admirable sense of duty and his stoicism during his final illness. The chink of tenderness that Monica had earlier revealed had sealed up again. Maddie sensed that her stepmother had arranged the order of service some time in advance of her husband's death. Nothing had been required of Maddie other than to read aloud the familiar Bible passage from Corinthians about the power of love – which she managed to do dry-eyed. As the final words rang out in the echoing stillness and she glanced across the meagre huddle of her father's acquaintances gathered there she wondered which of them had loved her father apart from herself – and Monica, of course, in her funny way.

Later, Maddie stood by the open grave in Earlham Cemetery and watched the coffin being laid to rest next to her mother's. Quite where Monica would go when her time came had never been mentioned and Maddie gave a little shiver to think of her father lying there till the Resurrection, flanked by both his wives. There is no giving or taking of marriage in heaven, the Bible said. It was probably for the good. She berated herself for her irreverent thoughts. It was as the vicar pronounced the final prayers and first Monica, then Maddie herself came forward to cast earth into the grave that her eyes filled with tears. She'd not been close to her father, but he was all that she'd had and she knew that he'd loved her.

As the handful of mourners trailed back to the line of waiting vehicles that would take them to a hotel for sherry and sandwiches, it began to rain.

'He left me what the solicitor calls a modest annuity,' Maddie explained to Lyle that evening. They were sitting in the drawing room after supper. Gussie was playing patience at the lacquered table near the crackling fire and exclaiming as the cards revealed themselves. 'It's a relief to have something. Everything else has passed to my stepmother, but on her death anything left will be mine.'

'It doesn't sound fair to you and the girls. You need the money now.'

'The will was drawn up before Philip ... went missing, Lyle, so my father had no reason to think we'd be in need. Nevertheless, I'm not planning to challenge it.'

'I didn't say you were.'

'It would have been useful, though ...' She stopped and bit at a hangnail. 'Yes, well. Monica has to have something to live on. She's only fifty-three.' She sighed.

'Philip's mother died at fifty-three,' Gussie put in to Maddie's surprise. She didn't realize that the old lady was listening. Gussie gathered up her cards, shuffled them and started laying them out again with the air of a fortune teller. She had been stranger than ever lately, more withdrawn, closer still to the dogs, which lay asleep on the floor around her.

'I wish I'd met Philip's parents,' Maddie murmured. 'but I never had the chance.' The Rose Anderson she'd discovered through her letters to her son had been warm and tender. How then could she have left little Philip at Knyghton while she returned to India thousands of miles away? It seemed so cruel. It was what women had to do, but thank goodness she'd never had to be separated from Sarah and Grace. Having lost her mother herself and known how it felt, perhaps she would have stood firm against the idea. She'd like to think so.

She surfaced from her thoughts to see that Lyle was watching her, a concerned expression in his eyes, and she smiled sadly at him. He rose and went to the window. It was still light outside. One of the dogs got up and followed, looking up at him expectantly.

'You want to go out, Jane?' he said, then asked Maddie. 'How about we stretch our legs for a bit?'

Maddie nodded and put down her mending. A walk would be pleasant.

'Is it all right if we take her?' she asked Gussie, who nodded. 'What about the others?'

The other dogs did not respond to Lyle's soft whistle, so it was just Jane who bounded ahead of them out of the back door and across the garden, where the long shadows of the trees threw patterns across the grass. A calm August evening, still warm, the sky streaked with pink, the air heavy with earthy scents. A blackbird called warning notes. Jane darted eagerly in and out of the undergrowth, reading the language of a hundred delicious smells, her stump of a tail wagging in ecstasy.

Under the trees Maddie stumbled on a root. Lyle stayed her and she linked her arm in his as though it was the most natural thing in the world. They continued in companionable silence over the loamy earth to the path down to the farm.

'I was going to say it's so wonderfully quiet here,' she shouted, as a fleet of Lancasters roared overhead, making them stop their ears.

As the sound died away they became aware of other noises carrying to them distantly on the evening air – dogs barking, shouts, a whistle. As they approached the farm the noises grew louder. 'Bloody hell,' Lyle muttered, dropping Maddie's arm suddenly and breaking into a run. Jane followed hot on his heels.

'What is it?' Maddie shouted in panic.

He called back to her, but his words were lost to a flurry of urgent barks that came from the field behind the hedge, then came the most awful sound she'd ever heard – a high-pitched, animal scream – and she ran after Lyle. He disappeared through a gap in the hedge, Jane bounding after, then she reached it a moment later in time to hear him shout, 'What the devil are you doing?'

A horrible scene met her eyes. Lyle was striding over the recently harvested field to where three rough-looking men, one bearing a sack, shouted commands to a small pack of hounds that were tearing at something dead and streaked with scarlet on the ground. A movement in the distance drew her eye. It was a hare zigzagging away across the stubble.

The Jack Russell sped towards the hounds. 'Jane. Here,' Lyle cried, but she ignored him and launched herself in among the slavering dogs with her tail wagging.

'Lyle, stop her,' Maddie shouted, but it was too late. As one the hounds turned on the newcomer, snapping and snarling. 'Oh, Lyle, no.'

The men stared at the carnage, stupefied. 'Get them off her, will you?' Lyle yelled, and as slowly as in a bad dream the man with the sack lumbered into action.

Lyle reached the dogs first and managed to seize Jane by the collar with Maddie crying, 'No, no!' He swung her high above the hounds' heads, a struggling white and brown ball spattered with red. Maddie screamed again, then saw Lyle had the dog cradled safe in his arms. The man with the sack swept the dead hare into it while the others called the hounds to heel.

'Get off my land,' Lyle shouted.

'Only a bit of harmless coursing, squire. Is the littl'un there all right?' said one of the men.

'If she is it's a miracle.'

Jane lay quivering in Lyle's arms. Maddie found a handker-chief and dabbed at the blood on the dog's side, murmuring soothing words. There was no wound there that she could see. Her ear was torn, though, and would need stitching. 'Jane, oh, poor Jane.' The hounds bounded about, tails waving, or sniffed at the ground, but their blood madness was ebbing and soon, one by one, they quietened and lay down, panting, surveying the scene with good humour.

The man with the sack hoisted it over his shoulder and set off across the field towards the road. The dogs leaped up and trotted after him.

'We're very sorry,' one of the other men muttered.

'I know you, you're one of Welbourne's men, aren't you?' Lyle's tones were more measured now.

'That's right, squire. We didn't think anyone would mind, a couple of hares for the pot.'

'It's cruel what you're doing.' Maddie's voice wobbled. 'A terrible way for an animal to die.'

The man eyed her dispassionately, but said nothing.

'Leave it to me, please,' Lyle told her firmly, then he said to the labourer, 'Your dogs were out of control. Not on my land, all right?'

The man nodded and began to walk away. The third man, who'd watched silently all this time, tipped his cap to Lyle and followed, whistling to himself.

'Poor old Jane,' Maddie whispered, stroking the trembling animal. 'Gussie would have been heartbroken if we'd lost her.'

'Here, you hold her,' Lyle said, his eyes cold, and Maddie

took Jane from him and cuddled her close. She could feel the dog's heart pounding as she hurried after Lyle's striding figure out of the field and back up the lane towards the house. Jane began to struggle, so Maddie set her down, anxious about her injuries, but the dog scampered along happily enough, though instead of running back and forth following scents this time she kept close. Lyle walked in silence, slightly ahead, and Maddie sensed that she'd done something wrong. Her resentment grew.

After a minute or two, Lyle stopped for her to catch up and she saw with relief that his eyes were warm again and that he was trying to be kind.

'You mustn't interfere like that. Those men, they're entitled to a hare or two for the table. They don't get paid much, you know.'

'But it's savage the way they catch them. You heard it scream.'

'It's unpleasant, I agree, but it's over in a moment.' He looked hard at her. 'I did my best for you. They won't forgive me for turning them off my field.'

'It wasn't for me,' she said, confused now, 'it was for the hare. And what about poor Jane?'

'If Gussie trained her dogs properly it would never have happened.' He glanced down at Jane, who was trotting at their heels. 'I'll stitch her ear myself. Hardly worth calling out the vet.'

'Can you do that? Won't it hurt her?'

'I can, and no, not much.'

*

Gussie, as predicted, gasped in distress when Maddie entered the gloomy sitting room carrying her beloved Jane, now wrapped in an old towel, just her muzzle peeping out.

'She's had ... an accident, but it's not as bad as it looks,' Maddie soothed, sitting on the sofa beside the old lady and lifting the dog onto Gussie's lap. 'Lyle's looking for his surgical kit.' While she went to light a lamp for him she explained briefly what had happened. Gussie looked appalled.

'I hate it when they hunt the hares. Such beautiful animals that harm nobody.'

'But you eat one when Mrs Flegg serves it up to you,' Lyle remarked, closing the door behind him. He'd brought with him a bowl of water and a small leather case, which he laid on the lacquer coffee table.

'Mrs Flegg never serves hare!' Gussie said, looking shocked.

'She certainly does.' Lyle grinned as he threaded a needle and proceeded to stitch up Jane's ripped ear with nimble fingers while Maddie positioned the lamp and Gussie held the patient down. Jane gave little whines of distress and the other dogs watched with interest. A generous daub of surgical spirit and it was done.

'What a brave girl,' Gussie said, feeding Jane a mint imperial which she crunched up with messy enjoyment.

'You'll have to stop her scratching the wound, or the others licking it,' Lyle said, putting everything away.

'I'll take her into bed with me tonight,' Gussie declared, hugging Jane so tightly that she struggled to escape. 'You'll all be jealous, darlings, yes, you will, but you'll just have to stay on the floor, won't you?'

Lyle and Maddie caught each other's eye and Maddie suppressed a smile. Lyle merely looked grim. It was growing dark outside. 'Drama over,' he said. 'Now I suppose we must put up the blackout.'

'I'll help.' Maddie rose, plucking a stray cotton wool swab from the rug as she followed him out into the hall where the lamplight cast them both in a golden glow. Lyle brought the framed blackout out of a cupboard and mounting the stairs, raised it across the tall window, where Maddie held it in place while he secured the fastenings. Downstairs again, they went from room to room drawing the curtains, then he held the baize door open for her and she could not help her arm brushing his hand as she passed through to the kitchen.

Maddie set the lamp in the centre of the table and handed Lyle a jug. 'If you'll fetch some milk I'll warm it.'

He lit a candle and went to the dairy while Maddie set out three cups. The stove was still hot and together they stood watching the milk shimmer in the pan as the lamp cast its intimate glow.

She was intensely aware of him close to her and glanced up and smiled. He smiled back tentatively and his eyes glinted. She swallowed and looked away, busying herself by refolding a tea towel on the rail of the stove. Very slowly, he put out his hand and touched hers where it rested on the rail and a rush of warmth surged through her. For a very long time nothing happened, then gradually his fingers curled around hers and she let them rest there. He drew a long breath and sighed and she turned towards him, her pulse pounding in her ears. He reached with his other hand and caressed her cheek and she made a small noise like a sob and rested her face against his palm. Then, with a soft rustle of cloth, he drew her towards him and she was in his arms and he kissed her softly, first her cheek, the tip of her nose and then her lips found his and they kissed, small nibbling kisses at first, then deeper, more searching, and she leaned into him, his arms tightening around her waist.

'Hang on ... the milk,' she breathed. He reached past her and moved the pan off the heat, then returned to kissing her once more. And now his lips were on her neck, her hair and his hands moving down her back to press her against his hardness and her body took over, she was melting into him and he was murmuring her name. It had been such a long time, she missed Philip so much, but Lyle wasn't like Philip, it didn't feel the same. Suddenly she felt ashamed.

She stiffened in Lyle's arms, but he seemed not to notice for he began to kiss her more deeply.

'Lyle, no, I can't.' She turned her head only for him to bury his face into the curve of her neck and fiddle with the top button of her blouse. 'Lyle, please.'

Finally she got him to understand for he released her and she stepped back and for a moment they looked at one another, tousled and out of breath.

'I'm so sorry,' she whispered, tucking back a lock of her hair. Her skin smarted from his kisses, the rub of his unshaven jaw. His eyes were wild, his face glowed with passion.

'What is it?' he rasped.

'I don't know, but ... it feels wrong.'

'Wrong how?'

'I don't know, I don't know. Philip ... We'd better take Gussie her milk.' Maddie eyed its wrinkled skin with distaste and reached for a spoon to skim it, then returned the pan to the hot plate and glanced up. Lyle was leaning against the dresser with arms folded, watching her with eyes full of misery. Maddie could think of nothing to say. When the milk began to steam she lifted the pan and shared it between the three cups.

He followed her upstairs where they found Gussie dozing on the sofa with Jane curled up asleep beside her. The old lady stirred when Lyle picked up the poker and prodded the embers of the fire. 'Isn't there any cocoa?' she asked, confused, when Maddie set the cup of milk on the table before her.

'You know there isn't, Gussie,' Lyle growled. 'Drink it up, it's good for you and it'll help you sleep.'

Gussie lifted the cup to her lips obediently. They were lucky to have plenty of milk, Maddie reminded herself as she forced herself to sip the warm sweetness, wondering whether it was not a little sour. She had rarely drunk milk before the war, but tonight it was part of this horrible evening, like a punishment. Suddenly she longed to be by herself.

'I'm going to bed, if you don't mind,' she said, taking up her cup.

Lyle nodded, then reached for a candlestick from the mantelpiece, lighting its wick in the flames. As he handed it to her, he would not meet her eye, merely returning her 'Goodnight'.

'I hope you and Jane are all right, Gussie,' she murmured. 'I'm so sorry about what happened. Come and wake me if you need help in the night.'

'Jane will be comfortable if she's in bed with me,' Gussie replied. 'But thank you, dear, for saving her from the nasty dogs.' Maddie saw her glance up at the picture above the fireplace, where the shape of the painted hare was just visible. 'Trouble always comes with killing hares. Remember that, Lyle. It's happened before with Flora.'

Lyle made a choking noise.

'Don't laugh, it's true.' In the leaping shadows of the room, Gussie's eyes glittered.

A witch they'd called her, Sarah's schoolmates. Of course that was nonsense, Gussie was a harmless old lady, a bit batty, maybe. But at that moment Maddie thought she sounded very witchlike indeed.

Upstairs, she readied herself for bed, her limbs heavy with sadness. As she slowly cleaned her teeth she had to stop for tears threatened. She dropped the brush into its glass and sought the bed, burrowing her face into the pillow. Too much had happened tonight. There was so much grief, she felt saturated with it. The shock of the violence and Lyle's anger with her earlier and then the ardency of his passion had broken something in her. And now she wept in earnest, wept for Philip, whom she had loved more than she had ever realized and whom she might never see again, and for her father, who had been so hard to love. Finally she wept for her daughters, so fragile, and for herself, lost, so lost and afraid. *Pull yourself together, Maddie, you're all they have.* But for once she couldn't. She was all played out.

A soft tapping sound broke through her sobs. She quietened and raised her head.

'Maddie,' came Lyle's urgent voice through the door. 'Are you all right?'

'Yes,' she whispered, then louder, 'Yes, of course. Go to bed, Lyle, I'm fine.'

'I wanted . . .'

'Leave me alone.' The words tore out of her. 'I'm sorry. I can't do it.'

'Maddie . . .' he started to say.

'Go away.' She heard a sigh, then the sound of his footsteps retreating down the stairs. After that she lay quietly awake for a long while, thinking how wrong everything felt. She did not love Lyle and it was certainly too soon for her to imagine being with anyone but Philip and yet still her body longed for him. No, she would not. That path would lead to unhappiness and confusion. She had to stop it now, put him back in his place or she and the girls would have to leave. Tomorrow she'd explain, when she felt calmer.

She heard Gussie crooning to the dogs as she shuffled past on the way to her room and the tick of their nails on the floorboards. Later, Lyle's measured footsteps. She heard him pause outside her door and held her breath, praying that he would not try to come in. Thank heavens, there was the sound of his own door closing and soon afterwards the only noises were the cries of owls hunting small creatures under the moon. And finally, she curled into a protective ball and slept.

Thirty-three

Maddie woke from a nightmare to pitch darkness, her skin clammy with sweat. She pushed back the blankets and for a while lay still, trying to forget her dream. The air was tense, heavy, as thick as black treacle and she smelled an acrid odour, slight at first, but – she sniffed it – getting stronger. She pushed herself up. Something was wrong, she was suddenly sure. She climbed out of bed, snatched her dressing gown from a chair and opened the door. A surge of smoke made her eyes prickle.

'Fire!' Her voice croaked. 'The house is on fire.' She coughed and covered her eyes with her arm. The children! She rushed through the smoke to hammer on Lyle's door, then without waiting for an answer staggered into the nursery, stumbling over a chair as she rushed to the windows and fumbled at the curtains. Moonlight flooded in. She threw open a casement, gasped in the fresh air then ran to the beds. The girls lay striped with silver, deep in slumber.

'Sarah, wake up! Come on now!' Sarah muttered something and wriggled away from her hand. Maddie seized her and dragged her from the bed. 'Grace!' The child was curled in a ball, as solid as a large snail, clutching her rabbit. Maddie snatched her up just as Sarah fell back into bed. 'No!'

Then Lyle was there, lifting Sarah as though he might a newborn lamb, and leading the way back to the landing. The dogs were barking behind Gussie's door, harsh frightened yaps.

'Gussie!' She whispered to Lyle as they set off down the stairs.

'I've banged on her door.' His voice ended in a cough. 'Let's go. I'll come back for her.'

They felt their way down along the banister in thick smoky darkness, Maddie pressing Grace's face to her breast and almost tumbling down the last few steps. Sarah was moaning in the hall as Lyle fiddled with the lock then the door creaked open and they stumbled out into the blessed night air.

'Take them well away,' Lyle's voice barked at Maddie as he staggered back into the house and she dragged the sobbing girls across to a bench at the edge of the lawn where she sat them down, tore off her dressing gown and wrapped them in it. Shivering with cold and shock, she looked back to the house in time to see the dogs run out of the door sneezing and coughing. She waited expectantly for Lyle and Gussie, but no one came. Phoebe spotted Maddie and bobbed across the grass towards her, but the others made little darts back into the house, their miserable yaps reaching Maddie across the quiet of the garden. What was happening?

'Don't you dare move,' she instructed the girls, wagging her finger, and flew back to the house, her bare feet chilled by the grass then cut by the gravel. She covered her mouth with her forearm and peered into the swirling darkness of the hall.

'Lyle?' she croaked, but there was no answer. There was no sign of flames, just coils of smoke that billowed out of the house to be taken away by the breeze.

'Maddie.' The sound came from behind her and she whipped round to see Lyle. He was half carrying, half dragging a dishevelled figure in a pale-coloured night gown streaked with smuts. Gussie's hair hung in grey rats' tails about her shoulders. Her expression was bewildered and her eyes rheumy. The dogs rushed around her whining, but she seemed not to notice. She shook off Lyle's arm and stared at Maddie, her mouth working.

'Are you all right?' Maddie stepped forwards to comfort her, but Gussie took a step back and would have stumbled had not Lyle steadied her.

'Flora?' she said warily.

'I'm Maddie, Gussie.'

'Maddie. Yes, of course.' Gussie's face crumpled and she began to shiver.

'Come here, Miss Gussie, I've brought a blanket.' They'd not noticed Mrs Flegg approach, but suddenly there she was, stout boots peeping out from under a ridiculous long macintosh, a mob cap over her curlers, taking charge of Gussie, leading her to the bench then soothing the girls who sat huddled together, tearful and wailing.

'I found Gussie outside the drawing room,' Lyle said to

Maddie. He rolled his eyes. 'The fire's in the kitchen.' He was turning away. 'Stay here, all of you. I'm going to help Flegg put it out.'

'Wait!' Maddie gasped, 'We should call the fire brigade.'

'No need,' Lyle shouted behind him and disappeared round the corner of the house.

She hurried back to the small group on the bench, where Mrs Flegg was tucking a blanket round Gussie.

'I'll fetch us warm drinks from the cottage,' she told Maddie, then stepped over the dogs, pressed shivering against their mistress's legs, and set off, an odd figure in her flapping coat. Maddie was wondering what was happening, how the fire had started, but Gussie had begun to shudder and moan and she should not leave her to find out. Instead she wrapped the blanket more tightly around the old lady, sat cuddling the children to her and waited for Mrs Flegg – or someone – to return. As the breeze slackened, distant sounds of activity reached her ears.

Before long the cook reappeared bearing a tin tray of gently steaming cups. 'They've nearly got it out,' she said tersely as she offered milk to the girls.

'Is there much damage?' Maddie asked, helping Grace, while Sarah sipped her drink and Mrs Flegg assisted Gussie. Sensing their mistress recover, the dogs settled, too.

'I don't know. Mostly smoke, I think. Flegg woke up and smelled it. Went down and saw flames, then Miss Anderson appeared behind him. What were you doing out there, Miss Gussie?' Gussie only shrugged and gulped down the last of her milk.

'Did you see what started the fire, Gussie?' It was Maddie's turn to ask, but gently so as not to distress her.

'I don't know. I heard a noise and went downstairs.'

Mrs Flegg and Maddie exchanged looks. Mrs Flegg's was puzzlement, but Maddie felt dismay. Gussie had not come up and raised the alarm. Instead she'd gone out into the garden and wandered about in her nightclothes. Was she out of her senses?

She looked up to see the bulky figures of Lyle and Flegg come into view from round the house, covered in soot and dripping wet.

'It's out,' Lyle growled. He looked exhausted.

'You're not hurt, either of you?' Maddie asked.

Lyle shook his head.

The Fleggs went off to fetch towels and warm water. Lyle looked anxiously at Gussie, now cuddling Jane in her lap. She returned him a ghost of a smile. 'I'm glad you're safe,' she said in a little girl voice. 'Thank you for rescuing me.'

'I think you rescued yourself,' he said, rather shortly. 'And the girls. Are they all right?'

'I think so,' Maddie said. 'Coughing a bit, that's all.' Grace made herself cough to underline this. It was then that realization kicked in. How close they'd come to death once again. Maddie began to shudder.

'No, I'm all right,' she said through chattering teeth when Lyle asked. 'I simply need somewhere safe for the girls to sleep.'

'I'll check the rest of the house,' he said. He was shivering now, but from cold and damp. 'If we open the windows, get rid of the smoke, we can go back to bed. Deal with the mess in the morning.'

She nodded, but when it came to it she could not do it. The nursery still stank of smoke and she was gripped by a nameless fear. It was then that Mrs Flegg came to the rescue. 'Come to us in the cottage.'

The girls and Maddie shared a single bed, piled with old bedding, in the Fleggs' spare room. While her daughters sank into exhausted slumber, Maddie, visited by memories of that night in their air raid shelter, could not sleep. Knyghton was safe, she told herself fiercely. Lyle had inspected every room as promised and had assured them. Still, she had not been able to let Sarah and Grace sleep in the nursery. She hoped that tomorrow she'd feel differently. When she finally fell into a doze, she dreamed of darkness and confinement and voices shouting. She couldn't breathe. She fought her way to consciousness to find Grace's arm clamped round her neck. She gently pushed it away and managed to sit up. Sarah was wrapped in a nest of blankets on the floor. Everything was peaceful. All she could hear were the consoling sounds of Mrs Flegg pottering in her kitchen on the other side of the wall. *Everyone is safe*, she told herself and got out of bed to go in search of a cup of tea.

Mrs Flegg said that Mr Lyle was up and gone out, but first he'd inspected the scene of the fire. A candle had been left alight and unattended, he'd told Flegg. It had burned right down and the heat from the metal holder had set the kitchen table smouldering. The table was ruined, but mercifully nothing else had caught light. Yes, Flegg was down there already, starting to clean up, but they'd have to cook their meals up here for the time being.

'Who left a lighted candle there?' Maddie sighed. Mrs Flegg, washing the porridge saucepan at the sink, turned her head to stare out of the window. In the garden below the little dogs could be seen running around a vague drifting figure that was wrapped in a shawl.

'Gussie?' Maddie whispered.

'I don't say nothing,' Mrs Flegg mumbled, scrubbing at a particularly stubborn patch of porridge.

Lyle came home early from work to help with the cleaning up. Flegg had managed to locate some old tins of paint in one of the sheds to use on the walls once the kitchen had dried out. He'd already chopped up the remains of the table for firewood. 'Oak makes a good blaze,' he told Maddie, who retorted that it was a good thing that it obviously hadn't the night before.

Apart from walking the dogs in the garden, Gussie was hardly seen that day. She retired to bed and took her meals in her room, Mrs Flegg trudging upstairs patiently with the tray and coming down looking worried, saying, 'Miss Gussie i'nt right.' It was Lyle who had a word with her during one of her short wanders outside with the dogs.

'What did she say?' Maddie asked Lyle.

'She doesn't remember,' he said shortly. 'I had to remind her that she was found outside after the fire had started. She doesn't remember being in the kitchen earlier or lighting a candle.'

'I've never known her this confused.'

'Nor me. Listen, Maddie. Sit down, will you?'

She did as she was bid, hesitantly, thinking he was going to refer to what had happened between them the evening before. Instead he said, 'I must take some of the blame. After you had gone to bed last night I ... Well, I don't know what made me do it, but I told her about the money problems. She was dreadfully upset. Went up to bed without saying anything, not even goodnight. When I turned in, her door was closed ...'

'She must have come down in the night, then.'

Both of them were silent. Given what Lyle had just said, perhaps Gussie hadn't been able to sleep. And now either she really couldn't remember or she was in denial about what had happened or ...

'She wouldn't have done it deliberately, would she?' There, it was out in the open.

'I hope not. Oh, Lyle, that's ridiculous. Of course she wouldn't.' Maddie thought for a moment. 'It doesn't make sense. Why would Gussie try to destroy Knyghton when she loves it so much? No, it must have been an accident.'

'You're right. It speaks of absent-mindedness, not an attempt to set the house on fire.'

'And she'd left the dogs upstairs in her room. She'd never do anything to hurt the dogs.'

Still, it was most concerning. Later that afternoon Maddie elected to take up a tray of tea to Gussie, including a cup for herself. She found the old lady standing at the window of her room, staring out onto the garden. At Maddie's entrance the dogs jumped up and formed a circle around their mistress as though to guard her, then one by one they lay down again.

Maddie set down the tray on a round side table. 'I'm afraid it's only bread and butter,' she said and Gussie turned and smiled distractedly, wringing her hands together.

'Why don't you sit down?' She plumped up the cushion on the bedroom chair. Gussie obeyed and Maddie poured the tea and sat on the bed to drink hers. It was pleasant just to sit in the room's homely atmosphere.

'Who gave you the dolls?' she asked. She liked the Spanish flamenco dancer best, with its dress flaring in tiers of ultramarine. Normally, Gussie would have smiled with delight at such interest, but today she did not answer, though she ate her bread and butter slowly.

'Lyle and I are a bit worried about you,' Maddie went on to say gently.

Gussie said nothing.

'Do you feel all right? Are you well?'

Gussie nodded and reached for her tea. 'Do you . . .' Maddie tried again. 'Lyle says you don't remember what happened last night. Perhaps you couldn't sleep. Did you go downstairs to the kitchen?'

'Why would I have done that?' Gussie snapped, surprising Maddie, for Gussie was never rude.

'I don't know, Gussie. I'm not blaming you for anything, it's simply, we don't know how the fire started. Lyle thinks a candle was left unattended, but nobody's accusing you of anything.'

'I'm not losing my marbles, if that's what he thinks.'

'Of course he doesn't,' Maddie said desperately. 'You are feeling all right, though?'

'Yes, perfectly all right. It's the broken night and the worry ...' Gussie stopped, her tea halfway to her mouth. Her hand was shaking, but then she mastered herself, laid the cup down and laced her fingers together in her lap. 'The worry ...' she repeated. 'I never thought we'd see another war, you know.' Maddie, horrified, saw Gussie's eyes fill with tears. 'So many losses. You must miss Philip. He was a dear boy, a very dear boy.'

'I miss him every day,' Maddie said softly. Last night, she'd betrayed her husband. And it was her eyes that filled now.

One by one the dogs rose and came to push their cold noses into the women's palms.

Thirty-four

France

September 1940

Once Philip had crossed the border into Vichy France he would be free. That was the hope that he held in his heart as he sat on the train, holding his papers ready. If he kept his mouth shut then he should be all right. The train was full, he was glad that he'd booked a seat. Tightly pressed between a portly matron peeling an apple into a napkin and a schoolboy with a satchel on his lap he sat back and closed his eyes so that no one would address him. He did not sleep, he was too anxious, and every time the door to the corridor slid open he blinked to check that it wasn't officialdom. Usually, though, it was a passenger leaving or entering the carriage, but several times between stations it was a French guard checking tickets and he would dutifully offer up his.

Before Philip left Paris, Monsieur Rambert had shown him a chart with the stations and he kept a careful eye on the ones they passed through. It was as the train approached Dijon, which he knew to be the final stop in the Occupied Zone, that two German officers entered the compartment and began to examine everyone's papers. Philip handed his over with lowered eyes. The officer spent some time studying them, consulted his partner then spoke to Philip in heavily accented French. Philip understood enough to realize that he was in trouble. There was something wrong with the travel permit, but what exactly he didn't know, and now the train was slowing as it trundled round a sharp bend. The soldiers clutched the luggage rail to steady themselves then Philip saw the platform of Dijon station slide into view and with much hissing and snorting, the train came to a halt.

'*Kommen Sie mit.*'

Philip stood up, shouldering his bag, and they ushered him out of the train and through the crowds on the platform to a small office, where a fleshy Kommandant sat behind a desk. The man examined Philip's papers and looked up at him with small piercing eyes.

'*Bernard Lavisse. C'est vous?*' The questioning began in a mixture of German and stilted French. He was a soldier, Phillip told them in his own imperfect French, lately discharged from the French Army, travelling south to see his mother. The Kommandant looked sceptical and his questions came faster. Philip's responses became flustered.

After a few minutes the man leaned forward and fixed

him with a gimlet eye. '*Vous n'êtes pas français,*' he pronounced then, triumphantly in English, 'You are British?'

'*Non, non, je suis français.*' Philip insisted, but his luck had run out.

The Kommandant snapped an instruction in German and the officers seized him. He was searched, then taken away in the back of a van to a nondescript command post in the city where they locked him behind bars in a narrow cell containing only a dirty straw pallet and a covered bucket. Philip sat on the pallet and waited, trying not to despair. It would be a prisoner-of-war camp for him, he reassured himself. He'd shown his army identity tag to them so surely they wouldn't shoot him as a spy.

After an hour or two he was brought water to drink and some oily, lukewarm broth, which he forced himself to eat before he lay down and tried to sleep, but what with the sounds of German voices and the slamming of doors, it was hard, and he could not still his thoughts. He tried to pray, but the words would not form, so he fixed his mind on memories of home to comfort himself. He could picture Maddie with her large calm eyes and softly waving hair, the determined thrust of her chin, but he could not remember the faces of his daughters. It was so long since he'd seen them. How they would have changed. He had to fight his feelings of desolation. *Be strong*, he told himself. *You'll get through this.*

Eventually, sometime in the small hours, he sank into a doze from which he was jerked awake by the jangling of keys as a soldier unlocked the gate of his cell. It was morning and they'd come for him. The man tied his hands together and he was led outside, to where an armoured truck waited with its engine running; a dozen unshaven, exhausted-looking men were being bundled into the back. His turn came then the doors slammed shut.

They were driven for some hours. Two guards were with them so they couldn't speak without being overheard. Philip glanced at the others hunkering on the benches in the gloom as the truck rattled along. Some were British by their looks, he thought. One of these, a youth with the cheeky face of an East End barrow boy, managed to form a covert V-sign, which he acknowledged with a raise of an eyebrow, confirming that despite his freshly dyed hair he himself must look more English than he'd imagined. Suddenly he longed for a cigarette.

Eventually the truck slowed and drew to a halt. The doors opened and the guards ushered them all out, he almost losing his balance in the process. He looked about. They were at the entrance to a train station, this one at the edge of a country town. They were herded past an impassive ticket collector onto the nearer platform. It was busy; there was an air of expectancy. Their German guards hustled them into an empty waiting room, then after an exchange of money and the word *zigarreten*, one left. The other watched him desultorily through the window as he walked off. Philip, sitting next to the barrow boy, stared at an advertisement on the wall for a patent medicine with a sense of fading hope and wondered what on earth he might do.

A nudge of his elbow. He glanced down, glimpsed the tip of a razor blade in the barrow boy's hands and his eyes widened in surprise. The rope lay loose around the boy's wrists. The remaining guard had his back to them so Philip duly presented his bonds and the boy worked on them quickly. Their eyes met. The boy mouthed 'now'. They both rose, throwing off their rope, and hurled themselves at the guard, quickly overpowering him, then Philip fumbled with the door handle and they were outside. A train was pulling in. They caught sight of the other guard, returning with his purchase, and dodged away in the other direction, through a chaotic throng of people and luggage towards a footbridge over the railway.

'Hey!' The other guard had seen them. They clattered up the iron steps and pushed past a man carrying a heavy sack, then skittered down to the opposite platform, where a goods train was pulling away. His young companion leaped up on to the link between two open wagons and heaved himself up and inside one, but Philip wasn't quick or nimble enough to follow as the train gathered speed.

He looked round the platform wildly. A gaggle of countrywomen carrying heavy baskets loitered gossiping near the station's high back fence. He pelted towards them, shouting desperately, *'Evadé anglais! Aidez-moi, aidez-moi!'* then pushed in among them. The women gasped, but seeing the German guards on the footbridge they took in the situation and quickly closed around him and he crouched down, hidden by their long skirts, and their baskets held like shields. Chattering loudly, this phalanx moved with him in the middle, further down the platform. He heard the soldiers run past panting, then they shouted to one another to give

up and return. Philip wondered whether the other prisoners had taken their opportunity and run, too. He hoped so.
Meanwhile, his rescuers were herding him through a narrow
back gate and onto the country road beyond, where, out of
sight of the soldiers, they released him.

'*Merci, mesdames, merci,*' Philip cried, steadying himself,
then, kissing his fingers to them in a Gallic gesture of thanks,
he ran for his life along the road. Ahead a patch of distant
woodland came into view. When he reached it he threw
himself in among the trees and lay there for a few minutes,
winded and spent. After he'd recovered a little he set off
once more, limping from cramp, but fear drove him on. The
guards may well have given up and returned to their other
prisoners, but it was possible that they'd sought back-up and
for the moment he could not call himself safe.

Half a dozen miles down the lane, exhausted and thirsty,
he passed the entrance to a muddy track almost hidden by
trees and turned down it, intending to find somewhere to
rest. After a short while he reached a quiet farmyard. There
was no one about so he crept in and tried the door of an
outhouse. It was locked. He followed the wall of a barn and
was able to slip inside. Apart from half a dozen straw bales it
was almost empty. He made himself a nest among them with
a ragged horseblanket and lay down. He must have passed
out, for when his eyes next fluttered open the light had grown
dim and there were sounds of movement outside and a dog
barked. Reluctantly, he hauled himself on to his knees. His
mouth was so dry. He had to find water. He listened until it
grew quiet again then clambered out from his hiding place

and went to the door. At that moment it was pulled open and he found himself staring down at the face of a young woman. Which of them was the more surprised, he didn't know. She drew breath to scream, but he clamped his hand across her mouth and murmured, *'Désolé. Evadé anglais. Je ne . . .* I won't hurt you. *Je suis ami.'*

When he felt her relax he released her and she pushed past him into the barn, wiping her face on the back of her hand, and turned to him. He tensed, expecting her to be furious, but instead she looked him coolly up and down. He was all too aware of how shabby he must appear, unshaven, his jacket open, covered in straw and his trousers streaked with mud. He probably stank, too. He felt ashamed and when she saw this she softened.

'Aie, aie,' she said, hands on hips and shaking her head. *'Vous avez faim?'*

'Oui. Et j'ai soif.' He mimed drinking.

She nodded. *'Restez.'* With that she slipped out through the door, smiling back at him briefly before closing it behind her. He waited, a pulse throbbing in his neck. Could he trust her? He didn't know. He glanced about for something he could use as a weapon if he needed it and picked up a vicious looking pitchfork.

A few minutes later, he heard a soft tap and her voice. *'C'est moi.'* His hand tightened round the handle of the pitchfork, but when she entered he set it against a wall for she was carrying a small rucksack and was alone. The rucksack, he discovered, contained a flask of water, which he drank immediately, a rough-hewn egg sandwich and an apple. He sat on a straw bale and wolfed them down as she watched him with curious dark eyes, her arms folded. When he'd finished, brushing the crumbs from his lips, he thanked her and introduced himself. Her name, he learned, was Sophie, and she lived here with her parents. They were out at the moment, visiting her grandmother, but they'd be back shortly. He asked if they might let him stay in the barn for the night and she bit her lip then said she'd ask.

An hour later, she came back and told him that her father had returned and said Philip could stay if he was careful to remain hidden. Philip slept deeply, wrapped in a thicker blanket she'd given him, and woke with the dawn, refreshed in spirit, though every bone and muscle ached.

When Sophie appeared with breakfast, a thin porridge, she had a scruffy collie bitch in tow that growled at him until a sharp word from her mistress made her lie down, her ears and eyes alert for danger. Philip talked to Sophie between spoonfuls of the gritty porridge, telling her how he'd escaped his German guards, hoping to amuse her and gain her trust, but at the mention of the goods train and the athletic barrowboy friend she frowned at some thought of her own. When she took the empty bowl from him she hesitated, before saying.

'*Vous voudriez vous laver?*' She pretended to wash her face and he nodded.

He followed her out into the autumn sunshine, the dog running ahead to the little farmhouse. In the simple kitchen there was no sign of Sophie's parents. She poured hot water into a basin, threw him a faded towel and left him to his ablutions. A few minutes later she reappeared with clean clothes for him, an old cutthroat razor and a square of mirror. This last he propped on the draining board, enabling him to shave. When he'd finished and had dressed himself in the baggy shirt, jersey and trousers he felt much better. Sophie smiled at him approvingly and gathered up his dirty clothes, which she proceeded to wash in the sink and hang to dry outside in the scrap of back garden. He hoped no one would see them from the road, but supposed she knew what she was doing. There was still no sign of her parents. Later, when he was washing the earth off some turnips at the sink he asked her where they were and she hung her head in apology for her lie, which she'd told simply to protect herself.

'Mes parents sont morts,' she muttered, then went on to explain that she'd lived here with her elder brother, but he'd gone to the market in the nearby town a week ago and had never returned. When she'd investigated, the stationmaster said that several local men had been put on a train going east towards the German border, guarded by Nazi soldiers. The man did not know what her brother looked like, but perhaps he'd been one of them. She didn't know what to do now, she said. There was too much work here on the smallholding for one person, though the Germans had already taken their livestock. There were just a few chickens left, but they would stop laying soon with winter advancing. Her brother had finished the sowing but there would be weeding to do and vegetables to dig and take to market so that she could buy milk and bread and perhaps a bit of meat. She brushed tears away and sniffed miserably.

'*Vous êtes courageuse,*' Philip said. Perhaps he could stay and help her for a day or two, he told her, but he shouldn't be here longer. It would be dangerous for both of them. If she were to be discovered harbouring an *évadé* . . . she could be punished. She'd have to ask a neighbour to help her.

She spread her hands. '*Restez ici un peu,*' she pleaded. She led him upstairs and showed him a narrow closet built into the wall of her brother's bedroom near where his bed stood neatly made, awaiting his return. The closet door could be easily hidden by the chest of drawers that stood next to it. He could conceal himself in there if anyone came. She looked at him triumphantly. He hesitated, trying to weigh up the relative risks. No one had come looking for him yet, but maybe they would, once the word of his escape at the station got about. On the other hand, if he left now, where could he go? His papers had been taken from him at Dijon so if he tried to travel by train he'd likely as not be caught. A day or two here might be best while he worked out what to do next and he'd like to help Sophie, who was being so kind. He folded himself inside the closet as practice and Sophie shut the door. He heard the scrape of the chest as she moved it into place. Yes, this was possible, although when she released him he saw there were telltale scuff marks on the floorboards. After they sanded these away and lightened the contents of the chest, she was able to lift it instead of dragging it. Philip was satisfied. That night he slept in her brother's bed on a feather mattress. It was the most comfortable he'd been since leaving the room above the post office in Normandy nearly three months before.

Three nights passed, a week, a fortnight. No one came to the farm except for a friendly neighbouring woman, who was anxious for Sophie's wellbeing. Philip retreated upstairs to the bedroom when he glimpsed her through the kitchen window. She was stepping over puddles as she pushed her bicycle to the door. He heard Sophie invite her in and listened to their chatter, then was struck by alarm as he remembered that a shirt of his was drying by the stove. What would the woman think if she noticed it? He felt so anxious he could hardly breathe. When he came downstairs later he was relieved to see that the shirt had gone. Sophie laughed and opened a drawer to reveal it crumpled up inside. She'd stuffed it there before admitting her visitor. He felt a rush of warmth towards her.

What she had to say next, though, roused his unease. The visitor had expressed concern that Sophie was here, working the smallholding on her own. It was too much work for one woman, and undoubtedly dangerous with German soldiers about.

'I told her I have Lulu here.' Sophie stroked the dog and smiled. 'Don't worry,' she said, seeing his doubt. 'I promised I would let her know if I needed help.' He was understanding her French much better now.

After the first day he'd recovered sufficiently to help with the dirty jobs indoors, laying the fire, shovelling hot ashes from the stove, sweeping the dusty flagged floor, while she was out digging up vegetables, collecting kindling, or, once a week, cycling to the town to sell eggs and bunches of dried herbs. As time passed he grew bolder and helped her outside, always alert to the advent of visitors, ready to dodge out of sight.

In the evenings they drew the curtains and he sat in her father's old wooden chair and fed the fire and told her about Maddie and his daughters and their life in London. He was grateful to Sophie, he said, but he had to get home to England. But how? Until they worked that out he had to lie low. Curled up in her mother's rocking chair, Sophie watched him over her mending, her dark eyes shining in the firelight, her lips soft and full, slightly parted in a way he found disturbing. This was another reason why he needed to leave. He took care to keep his distance, but he could not help the way that the earthy scent of her bewitched him.

One evening as they sat by the fire, listening to the wind get up outside, Philip dared ask her why at twenty-eight she still wasn't married. He knew at once that he'd hit a tender spot, for her face clouded and for a moment she bent over her needlework and did not reply. Finally she brushed back a lock of her hair and told him how she'd become engaged during the early days of the war, but her fiancé had been killed in a fight. Had he lived, she would have moved to the town, become a butcher's wife, but all that was gone now. She felt responsible for his death, she said, tears pooling in her eyes, for the fight had been about her. He'd seen her flirting with a handsome young French soldier in the market. She hadn't meant anything by it, it was a bit of fun, but Jean-Baptiste had nursed a jealous streak and a brawl had started. He'd fallen and struck his head and that had been that. Now that her brother had vanished, she could not think to marry and abandon the family farm. She had to trust that one day he'd return.

Philip was silent after she'd finished her tale and returned to her sewing. He stared into the fire. Her story was a tragic one, and it stirred memories of his own. Memories that he'd buried deep under layer upon layer of regret. Memories of an event that had ruined his youth, nearly broken him, which he had had to forget in order to survive. And now this girl's loss had unwittingly awoken them. He threw a handful of sticks on the fire and watched the flames lick at them greedily, until his eyes were dazed by smoke and the sound of the wind in the chimney roared in his ears.

That night, he lay on his bed in the darkness listening to the gale whipping round the house, rattling the tiles, and tried to put Flora out of his mind, but when finally he dropped off his sleep was fitful and she visited his dreams. He'd blocked her out of his thoughts, it was the only way he could go on, but now the carefully constructed barrier was crumbling.

He woke late the next morning and dressed in a daze, wondering why the dog was barking. When he hurried downstairs the animal was scrabbling at the door to go out. In the yard he found Sophie shooing chickens, her hair blowing in the wind. The fence around their run had blown down during the night. As he helped her, he remembered a trick he'd used as a boy at Knyghton, and fetched the old horse blanket from the barn. When he threw it over a hen one at a time it lay quiet so he could scoop it up and return it to its shed while Sophie rummaged in an outhouse for a mallet and rusty wire to repair the run.

The weeks became a month, then several months. Philip's spirits darkened. Each time Sophie returned from her weekly trip to the town, the news was the same. The Germans had set up a command post, they were guarding the bridge on the road into town. When she queued for bread soldiers idled about watching. One, with kind eyes, asked to buy some dried lavender and she dared not refuse, though his coins felt dirty to her touch. She did not know how to help Philip without putting them both in danger and Philip dared not set off on his own again.

'Who can I trust?' she said. 'Because of Jean-Baptiste his family hate me, and they have many friends in the town.' She did not have a map. All she knew was that it was a long way to anywhere. He was welcome to stay. She was still using her brother's ration cards so there would be enough for two. Her eyes were calm when she said this, and they lingered on his face. He was trapped, he realized, and he swallowed, but assured her that he'd not do anything rash, instead would bide his time.

There was too much time to think. As he mined vegetables from the frosty ground or repaired the rotting barn door Philip thought of Maddie and felt deep shame that he'd never told his wife about Flora. He'd put it all behind him by the time he'd met Maddie, cut himself off from Knyghton and its tragedy. The last occasion he'd seen Gussie was when she'd been in hospital and he'd been able to visit her because he'd been in Norfolk for training exercises. And Maddie had not asked much about his childhood and youth. He sensed that she too had her secrets, her pain, and they'd respected this in each other. She did not probe him like some girls would. Instead there was something enigmatic about her and that was part of her appeal. He loved how she lost herself in her work, too. As someone not at all creative he was awestruck by her ability to pluck pictures out of the air. When she drew and painted it was as though she was somewhere else, a land of the imagination where he could not follow. He wondered what she might be doing now, and whether she thought that he was alive or dead. 'Missing, believed killed.' That's what they'd have told her. The very thought brought anguish. If Flight Lieutenant Simon Winthorpe had got home safely he'd surely pass on Philip's message to Maddie that he was alive. He must cling to that hope or go mad.

It was rare that anyone visited the farmhouse. Sophie collected her post from town. Then, near Christmas, as snow lay on the ground and icicles hung from the gutters, her neighbour came to the door once more and invited her to Reveillon, the Christmas meal after midnight communion. The fare would be sparse, but the woman didn't like to think of Sophie being on her own. From upstairs in his room, Philip heard the woman try to persuade her and Sophie's weak excuses.

'You must go,' he told her after the visitor left, shaking her head in puzzlement as she crossed the snowy yard. 'I'll be all right. It would be a shame for you not to go out and enjoy yourself and people might become suspicious if you don't.'

It was that which finally made her decide she should go.

*

After Sophie had departed, first to attend the midnight ser-vice at church, then to join her neighbours for their Christmas meal, Philip damped down the fire, settled the dog by the hearth and went up to bed for there was nothing else to do and he would not risk drawing unwanted attention by showing a light.

He wondered what Maddie and the girls would be doing to celebrate Christmas 1940, the second of the war. Going to her parents, perhaps. Monica usually roasted a brace of pheasants for dinner at Christmas. Perhaps it was easier to imagine what they wouldn't have: Christmas pudding, chocolates, an iced cake. His mouth watered at the very idea of such food from Christmases past. He'd had to wring the neck of one of the chickens that morning, which Sophie had roasted as a contribution to her neighbours' feast. She'd cut some scraps off where no one would notice for him to eat in the morning and had licked the juices from her fingers with eyes closed in ecstasy. He wondered if she'd bring back anything from the feast or if the meal would be so very meagre that everything would be eaten. There was little else in the larder now except bread and chicken fat. And a few turnips in the barn – he had always disliked turnip.

At Knyghton, once they were old enough, he and Lyle had attended the midnight service at Monksfield church. Susie Welbourne's father had picked them up in his motor and brought them back afterwards. He'd loved the candlelit church, decorated with greenery, and the cheerfulness of the congregation, the men smelling of beer from the pub and belting out the carols, and afterwards walking up the snowy lane to Knyghton with the stars blazing overhead. It hadn't always snowed at Christmas, of course, but that's how he remembered it. The last time he'd visited a church had been back in May, when he'd hidden in that chilly crypt. He wondered what the German soldiers did here, the devout among them anyway, and shivered at the thought of them kneeling in the church alongside those they'd vanquished. Would they beg God for forgiveness? He was not crude enough to believe that all of them were bad, but many of them would have done cruel things under orders. The sound of gunfire erupted in his mind, the screams of his comrades as they fell to the ground. His skin prickled with terror and revulsion. Why hadn't those gunners refused to carry out their leading officer's command?

His thoughts drifted on in the darkness. Outside, all sound was muffled by the snow. It was therefore a shock when the dog's furious barks pierced the silence, its nails skittering on the flagstones. He sat up, expecting to hear a knock, the harsh shouts of German voices, but there was nothing. His mind raced. Should he hide in the cupboard? But what was the point if Sophie was not there to move the chest into place. The dog's barking intensified. It scrabbled at the door. Who was there?

Philip peered outside through a chink in the curtain. At first the fallen snow dazzled, then he saw something, a movement and the shape of a great pale-coloured animal separated itself from the shadows. It was a deer, a large white stag with branched antlers and gleaming eyes. It stood alert, its ears twitching. The dog's barks grew more frantic, but the stag seemed unbothered. A sense of awe stole over Philip as he lifted the curtain and stared, bemused. Never had he seen such a beautiful wild creature and here it was in the farmyard, as though it had come for him alone. All his dark thoughts fled. He was caught up, transfigured by this encounter. For a while the stag stood there, gleaming like silver fire, and then it wandered off past the barn. He held his breath as he saw it take the fence with graceful ease, and bound away across the field. All that was left were its hoof-prints in the snow.

The dog quietened. Philip dropped the curtain and sat in silence, the spell still upon him. And from far off he heard a church bell tolling the hour. It was midnight. Christmas was here. Had the deer been real? Of course it had. He'd seen its prints. The dog had barked. He knew that he'd been sent a precious gift, something to give him hope, and was humbled that in all the great universe there had been something so special just for him.

Later, when Sophie returned, her cheeks pink and her eyes shining, a bag of parcels hanging from her arm, he tried to explain the wonder of what he'd seen, throwing up his hands in frustration at his workaday French. It was then that she smiled, drew him to her and kissed his mouth with her cold lips and he felt himself respond. After a moment he put her gently from him and she lowered her eyes and busied herself unwrapping the parcels. He exclaimed at the slices of ham, some boiled eggs and a bit of fruit pie they'd sent her home with together with a dusty bottle of wine without a label. A veritable feast! Philip fetched the present he'd made for her, a rack from which to hang her drying herbs, fashioned out of some bits of wood he'd discovered at the back of the barn. She had a present for him, too. The black scarf that she'd been knitting. She wrapped it twice round his neck and kissed him again. This time he held her close. He was shocked at how thin she was. He could feel the sharpness of her shoulder blades.

'*Ma chère Sophie*,' he murmured. 'I can never thank you enough for all that you're doing for me, but I truly hope that I can leave you soon.'

'I do not want you to go, Philip.' She looked up at him, her eyes appealing. 'It's too dangerous. Please stay. No one has come looking for you here.'

It was true. Whether it was because the farm was so hidden and out of the way or because there was nothing about a girl and a few chickens to attract the interest of the occupying administration, he had no way of knowing. Surely, though, it was simply a matter of time before some unrelated incident generated a search of the area or the authorities decided to commandeer all remaining livestock. And then . . .

'Sophie . . . I'm not safe. Even you say I look English.'

She turned from him and crossed her arms and he sensed that she was trying not to cry. He'd feared this, that they were becoming too close.

'Madame Berger has seen you,' she said in a dull voice. 'She took me aside.'

His heart quickened and his palms prickled with shock. 'Don't worry.' She came and hugged him. 'She will not tell. But her husband . . . He is a different matter. I do not trust

him. The way he looks at me as though he wants to eat me.'
She shivered then took a deep breath. 'There are new posters
up in the town. I've seen them. Anyone they catch harbouring
the enemy. There will be no mercy. I did not want to tell you,
but . . .' She spread her fingers in an expressive gesture.

He clasped her hands between his. They were rough and
calloused, the nails broken, but they were also warm and
strong. Holding them calmed his fear. 'What did you tell her?'

'The truth. She'd seen you working outside in the field and
guessed. What other explanation could there be?'

'That I'm a cousin, come to help you?'

She laughed. 'They know my whole family, Philip. That's
what it's like here. My mother and father grew up as neighbours. Everybody knows everybody else. None of my cousins
have such pale skin and hair the colour of autumn leaves.
You don't fit in.'

He knew that. Even though his French had improved he
could not easily pass as one of them. He released her hands and
ran his fingers through his offending hair, lost in thought. If
someone else knew who he was then that changed everything.

'Philip.' Her voice, husky with emotion, drew his eyes to
hers. 'I did not tell you what else Madame Berger said. She
took a breath and glanced past him fearfully to the window.
There was no one there.

'She says there is a doctor in town who can be trusted.
He may know how to help. He's not the old one my family
went to, but a younger man, fresh from Dijon. He treated
her brother for his heart. His pills have made a difference,
she said.'

'It's not my heart that's the problem,' Philip said lightly, but she'd awoken hope. If this doctor could indeed be trusted ...

She brushed away his jest and explained that while Mme Berger's brother had been waiting to see the doctor the wounded patient who was seen before him could be overheard speaking English. 'Should I try to find out more?'

'Yes,' he told her.

She hung her head and examined her hands. 'I wish you would stay with me,' she sighed.

'Sophie, I can't. I must go home. Even if I die trying. I have a wife, whom I love, and children. And I can't go on risking your safety.'

'I had hoped ...'

'I know. You're a lovely woman, Sophie, and you'll find someone who deserves you.'

She looked up at him proudly, her eyes flashing. 'Don't worry about me. I will not beg.'

'I did not think that you would,' he said humbly. 'So will you find out more about this doctor?'

She nodded, then busied herself assembling a meal while telling him gossip she'd learned from her neighbours. The Jewish dentist in the town had been picked up by the authorities. The elder of the baker's two pretty daughters had been wearing new silk stockings and expensive scent, which made you wonder how she'd got them.

After they'd eaten, it began to snow so Philip went outside to feed the chickens. Then they sat by the hearth as darkness fell. They taught each other Christmas carols and cracked hazelnuts, throwing the shells onto the fire, making it leap and crack.

He thanked her for the lovely day and bid her goodnight, then went up to his room where he shut the door and sat on the bed in the darkness with a blanket round him, listening to the wind rattling the roof tiles. Whether or not Mme Berger and her brother could be trusted, surely no Nazis would come looking for him on a night like this. For the first time in a long while he didn't feel afraid. Instead he understood that he was waiting for something. Here it came, a gentle knock. The door creaked open and Sophie entered wrapped in a dressing gown, her hair tousled and her full lips soft and smiling in the candlelight.

For a moment they froze, looking at one another, then Philip slipped the blanket from his shoulders and stood up. She turned and shut the door and waited as he came, took the candle from her and held it up, staring down at her. Slowly, not taking her eyes off him, she untied her gown and let it fall to the floor. Now she was naked, the sharp angles of her bones softened by the candlelight. He reached and touched the nipples of her small high breasts and she flinched, then began to shiver. Desire surged through him. She touched the livid scar of the bullet wound on his shoulder with her finger, then reached and pinched out the flame and drew him down onto the bed. His mouth was everywhere, nibbling, licking, sucking, making her moan with pleasure, and he was lost. Nothing mattered but this, here and now. He plunged inside her, making her gasp, and when the release came it was as though all the fear and tension of months poured out of him. After that, exhausted, he slept. But when he awoke in the morning to find her sleeping beside him, he thought instantly of Maddie and knew that nothing had changed for him.

He climbed out of bed, went downstairs. He lit the stove with the last of the kindling then stared out of the window as he waited for the kettle to boil. Outside, the snow lay banked up against the outhouses. It was impossible to say how long it would be before Sophie could visit the town, though she would need to soon before the food ran out. His thoughts ran ahead. Her father's old gun and a few cartridges were hidden under the floorboards of her bedroom. He weighed up the wisdom of trying to shoot birds or rabbits, even the deer, possibly attracting unwanted attention, against the likelihood of starvation. As he spooned dried camomile flowers into a teapot, he remembered with distaste some vicious metal traps he'd seen in the outhouse. He'd had to kill men, but as with Flora's death he'd pushed unwanted thoughts about that behind a door in his mind. He had no qualms about killing animals if done cleanly. If he checked the traps daily he supposed he'd be doing his best.

He sighed as he trudged upstairs with the mugs of tea. When he pushed open the door of his room there was Sophie awake and smiling at him from the bed. Again desire stirred in him and again he gave in to it. Here, in this distant pocket of the world, it was he who was trapped. This time when he came he cried out 'Maddie!', and hearing him, Sophie wept and pushed him away.

Many weeks passed. It wasn't until a chilly spring night in the middle of March that Philip shouldered his old rucksack, gave Sophie one last searching kiss and stepped silently out into the shadows of the lane. A gibbous moon rising above a line of hills lit his way towards the town, the dark mass of which he could see huddled on the nearest slope, several miles away. Sophie's father's old clothes hung baggy on him, but with the beret covering his hair he hoped he might look to a casual observer like a French peasant, though it being well after curfew his intention was to keep out of sight. While alert and fearful as he passed fields and copses and farms, he could not help a feeling of cautious optimism. He'd been on edge since the summons to the doctor's house came two days before. At every step his courage grew. He was on his way again.

As expected there was a guard post at the edge of the town, but he hid himself, then, as the sky began to lighten, skirted some wasteland and climbed an escarpment that brought him up short at a high chain-link fence. Somehow he scrambled over this into someone's back yard where he was confronted by a barking terrier dog. A man shaving met his eye through the window, but on seeing Philip's pleading gesture obligingly turned his back to continue his task. Weak with relief, Philip dodged the dog and escaped over another fence, jumping down into a narrow alley. From there he emerged into a crisscross of cobbled streets, following the summons of a church bell to the town centre.

He arrived in the main square just as shops were opening up. A queue was already forming outside the baker's and the butcher's as the church clock struck eight. A pair of German sentries stood on duty outside the old town hall, beneath a swastika banner, one of them rubbing his eyes with tiredness. An officer in pince-nez sipped coffee and read a paper at a table of a pavement café. He raised his eyes to glare at Philip, but Philip hitched up his trousers in the manner of a shambling old man and limped on.

The doctor's surgery was, as Sophie had explained, in a street that ran off the opposite side of the square, where the houses were bigger with railings at the front and little balconies. Philip stood aside as half a dozen soldiers on a drill marched past him, their leading officer barking instructions, then turned his attention to the surgery. It was still closed, the windows barred and shuttered. Checking that the soldiers had gone he knocked on the painted front door. After a wait it cracked open, but instead of a maid looking out, he met the eyes of a sharp-featured man in a tailored suit and with glossy dark hair. He knew it was the doctor himself for he was wearing a stethoscope round his neck.

'You've a prescription for my wife Sophie,' Philip said in fluent French.

'Ah, yes, for her nerves,' the doctor replied in a kindly manner and with a glance down the street. 'Come in, won't you, while I fetch it.' He opened the door wider and Philip stepped inside.

Thirty-five

Norfolk

Late August 1941

It was two days after the fire. The Fleggs, Maddie and Lyle had spent hours clearing up and repairing the kitchen and all of them were exhausted. Tonight Lyle was distracted and silent through the evening meal. Maddie felt his mood like a leaden weight and found it difficult to swallow the stew that Mrs Flegg had cooked in the cottage. Sarah and Grace ate with them tonight, because no one had time to make separate meals but Grace was naughty from tiredness and refused to eat her lumpy semolina. Maddie insisted that she should, while privately sympathetic. In the end Lyle growled at Grace to 'Do as your mother says,' and this surprised the child so much that she picked up her spoon. Gussie was still in a world of her own, feeding the dogs crusts from her plate and talking to them as though they were infants.

When Maddie came slowly downstairs after saying goodnight to the girls she found Lyle waiting for her in the hall. 'Would you like a walk?' Seeing her hesitate he added quickly, 'Just a walk, I promise you. We have to talk.'

It was a golden summer evening after a hot day and the air was limpid. As they walked through the garden to the lane, a thrush sang a full-throated solo somewhere unseen in the chestnut tree. The air was so still that the sound of sheep bleating reached them from far away. For this single precious moment it was all so beautiful, Maddie thought. Maybe they'd have a night off from the planes, the sirens and the faraway explosions.

As they came out of the trees on the lane towards the farm, Lyle took her hand. Gently, she freed herself and tried to frame what to say.

'The other night. I thought you wanted . . .' Lyle began.

She stopped and turned to him. 'I thought I did, too, but . . .' Then she burst out, 'It's wrong, Lyle. Don't you see?'

'How can it be wrong? I'll marry you, Maddie. Will that do?'

She stared at him, stunned, then shook her head. 'I'm still married to Philip.'

'Maddie . . . you must face the truth. He's not coming back.'

'It's not that simple.' How could she explain that although that's what her head told her her heart said otherwise.

'It is simple. Very simple. You know what they believe happened to him. I love you, Maddie. I'd like you to be my wife.' His eyes were upon her, warm and pleading, and once more she felt her insides melt with desire.

'I don't know how I feel about you. Only that ...' As she gazed up at him she faltered and suddenly she was in his arms again. They kissed each other deeply and she shivered with desire as his hands moved over her body.

Finally she pushed him away. 'We mustn't do this,' she sighed. 'Someone might see us. I have to think of the girls.' The thought of the villagers gossiping about her and Lyle was insupportable.

'The girls will need a father.'

'They have a father ...' she started to say, then bit her lip. 'I don't know, Lyle.' She pushed her hands into the pockets of her jacket and stared into the distance, unseeing. Her thoughts were so confused. She loved Philip, she couldn't transfer her affections at will and it certainly felt wrong to encourage his cousin. Could she ever see herself marrying this man? She was fond of Lyle, there was no doubt, and, God knows, she was attracted to him, but he was complex and the weight of gloom he carried oppressed her. What if it got worse after they married? Oh, everything was so confusing.

'We ought to go back,' she said listlessly. 'Unless we really are going to walk.'

'Let's walk. We'll talk about normal things. I promise.'

They continued their amble down past the fields and stood at the breast of a low hill to watch the sunset. 'These skies go on forever,' she murmured.

'If only it could always be as peaceful as this,' he sighed. 'If we win this war ...'

'When ...' she said automatically. 'When, not if.'

'All right, when . . . I'll have to decide what to do about the farm. We can't go on like this. I'm mortgaged up to the hilt.'

'Marry Susie,' she said, smiling.

'I've tried that idea.'

She whipped round. 'What?' she said, outraged.

'In a moment of despair I asked her. Do you remember that letter you brought to me in the kitchen garden? It was from her. She said no. Told me I don't love her enough. And it's true, but I had to get the matter out. Everyone – her father, Gussie – seems to think I should. But in the end she saw right through me.'

'Perhaps you didn't ask her properly. The two of you have such similar upbringings. She'd know about farming and would understand you. The perfect wife – and surely her father would be more helpful than you say. Especially if she's his only child.'

'We'd fight like cat and dog. She likes things done her way, does Susie.'

'So do I,' Maddie said lightly. 'I'd not be much use to you, Lyle. I don't understand farming and I wouldn't be good at being a farmer's wife.'

'You'd learn.'

'I'm not sure that I'd want that kind of life.'

She looked away, her attention caught by a movement in the trees. Some large animal, she thought, a deer maybe, but whatever it was it had gone. She shivered. A breeze had got up and now that the sun was setting it was getting chilly.

They wandered back to the house together. In the drawing room Gussie was by herself playing cards again. The moment that Maddie had settled herself with a pile of mending there was a distant rumble like thunder. Soon after this came the faraway sound of explosions. 'Poor old Great Yarmouth,' Lyle murmured. All the peace and serenity of the evening was gone and fear and uncertainty had taken its place.

Thirty-six

'What an attractive coat.'

Monday morning started in an ordinary manner, except that Christine Sutton arrived five minutes early and wearing a navy blue jacket with white piping that Maddie hadn't seen before. It wasn't these things alone that engendered a sense of unease, it was also that today Christine's smile didn't meet her eyes. Still, it didn't occur to Maddie that anything might be actually wrong.

'I'm going to meet up with a friend afterwards,' Christine said as she carefully hung up the jacket and picked some thistledown off a sleeve.

'How very nice,' Maddie said, wondering if it was the mysterious man again. 'Grace is upstairs. She's cross because Sarah has gone down to Aylsham with Mr Anderson today.' She left Christine to make her own way up and hurried to the kitchen to fetch a cup of tea, her mind already on her morning's work.

Once she'd settled at her desk and lost herself in her painting the real world retreated and the sound of the front door closing hardly registered. She glanced out of the window to see Christine holding Grace's hand as they walked together up the drive and her eyes narrowed. Grace was carrying a small rucksack on her back. Perhaps they were going into the village this morning. Grace would have her library books in the rucksack – and Rabbit, of course. Satisfied with this answer, Maddie returned to her work.

Usually she had to be interrupted at twelve when it was Christine's time to leave, but today when she surfaced and consulted her watch it was nearly a quarter past. Quickly she dropped her brush into the water jar, laid out her picture to dry then put away her paints. Craning to see out of the window she saw that Christine's bicycle wasn't parked in its usual place. Indeed, when she went downstairs and opened the front door to look it wasn't anywhere. Perhaps they'd returned and Christine had left without Maddie noticing. She shut the front door and went along to the kitchen where Mrs Flegg was stirring a pan of soup on the stove.

'Are Grace and Mrs Sutton back?' she asked.

'Haven't seen 'em,' Mrs Flegg said. 'Mrs Sutton didn't say they were going out.'

'No, nor to me. How strange. I suppose they caught the bus into Monksfield.'

'I wish she'd said. We needed some blacking.'

'I can go out later, if you like.'

'No need. Flegg's running low on cigarettes. He'll go.'

'We'll have to push lunch back a few minutes. I hope that doesn't put you out.'

'A good thing Mr Lyle and Sarah are having theirs out today.'

One o'clock came and went. At half past the soup was congealing in the pan and Gussie was pacing the dining room like a hungry cat. Maddie said reluctantly that they should eat, but all the while she was alert to signs of the travellers' return. She hardly noticed the soup as she spooned it down.

'She didn't bring her bicycle this morning,' she said suddenly to Gussie, the oddness of the fact falling into place. 'She was meeting a friend, she told me.'

'That doesn't explain why she's back late with Grace.'

'No.' Perhaps the friend had a car and was dropping Grace off before he and Christine went off on their outing – she'd decided the friend was a 'he'. Maddie's thoughts ran on. The car could have broken down or run out of petrol. There'd be some perfectly sensible reason why they were late.

'I do hope they haven't had an accident.' Maddie's head snapped up at Gussie's words.

'I'm sure they haven't,' Mrs Flegg reassured her as she piled the empty dishes. 'Now don't you worry, Mrs Anderson, there'll be some reasonable explanation.' She began to recount a long story about why her nephew in Sheringham was late back the previous Friday. 'And it turned out he'd stopped to help a woman find her dog what had run off.'

'Our dogs are all here,' Gussie murmured, checking anxiously.

Maddie stood up and went out to look out of the window. After a moment she said, 'I must go and look for them.' She ran to fetch the bicycle out of the shed.

An hour later, she returned exhausted to Knyghton to find them still gone. She'd been into Monksfield and back, visited the library, several shops, the tea room, the church and finally the rectory, where she enlisted Anna's help, while Mrs Clairmont watched Milo who was taking a nap. By now, Maddie was extremely worried. 'Nobody has seen Grace or Christine Sutton all day,' she gasped to Mrs Flegg, her voice quivering with unshed tears.

'I've sent Flegg down to see if Mr Lyle and Sarah are back at the farm yet,' Mrs Flegg said with her hands on her hips and just at that moment the farm truck bounced up the drive in a cloud of fumes and Lyle and Flegg stepped out.

Lyle came to her at once. 'I've left Sarah with Robert. She was helping with the horses.'

'She'll love that. Oh, Lyle, I'm so glad to see you,' Maddie said, clutching his arm. 'There's no sign of Grace and I've run out of places to look. I don't know what to do.' She described where she'd searched, of whom she'd enquired and he looked thoughtful.

'There has to be a reasonable explanation,' he reassured her. 'Perhaps they didn't go into Monksfield after all. Where else might they have gone? Think, Maddie.'

'I don't know! Christine has never taken Grace anywhere other than Monksfield to my knowledge.'

'Christine lives in Carshall, doesn't she?'

Maddie nodded, tucking a strand of hair behind her ear.

'Yes. Can we go there? I've got the address on a letter some-where. It's something Cottages, I think.'

Grove Cottages was a line of four small, detached white-painted properties on the edge of Carshall's large village green. An unguarded pond near the road was enough to ring alarm bells in Maddie's mind as the truck pulled up outside No. 2 and she couldn't help going to stare into its muddy depths.

'Come on,' Lyle said, drawing her away, and she followed him through the gate of Christine's house and across a neat front garden to a white-painted front door. His knock was not answered so Maddie went and peered through the window, though she could see little because the nets were pulled across. Lyle strode along to a high side gate, rattled the latch uselessly, then reached over the top and drew back a bolt. This time when he tried the gate creaked open.

Beyond the long strip of back lawn ploughed fields rolled away into the distance. Maddie rapped on the back door then shaded her eyes to look through the downstairs windows, before standing back to squint at the ones upstairs. Their cur-tains were tightly shut. For a moment she thought she saw a movement, but it was simply the reflection on the glass. There was, she concluded with a heavy heart, no one in.

'Coo-ee. May I help you?'

They turned at the shrill voice to see an elderly lady staring through her spectacles at them over a hedge, a pair of shears in her hands.

'We're looking for Mrs Sutton.'

'I didn't think you looked like burglars, but you never know these days.'

'I'm Maddie Anderson and this is my brother-in-law Mr Lyle Anderson of Knyghton. Mrs Sutton minds my little girl twice a week, and she came first thing this morning as usual, but they haven't returned from an outing. Have you seen them? We're actually very worried.'

'No, dear, I haven't. Where did you say they went?'

'That's it, we don't know. Mrs Sutton left no explanation. I assumed they went into Monksfield, but no one I've asked there has seen them.'

'No one's been here today since she and her husband left this morning.'

'Her husband?'

'Yes, they went off in his car after breakfast.'

'I didn't know ... that's odd.' Was this the old husband or a new one – or ...? She wasn't sure how to ask.

Lyle took her arm gently. 'Come on, Maddie. It's plain there's no one here. Thank you,' he said to the neighbour. 'If they return perhaps you would send word to Knyghton.'

'Knyghton. That's the farm off the road to Monksfield? I in't lived here so long meself. Twenty years come February. Yes, I'll send word. I hope you find your little girl.'

Maddie thanked her and they left, Lyle relocking the side gate while Maddie climbed into the truck.

'Christine's lied to us,' she said to Lyle as he started the engine. 'Why would she say she was separated from her husband when she wasn't. Or—'

'I don't know, Maddie. Where now – back to Monksfield?'

'We should call in at Knyghton on the way in case ... but then Monksfield, yes. There must be someone who saw them. The bus driver, how do we find him? Oh, Lyle,' she sighed as he turned the truck, 'I'm beginning to think we should go to the police.'

Thirty-seven

The rest of the day passed in an endless nightmare. Maddie telephoned the police from the rectory. The rector contacted the bus company, who said they'd make enquiries. A Constable Rallison arrived from the next big village and methodically asked Maddie all the questions that had already been posed by everyone she'd spoken to. She tried not to sound impatient as she trotted out the story again. He licked his pencil and wrote laborious notes in his book.

'We'll need a recent photograph of your daughter, Mrs Anderson,' he said, but before Maddie could tell him that all her photographs had been lost in an air raid they were interrupted by the bus company ringing back.

'The driver on that route was a Miss Flossie Jary,' the rector said after he'd finished the call. 'She remembers picking up a woman of Mrs Sutton's description and a little girl. They didn't come to Monksfield at all. She picked them up on her return route and she dropped them off at the train station.'

'The train station?' Maddie echoed, bewildered. 'But where were they going?'

'That's what we must now find out,' Constable Rallison said before riding away on his bicycle. An hour and a half later he returned with news. The woman who'd been on duty at the station ticket office that morning had only the vaguest memory of the travellers, but a guard remembered seeing the two of them catching a train to Sheringham. 'Perhaps your Mrs Sutton fancied a day by the sea,' the constable suggested.

'She should have said . . .' Maddie cried in dismay.

'Perhaps that's the explanation, Maddie, and they'll be back soon.' Lyle said consolingly, but Maddie knew in her heart that they were wrong.

By nightfall there was still no word. There was nothing for it but for the Andersons to return to Knyghton. There Maddie found Sarah safely back from the farm and in an agitated state at the upheaval. She made reassuring noises and managed to get her to bed, but later, when it was her turn, she could not sleep and was not surprised when in the small hours the door of her bedroom opened and the ghostly figure of her elder daughter in her white nightdress crept in and, with a sob, ran to the bed. Maddie lifted the covers and drew her in. It was comforting to have her there and both managed to doze off. Maddie woke as the cold fingers of dawn crept round the edges of the curtain. Instantly she sat up as realization flooded in. Although Sarah lay safely beside her, gently snuffling in her sleep, Grace was still gone. *I've not even got a photograph of her,* she remembered.

Constable Rallison was a sympathetic young man, but of

a dramatic turn of mind. After his visit to Knyghton later that morning Maddie overheard Lyle remarking morosely to Flegg that what was turning into a full-blown case of child kidnap had clearly been the most exciting thing ever to have happened on the man's watch. Certainly the officer had spoken importantly of telephone calls from the chief of the Sheringham police and a journalist from the local newspaper. He had instructed in a most pompous manner that the Andersons should try to be calm and let the professionals do their job.

Child kidnap! *Surely not*. Christine Sutton was fond of Grace. She'd never hurt her – *would she?* There must be some reasonable explanation for their disappearance and the pair of them would suddenly appear and everything would return to normal. But as the hours went by, there was no news. Maddie and Sarah spent the day at the rectory so Maddie could be near a telephone, but also to get away from Gussie's fussing and Mrs Flegg's doomy pronouncements.

Lyle appeared at lunchtime to ask what was happening. Maddie felt too weak to answer him and merely shrugged. Mid-afternoon the telephone rang and she sprang to life when Mrs Clairmont held the receiver out to her. It was Rallison.

'I'm afraid we have not located your daughter, Mrs Anderson. There have been no sightings.'

'Not Sheringham beach, then?'

'Unless they climbed over the barbed wire, no. We're continuing with our enquiries. You're not to worry, I'm sure we'll find them.'

Maddie replaced the receiver and stood up shakily. 'Nothing to report,' she muttered and sank into deep gloom.

On the second day since Grace and Christine's disappearance, Rallison pedalled up to Knyghton full of news of a sighting. A middle-aged couple sitting on a bench had seen a woman of Christine's description marching a little girl along the seafront. At one point the girl had shaken off the woman's hand and exclaimed, 'You can't do that, you're not my mummy,' and the woman had said, 'Come along, Grace, there's a good girl,' in a stern voice, then more gently, 'I'll buy you an ice cream!'

So they were definitely in Sheringham. But where and why, and why, Maddie asked the constable, were the police taking so long to find her in a small seaside town? And were they with this mysterious man who may or may not be married to Christine?

'I'm sure everyone's doing their best, ma'am,' the constable told her importantly as he left. 'Just thought you'd want reassuring.'

'At least they know roughly where she is,' Lyle said. 'I must go down and see how they're getting on with the ploughing, but I'll be back as soon as I can.'

After he'd gone, Maddie could settle to nothing. It was no good, she could not wait. She felt braver now her worst fears were allayed. Her daughter was alive and she knew roughly where she was. Sarah had gone to play with Nadya and Anna would look after her. What mother would not go in search of her missing child? Gussie had shut herself in her bedroom and would not reply to her knock so Maddie went outside to find Flegg to beg him to take her to the station in the trap.

She packed a few essentials in a shopping bag and sat alongside him, comforted as ever by his solid presence. 'Mr Lyle won't be pleased,' she sighed, as Flegg spoke to the pony and the trap jerked into motion, 'but I feel I have to go. Would you fetch Sarah for me later?'

'Don't you worry, Mrs Flegg and I will look after her.'

'That's very good of you. Thank you, Flegg. I don't know what I'd do without your kindness.' As they turned out of the drive and down the lane, she remembered Mrs Flegg's initial hostility to her arrival as a refugee with two little girls. Flegg, though, had been kindly from the moment that he'd picked them up from the station. He exuded goodness, as steady and as solid to the core as the old chestnut tree by the gate. She remembered all the hours he'd spent with the girls, showing them how to grow things in the vegetable garden, and letting them search for eggs.

'I'd do the same if she were mine,' Flegg said, his voice full of feeling. 'That I would. Given the chance.'

She glanced at him curiously and to her alarm saw sadness in his face. And then it struck her. This had happened before. Not in this way, no. But the Fleggs had lost a child. For a while they had been parents. A girl had lived with them in their home, but she'd not been theirs, they'd just been lent her for a while. Then her fate had been taken out of their hands.

'Flora,' she whispered, but Flegg was busying himself with turning out into the road and did not answer.

'Flegg,' she said cautiously when they'd got going again. 'Do you know what happened that day when Flora . . .'

For a moment he did not reply, but his big hands tightened on the reins. Finally he shook his head. 'Mr Philip and Mr Lyle, they both grew too fond of her, so Mrs Anderson sent her away to the parson's. She'd have been all right if she'd stayed there, that's all I know.'

'They say it was my husband's fault, that it was his gun . . . I didn't know a thing about that before we came here, Flegg. I'm sorry, it must have stirred it all up again.'

'Whatever happened, it was an accident,' Flegg mumbled. 'And it's all water under the bridge now. You must get along and find Grace. That's the important thing.'

'Yes. Thank you, Flegg.'

From Sheringham station it was a short walk into the town. Maddie expected to see Christine and Grace around every corner, ahead of her on the pavement, coming out of the greengrocer's, sitting in the window of a tea shop, but although she saw plenty of women with small children none of them were the ones she was looking for. She was nearing the seafront now and the scent of salt and the mournful cries of gulls brought happy memories of childhood holidays that seemed all wrong today. There was the ice-cream kiosk, still open, but there were no donkeys waiting patiently on the sand. Instead the beach was festooned with coils of barbed wire and the tide was in. Waves crashed on the shale and the water was a dirty grey. She shivered in a chilly wind. Feeling dismal she sat down on a bench with a good view of the promenade, pulled her jacket around her and wondered what to do next. It was all very well coming to the rescue, but she had no idea where to look for her daughter. The police had visited the hotels and boarding houses, Constable Rallison had told her, so there was little point in doing the same again. If Christine was lying low with Grace in a private house she had little chance of finding them. Oh, she did feel faint. Perhaps if she bought tea and a bun at the kiosk and sat here for a while to recover her strength she might see them pass. Christine with her love of bracing walks wouldn't keep Grace in all day, would she?

After a fruitless half hour watching people stroll about, Maddie got up, returned her cup and saucer to the hatch then set off back towards the high street and the main shops. Here she wandered about for a while, her attention alert to any little girl she passed in the busy street. She wished yet again that she had a photograph of Grace to show people. She came to the police station and paused in shock at a poster pinned to the noticeboard outside. 'Missing', it said, and described Grace and what she'd been wearing when Maddie last saw her. Her courage stoked by this concrete evidence of the search Maddie entered the building and introduced herself to the policeman behind the counter, who viewed her kindly and brought her a glass of water. No, there had been no further developments, but his colleagues were actively looking. 'We don't think your little girl can be in danger, if she's with her nanny,' he soothed.

'But the woman must have gone mad. I want Grace back.'

'Of course you do, ma'am. But the best thing you can do is go home and let us do our job.'

She took up her bag and left, wondering what to do next.

She wasn't willing to go back to Knyghton without Grace. The question was, what were Christine's intentions? She'd spoken of meeting a friend, but why had she taken the train when she had a husband with a car? Was the friend someone else entirely or had he or she been a lie? All things she could not answer.

During this time she'd been walking aimlessly and now the shops petered out. She passed a nonconformist chapel and a library and then the houses began. She trailed along the terraces, but was unable to see beyond the net-curtained windows. Soon she began to give way to despair. She paused, gazing about her, and an older woman on her knees looked up from scrubbing her front step. 'You look a bit lost, dearie,' she remarked. 'Can I help?'

'I'm looking for my daughter.' Maddie said and went on to explain. 'Have you seen anyone unusual here?'

'Plenty, what with the war, but not the sort you mean. We had a policeman asking this very morning. I am sorry for your trouble.'

'Thank you.' She was much heartened to hear that the police had been going door to door and continued her way along the road and into a small park. She passed children playing on swings or walking with their mothers, or ambling together in groups, chattering, buffeting Maddie as they passed.

She came to the far side and turned into a shadowed side street where the houses were taller with stubby front gardens and steps up the front doors. A car was parked outside one and a man in his shirtsleeves with his back to her was packing bags into the boot. She watched him light a cigarette then hurry away into the house. As she idled past the car she glanced at the open boot and her eyes widened. A little rucksack lay next to a holdall and she knew it at once. She'd seen it bobbing up and down on Grace's back the last time she'd seen her, walking away down the drive at Knyghton, her trusting hand in Christine's. In a second everything snapped together. This man must be Christine's 'friend'.

She glanced at the house. The front door stood wide open. When she tiptoed up the steps, her heart thudding, she stared into a long narrow hall, but there was no one in sight. She entered, on full alert, and heard voices from somewhere deep in the house, then a child began to wail. 'Grace,' she murmured. It had to be Grace. Part of her knew she should retreat, write down the car licence number and go to fetch help, but she could not bear to leave. The child's thin wail drew her on. She pushed open the door at the end of the hall and froze as three people in the kitchen looked up at her in astonishment. The man she'd just seen stood with arms akimbo watching Christine who was bent doing up the buttons on the coat worn by the wailing child, a coat Maddie had never seen before.

'Grace.' Maddie hurried to her, pushing Christine aside to fold the little girl into her arms. 'Oh, Grace, are you all right?' She lifted the child up and Grace burrowed into her shoulder, still shuddering with sobs.

'Where's she come from then?' the man demanded of Christine in a London accent.

'It's Mrs Anderson.' Christine's voice trembled.

'I guessed that much, you silly girl, I mean how did she find us? Come on, we need to get out of here.'

Together they seized Grace and tore her from Maddie's grasp. 'No, no, no,' Maddie cried out, but the man's arms were around her in a tight grip. Christine wrestled with a frightened Grace, trying unsuccessfully to soothe the child in a voice high-pitched with panic.

'Get the brat into the car,' the man ordered and Christine grabbed Grace by the wrist and dragged her past them towards the hall.

'Don't hurt her, Reg,' the woman quavered over her shoulder. 'I don't want us done for murder,' then to Maddie she said, 'I'm sorry, Mrs Anderson.' Tears filled her eyes and she was shaking.

'Don't worry,' Reg growled. 'She's just going in here.' At this he pulled opened a wooden door next to the door out to the hall to reveal a dark cold space with wooden steps disappearing downwards.

'No!' Maddie screamed as he shoved her into it, steadied her on the top step then slammed the door. She fell against it, drumming it with her fists and crying out, but to no avail. She heard the key turn then bolts being shot across. Reg's moving feet broke the line of daylight at the bottom of the door.

'There, you can shout all you like,' cried his muffled voice, then the line of light shone steady and she heard his retreating footsteps before the front door slammed shut, shaking the whole house.

Maddie threw herself against the door, but it was a stout one and as she was teetering at the top of the steps, she could bring no real force to it. She was like an imprisoned bird, fluttering uselessly against the bars of its cage and crying out in fear.

'Mrs Anderson, that'll do you no good.' Someone spoke sternly from the other side of the door and Maddie froze. It was Christine.

'Let me out,' Maddie begged. 'Christine, why've you done this?'

'I can't let you out. My husband would be furious. I'm here because I told him I needed to spend a penny.'

'That man's your husband?'

'Yes, Reggie's come back for me. Isn't that marvellous, Mrs Anderson? And now with Grace we're a family. I can't have kids of my own – did I tell you that?'

'No.' Maddie couldn't in truth remember.

'I'm sure I did. I always wanted kids. It's hard looking after other people's when you're desperate for one of your own.'

'So you've stolen mine. You could have adopted one.'

'It's like Reggie said, you don't know what you're getting when you adopt. And I love Grace and she loves me.'

Maddie couldn't believe her ears. 'But she's my daughter.'

'But you don't look after her, do you? You leave that to other people.'

'That's ridiculous.'

At that moment they heard footsteps in the hall and Reggie's voice: 'Christine, we have to go.'

'Just coming,' Christine called back. 'I'm putting Mrs Anderson right on a couple of things.'

'Confound it, Christine, come on.'

'I'm not letting her out if that's what you think. Give me

a moment, please. Now,' she addressed Maddie through the door, 'don't worry, we'll look after her. She's used to me and she's met Reggie before. I would have introduced you to him, but you said you didn't want him coming to the house.'

'I didn't know he was your husband. You didn't tell me.'

'Didn't I? You didn't give me a chance. Grace will be very happy with us. Goodbye. I'm sure someone will hear you shouting eventually and let you out. That's what Reggie says, anyway,' she added doubtfully.

'Christine!' Maddie cried. 'Please, let me out. You can't do this to us. Grace is my daughter, not yours ...'

She heard departing footsteps and then the front door close.

After a moment the walls of the house vibrated with the sound of the car engine, then she heard the vehicle accelerate away and soon there was silence. Grace had gone.

Huddled in the gloom at the top of the cellar steps, tears ran down Maddie's face. A chilly draught blew up from the darkness below, bringing with it a musty smell of coal mixed with earth and damp. Her limbs began to prickle with panic and each breath was a shallow gasp. Maddie thought of Grace and berated herself for believing she could rescue her without help, then she started to shudder and pulled her jacket tightly round her. Too crippled by fear even to cry out, she remained there for a long time hunched into a tense ball, her eyes fixed on the line of daylight at the bottom of the door. Her mind fell into a nightmarish daze. Voices taunted her. *No one else knows you're here. You won't be found in time. You'll never see your family again. Grace, oh, Grace.*

A thud broke into her thoughts and she lifted her head. The sound came again, then children's voices from outside in the street. They were playing football. She stirred, sat up and cried out once, twice, but they did not hear. A minute or two later came a slapping sound from somewhere deep in the cellar and a rattle of metal. A bolt of terror shot through her, but then came the patter of a child's feet. 'Here, Taylor!' A boy's voice followed by the thud of the ball on the road. Then came the rattle of metal again. The lad must have stepped on a loose plate or drain grid, she thought as his footsteps retreated.

These ordinary sounds were comforting, and gradually Maddie felt her stiff limbs relax, though she still couldn't bring herself to move. She did not know what she feared about the darkness all around, what was waiting further down the steps to attack her, but there was something. It made the hairs on her limbs stand on end. *You have to move, Maddie. If you're to get out and find Grace*; but still she couldn't. She brooded on the metallic sound she'd heard and sniffed at the smell of coal. Probably there was a coal chute from the front garden opening into this cellar and the boy fetching his ball had trodden on its cover. And if there was such a chute she might be able to reach it.

It took a great deal of courage, but gradually she uncoiled and began to lower herself with gritted teeth slowly down the steps into the terrifying darkness. At each step she expected something to reach up and seize her, but nothing did and eventually her shoe touched gravelly earth at the bottom. She tried to stand upright, but struck her head against something hard and cried out, rubbing her throbbing scalp. With her other hand she reached up tentatively and her fingers found the edges of a wooden beam. She clutched onto it, glad of something to steady her. The darkness pressed against her eyes as she moved forwards. Something scuttled away to one side and she gasped, then froze, listening out, but all she could hear was the football game outside. She stared in the direction of the thuds and the children's voices and wondered if she was imagining a cloud of greyish light ahead. Her hands moved along the beams as she shuffled towards it, stumbling on lumps of coal. Then she felt the line of another beam at right angles to the first one and ducked under it. Reaching out she felt a cold concrete wall. She'd reached the extent of the cellar. And then, looking up she could see what she'd hoped for, a glimmering rectangular outline of a coal chute set into the top of the wall. She remembered the one at home in Norwich. The coalman could pull it outwards and pour sacks of coal into the cellar. Woe betide him if he hadn't fitted it snugly back into place to avoid the rain getting in. Monica used to give him a piece of her mind.

Full of purpose now, Maddie's fear fell away. She climbed up onto a low mound of coal, reached up and pushed the chute, but it was heavier than she thought, or else stuck. With another shove it grated a little and daylight flooded the cellar. One more try and she'd pushed it to one side. This done, she fell against the wall, exhausted but full of triumph. But how could she get out? She wasn't tall enough haul herself up through the chute and anyway she'd already cut her hand on the edge of the hole. She clamped her handkerchief on the wound and glanced hopefully around the cellar, blinking in the grey light, but there was nothing she could usefully stand on. The floor was bare earth, not a place to store junk.

After a while, she did the only things that she could think of: shouted for help and threw lumps of coal through the hole to attract attention. When finally, a young boy's face filled the rectangle of daylight overhead she could hardly contain her relief. 'I'm stuck here,' she told him with a catch in her throat. 'Can you fetch your parents, please.'

In the end the police were called and broke into the house to let her out. Maddie sat on the doorstep, filthy and shaken, while the officers dealt with a small crowd that had gathered. A neighbour said Reggie Sutton had only moved in recently. A quiet sort, seemed nice enough, no trouble. *No trouble, my foot*, Maddie thought grimly. 'We need to find Grace!' she said in a thin voice.

"Ere, Mrs, what's this?' One of the young footballers bent to pick up a scrap of paper fluttering against Maddie's skirt and gave it to her. She unfolded it with trembling fingers. As she studied the pencil drawing on it her eyes widened. It was a map. Wordlessly, she passed it to one of the policemen, who examined it, then smiled at her broadly. 'I know this place, Mapleton Street,' he told her, tapping the paper. 'It's in Yarmouth. They've gone to Great Yarmouth!'

It was hard going back to Knyghton without Grace, but the police were immovable. Maddie was not to be included any further in the operation to rescue her daughter. A shy rookie constable drove her home. Grimy, exhausted and traumatized by her ordeal, she stepped out of the car wrapped in a blanket to be greeted by a line-up of the whole household plus the rector's wife, Anna, Nadya and Milo. Sarah ran to her mother with a cry and Maddie folded the child tight against her breast. 'It's all right,' she whispered in her daughter's ear, 'the police will find Grace soon and bring her home. I know they will.' She thanked the young rookie, who started to make a speech about how brave she was, then seeing Lyle frown stopped suddenly, realizing he was making a fool of himself. Maddie thanked him and he climbed back into his car and drove away.

Everybody crowded round Maddie, all talking at once. Lyle hugged her then said, 'My dear girl, you're shivering.'

'I'm cold,' Maddie said, 'and ...' She swallowed a sob.

'You poor thing.' Lyle led Maddie indoors, with Sarah still clinging to her hand, They sat her down on the sofa in the living room while Mrs Flegg and Anna went off to the kitchen to heat some water for a bath and the rector's wife rubbed her feet with a towel to warm them. Lyle started to lay a fire and Gussie sat in her favourite chair with her sewing in her lap, as tranquil as though nothing out of the ordinary was happening.

'The police telephoned to tell us what had happened and that you were on your way home,' Mrs Clairmont explained, 'so Alwyn dropped us off here to let Mr Anderson know.'

Lyle poked a lit match into the kindling. 'We were extremely worried about you,' he said sternly as they watched the flame lick up the screw of paper underneath. 'When Flegg came back and said he'd dropped you at the station I knew at once what you'd done. It was dangerous, Maddie, and stupid. And very brave, of course,' he said, and rising, came to sit on her other side.

Maddie sat in silence until Anna came in to say that her bath was ready. She allowed Anna to take her upstairs to the bathroom. There she caught sight of herself in the mirror over the basin as Anna helped remove her filthy clothes. Her unkempt hair and the coal streaks on her teary face brought back the horror of the dark cellar.

'Don't worry, Maddie,' Anna said, smoothing her friend's hair. 'We'll make you clean and lovely, ready to welcome Grace home.'

She nodded, but daren't speak her worst fear out loud: *What if they don't find her and she never comes home?* 'Maddie,' Anna said sternly, as though she'd read her mind. 'At least you know where she is. Mrs Sutton won't hurt Grace and soon the police will bring her home.' At last, Maddie nodded and relaxed. She lowered herself gratefully into the hot soapy water and allowed Anna to wash the coal dust out of her hair with gentle fingers.

Later, after Anna, Milo and Mrs Clairmont had been collected by the rector in his battered old Austin, the four remaining Andersons sat down to supper, though no one felt much like eating, being conscious of the empty fifth place at the table. Sarah asked twice what time Grace was coming home and, picking up on the air of anxiety, would not take Maddie's 'Soon, dear,' as an answer. The little girl was allowed to stay up for a while and play Snap with Gussie until she fell asleep over the cards, whereupon Lyle lifted her into his arms and took her upstairs. Maddie followed to tuck her into bed.

'She went off straight away,' Maddie said when she came down a few minutes later. 'Tired out, poor mite.'

Now that there was just the three of them they sat around the fire in the twilight and Maddie falteringly repeated what she'd already passed on to the police, that Christine's errant husband had returned and had appeared to make amends to his childless wife by colluding in this ridiculous plot. Christine had justified the kidnap of Grace by convincing herself that Maddie didn't look after her daughters well enough.

'She must be out of her mind. But perhaps she is. She spoke at her interview of having recovered from nervous exhaustion. Perhaps she hadn't got better after all. Oh, to think that I've let her look after Grace all these months.'

'It's hardly your fault,' Lyle muttered.

'I feel it is. She's right about one thing – I should have looked after Grace myself. She's much more important than my work.'

Something occurred to Maddie that made her prickle all over. 'Christine was disapproving about Grace's imaginary friend. She said I shouldn't allow Grace to invent things. It was like telling lies. I think that's another reason why she decided I wasn't a suitable mother. Was she right and I wrong?'

Lyle frowned. 'Christine was the one who told lies.'

Gussie, who'd been keenly listening, finally spoke up. 'Grace's friend was not imaginary. Do you see nothing?'

Lyle and Maddie exchanged wary glances. 'What do you mean, Gussie?' Maddie said. 'Grace's friend was not real.'

'Not real in the way that you mean, but Flora's still here. I've seen her. Out of the corner of my eye, like a flicker of light sometimes, but I know it's her.'

'A ghost, you mean? I know you say there are ghosts here, Gussie, but I've never seen or heard such a thing,' Lyle said. 'And anyway, Grace called her friend Sebby.'

'Just because you haven't seen a ghost, Lyle ... doesn't mean there aren't any.'

Lyle shot Gussie a look of disgust.

Maddie bit her lip, wondering if Gussie really did see ghosts and thinking of the pictures she'd drawn of Flora. Then she shrugged. None of this seemed important at the moment. She wanted her real flesh and blood daughter back. It felt as though there was a yawning hole inside her and nothing could distract her from that.

The minutes crawled by and she dreaded the thought of bedtime coming around again. She hugged herself. At least tonight she knew what had happened to her daughter and could dare to believe that everything would be all right. Christine might be off her rocker, but Maddie did not think that she'd harm Grace. *Would she?*

Lyle got up to light the lamps and draw the curtains. It was dark outside now and far away they could hear the air raid sirens sound, then the rumble of distant planes. Shortly afterwards the explosions began.

Maddie covered her eyes, knowing that bombs would be dropping over Yarmouth and wondered exactly where the house in Mapleton Street was where Reggie would have taken them. *Please let Grace be all right,* she prayed. She glanced up to see Lyle watching her with concern, and when he suggested that they listen to the news, she guessed that it was to mask the sound of the raids. By the time the wireless set warmed up, however, the newscaster was halfway through a terrible story about the sinking of a naval ship with all hands and Maddie rose to her feet unable to bear it. 'I'll fetch us some tea, shall I?' she said brightly. 'No, Lyle,' she assured him when he offered to help. 'I'm perfectly capable of doing it by myself.'

Ten o'clock came and went and she was nervy with waiting. What could the police be doing that took them so long? If they had the address in Great Yarmouth, surely it wouldn't take so long to find Grace. The raids would have interrupted them, she decided humbly, thinking that the fate of one small girl had to be measured against the lives of many other people. Her tea still lay untouched. She drank it down cold and gathered up the cups.

'You should go to bed,' Lyle remarked, 'you look exhausted. Even if they've found Grace they won't bring her back tonight. Not with the raids.'

'They wouldn't put her in a police cell, would they?' Gussie asked.

Maddie's eyes widened with distress.

'Of course not, Gussie,' Lyle said crossly. 'I'm sure she'll be somewhere comfortable and safe, Maddie, and they'll bring her back in the morning.'

Maddie let out a little moan.

'Go on, go to bed.'

'I won't sleep, there's no point.'

'Have one of my little pills,' Gussie said, putting aside her cards. 'The doctor prescribes them, they're very good. You'll sleep like a baby.'

'That's kind of you, but I don't want to be dead to the world when Grace comes home.'

'Nonsense, dear. You need a proper night's sleep. I'll be going up myself now so I'll leave the bottle in your bedroom.'

They wished Gussie goodnight and she departed with the dogs flowing round her. They heard her voice in the garden as she let them out briefly, then the sound of their claws on the stairs as she went up to bed.

Maddie and Lyle sat before the dying fire for a while longer, Lyle nursing a glass of whisky. Maddie leaning forward in her seat, her hands twisting uselessly in her lap.

'Go to bed,' Lyle ordered.

'I think I will.'

'And take one of Gussie's wretched tablets.'

'I don't want to. Grace might come home or Sarah might need me.'

He sighed.

She glanced up at him. 'What do you think of what Gussie said earlier?'

'About ghosts? Pure nonsense, of course. Gussie has always been odd, but I'm wondering if the old girl is losing it.'

'Perhaps she is, Lyle. But there may be a grain of truth in what she says about Flora haunting us. I'm not the sort to see ghosts, but think of those drawings I made of her and how accurate you thought they were.'

'You must have seen my photograph of her.'

'I hadn't. Not then.'

His demeanour had changed and she was hurt by his tone. He didn't believe her, that was evident.

Instead she went on bravely, 'I sense that Gussie knows something important that she's not telling us. I don't mean supernatural.'

'What sort of thing?' His eyes narrowed as he replenished his glass then sat back in his chair.

'If I knew that . . .' She shrugged.

'Gussie likes to gives that impression.' He sipped his drink and laughed. 'It's part of the general air of battiness. Listen, Maddie, I'll tell you all about my dear aunt, if you like. I would have before, but it seemed fair to let you get to know her without my interference.'

There was a shushing sound as a log in the fire fell into ashes. Maddie looked at him expectantly and he went on.

'As far as I can tell Gussie's always been the way she is. Childlike, delicate. She was born six weeks early and nearly died.'

'That certainly explains her fragility and why her mother was worried about her.'

'Indeed. George and William were very affectionate and gentle to their elder sister and Gussie loved her little brothers back. Philip and I were fond of Gussie. She had an affinity with young children. As I grew older I thought her a bit strange, tied to the house as she was and having no interest in the outside world.' Here he glanced up at the portrait of Eleanor Anderson over the fire. 'My grandmother protected her always. And as you know, Gussie has a fierce love for Knyghton and for the Anderson family and that's it. Her only friends are animals. That's been her life. But it's about more than love of her home. Gussie's always liked to project the impression that she's the keeper of Knyghton and its secrets. She may appear innocent, but she liked to snoop around and find things out. And she could be awfully manipulative. She didn't like Flora when she came, regarded her as an interloper, a cuckoo in the nest, if you like, and made it clear. Here's another example: she played her part in persuading my mother, Daphne, to leave.'

'With the awful Mr Sugden?'

'Yes. And this manipulative tendency is why I suspect her of causing that fire. You may wonder why she'd endanger the house she loves and her dogs, but I think it was about power. A hint to me that if I can't save Knyghton then no one else should have it. I don't seriously believe that she intended to burn the whole place down, but it was a stupid thing to do.'

'Very stupid. I suppose it's likely that you're right. After all, who else would be so careless as to leave a lit candle in the kitchen? And Flegg did find her wandering about outside.'

Lyle sighed. 'Strangely, though, Maddie, I feel sorry for Gussie. She couldn't help her odd upbringing. And Fate has been unkind to her.'

'Her parents died, and her brothers, and now Knyghton itself is under threat?'

'Yes. After my grandmother's death she grew markedly different. Less focused. Preoccupied.'

'Eleanor died not long after Flora's tragedy, didn't she?'

He nodded and sipped his drink. 'Six months or so. The doctor said her poor heart was worn out by it all.'

Maddie's mind was working. 'So you could say that Flora's death caused Eleanor's?'

'Not directly, but it must have had its effect. What are you getting at?'

'I'm sorry, I'm not making sense.' Maddie rubbed her eyes and stood up. 'You're right. It's probably time for me to turn in.'

Lyle set down his glass and came to her. 'Poor Maddie.' He took her by the arms and drew her to him and she laid her head on his shoulder. Gently he rocked her. 'Grace will come home tomorrow, I'm certain.'

She had managed to hold in her grief, but now she let out a sob.

'Shh,' he said and he bent and kissed her cheek and stroked her hair. Then he took her face in both hands and began to kiss her. She wriggled away.

'Maddie, please let me,' he whispered, and tightening his grip, pulled her closer. His arms were round her now and his mouth moved down her neck and he stroked her breasts through her blouse and fumbled at the buttons.

'Lyle!' she cried, shocked. 'Don't. Lyle. Please.' With all her strength she pushed at him violently. 'For God's sake,' she cried. He staggered, then recovered himself, wiping his mouth on his sleeve and the fire left his eyes. He hung his head.

'I'm sorry. You're so beautiful. Why won't you let me have you?'

'We've been through this before,' she hissed. 'Just leave me be.'

She turned and flounced out of the room.

Upstairs, she undressed and sat on the bed in her night-gown, staring at the bottle of sleeping tablets Gussie had left on her bedside cabinet. Finally she swept it into the drawer and considered pulling the chest of drawers across the door in case Lyle tried to come in. But suppose Sarah needed her? Instead she tiptoed out and down the corridor to the nursery, where she climbed into Grace's empty bed. Here she lay in the dark with Grace's pyjamas pressed to her face, imbib-ing the milky fragrance of her and cried herself quietly to sleep. She dreamed of being trapped, held down, unable to escape to save her daughter who was somewhere far away in the darkness.

Thirty-eight

France

March 1941

Early one morning at the end of March Philip disembarked from a bus near Marseilles railway station. He was exhausted, his clothes ragged and dirty, and he dawdled for a moment, bewildered by the crowds, the noise and the bright spring sunshine, before he pulled his cap down over his eyes and made his way towards a down-at-heel café. There he ordered toast and coffee and ate hungrily, pondering what to do next. As he counted out the last of the money the doctor had given him to pay for his food he felt the patron's curious eye on him and wondered if he should take a risk. *'Je cherche une carte de la cité,'* he told the man, who glanced about quickly then fished a dog-eared map from a drawer behind the counter.

'Vous voudriez quoi?' the man growled, unfolding the map.

'*Le Consulat American.*'

'*Ah, vous êtes American.*' His voice was heavy with irony, but he pointed to a spot on the map that was already well-worn. How many British evaders had the man already helped, Philip wondered, and thanked him, before going on his way. Outside he set off in the general direction that the patron had shown him, but he must have turned off too early, for he soon found himself in a maze of gloomy streets so narrow that the buildings almost touched overhead.

He dodged round shopkeepers preparing for the day, raising shutters or washing the cobbles outside their shops. At a window above an apothecary a girl was pegging dripping sheets onto a line and he raised his head, welcoming the cool water on his face. He walked on, following his nose, not daring to ask for directions. Before long he came to a tiny square where women were gossiping and laughing as they washed clothes in a gushing fountain, and he smiled his thanks as they made space to let him fill his water bottle. As he continued along the street, he was astonished to see the silhouette of a tall sailing ship filling the narrow slice of sky ahead, an illusion of distance that told him he'd reached the sea. Now the buildings became grander and the street opened out suddenly onto a wide concourse marking the tip of a long, narrow harbour, like a finger driven into the land. This he knew from the map was the Old Port. Warehouses sprawled on either side and a great ugly gantry spanned the water. The sailing ship he'd seen was beyond this, further out to sea than his first sight of it had suggested.

The sea was beautiful, the deep blue of the Mediterranean,

and the air smelled excitingly of salt and oil and of the fish being unloaded from boats in glittering heaps and sold from carts crowded by customers. And now, despite the presence of a pair of strutting gendarmes, his spirits rose. Marseilles was a gateway to the Mediterranean and the Middle East and, to the west, the Atlantic Ocean and the route home. If only he could find a ship that would take him.

Feeling the sun on his back and seeing the life of the busy port around him, all the fear and the frustration of the last few months began to fall away. He had nowhere to stay, and no clear route home, but still freedom felt tantalizingly close. For the time being at least, Philip was content to sit down on a bench in the shade, next to a man reading a newspaper, and take stock before trying once more to locate the American Consulate.

Since he'd left Sophie's farmhouse he'd been hidden in the attic of a friend of the doctor for the best part of a week until he'd left the town early one morning buried beneath a pile of stinking rubbish in the back of a cart, clean clothes safely folded in a bag. The driver had dropped him off at an inn on the border with free France, where the proprietor allowed him to wash and brought him a meal before explaining where he could cross the line unnoticed. As night fell, Philip followed the line of a hedgerow between fields, crawled between the coils of a barbed wire fence and walked to the lane beyond. It should have felt like a triumph, but it had been too easy for that and having little idea of where to go next he wandered the lanes, taking his direction from the sun in the day, sleeping in deserted shacks at night. On one occasion he broke the lock on a shed in a cemetery outside a village and slept inside surrounded by battered flower urns, spades and a half bottle of what turned out to be rather good brandy.

Then his luck ran out. In Lyons, after asking directions in a charcuterie of a sharp-faced woman behind the counter he was picked up by a pair of gendarmes and spent several days in a cell before he managed to escape and continue the long walk to Marseilles. The bus driver had stopped to pick him up a few miles outside the city, and for that he was grateful.

He ought to get going. As he walked back into the mass of busy side streets, where it was possible to be more anonymous, he remembered the name of the square the American Consulate was in – Place de Félix Baret. He spotted a second-hand bookshop where he found an old guidebook with a map tucked into the back. He could not afford to buy the book, but he worked out the route. He'd come some distance out of his way, he realized, but he was able to orientate himself using the port as a lodestar and thought he had it now. The bookseller was watching him curiously so he quickly slotted the book back into its place on the shelf and left.

Place de Félix Baret turned out to be a huge rectangular open space lined with grand buildings in a classical style and populated by trees bursting with the high-pitched twitter of birds. Philip joined the short queue of people waiting outside the American Consulate, but it was an hour before it was his turn to enter a tiled hallway, climb the stairs and present himself to a harassed-looking young man in the office. It was a tremendous relief to be himself again, to explain his position in English and be readily understood.

'May I ask you to wait a moment, please, sir?' the young man bade him and rose to knock on a nearby door. A moment later Philip was ushered into this inner office and spoke with the consul himself. Later that day he returned and to his delight was furnished with non-combatant identity papers and given an address very near the Old Port where he'd sat that morning.

'It's the British and American Seamen's Mission,' the consul said. 'Ask for Mr Caskie.'

When Philip presented himself at the white-painted hostel that occupied the meeting point of two cobblestoned streets he was invited in and interviewed by a middle-aged Scotsman in a clerical collar. The Reverend Donald Caskie was welcoming and sympathetic, but he explained with great sternness the conditions under which he would agree to help Philip.

'The French police are under instructions from the Gestapo and so we are watched constantly and regularly subjected to raids. We are only allowed to help civilians here and you must follow my rules exactly. I see from your papers,' he said with a knowing smile, 'that you are indeed a non-combatant, and luckily I happen to have a free bed. I will do my best to get you home via Spain, but the timing is mine. It may be days or weeks before I call you and it's my decision whom I call when, because I know what I'm doing and what is most likely to work. Do you understand me?'

'Perfectly. Thank you.' Philip was intensely grateful for the man's kindness, but secretly disappointed that there would be another delay.

'Do you have any questions?'

'Yes. Is there any way that you can let my family know that I'm safe?'

'I will do my best,' Caskie said gently and Philip had to be content with that.

After producing some clean clothes for him from a secret stash Caskie showed Philip upstairs and into a simple dormitory where four other men were resting on their beds, reading or playing cards. They nodded in a friendly way, but no one spoke to him as he pushed his knapsack under the spare bed then investigated a pack that Caskie had given him containing a towel, a razor, soap and a toothbrush. One of the men pointed him towards a bathroom along the corridor. After he'd showered and dressed, he began to feel more human. Philip bundled up his filthy old clothes as instructed and took them downstairs to be burned. It was enormously pleasurable to be served a simple meal of soup and bread in the quiet dining room and he forced himself to eat slowly to prolong the enjoyment. Once he'd finished he returned to the dormitory, lay down on his bed and quickly fell into a deep slumber.

Everybody had to help out at the Seamen's Mission, he quickly found. The following morning, much refreshed, he was dispatched with another evader through the narrow winding streets to queue outside a little Greek grocer's shop, whose owner, it became apparent, was ready to help Caskie's waifs and strays. They both handed over ration cards and gratefully packed away the supplies the grocer sold them, cheered by the smell of the newly baked bread. Housework and cooking were also part of the remit and if there was no meat and the vegetables were past their best at least there was sometimes fish. Philip was simply glad to have regular meals. The comings and goings at the hostel were mysterious. Sometimes extra bodies appeared without explanation and slept on pallets on the dormitory floor or someone who'd been there when he went to bed wasn't there in the morning.

There was an air of general caginess in the dormitory, but he understood why. Caskie promoted a 'need to know' policy. No one readily shared any information because they did not know who might overhear and who might betray.

'Marseilles is riddled with spies,' Caskie had confirmed at their first meeting. 'Keeping mum is the only thing to do. Lives are at stake, including yours.'

One day Philip was abruptly woken at first light by the sound of loud voices speaking French outside, then the door of the dormitory was thrown open to reveal Donald Caskie. 'It's a raid,' he murmured, with remarkable sang froid, and at once all the men leaped out of bed. Philip knew by now that it was vital to hide evaders who had no civilian identity papers. He assisted by raising a floorboard to enable a wiry flight officer to wriggle into the space underneath. The plank was then nailed back down while someone else hid the man's possessions and then everyone climbed back into their beds. Just in time, for downstairs Caskie could be heard admitting the gendarmes, who clattered up the stairs and swarmed through the rooms, nosing into everything and asking the men they found for their papers. No combatants being evident, they questioned Caskie for a few minutes and eventually departed, disappointed. Once it was apparent they'd gone for good, men rose from their hiding places like the dead at the last trump. The mission had survived another raid.

Thus the days and nights passed. Caskie was always busy. Even late at night he could be found sitting behind his desk, in a halo of light from a hooded lamp, working out the next day's schedules. He would usually make time for a chat if a man needed it, indeed he clearly regarded it as an important part of his work to minister to the souls of the poor wretches to whom he gave sanctuary. As for confidentiality, Philip had no doubt that the man could be trusted. He was used to Caskie being guarded when it came to names or sensitive information. The priest was a man who would keep your secrets.

One evening, Philip found himself telling Caskie about Maddie and how dreadful he felt that he'd betrayed his marriage vows. Did Caskie think he should confess his affair with Sophie to Maddie once he got home? Caskie studied him and said nothing for a moment, but Philip could sense his deep concern. Finally, Caskie replied, 'I cannot advise you, only you will know what seems right. But I urge you to reflect. You will have been missing for well over a year by the time you return and you don't know how matters will have been for your wife. She may well have been told you are dead – although I hope the good news that you are safe and well will reach her soon. Depending on what you find you will need to treat her gently. It will not be easy for either of you. You cannot simply return to the relationship you once had. It is likely gone for ever and you will both need to forge a new and stronger one.'

Philip hung his head under the weight of this realization. 'You're right, of course,' he whispered. 'We will both have changed.'

'Would you like me to pray with you?'

Philip would normally have been embarrassed by such a suggestion, but here, in the gloom of this bare-walled room with this man of such sincerity, humility and strength of spirit, it felt right. He squeezed his eyes shut and joined in when Caskie murmured the familiar words of the Lord's Prayer in his comforting Scottish accent, and when Caskie called down God's blessing on him, he echoed Caskie's 'Amen'. After that conversation, although nothing had materially changed, Philip somehow felt better, more prepared for whatever lay ahead.

A fortnight, three weeks passed, then one evening in early April, Caskie drew him aside. 'You must be ready tonight,' he told Philip in a low voice. 'I'll call you at two a.m.'

Philip went to bed early and fully dressed, but could not sleep for excitement. Still, he'd fallen into a doze by the time Caskie roused him and felt muzzy as he gathered his bundle in the moonlight, pulled on his beret and crept downstairs to find Caskie and three other men waiting in the hallway.

Caskie shook hands with all of them and they thanked him effusively, then he showed them outside, entrusting them to the care of a stocky Frenchman wearing a dark trenchcoat. Soon they were sitting huddled together in semi-darkness in the back of a van, which bumped slowly and quietly over the cobbles and carefully around tight corners until they reached a main road. Once they left the city behind the van picked up speed. Philip was on his way home.

One of Philip's companions, an RAF pilot named Collins, seemed somehow to know that they were heading for Perpignan, two hundred miles west along the coast. The tricky bit, he said, would be crossing the border at a safe point with their guide and climbing the Pyrenees into neutral Spain. After that, they would be transported south all the way to Gibraltar and from there shipped home. Philip closed his eyes in relief at the prospect. He'd had enough adventure for a lifetime. The men were mostly silent as the van rattled along, each lost in his own thoughts, presumably, like him, still traumatized by their experiences and hardly daring to hope that their ordeal would soon be over.

One of them was very young. Philip didn't know his name, but when the boy lit a cigarette Philip saw in the flare of the match how pinched and unhappy he looked and guessed that he'd experienced the worst of war and as a result could no longer live with himself. Philip heard again in his mind the rattle of machine-gun fire and his body quaked with his own remembered terror. *Quiet*, he told himself and tried to stay calm by thinking of Maddie's face, which led him to turn over the conversation that he'd had with Caskie. He wondered if Maddie knew by now that he was alive and whether she was still waiting for him or . . . *Stop torturing yourself.* Finally he fixed his thoughts on the here and now of the sound and vibration of the van on the road, thereby finding strength, and so the hours passed.

At Perpignan they stepped out blinking into early morning sunshine to see a breathtaking view of snow-capped mountains. They followed their driver into a terracotta-roofed inn with pretty shutters. There they were greeted by a plump woman, who appeared to be expecting them. She showed them to a table and brought them breakfast. While they were eating the patron entered, cast an eye over them all as he spoke to the driver in dialect and handed him an envelope, before retreating. The driver read the note inside and frowned, then tore the note into little pieces.

'Is everything all right?' Philip asked him in French.

'Yes. We have to change your route,' the man said brusquely, dropping the pieces into an ashtray. 'The usual one is guarded. It's not a problem.'

Philip nodded, satisfied. They all had the right papers, even if they were stopped. Their guide arrived, a tall, sinewy man who studied the four desperate men he was expected to lead over the mountains. After an urgent conversation with the driver about the change of plan, his expression was grim.

When they set off again this time it was on foot, a steady, zigzagging climb through the foothills towards the mountains looming above. The guide strode nimbly, but the men in his care quickly grew tired. He urged them on, and Philip caught the tension in his voice. They must be approaching the border soon. The air grew colder and coils of mist obscured their view.

Then, at the top of a steep incline, calamity. A Nazi patrol was waiting and everything happened very quickly. The guide raised his hands in surrender, as did Philip and the RAF pilot, but the other two men panicked and started to scramble back down the hill. One of their captors raised his rifle. Several cracks of gunfire and both fugitives fell and did not move again. Philip, the guide and the pilot were frog-marched down past their bodies and around the shoulder of the hill to the border checkpoint that they'd hoped to avoid. Here they were handed over to French guards, handcuffed and herded roughly into the back of a van.

'*Je suis désolé,*' their guide muttered. 'The letter at Perpignan. It must have been a trick. We have been betrayed.' Philip and the pilot said nothing. There was nothing to say. Philip thought of the twisted bodies lying on the mountainside. How near they'd all been to freedom and now two of them at least would never go home. He tried not to think of their families waiting for news of their return, having previously been told by Caskie's contact that they were safe. It was rotten luck, rotten. Oh, why had they tried to run?

On arrival back in Perpignan, he and the pilot were locked together in one police cell, their guide into another, but soon he was released and they never saw him again. Philip and his companion, however, lay on their pallets and awaited whatever was to be their fate.

Thirty-nine

Norfolk

Late August 1941

Maddie rose early after her troubled night in Grace's bed. At nine, she heard the sound of a vehicle crunching along the drive and flew to the front door. It was a police car and she waited in the doorway, her heart in her mouth, as it stopped in front of the house. A small pale face appeared at a side window and little hands battered the glass.

'Grace,' she cried, running forward. She snatched open the rear door and the child tumbled out into her arms and at once began to cry noisily, kicking Maddie's legs angrily.

'Somebody's pleased to be home,' laughed a burly officer, as he and the driver stepped down from the vehicle.

'Thank you,' Maddie cried. 'Thank you a thousand times.'

She hugged her daughter tightly, stroking her hair and murmuring soothing words until the child fell limp.

The rest of the household were assembling on the doorstep. Sarah charged forward followed by the dogs and they danced up and down around Maddie and Grace, making a joyful noise. Lyle came out and shook the policemen by the hand. Shortly afterwards Constable Rallison came cycling furiously up the drive, having presumably heard the good news and determined not to miss a thing.

Lyle invited the officers into the kitchen where Mrs Flegg quickly cleared the table, assembled chairs and made a big pot of tea. Grace snuggled exhausted on Maddie's lap, thumb in mouth, Rabbit in hand, her eyes unfocused. Gussie, who didn't like crowds, retired to the drawing room.

The burly officer slurped his tea and told his tale with much skill and enjoyment. The house in Great Yarmouth where Christine and her husband had taken Grace belonged, it had turned out, to Reggie's elderly aunt who was in hospital and didn't know a thing about what her nephew was up to. There was no one in when the police arrived late the afternoon before, but a pair of officers had been left to watch the place at a discreet distance while two others drove round the town looking for Reggie's car. It was thought that perhaps Reggie and Christine had discovered the loss of the map and, fearing discovery, made other plans.

The air raids interrupted the police operation, but it resumed at dawn. Reggie's car was eventually identified parked outside a beachfront boarding house where the fugitives were discovered tucked up in bed upstairs. The perpetrators were now in custody and Grace, of course, brought straight home.

'All's well that ends well, eh?' said the burly officer with a satisfied smile as he held out his cup for a refill.

'Indeed,' Lyle said. He sounded a little impatient. 'We're much obliged to you.'

The policemen took the hint and went on their way soon afterwards, Lyle hurried off to the farm and Maddie was left in peace with Mrs Flegg and the girls. Grace was sound asleep, so Maddie carried her up to the nursery, laid her on her bed and unbuckled her sandals. She noticed how clean and tidy the girl was in a new frock, the efforts of Christine, she supposed. Christine must have longed for a little girl of her own to dress up in pretty clothes, but Maddie could muster no sympathy for her. To rob Maddie of her child, justifying it to herself as an act of rectitude, was ridiculous.

For the moment though, as Maddie tucked the blankets around her beloved younger daughter, none of this mattered. Grace was home safe and Christine and Reggie were brooding over their sins in a police cell. And Maddie had shown courage and played her part. If she hadn't tracked the pair down in Sheringham the police would have missed them and they might have got away. She shivered at the thought, then looked up as the door sighed open. It was Sarah. She slipped into the room and together they nestled on Sarah's bed and watched Grace sleep.

'Was it Nanny Sutton who took Grace?' Sarah whispered. She'd been listening downstairs and discovered the story for the first time.

'Yes,' Maddie admitted, drawing Sarah close. 'She and her husband wanted a little girl of their own, but that was the wrong way to go about it.'

'I knew she was bad,' Sarah said. Maddie looked askance at her daughter. 'She wasn't kind to Grace. She stole her rabbit.'

'How do you know that?'

'Grace saw her with it.'

Maddie frowned. 'Why didn't you tell me? All that searching.'

'Oh, it was after that. Grace said she saw her leave it under the bush then pretend that she'd found it.'

'Oh, Sarah.' Why would the woman have done that? Was it to punish Grace by depriving her of Rabbit or to win her gratitude for finding it? The latter, surely. Maddie thought of all the trouble Christine had taken to endear herself to Grace, how Christine had feared to upset the child. Maddie should have followed her instincts and got rid of the woman months ago. Advertised again. There would surely have been someone better.

It was because of the war that it was difficult. This beastly war, it ruined everything and sucked the joy out of life. She didn't care about sounding selfish. Her thoughts ran in and out of one another in a great self-pitying tangle. She didn't think she could ever leave Grace with a childminder again. Even if it meant she couldn't work. It would be another year before Grace went to school, she'd have to last out till then.

She sighed. Maybe coming to Knyghton had been a mistake after all. If she and the girls had remained in London, found somewhere else to live, she would never have got herself into the mess she had. She wouldn't have got caught up with Lyle and with the tragedy of Flora. Nor would she have learned so much about her husband at a point when she'd lost him and could never confront him about the awfulness of it. Maddie let out a sob, then remembered Sarah's presence and stifled it. She had to go on being strong for the children.

While she was tidying her bedroom later Maddie remembered Gussie's sleeping pills. Fearing the girls getting their hands on them, she took them from the drawer and went and knocked on Gussie's bedroom door. There being no answer, she opened it and went inside, intending to leave the pills somewhere safe. Her nose wrinkled. The room needed airing – it smelled strongly of dog. In the excitement Mrs Flegg hadn't yet done her rounds. The curtains were half drawn and the bed hadn't been made. Maddie crossed to the chest of drawers and dropped the bottle inside a top drawer onto a pile of hair curlers. Then she went and threw open the window, having to lean over a small suitcase that had been left open on the floor there. Curious, she looked down and saw it was the case of photographs that she and Gussie had examined together, but which had never been returned to the loft. Gussie must have been going through them again.

Thinking that they might fade if left in the sun she bent to close the lid of the case, and her attention was caught by the print on the top of the pile. She picked it up. It was a picture of Gussie and her two brothers as adolescents, Gussie, slight and looking uncomfortable in a frilled blouse and stiff skirt, seated with her hair pinned up, the boys standing behind her in dark suits and white shirts with starched collars and cravats. Maddie wasn't sure which was George and which was William. They must have been close in age. That the three were siblings was obvious. Though Gussie's hair was light-coloured and the boys dark, there was something about the set of their eyes and their expressions that marked them out as related. She'd seen this picture before, of course, but another must have diverted her attention because she'd hurried past it.

Wanting to compare them with their parents, Maddie shifted the case and rummaged until she came to a pair of oval photographs set side by side in a cardboard frame. Eleanor and her husband, both still young, taken, she supposed, soon after their marriage. She sat down on Gussie's bed and set the photographs before her on the rumpled eiderdown, noticing the likenesses, but also the differences. Gussie looked more like her mother in her nose and lips, she decided. The boys favoured their father – it was the shape of the eyes. Maddie glanced up unseeing, thinking of how Lyle looked like his grandfather, but Philip with his reddish hair must be more like his mother than his Anderson father. Again she looked down at the photographs and an uncomfortable feeling stirred in her, though she couldn't think why.

She was just returning the pictures to the case when she heard light footsteps out in the corridor, then Gussie entered, followed by Phoebe the Pekinese. Maddie rose quickly.

'Oh, you made me jump!' Gussie fluttered, pressing her palm to her breast.

'I'm sorry. I was returning your sleeping tablets and saw the photographs. I hope you don't think I was snooping.'

'No, of course not,' Gussie said. 'I wanted my cardigan.' The dog scrambled up onto the bed, but Gussie took it up into her arms and fondled its ears.

'I was struck by the family likenesses,' Maddie said.

'Yes, I—'

Just then from downstairs came the sound of the doorbell followed by urgent barking. Phoebe struggled in her mistress's arms, then tumbled awkwardly. Maddie moved to save her, but her foot jolted the case so that half a dozen photographs slid to the floor. 'Oh, drat.' The dog righted itself and tore out of the room to join the melee below, while Maddie gathered up the fallen pictures. It was when she picked up the one of the household that showed Tilly in the background and stared at it that the uncomfortable feeling swelled once more inside her.

She looked at Gussie. Gussie stared back at her and a bolt of understanding passed between them, though the old lady said nothing. Instead, Gussie took up a cardigan from the bedroom chair, nodded to Maddie and left the room. Maddie stared at Tilly in the photograph then laid it on top of the others in the case and closed the lid.

She fetched the cracked photograph of Flora from Lyle's bedside. Back in her own room she studied it by the window and tried to do the maths. If Flora had been the same age as Philip and Lyle, she'd have been born around 1908. Gussie would have been in her late thirties then, George and William not far behind.

Maddie blinked. Her suspicions might all be nonsense. *I'm becoming cynical*, she thought. Yet the mystery concerning

Flora's life and death haunted her more than ever. She longed to clear her husband's name – for his sake but also for her own.

She stared at a teardrop-shaped stain on the wallpaper and pondered her next move. She could not tear herself from the idea that Gussie knew something that she wasn't saying. Maddie would have to tread gently, tease the secret out of Gussie, or the old lady would take fright and clam up. She brooded about the right approach as the day passed.

In the afternoon a detective arrived to question Maddie and Grace, but Grace would say little about what had happened, only shook her head when Maddie asked if anyone had hurt her. Maddie watched her go off to play with Sarah in the garden, her relief that the child was safe tinged with continuing concern. She knew from her own experience how such things could lie buried for years. One could only hope that Grace would be all right. The important thing now was that the detective said that Christine and her husband had that morning appeared before a magistrate, charged with child abduction. Maddie should expect to be called as a witness when the case came to court, but Grace was too young to give evidence. The pair had not been granted bail so Grace was in no further danger at present. Maddie felt the tension begin to drain away.

That night, though, she dreamed that she was lying in that dark cellar again, with something or someone sitting on her chest, pressing the life out of her. When she woke in the darkness of her bedroom her limbs were prickling with fear and she could not move. She thought about the horror of her experience, but also how she would overcome it for the sake of her daughter. Love for Grace had made her strong.

Slowly, the fear ebbed, but Maddie was wide awake now. She climbed out of bed and felt her way to the window where she twitched back a curtain and looked out. The back garden was bathed in liquid moonlight that picked out the shapes of the trees, their leaves shivering in the breeze, like a restless sea. It was all so beautiful. A fox emerged from the treeline and trotted across the grass, dipping its head from time to time as though following a scent. She had locked up the chickens herself that evening, so they at least were safe from its hunting. The fox sat down for a moment, with its brush curled round itself, raised its elegant head and licked its lips. Maddie smiled, visited by the memory of when Philip had first spoken to her in Norwich Museum while she'd been sketching one of this fox's relations, and now it seemed, just for a moment, that Philip was with her. She heard his voice in her head and found that she was blinking away tears. Leaving the curtain open so that moonlight flooded her room she returned to her bed where she lay quietly musing until she fell asleep.

Forty

The following morning was sunny. Maddie, who with Grace's assistance had been tidying the nursery, shook her duster out of the window and noticed Gussie sitting on the garden bench, Phoebe on a towel on her lap. She was combing the little dog's flyaway hair. Maddie waved to her. Gussie shaded her eyes with her hand and waved back.

'I'm about to make some tea,' Maddie called down. 'Shall I bring it outside?' and Gussie nodded.

A few minutes later she sat down beside Gussie on the bench, a tray of tea on a table between them. Gussie continued to comb Phoebe, who sat patiently on her lap, murmuring endearments to her. Maddie kept a close eye on Grace, who was throwing a ball for the other dogs on the lawn nearby.

'She'll be all right,' Gussie said.

'Who, Gussie?' It had taken a moment for Maddie to realize that she speaking about Grace and not Phoebe.

'Now that woman has gone.'

'Christine Sutton?'

'Yes. I never liked her.'

Maddie gave her a sharp look.

'Sly, she was,' Gussie said vaguely. 'She shoved Phoebe hard with her foot once when she thought no one was looking.'

'Oh, Gussie, I'm sorry.'

'Good girl, there, off you go.' Gussie finished fussing with Phoebe and the dog jumped down to join the others. Gussie shook out the towel and brushed hair from her skirt.

'Looking at those photographs, Gussie, made me wonder. Was Flora's father Mr Simpson? Her real father, I mean?'

Gussie shook her head, but did not look at Maddie. 'Mr Simpson wasn't Flora's father. He married Tilly when she was already expecting.'

Maddie drew a deep breath of excitement. 'They hadn't simply ... you know ... done things the wrong way round?'

'No, it wasn't like that.'

Gussie was infuriating.

'Do you know who Flora's real father was?' For a moment Gussie's lips worked silently and Maddie saw triumphantly that she knew the answer. Lyle had been right. Gussie's head may be in the clouds, but occasionally she revealed that she took in more than the casual observer might think. Anything where Knyghton was concerned, Maddie realized, and the people whom Gussie felt belonged to her, Gussie would squirrel information away for when she needed it.

She steeled herself for an answer that might change her picture of the Andersons, alter her sense of Philip, for ever.

'I don't know,' Gussie said finally. 'Only that Mr Simpson

came to the door once and my mother went out with him to the garden. I watched them from a window. She gave him some money. Then she fetched Tilly and left them together. Tilly was crying and he put his hand on her shoulder, to comfort her, I suppose, but she stepped away. Next thing we all heard they were getting married. Mother lent her a dress and went with her to the church. Flegg had made the pony and trap all pretty with flowers and wore his Sunday suit. He gave Tilly away. Mrs Flegg said it was because she was an orphan and had no one else. And that's the last we saw of Tilly except for the begging letters. She never even brought the baby up to see us, and you'd have thought she would have after my mother's kindness. Years later, when Mother received a letter from Mr Simpson to say he couldn't look after Flora, Mother went and fetched her and you know the rest.'

'Surely you couldn't say for certain that Mr Simpson wasn't Flora's father.'

'I heard Mrs Flegg say to Flegg once when she didn't know I was listening. It was soon after Flora came to us. She said, "Poor mite, I suppose he doesn't want her because she's not his."'

So the Fleggs knew, too. 'And she was definitely talking about Flora?'

'Yes,' Gussie sounded impatient.

'Very mysterious,' Maddie sighed, trying not to show her frustration. A thought occurred to her. 'Gussie, would you watch Grace for me for a few minutes, please?'

'Of course. Dear child. She's happy with the dogs, isn't she?'

Maddie stacked the tray and returned with it to the kitchen where Mrs Flegg was stirring the contents of a saucepan. Maddie began to wash up and wondered how to broach the subject of Flora. Once again she decided she must start with Christine Sutton. She dried her hands on a tea towel and turned to face Mrs Flegg.

'Mrs Flegg, I feel so dreadful for having employed Mrs Sutton.'

'How was we to know she was a wrong-un, Mrs Anderson?'

Maddie bit her lip. 'Her references were in order, but I should have taken them up. Spoken to the mothers.'

'You can't beat yourself up about that. Them as employed her might not have known the kind of person she was.'

'No. Gussie didn't like her, though. She says Mrs Sutton was sly.'

There was a pause. Mrs Flegg continued to stir. 'Reckon Miss Gussie was right.'

'I wondered if she was right about something else. I know you don't like me talking about Flora, but I need to know more about her for my husband's sake. Do you see?'

Mrs Flegg coughed, but said nothing. Maddie watched her stir the pan, then took a breath and said, 'Gussie says that Mr Simpson wasn't Flora's father.'

Mrs Flegg's hand finally stilled on the spoon and for one awful moment it struck Maddie that she'd been utterly tactless. It couldn't have been Flegg, could it? No, not that dear old man. But Mrs Flegg merely looked thoughtful.

'No, Albert Simpson weren't her dad. Tilly told us Mrs Anderson had fixed the wedding. Simpson had tried courting Tilly once but she wouldn't have him and then we found out why.'

'Why, Mrs Flegg?'

'Well, she'd been carrying on here, hadn't she? I saw them together.'

'Carrying on with whom?' She twisted the towel in her hands, dreading the answer. If it was Philip's father, William . . . then . . . no, she couldn't bear it.

'Don't tell anyone, mind, but it was old Mr Anderson, Miss Gussie's pa. He had his eye on Tilly the moment she arrived. She was a very pretty girl.' Mrs Flegg wrapped a cloth round the saucepan handle and lifted the soup off the heat. 'And he was a very charming sort of man. One for the ladies all right.'

Maddie's mouth dropped open. Eleanor's husband, Philip's grandfather! So Flora was . . . Gussie's much younger half-sister! Philip and Lyle's aunt! It was shocking – poor Eleanor, left to deal with it.

'And his wife knew all this?'

'I reckon she did. She had a lot to put up with, that poor woman. It must have nearly broken her but she knew her duty. That's what you did in those days, Mrs Anderson, just kept mum and got on with it. Not that I approved of such goings on, mind. Far from it.' Mrs Flegg shook her head as she untied her apron.

Maddie leaned against the sink, hardly able to focus. The mystery surrounding Flora was finally starting to unravel. If Flora had been part of the family then that would explain her arrival at Knyghton.

'So that's why Eleanor took Flora in?'

Mrs Flegg nodded. 'Old Mr Anderson was dead by then. Of course, the boys had no idea about any of it. Mrs Anderson told nobody what her husband had been up to with Tilly.'

'So Flora herself didn't know?'

Mrs Flegg was silent again. Then she said in a hard, unnatural voice, 'You'll need to ask Miss Gussie about that. We was told to say nothing and nothing is what we said.' She fitted a lid on the soup saucepan with more force than necessary, then bustled, grim-faced, into the scullery where Maddie heard her pottering about in the larder. She tried to process what the woman had said, but couldn't make sense of it.

When Mrs Flegg returned with a jugful of milk and started measuring ground rice into a bowl. Maddie dried more cutlery and said carefully, 'What exactly do I need to ask Gussie?'

'I'm not saying nowt. Are you going to take all morning drying that knife or can I have it here?'

Forty-one

London

September 1941

The first sign that something was wrong came after Philip disembarked at Southampton very early in the morning. He passed a shocking number of bombed-out buildings around the harbour before he found a kiosk with a working telephone, but when he asked the operator for his home number she told him it was no longer in use. He replaced the receiver and stood thinking for a moment until the next person in the queue knocked impatiently on the glass.

Despite his anxiety about Maddie and the girls he slept on the train to London, stumbling out into the vast echoing space of Waterloo station shortly before ten. He checked the instructions he'd been given on the ship and took the underground to Marylebone. Though he yearned to get home, duty must override everything. He spent much of the day being debriefed by a pompous major sitting across from him behind a desk in what in peacetime was an elegant hotel bedroom. The man had cross-questioned him with urgency about the massacre that Philip survived and assured him that the matter would be passed on upwards. Philip told him, too, the news he'd heard at the internment camp near Perpignan, about Simon Wingate, the pilot he'd met in Paris, that he'd been shot trying to escape before Philip's arrival. Oh, the relief when shortly after three he was free to go. He tried telephoning Maddie again, without success, before committing himself once more to the depths of the underground.

The walk from the station at West Kensington was the first real opportunity he'd had to view the destruction that war had wrought upon London. He noticed with dismay the gaps between buildings, the bomb craters, how the once familiar had become strange. Dread dogged his footsteps, and his pace slackened as he rounded the corner into Valentine Street. When he reached the spot where number 38 had stood he stared in disbelief at the jagged silhouette of the back wall, the stumps of old beams probing the air, all that remained of the house he'd dreamed of as home. Much of the rubble had been cleared away and the ground was covered with a misty pink blanket of willowherb, humming with summer bees. As the initial shock faded, panic possessed him. Were they dead, then, his precious three girls, whom he'd thought about and longed for all the time that he was lost in France? He fell to his knees and began to shake.

After a while he mastered himself sufficiently to go and

ring the next-door neighbour's bell – what was her name? 'Nosey Norah,' Maddie had called her. Norah Carrington, that's right. She hadn't liked Maddie for some reason he couldn't fathom, but she'd been polite enough to Philip.

There was no answer, but he was sure he heard sounds within, so he knocked again, then shielded his eyes to peer in at the window of the dingy sitting room where a smudge of orange on the mantelpiece was the only colour.

The rattle of a sash drawn up overhead sent him stepping backwards. Norah's pinched face poked out of an upstairs window.

'Mr Anderson!' she said in surprise.

'Miss Carrington. Maddie, the girls ... what happened?'

'They got out all right,' she said in her cracked voice.

'Thank God.' He closed his eyes briefly then asked, 'Where are they?'

'I don't know!' she snapped. 'You'll have to ask that old cow at number 21.'

'Mrs Moulder, you mean?'

'They was there for a while then they went off to the country. I don't know where. Nobody tells me anything.' She paused then said. 'Wait there, will you. I have something for your wife.' She withdrew and the window squealed shut.

Philip waited on the doorstep, his mind working. They were safe, but not in London. Where would they have gone, then – her parents in Norwich? He glimpsed Miss Carrington's unkempt, angular figure lope into the sitting room and seize the orange blob from the mantelpiece, then a moment later the front door creaked opened and she held the item out to him. 'This came for your wife.' It was an orange envelope. 'The boy didn't know where to deliver it and Mrs Moulder was away staying with her nephew so I said I'd take it. I didn't open it, of course. '

A telegram. Philip took it from the woman, staring at her, appalled by her negligence. After a second's hesitation he tore it open and unfolded the sheet of paper inside. *'Lt Anderson alive and well in France,'* the first words said. It had, it seemed, been dispatched by some army outfit in Edinburgh – Donald Caskie's contact, no doubt. He frowned and checked the date on it. The third of April, shortly after he'd arrived in Marseilles, in fact, and now it was September. So Maddie wouldn't know, wouldn't have heard that he'd survived, because this wretched woman had kept the telegram on her bloody mantelpiece. Anger surged through him but somehow he held it in.

'I kept it safe,' she whined, sensing his distress.

'You should have given it to Mrs Moulder when she returned and she'd have sent it on.'

'She doesn't talk to me,' Nosey Norah mumbled, staring at the sky. She had a mad look about her. Was she mad, or was this some sort of revenge on all the perceived slights she took from her neighbours? Philip hadn't taken much notice of the woman, but Maddie had often complained about her.

Philip folded the telegram away. There clearly wasn't any point in continuing this conversation. 'Thank you, Miss Carrington,' he said, shouldering his kitbag. 'I wish you good afternoon.' He touched his cap and withdrew, closing the garden gate behind him.

'My windows haven't been the same since that bomb,' she cried after him. 'Reckon I'm due some compensation.'

He ignored her as he crossed the street in the direction of Mrs Moulder's house, flinching when Norah's door slammed.

'Here's Maddie's address,' Mrs Moulder said, fumbling with her spectacles and smoothing the page of her engagement book. She appeared older and more frail than Philip remembered. 'Knyghton in Norfolk. She said it was her aunt's place.'

'Gussie?' Philip murmured in surprise. 'She's my aunt, not my wife's. Why should Maddie have wanted to go there instead of her parents' home? She doesn't even know Gussie.' His heart sank to think of his girls in the house he'd been so determined to escape.

'There's no telephone number, I'm afraid,' Mrs Moulder said, peering at her own spidery handwriting.

'They don't have a telephone,' he sighed. 'They are rather ... old-fashioned.'

He went on his way, thanking Mrs Moulder warmly for looking after his family.

As the train trundled towards Norfolk his mood changed with the regularity of the stations they passed through. He was going to see Maddie again, and his daughters and the thought excited him, but the loss of their house was terrible and he was certainly not looking forward to seeing Knyghton and its other occupants. The place was clouded by memories of his youth, memories of loneliness, heartbreak and tragedy. And now, he supposed, Knyghton would have entwined Maddie and the girls in its strange grip, too. Gussie had been even odder when he'd seen her in hospital and Lyle he remembered with contempt. No, he'd never have suggested that they seek refuge there if he'd had any say in the matter. He wished he'd warned Maddie.

The sun was beginning to set when he changed trains at Norwich. As he waited for the connection he thought about his and Maddie's happy courtship in the city and wondered how Maddie's parents were. He should have telephoned them, he thought suddenly. Well, soon he'd be able to ask her in person. On the train he counted the stops until the nearest station to Monksfield and Knyghton slid dimly into sight. *Well, this is it, chum*, he told himself as he stepped down onto the platform.

There were no cabs available this late in the evening, but since the moon was rising and he was used to walking he set out on foot. It wasn't long, though, before a passing doctor stopped in his old Austin car and offered him a lift as far as Carshall. When he heard Philip's story, though, he was so moved that he insisted on taking him further. Philip thanked him and asked to be dropped at the bottom of the lane to Knyghton. He needed the walk to prepare himself, he said.

After the doctor's car pulled away Philip set his face towards Knyghton. As he walked in the cool night air, familiar scents of white meadowsweet and freshly turned earth rose around him, stirring nameless memories. Above the trees hung a full moon trailing wisps of cloud. Soon he reached the cover of the canopy where moonlight dappled the loam beneath his feet and here was the old gate and the same old hand-painted sign. Philip touched the gatepost lightly for luck as he passed and thought that of all the versions of his homecoming he'd imagined, deep in France, this had never been one of them. Then he shrugged his kitbag more securely onto his shoulders and strode up the drive, hoping that someone would be up to welcome him.

Forty-two

Maddie felt restless that evening, but couldn't say why. She simply couldn't settle to anything. Lyle had gone out on a moonlight Home Guard exercise in Monksfield Woods while Gussie sat playing patience and muttering to herself. Otherwise, all was quiet. The planes hadn't visited Norfolk tonight.

She'd been sketching in her book. She'd had an idea to write a children's story, but it wouldn't quite come to her. She knew the appearance of the central character – or the girl's face, at least – and that there would be animals, a hare, perhaps. She knew the source of her inspiration, but not how to turn the idea into a story with pictures yet. It would manifest itself if she pegged away at it. She finished drawing a thumbnail sketch of a mouse on its hindlegs carrying a flower. Outside an owl hooted, making her look up. The curtains shivered in a sudden breeze from the open window that brought with it the scents of the garden. She put down book and pencil, stood up and stretched.

'I'm going out to get some air, Gussie.' The dogs were piled on top of each other peacefully asleep and did not stir.

'That's spades out!' Gussie said triumphantly and smiled up at her. 'Don't catch a chill, dear.'

'I won't, I promise,' she said, buttoning her cardigan.

When Maddie slipped out of the back door the garden seemed like a different world, bathed in moonlight, each branch, each leaf, the roofs of the outhouses and the wall of the kitchen garden tipped with silver. The white stripes between the black beams of the house gleamed as though the building was electric. The only sounds were her feet softly treading the grass and the hoot of the owl. As she drifted around the side of the house she was startled by the sight of the moon rising above the trees, huge and close tonight, the colour of old bone, scarred with lines and craters. The ancients had seen a man in the moon or in some cultures a hare. Maddie stood staring at it for a while tracing the patterns, trying to see what they had and feeling peacefully alone, but not lonely, caught up in the moment.

Philip turned the corner of the drive to see Knyghton before him, silent and glowing in the moonlight. He glanced about then stilled suddenly, seeing a figure standing some way off, its back to him, staring up at the moon. It was Maddie. With the moonlight pouring over her she seemed so wild and graceful, he was minded of the deer he'd seen in France last Christmas night. For a moment he could do nothing but stand and watch her, hope and longing coursing through him, but fear, too, fear that she wasn't real, that she'd vanish like a phantom if he approached. He licked his dry lips and shrugged off his kitbag.

Maddie must have sensed the movement, for she turned and saw him and for a moment froze as though terrified. And then something – a cloud or passing bird – caused the moonlight to flicker, breaking the spell. 'Lyle?' she said in a shaky voice and his heart almost broke. She took a step towards him, then hesitated. 'Oh, God, Philip, it really is you.'

'*Maddie*,' he breathed, his voice hoarse with longing, and he opened his arms to her. She staggered and almost fell, whimpering, but recovered herself and now she was running across the grass towards him, sobbing, 'Philip, Philip,' then slammed warm, solid and very real into his embrace, hammering at him furiously with her fists. He grasped her arms and held her tight as she sobbed and struggled until she fell slack with exhaustion, then he buried his face in her hair, breathing in the familiar flowery scent of her, soothing her, whispering her name.

'I'm sorry,' she managed to gasp. 'It's the shock. They said you're weren't coming back. They said you were . . .'

'I can imagine.'

She nodded. 'I nearly believed them.'

'I nearly was dead, several times.'

'But you're here now. How can that be? Why didn't you let us know?' She stared at him, gazing from head to toe as though to convince herself. Then she laid her cheek against his chest and he folded his arms around her.

'There's hardly anything of you. Philip, where have you been, what happened to you?'

'All in good time. Sarah and Grace, are they all right? Can I see them?'

'Yes, they'll be asleep, of course . . .'

'I must see them, Maddie. All these months . . . it's been the thought of you and the girls that's got me through.'

'Let's go inside.'

Philip released her so he could gather up his kitbag. As she reached out her hand to lead him he heard a grinding sound and turned to see the flickering silhouette of a man on a bicycle careering up the drive towards them. A creak of brake rods, a shouted oath, but the bicycle didn't stop and Philip felt the full force of its crash into his side, with Maddie screaming, 'No, Lyle!', then all was confusion, both men wrestling together on the ground, the bicycle thrust aside, its front wheel spinning. From inside the house came the muffled sound of dogs barking and a child began to cry.

Maddie's eyes shot sparks and she strode off round the side of the house. After a moment the two men dusted themselves down, gathered their possessions and followed her sheepishly to the back door.

It was several hours before Maddie and Philip found themselves alone. They sat side by side on Maddie's bed, fully clothed, eyes red-rimmed, bowed by deep tiredness. *All the times I'd dreamed of this homecoming, I never thought it would be like this,* she thought. *There'd have been tears, but of happiness, not anger and frustration.*

She'd scooped the crying Grace from her bed, woken Sarah and taken them downstairs where they found Philip and Lyle in the hall glaring at one another before Lyle stormed off towards the kitchen. She felt so confused she'd been unable to speak to Philip, but then she forgot this for Sarah ran to her father and he swept her up, murmuring endearments. Grace, however, buried her tear-stained face in Maddie's shoulder and clung tightly to her.

'I'm sorry . . .' Maddie said with pleading eyes.

'She's too young to remember me,' Philip told Maddie gently. Together they returned the girls to their beds and sat with them until they fell asleep.

'They've missed you, though, Philip,' she said as she pulled Sarah's blanket over the child. 'Both of them. We all have.'

'I know. And I'm sorry, so sorry to hear about your father.'

Philip tucked Rabbit into the crook of Grace's arm. Then he picked up the candle and led Maddie downstairs where they found Lyle in the drawing room drinking whisky.

She left the two men together while she prepared a scrap supper for them and was content to find them on her return speaking civilly to one another. As the level in the whisky decanter grew considerably lower, Philip hesitantly told them the outlines of his story. Maddie listened, appalled, eventually sharing the relief he'd felt after he'd escaped from an internment camp in the shadow of the Pyrenees, then with help from an Andorran shepherd made his way across the mountains into neutral Spain and down to Gibraltar, from where he'd taken ship for home. Horrifying as it all sounded, she knew it wasn't the full story. It was like one of her sketches, lacking depth and detail, and her heart nearly broke under the weight of this knowledge. Something had changed in him. There was tautness in his manner, a nervousness in his speech and he smoked incessantly as he spoke, lighting each cigarette off the last.

Lyle, too, was chastened by the tale, for after Philip finished, he rose groggily from his chair, slapped his cousin on the shoulder and said he would leave them together. 'Very glad you made it through, old man,' he slurred, and thankfully there was sincerity in his tone.

'And thank you for looking after my family,' Philip said, putting his arm around his wife. 'It was a terrible shock to find what had happened to our home. I don't mind saying that I was surprised when our old neighbour told me that they'd come here.'

'Everybody at Knyghton has been welcoming,' Maddie said quickly, keen to clear any doubt. She bid Lyle goodnight and began briskly to tidy up the remains of supper to hide her emotion.

'Bed, I think,' Philip said, yawning and she felt her stomach tighten. Of course, she was delighted by his return, but everything was moving too fast. She wanted badly to be by herself and to think about what had just happened, how the husband she'd been told was dead had almost magically reappeared. She needed to accommodate herself to this.

As they sat side by side on her bed, which she must now think of as 'their' bed, she could not think what to say to him. There was six inches between them, but the gap might just as well have been as wide as an ocean.

Silently, she stood up and began her bedtime routine, changing into her nightgown while he watched, then he started to undo the buttons on his shirt. 'I have nothing to change into,' he admitted. 'Everything in there ...' he nodded at his kit bag, '... is filthy. And I'm none too clean myself.'

'Go to the bathroom,' she soothed. 'And I'll fetch some warm water.'

It helped them both. She undressed him as though he were a child and almost wept as she saw how emaciated he was, touched his bruises and the livid scar on his shoulder as he stood in the bath and she gently washed him then wrapped a towel round him.

In bed they lay spooned together, and she quickly heard his breath grow even. She wished she, too, could sleep, but her mind was too active thinking of what he'd endured and of the deep enmity between him and Lyle, wondering how things could ever mend between them all.

Here at Knyghton, she'd been safe, looking after the children, calmly continuing with her work while Philip had been suffering and she did not know what to say to him about it. She'd suffered, too, but even the fright about Grace and being shut in that cellar could not be compared to what he had been through.

She must have slept, because she surfaced in the night to feel the bed empty and cold beside her. For a moment she wondered if she'd dreamed of Philip's return, but then the door opened softly in the darkness and he entered, bringing with him the chill of outdoors. He climbed back into bed and fell asleep instantly. In the morning, when she asked him where he'd gone, he couldn't remember.

Witnessing the Fleggs' joy and Gussie's warm welcome to Philip the following morning and the way Sarah and Grace capered about, Sarah not letting their father out of her sight, made Maddie hope that all would be well once more. Yet Philip already seemed restless, directionless and any unexpected sound made him start. Often he'd begin to speak, then fall silent, as though the effort were too much. She resolved not to bother him with questions for the moment and sent the children over to play with Nadja and Milo, knowing that her husband needed to rest.

Philip sat in the farm office a few days later recording the details of a seed delivery in the big ledger. It helped, he'd found, to immerse himself in small tasks, and since paperwork was what he was good at and Lyle hated it, he was making himself useful. It made him feel rotten to be keeping out of Maddie's way, but he was finding he couldn't bear her anxious eye on him, the constant small attentions, though he could see that she was holding herself back and was grateful. He'd been used to fending for himself for so long now and keeping his own counsel, that such behaviour was ingrained in him.

He wanted things to become normal between them again. Seeing how beautiful Maddie was in the moonlight the night of his return he knew that he loved her more than ever, but it was as though there was a spreading silence between them that he lacked the courage to cross.

The downside of this office work was that he was in regular contact with Lyle. His cousin was civil and glad of Philip's help with administration, but there was no warmth between them. This had been the case between them for years, ever since that terrible day fifteen, no, sixteen years ago when Flora had died. Each had blamed the other, but probably neither knew who'd fired the fatal bullet and it was too long ago now for the truth ever to be revealed.

It was something more than the familiar froideur between them though, Philip decided as he returned the ledger to its shelf and freed the next slip of paper from the metal spike on the desk, a bill that needed urgent payment. Lyle actually resented his return. Philip sat for a moment, the bill in his hand, considering this. Through the dusty small window looking out onto the yard he could see Lyle speaking urgently to the prettier of the two land girls and gesturing towards the barn. His cousin looked utterly fed up about something, but then Philip had hardly seen him smile since he'd arrived. The farm, it was obvious to him as he went through the ledger, was in financial difficulties, though how extensive these were he couldn't tell. But that couldn't be the reason for Lyle's resentment towards his cousin.

The incident with the bicycle still troubled him. Lyle had insisted that it was an accident, that he'd been so shocked to see Philip that he'd applied the wrong brake, the one that didn't work. Philip hadn't challenged this explanation, but he was still haunted by the suspicion that Lyle had deliberately ridden into him. He'd sensed his cousin's anger. And that suspicion had been fed recently by his observation of Lyle over the last few days, the way his cousin looked at Maddie and the careful, polite way that Maddie treated Lyle. Was there something between them? No, the thought was unworthy of Maddie, who'd welcomed him back with all the warmth he'd wished for. Yet still that worm of unease stirred in Philip's mind when he was with them.

He laid the bill down on a pile of others on the desk then drew another off the spike and smoothed it out, but he could not concentrate on it. Instead he was remembering the conversation he'd had with Donald Caskie towards the end of his time in Marseilles. Philip had confided in him about his guilt over the French girl, Sophie, and Caskie had thrown the problem back at him asking him to be considerate of Maddie. Maddie had been told that Philip was probably dead so it was perfectly reasonable for her to have looked elsewhere ... but to Lyle? A rush of jealousy shot through Philip with such force that his hand shook. *Anyone else,* he thought, *but not Lyle.* It felt as though a great faultline had opened up before him and he'd fallen down it. It was exactly how he'd felt all those years ago when they'd tussled over Flora. Were he and Lyle to be rivals in love once again? He closed his eyes briefly and waited for reality to reassert itself. He mustn't think about it now, he was too tired and strung out. He must bide his time. Maddie, of course, wouldn't know about Flora. He'd never found the courage to tell her. Should he have done? It was one of the reasons he hadn't introduced her to Knyghton. Again, that worm of unease.

He hadn't wanted to come back to Knyghton, but here they were. Sometime, he knew, he would be called back to his regiment and have to leave Maddie here. What would happen then? Through the window he saw that Lyle was standing alone with his back to him, hands on hips, staring into the distance. As though aware of being watched he swung round and met Philip's eye through the glass. Philip nodded and hastily returned to his work.

That night, he turned to Maddie and they made love for the first time, tenderly at first, then fiercely, and he was ashamed to find tears on his cheeks afterwards. Maddie kissed them away and held him close and they lay listening to the distant sounds of explosions and the reply of the ack-ack guns.

'It must have been dreadful for you in London,' he whispered, thinking of what his little family had endured.

'Terrifying,' she murmured. And she spoke for the first time of the night their house was bombed and how she was sure they were going to die under the heap of rubble.

'My poor darling. You've had to be so brave.' He remembered her childhood fear of tight spaces. 'Thank God you've been safe here.'

'We haven't exactly,' she said, and she explained in broken words how they'd not initially felt welcome at Knyghton, and described the series of events that had led up to the abduction of Grace.

Outrage coursed through Philip's limbs as she recounted the details of her imprisonment in the cellar in Sheringham, and how Grace was eventually recovered. 'It's about time they installed a telephone here,' he said. 'Ridiculous, all that running about.'

'It's all over now,' Maddie assured him and explained that the Suttons were in custody, awaiting trial.

She seems so calm, Philip thought, realizing how strong his wife was now. She'd lived through the most frightening experiences and shown a bravery he never knew she'd possessed.

'I'm proud of you,' he said, planting a kiss on her forehead.

'It's nothing beside what you've been through,' she sighed. 'How you survived I don't know. All those good folk who helped you. It's wonderful to realize there are so many brave people in France who are on our side.'

'The worst bit was not having enough to eat. I know a few tasty ways to cook a squirrel now.'

'No thank you.' He felt Maddie's face muscles tighten in disgust and smiled to himself. The account of his adventures that he'd given that first night had been heavily redacted. He had not described the horror he'd woken from near Dunkirk, nor the brutality of the soldiers who'd set the farmhouse alight, nor the beatings at the internment camp near Perpignan. He wanted to forget these and there was no point in disturbing Maddie with them. No, he would put the past year behind him. He would have to, anyway, in order to muster the courage to return to the front. He sighed in the darkness.

Maddie was silent and he'd thought she'd fallen asleep when she spoke. 'Philip?'

'Mmm.'

'There is something else I must tell you. Something that may make you angry.' He heard her intake of breath.

'No. Don't.'

'But . . .'

'I don't want to know. Not tonight anyway.'

'Mmm.' She fell silent again and soon, by her breathing, he knew she was asleep. Telling her about Sophie would have to wait for another time.

The following day being the last Saturday before the start of the autumn term, Mrs Clairmont had organized a Sunday school treat for the children, though wartime conditions dictated that it would only be a picnic and games in a meadow behind the rectory. Flegg fitted Bonnie between the shafts of the trap and took the girls there himself in their patched summer dresses with packets of sandwiches, leaving Maddie and Philip much needed time alone together. Maddie would have loved to attend, but Philip was not up to large social gatherings. She accepted Anna's offer to keep an eye on the girls and remained at Knyghton, where Philip was easily persuaded not to go down to the farm. She'd noticed Lyle's strange mood and hoped to try to clear the air. The rivalry between the two men could not be allowed to continue.

'Let me show you where I've been working,' she said, after the girls had gone. On the way upstairs she told Philip about the picture book she'd been illustrating and how pleased her editor and the author had been with the result. Philip followed her along the landing, hesitating a moment before entering his old bedroom.

'I like it because it doesn't get the glare of the sun in the mornings,' Maddie said, chattering to hide her nervousness as she watched him wander the room, open the wardrobe door and quickly close it again, then touch a gouged mark on the wooden mantelpiece. His gaze went to the floor by the bed, and she knew he was thinking of the old hiding place. She bit her lip.

'I found your parents' letters,' she said gently. 'Lyle told me where to look.'

'Lyle?' He spun round. 'How did Lyle know?' His eyes flashed with anger. Maddie quickly explained that it had been by accident.

'He was never usually one for sneaking about, I'll give him that.'

Maddie didn't like to say that Lyle had subsequently searched for the letters, but not found them.

'I suppose you read them,' he said dully.

'I thought I'd lost you,' she whispered. 'Of course I read them. It helped me feel close to you and ... to get to know you better.'

He sat down on the bed and stared down miserably at the floor. 'That's the trouble with this place. It drags you back into the past. And what's the point of going over it all? We can't change anything, after all.'

'No, we can't,' she said, thinking of that awful day when she lost her mother. 'But I was glad to know what had happened to you all the same. You never told me very much, Philip.'

He shrugged and managed a smile. 'You're right. I'm sorry.'

She sat down next to him and took his hand, then drew a deep breath. 'I told you about my mother, how she was killed in an accident, but I didn't tell you everything. You never asked much, you see, and I didn't want to bother you with it.' She didn't look at him. She might dry up if she looked at him. 'But it still affects me and now that I've lost Dad and because I nearly lost Grace I think about it more.' She stopped, wondering whether to go on.

'What do you think about, Maddie?' he said softly.

She turned to face him. 'When I was locked in that cellar I was so frightened, but I had to overcome that fear and I did. That's what I mean. Sometimes you do need to face the past.'

'I still don't understand. You've always had that fear.'

She closed her eyes and remembered. 'At my school there was a girl in the class above, Hillary, who disliked me. I don't know why, but she used to take things of mine – pencils, a cardigan. I know it was her. She was a bit like our old neighbour, Norah Carrington, a little strange. The pencils reappeared in my satchel, but snapped in half. The cardigan turned up in the lost property box, but with a hole in the sleeve that I know I hadn't made. Then it got worse. She used to pinch me when she passed. I didn't tell anyone. It never occurred to me to complain.'

'You were only six?'

'Yes. That awful day, when the bell rang for home time, I left the classroom with the others, but had to run back for my hat. While I was looking for it in the cloakroom Hillary came in, chatting to another girl. I thought she hadn't seen me, so I shut myself into a walk-in cupboard full of games equipment meaning to wait until they'd gone. The only thing is that when I tried to push the door open it was locked. I don't know to this day whether the latch had clicked shut by itself or whether Hillary had done it, but I hunched there in the dark for ages with the smell of rubber and dirty socks. I didn't like to make a row in case Hillary was still about and by the time I did, everyone had left and nobody heard. And in the meantime ...' She took a deep breath, but feeling the firm pressure of Philip's hand she went on.

'In the meantime apparently, my mother was looking for me. She'd come into the school then gone home and come back again, getting more and more frantic. I don't suppose she saw the car that hit her. As I grew up I always thought it was my fault that she died and I could never escape the fear of confined spaces. So there we are.'

She and Philip sat together silently for a moment after that. She glanced at him, wanting his reaction. Finally he cleared his throat and said, 'You've been extraordinarily brave, Maddie, I see that now.'

'I should have told you before.'

'You've always been het up about lifts or crowded spaces, but I never thought to ask why. But you survived being buried under rubble in the shelter and locked in a cellar.'

'For the girls' sake. I had to.'

He drew her close and she clung to him. After a while she gently pulled back. There were things that he had never told her, but it was no good posing him direct questions.

'You haven't asked me about my drawings,' she smiled.

'No, that's remiss of me. Come on, show me.'

She rose and went to the desk. 'Of course, my Sammy Squirrel illustrations are all with the publisher, but I still have the first versions of two that Mr Edwards asked me to redo.

Now, where are they?' She started to sift through papers. 'Here.' She laid them out for him to see and watched his eyes light up with pleasure.

'They're jolly good. What's wrong with them? You should have stood your ground.'

'He said they didn't quite reflect that part of the story and once he explained I realized what he meant.'

'Did he pay you for the extra trouble?'

'Oh no, Philip, that's not how it works at all.'

He frowned. 'I think you're very good-natured about it.'

'I have no choice.' She sighed, touched by his belief in her, but frustrated at his continued failure to understand. 'I'm not a proper artist, I'm an illustrator and I must follow instructions.'

'Mmm. May I?' He drew the pile of papers towards him and started to go through them, admiring some delicate studies of the girls and a sketch of the hare from above the front door of Knyghton.

Then, as she'd planned, he came to the portraits of Flora. His hand stilled and a frown crossed his face. 'Who is this supposed to be?'

'I think you know,' Maddie whispered and was dismayed to see the blood drain from his face. 'You never told me about Flora, Philip.'

'Who told you? Lyle, I suppose. And you believed his lies.'

'Stop it, Philip, please. It's not as simple as that. I don't believe in ghosts, but it's as though Knyghton is haunted by Flora and the secrets around her. I don't know why, exactly, I felt an urge to draw these. Lyle said I'd seen the photograph of her he keeps by his bed, but if I had I don't remember it.'

'How do you know what he keeps beside his bed?' Philip's tone was bitter now.

'Oh, Philip, don't be silly. The bedrooms here don't clean themselves, you know. And it wasn't just Lyle who told me the story.' She went on to explain briefly all that she'd learned about the tragedy, the rivalry between Lyle and Philip, what she'd discovered about the inquest.

'All this is the past, long gone,' Philip said. 'There's nothing to be done about it. It wasn't my fault.' His voice twisted with pain.

'It hasn't gone, Philip. That's the point. It affects all of us. You, Lyle, me, Gussie, the Fleggs and the girls. The whole village. It's something nobody wants to talk about.' She explained how Sarah was teased at school because of being an Anderson of Knyghton, Gussie regarded as a witch. 'Flora's death still haunts Knyghton. It's like a pall hanging over everything.'

Philip's expression turned sullen.

'It's time that the truth came out. Did you know that Flora was your aunt – and Lyle's?'

His eyes widened in shock and he shook his head wordlessly.

'I thought not.' She told him what Mrs Flegg had said and Gussie confirmed, and saw that he could hardly take it in. He sank down onto the bed, shaking his head in disbelief.

She sighed and laid a comforting hand on his shoulder. Poor Philip, after all that he'd been through to come home, only to face more pain.

He sat staring at the floor. Finally he looked up and said, 'If all this is true, I suppose it makes sense. Certain things my grandmother did. No wonder, seeing our interest in the girl, that she tried to send Flora away again. Poor woman, she had so much to put up with. And Gussie's behaviour back then. It was clear that she didn't like Flora, but now I understand why. Her father had hurt her beloved mother by his affair with Tilly and Gussie took it out on the child.'

'None of it was Flora's fault.'

'Of course not. I loved Flora, Maddie, I can't deny that, but it was calf love, a silly romantic thing between us, that's all. We were both very young. I never touched her. Not brave enough.'

Maddie felt a rush of gladness. 'And was it the same with Lyle?'

'I don't know about Lyle.' He spoke hesitantly. 'Flora was mesmerized by him, I could tell. Girls were. Young Susie Welbourne was always hanging about. I suppose she's married with a brood of children by now.'

Maddie shook her head. So Lyle had kept Susie on a string for a long long time, it seemed. Or maybe it was Susie's fault. Maddie didn't know and it wasn't her business any more. Not now Philip had returned. She felt herself blush at the thought that she'd been tempted by Lyle.

'Maddie?' So he'd noticed.

She could not look at him.

He tipped her chin so that she had to.

'I hate to ask this, but was there ever anything between you and Lyle?'

Her face grew warm. She pushed his hand away. 'Not really,' she sighed. Then she looked at him with direct gaze. 'I thought there might be,' she said. 'Everybody said that you weren't coming back and I felt . . . lost, I suppose. Oh, Philip, nothing happened, I didn't let it. Do you believe me?'

He studied her then slowly he nodded. Then he leaned and kissed her, gently at first, then more deeply. And she kissed him back.

Finally they drew apart. 'Poor darling,' he said, 'you've been through the mill, haven't you?'

'Nothing to what you've endured,' she whispered.

'At least I wasn't made to believe you were dead,' he said.

At that moment, there was a knock on the door and Gussie put her head round. 'Oh, here you are. Mrs Flegg's putting lunch on the table and you're late.'

That night after they made love Philip lay back and wondered again if he should tell Maddie about Sophie. It had been a day of confessions, but this one was too difficult. He had not fallen in love with Sophie, though he'd been fond of her and very grateful. She'd risked her life to help him. He knew that she'd felt something much deeper for him, but she'd also known how much he loved his wife. He tried to remember what else Donald Caskie had said and realized how wise the priest had been. Maddie had endured much while Philip had been missing. *Lyle.* The very thought of his cousin and Maddie together made him tense suddenly.

'Philip?' Maddie murmured.

He leaned over and kissed her. 'Go to sleep, darling.'

Then he fell back on the pillow. She'd said that 'nothing' had happened, but something must have or she wouldn't have mentioned the matter. And whatever it was had certainly possessed Lyle. The man's resentment of him was palpable.

He'd never thought of himself as a jealous man. It was specifically because the object of his ire was Lyle. It was as though the same old struggle was re-enacting itself. He closed his eyes and Flora's face floated into his mind, those serious grey eyes in which fear or delight could clearly be read. Would he ever be able to put the tragedy of her loss behind him?

He'd loved Flora, he'd readily admitted that to Maddie, although he'd portrayed it as an adolescent pash. That summer when he'd returned for the school holidays to find that she had grown into a willowy young woman with stars in her eyes, he'd been struck with the lovesickness that poets write of. They'd spent deliciously happy hours together reading and talking. Sometimes Lyle joined them if he was free and they'd walk through the fields to picnic by the river and swim. Over the next year in term time he and Flora sometimes wrote to each other, simple friendly letters. He'd kept a bundle of them in his desk. They must have been lost in the ruins of 38 Valentine Street like almost everything else. There had been a photograph album he'd once put together, he remembered, and a mysterious ornate silver key that he'd found after his grandmother's death, but which didn't seem to fit anything. Those things would be lost, too.

It had been when he came home after exams the following June that he found everything had changed. Flora was as sweet and welcoming as ever, but her eyes were no longer for him. He noticed it at once whenever Lyle sauntered in, she'd blush and then grow pale and her hands would flutter over the pages of her book. And Lyle would look at her lazily through narrowed eyes, an expression he'd recently learned to use that enraged Philip.

Gussie snooped about and then his grandmother had interfered. Suddenly Flora was sent to the rectory. 'To stay for a while,' Philip was told, but a week became a fortnight, and he wondered if she would be allowed to return. Nobody forbade them to see one another, but if he called by he was usually told that Flora was out or busy or the rector's wife would keep a strict eye on them. He'd been pleased when Flora was invited back to Knyghton for the night of the harvest supper.

Late that afternoon he was out in the top field with a rifle, watching for rabbits fleeing as the reapers closed in on the final patch of restless golden corn. When he'd shot one he collected it up and dropped it into a bag for the purpose.

He reloaded and moved on, following the reapers to the last field, where Lyle joined him and they took turns to take aim as the hapless creatures ran to and fro, looking for escape. Poor beggars, yet they were pests in a cornfield. They dug holes and ate the young shoots and their numbers had to be checked. From time to time, the arcing scythes sent a hare running and the boys lowered their guns and let it go. They had nothing against hares.

The late afternoon sun dazzled. It flashed off the metal blades, almost blinding him.

He blinked as he concentrated intensely on the edge of

the corn. Out of the corner of his eye he saw a fleeing brown shape that for a moment unnerved him. He'd raised his gun and fired just as his mind said, 'Hare' then heard a second shot echo round the field.

'Damn the sun,' Lyle spluttered. 'Still, one of us got 'im.' He ran across to claim their prize.

Had she cried out? Why hadn't they seen her? Had it really been the sun?

Philip sighed and turned over. He had to accept that he would never know the answer.

Forty-three

After lunch the following day Philip fell asleep in a deckchair in the garden, while Sarah tried to teach a ball game to Grace. Gussie was upstairs taking a nap and Lyle had gone off on his bicycle with a vacuum flask and a fishing rod saying he was intending to 'tickle some trout'. Maddie kept one eye on her daughters and the other on her husband. Sunshine creeping through the foliage cruelly picked out the lines on his face and the bruised skin beneath his eyes and her heart went out to him. His experiences had aged him, but she probably looked older, too. She certainly felt older. Less naïve, she hoped, more able to stand up for herself and her family.

A shadow flickered at the edge of her vision. A wren had landed on a nearby branch. Maddie stared at it with bated breath, noting the many different browns of its plumage and its quick movements, consigning its stubby shape and turned-up tail to memory so that when it flew off she reached down for her sketchbook, flipped it open and was able to draw it easily in small swift flicks of the pencil. Realizing she needed a softer lead for shading, she rose and went inside to fetch one.

The door to Philip's old bedroom stood open and she was startled to see a still figure inside bent over the desk. She drew a sharp breath, but Gussie didn't appear to hear. She was too busy examining a leaf of paper that gleamed like ivory in the pale light. Taking a step towards her Maddie saw what it was and her heart skipped a beat.

'Gussie?'

Gussie glanced up and Maddie was surprised to see tears glittering on her cheeks. She'd never seen the old lady cry before.

'What's the matter?' she said gently, but Gussie simply shook her head, then held out the page. Maddie took it from her. It was the picture of Flora's face. She did not study it, she was more concerned about Gussie, who seemed frailer than she'd ever been. She swayed slightly and Maddie put out a staying hand. Then she led Gussie slowly back to the safety of her bedroom and helped her onto her bed, pouring her a glass of water from a carafe and sitting by her as she sipped it. Still Gussie did not speak.

Maddie waited until the colour came back into the old lady's face then chose her words carefully. 'Gussie, what happened years ago has been allowed to cast its shadow over Knyghton for too long.' Gussie would not look at her, but Maddie bravely went on. 'There's so much that I know about Flora now.' She thought of all the secrets, of the girl's birth that had made her Gussie's half-sister and Lyle and Philip's aunt, and of her tragic death. 'I suppose no one will ever know who fired that fatal bullet. It was an accident, wasn't it? She ran onto the field recklessly, in a panic. But why? That's what we don't know.'

Gussie picked a tiny feather from the eiderdown. 'I told her,' she burst out and Maddie blinked. 'I told her who her real father was and why Mother had sent her away. I didn't want her here. Why had she come back? She upset everything. She shouted at me then, that she didn't believe me. And then she ran. I never told anyone before. Everyone would have blamed me, and it's true, it was my fault. And it was my fault that Mother died. "Too much grief," the doctor said, that's why her heart failed.'

Maddie closed her eyes briefly, but said nothing, trying to take all this in. She could hear the happy sounds of Sarah and Grace playing through the open window.

'It was my fault, wasn't it?' Gussie was looking at her anxiously now, like a child wanting reassurance.

'It wasn't your fault that Flora was killed, no,' Maddie managed to say. She wanted to add, *It was a cruel thing to say to a young girl, to unmake her like that, to tell her she wasn't wanted. No wonder she panicked and ran to find the people she loved most, the boys whom she'd just discovered were her nephews.*

'Gussie confessed to me,' she told Lyle and Philip late that evening when they were sitting in the drawing room. Apart from a brief appearance for supper Gussie had kept to her room for the rest of the day. 'She was jealous, deeply jealous of Flora, whose birth, the result of your grandfather's adultery, must have hurt your grandmother so deeply and who'd lately taken up so much of Eleanor's attention and threatened the peace of the household. Gussie thought Knyghton was rid of Flora, but that evening she'd come back. And all these years Gussie had kept her part in the tragedy to herself and the guilt has eaten away at her.'

Lyle rose and went to stand before the painting of Eleanor over the mantelpiece. 'Flora's death killed my grandmother,' he remarked. 'She never got over it.'

'That's true,' Maddie murmured. 'Gussie admits her part in that, too.'

Philip swirled the whisky in his glass and sighed. 'Poor old Gussie. She's never had much of a chance at life.' He was silent for a moment, lost in thought, then he frowned and said, 'I've remembered something. You know when I visited her in hospital that time, Maddie, the day I first met you?' Maddie nodded. 'Well, she said something very peculiar. She said, "It had to be you, Philip, it had to be you." But when I asked her what she meant, she closed her eyes and mumbled, "Knyghton. It was because of Knyghton." I dismissed it at the time, thought she was still woozy from the anaesthetic. Now I believe I know.'

It was Lyle's turn to frown. 'What did she mean?'

'I don't see how we'll ever know which of us killed Flora,' Philip went on. 'But the police seemed determined for a while to pin the blame on me. Yet why would either of us want to hurt Flora? We both loved her ... And the circumstances ... Flora should have kept away from the guns. It was very obviously an accident. We hadn't been drinking, though somebody said we had. The sun blinded me, that's all.'

Maddie's eyes widened. 'Are you saying that Gussie tried to make you shoulder the blame?'

'It's a possibility, don't you think? Lyle?'

All this time Lyle had been brooding in silence, turning his glass in his hands. He lifted his head and said in a low voice, 'Because if one of us was to go to prison it shouldn't be me because of Knyghton? You must ask her straight out, old boy.'

The following morning, Maddie watched from a distance as Philip strolled with Gussie across the grass deep in conversation, the dogs trotting behind. They stopped, and when Gussie turned to face him, her anguished expression startled Maddie. Then Gussie tottered and started to fall. Philip grabbed at her arm, but her slight figure slipped through his grasp and she slid to the ground. The dogs tumbled about their mistress, nosing at her and whining.

'Gussie!' Maddie began to run across the grass.

'It's the guilt that she's carried all these years,' Philip murmured to Maddie in the hall after they'd shown the doctor out. Gussie was resting on her bed with Mrs Flegg in attendance. The doctor was not the youngish chap who'd given Philip a lift on his first night home, but an older man who'd tended the Anderson family for years. Gussie had apparently been prone to these blackouts at times of high emotion in her life, and now that she'd come round she seemed as right as rain, if subdued.

'What did she tell you?' Maddie asked.

'It was as I thought. When the police interviewed her after . . . the accident, she told them I'd been angry with Flora because she preferred Lyle to me. Nonsense, of course, but if the blame had for any reason fallen on Lyle he might have been sent to prison and then what would have happened to Knyghton? Gussie always put Knyghton first.'

'But the coroner threw out the idea that you were to blame?'

'There was nothing to substantiate it. Phew!' he added, passing his hand through his hair. 'We know everything about the matter now, don't we, and I feel as though I've come out of a long tunnel.'

'You and Lyle can be friends?' She smiled.

'I wouldn't go that far.' His eyes glittered in the gloom of the hall. 'Not while we're rivals for you.'

'What rubbish, darling,' Maddie remarked. She leaned forward and kissed him hard on the mouth.

'It was finding this that made me decide to come to Knyghton,' Maddie said. She dug the package containing the photograph album out of a drawer in the dressing table and handed it to her husband.

Philip reached inside and drew out the book. 'Ah, yes.' He turned the pages, smiling to himself. 'Grandmother gave me the album for my birthday once and I collected the photographs to remind me of the times when it was idyllic here. We were evenly matched then, Lyle and I. He always caught more fish, but I was a better shot with a stone. My grandmother looks formidable here, doesn't she, but she was actually very kind.'

Maddie watched as he came to the final page. He stared at it and frowned. 'I hadn't noticed her before,' he said, showing her the blurred figure in the background that had intrigued Maddie from the start.

'Flora.'

'From those early days when she used to follow us around. A great nuisance we thought her. She was shy and hardly spoke to us.'

He closed the album and tried to slide it back into the envelope. 'Hello, there's something else here.' He fished out the small white packet and shook the key out into his hand, then smiled.

'I thought you'd remember what it was for,' Maddie said.

'I don't, actually. I found it after Grandmother died. Gussie had left the button box open on the coffee table and a dog must have knocked it over. It was there among the buttons spilled on the floor. No one knew what it was for so I put it in an envelope in my room for safety.'

'I see,' Maddie said, taking it from him and turning it over. 'Should we check with the household in case they've remembered it?'

'I suppose so,' Philip said, dropping the envelope into his jacket pocket. 'As I say, they didn't back then.'

Gussie was embroidering a handkerchief in the drawing room and looking perkier than she deserved, as Maddie set down the tea tray on the lacquered table and laid out the cups. She had just finished pouring the tea when Philip entered. She smiled a welcome then her eyebrows shot up in surprise as Lyle passed the window on his way to the back door with his fishing rod.

'He was whistling!' she said, setting a cup of tea in front of Gussie.

'A man can whistle if he wants,' Philip said mildly.

'But Lyle never does,' Gussie put in. 'He seems unusually cheerful, I must say.' She raised the cup to her lips and made a moue as she tasted the tea.

'Sorry. I gave lunchtime's tea leaves a second pressing,' Maddie murmured.

A moment later, Lyle joined them. He did look cheerful, Maddie thought, amazed, but glad.

'Hot and wet is the best we can do this afternoon,' she said, handing Lyle the cup she'd poured for herself.

'Hot and wet will do the trick,' he said with a smile. She rose to fetch another cup from the kitchen.

When she returned Lyle was in the middle of some story about assisting with an army lorry that had broken down by the church, from which she surmised that he'd been into Monksfield. She sat down and helped herself to tea and a rock bun. Lyle pulled a set of keys from his jacket as he searched for cigarettes and seeing them obviously reminded Philip, for he dug into his own pocket and brought out the envelope containing the silver key.

'Does this mean anything to either of you?' he said, laying it on the lacquer table.

Lyle squinted at it and shook his head. 'Where did you find it?'

While Philip explained how he'd found it in the button box, Gussie leaned forward, picked it up and turned it over. 'You didn't say before where you found it,' she said, looking up at him. 'Mother kept it there because she said it would be safe. I think she meant from Father. Father would never think to look in a button box.'

'I didn't know that it was important after all. Do you know what it's for?' Philip asked, but Gussie shook her head.

Just at that moment, Grace and Sarah sidled into the room, asking for cake. They sat down on the sofa on either side of their mother and were each given a bit of rock cake on a plate. After she'd finished hers, Grace put out her hand and picked up the key.

'Don't play with that, dear,' Maddie said and Grace put it down obediently, but then she slid off the sofa and crawled round to the other side of the lacquer table. 'What are you doing?' Maddie said, craning her neck to look at her daughter between the carved legs.

'Here,' Grace said, touching the underside of the table.

Sarah slid down to join her sister then she reappeared and picked up the key.

'Sarah?' There was a scrabbling noise.

'Come and see, Mummy.'

Maddie joined the girls on the hearthrug to look. In the side of the small but heavy table, hidden under the lip of its surface, was a tiny keyhole. Sarah fitted in the key, jiggled it about then turned it. Everyone gasped as a shallow drawer sprang out. Sarah peeped in then sat back on her heels, disappointed. 'It's only papers, Mummy,' she said.

Maddie reached in, gathered them up and passed them to Lyle.

'Oh, Mummy!' Grace cried. Her little hand slid into the

drawer and grabbed something else there, a large square, black leather-covered box. She struggled but couldn't open it so passed it to Maddie, who popped it open and gasped to see a gold and diamond necklace and a pair of matching earrings arranged on a velvet lining.

'Mother's diamonds,' Gussie cried, and Maddie stared up at her. 'The ones in the portrait!'

'What are the papers?' Philip asked Lyle, who was busy unfolding them.

'I'm not certain,' he said, passing one over to him, 'but they appear to be old government bonds. If they are,' he added cautiously, 'then perhaps Knyghton's troubles are over!'

Forty-four

Late December 1941

The Anderson family arrived early for the wedding at Monksfield church. There was something particular they wanted to do beforehand.

'Be careful, it's slippery,' Maddie called as the girls ran ahead up the graveyard path, which sparkled with frost. She and Philip and Lyle with Gussie followed more carefully, Maddie carrying a bouquet of winter hellebores in her arms.

They reached Flora's lonely grave and gathered round it while Lyle laid the bouquet, then Philip read Flora's favourite poem, the one that began 'There is a garden in her face/ Where roses and white lilies blow'. Flora had been lovely and unspoiled, like the girl in the poem. And if she'd lived, like that girl she'd have taken a boy of her choosing. After this simple ceremony they all stood in silence for a moment. Even the girls were solemn.

Maddie had explained to them both the afternoon before. 'Flora was Daddy and Uncle Lyle's relative whom they loved very much and she died a long time ago in an accident. Daddy and Uncle Lyle want to remember her on Uncle Lyle's special day so we're going to have a little special time at the grave.' Lyle had asked the Fleggs if they wanted to come, but Mrs Flegg sniffed and said it was mawkish. 'We'll just go to the wedding, if it's all the same to you, Mr Lyle.'

Lyle helped Gussie, Philip took Sarah's hand and Maddie Grace's as they walked back down the slope and into the little church. It was a chilly Saturday after Christmas, but the congregation already gathering was warming it up nicely. It was splendid, Maddie thought, to have the Christmas tree there glittering with baubles and the season's white hangings. Just right for a wedding. The steady flames of the Advent candles pierced the gloom. The carved angels looked down from the roof, silently plucking their lutes and singing with joy.

Lyle took his place in front, Philip, his best man, next to him, checking in his top pocket for the ring. How handsome they both looked, Maddie thought proudly, watching them whisper to one another from the pew behind, Lyle's tawny head against Philip's reddish brown one, Lyle in a grey suit with matching tie, Philip trim in his uniform. The cousins had grown closer over the past months and she was thankful.

'The bride's late,' Gussie remarked to her over Sarah and Grace's heads.

'Brides are always late,' Maddie smiled back. 'It's to keep the groom on his toes!'

Just then the organ creaked into life with bright

discordance and she looked behind her hopefully. There was Susie, entering the church with her father, in a fetching blue coat and hat and red lipstick. She drew off her gloves as she slipped into a back pew and Maddie caught the sparkle of her sapphire ring. It had been a surprise when two weeks after Lyle's announcement Susie had declared herself engaged to the new doctor who'd given Philip a lift to Knyghton on the evening of his return. They'd met apparently at a local musical recital and were to marry in the spring.

And now the bridal march staggered into action. 'Stand up, girls,' Maddie whispered, as the rest of the congregation rose to their feet. Necks craned and there was a collective gasp as the bride appeared at the end of the aisle. Tears of happiness sprang into Maddie's eyes for Anna looked simply radiant, the dove-grey frock of Mrs Clairmont's that Maddie had adjusted for her a perfect fit and her face full of shy joy.

Behind her and slightly to each side Nadya and Milo walked solemnly behind their mother as she progressed down the aisle towards Lyle, who now stood at the foot of the altar steps smiling to welcome her. When she reached his side he put out his hand and squeezed hers. Nadya drew her brother back to the seats appointed to them and the rector beamed at the congregation then peered over his service book and smiled at the couple. The music squeaked to a halt and he began: 'Dearly beloved . . .'

In the drawing room of the rectory where a small party of friends and relatives gathered afterwards everyone agreed what a beautiful service it had been. It was a shame that there could be no Polish family from Anna's side and that she couldn't even contact them to tell them what had happened, but the rector had inserted a special prayer for them. Anna had asked Mr Clairmont to leave out the question about being 'given away'. It wasn't appropriate for a widow with children, she told him firmly.

When Lyle had conveyed the news that Anna had agreed to marry him, the other Andersons had been open-mouthed with surprise because he'd kept the courtship so secret. He'd taken to Anna as soon as he'd first met her, he told them, and been enchanted by her children. Lately he'd been taking Milo fishing in the village stream and had developed quite a rapport with the child.

Looking back, Maddie saw that the events engendered by Philip's return and the bonds that had solved his financial problems had finally settled something in Lyle and he'd come to realize where his path to true happiness lay. Not with Susie or Maddie, but with the lovely Polish widow who radiated kindness and who, like him, carried a heavy burden of sorrow.

Maddie watched them together cutting the ersatz cake, Lyle open-faced and laughing as she'd never seen him before. They were well suited, she thought. And Anna had even charmed Gussie.

'She reminds me of my dear great-auntie,' Anna had confided in her sadly. Another relative whose fate Anna did not know. Maddie, who'd once tried and failed to imagine Susie living with them at Knyghton, was relieved all over again that Lyle was marrying Anna instead.

As for Maddie, she'd politely offered to find somewhere else to live while Philip was away, after he'd been called back to his regiment in October, but Lyle and Anna would have none of it. They must remain with them at Knyghton. There were several more bedrooms that could be opened up and, remarkably, Mrs Flegg's widowed elder sister had declared her wish to move in with the Fleggs and was quickly engaged by Lyle to assist with light housework. Somehow they would get by. Grace was already spending a lot of time with Milo and they'd both start school in the autumn. Maddie had a new contract to illustrate a sequel to the last book she'd worked on, and had secretly started to write a story of her own for older children about the adventures of a young evacuee in wartime. She'd not yet shown it to anyone, but she had the girl's face firmly fixed in her mind – Flora as she imagined she had looked as an eight-year-old child.

Maddie felt Philip's hand on her shoulder and turned to smile at him, only to read the sober message in his face. 'I'm afraid my taxi's here,' he murmured.

'I wish you could stay longer,' she whispered, brushing his cheek with her hand. She watched him saying his goodbyes, dear Philip, bending to kiss Sarah and Grace.

'Do as your mother tells you,' he said. 'I'll be back again soon, I'm sure.' They'd been lucky so far. He'd been stationed in Scotland, training new recruits. Maddie hoped against hope that this was where he would stay. For a good while yet, anyway. He'd been lucky to have his leave extended beyond Christmas to attend the wedding and now time had run out. Together they went out to where the taxi waited in the drive. As the driver stowed Philip's case and overcoat in the boot of the vehicle, Philip and Maddie stood together in a close embrace.

'Don't do anything brave, will you, Philip? You've proved yourself already. Think of us here.'

'You must be positive, darling. It's more hopeful now that America's in it with us.'

'Every time you come home it's harder to say goodbye all over again.'

He laughed. 'I take it you'd still rather I came home?'

'Don't be silly.' Despite her misery she smiled. He kissed her soundly before letting her go.

She watched, hands in pockets, as the taxi spluttered away down the drive in a cloud of exhaust fumes and was gone and wondered as she did each time if she would ever see him again.

And as she did each time she regretted that they hadn't spent more time together, just the two of them, that they hadn't talked more. After that first night Philip had rarely spoken about what had happened in France. It had marked him, that was clear. He was quicker to anger, he startled at loud noises, slept restlessly, whispered broken words as he tossed and turned, words she could never quite hear. The war had changed him. It had changed them all. It had picked them up and thrown them about and left them to lie where it willed. One day it would end. *We must have hope that it will be soon,* she thought as she turned to go back inside.

London

Autumn 1977

Grace glanced up from her reverie as the door of the café opened. Her eyes widened as a woman entered in a draught of cool air. A flame of auburn hair, pale skin, that furrowed frown as she gazed about ... Grace would have known her even without the photograph. She rose trembling to her feet.

'Marguerite.' Her voice was hoarse with emotion.

'Grace.' The frown was replaced by a smile as the woman stepped forward and they briefly shook hands. 'I am sorry that I am late.' She spoke with a musical lilt. 'So many people. What is happening?'

'There's a protest march against racism.'

'Ah oui, we should have joined them maybe.' Marguerite folded her elegant camel coat over the back of the chair opposite and sat down.

'You're probably right. I've started tea, I'm afraid, but I'll order more. Or coffee if you'd prefer. The cakes aren't very special ...' *Grace wished she could stop gabbling, but Marguerite, leaning on the table, chin in hand, was smiling as she listened.*

'English tea would be very nice,' she said. When the waitress had come and gone Marguerite said, 'Oh, Grace, I am so pleased to meet you.'

'And I you. I'm sorry. It's still a bit of a shock for our family. My sister Sarah . . . it's harder for her than for me.'

'I understand. Please don't apologize. I'm lucky. I've always known who my father was, you see, and also that he did not know that I existed.'

'I'm sorry that you found us too late.' How would her father have reacted to hear he had another child? With horror? Embarrassment? They would never know. Grace's father had been dead for five years and it was her mother who was left bearing the brunt of the news.

When the letter addressed in a foreign hand to 'Lieutenant Philip Anderson' had arrived at his widow's London flat via the office of his old regiment, naturally Maddie had opened it. The contents had shocked her so deeply that she forgot about the pie in the oven, which burned to a cinder, and had to cancel the afternoon's meeting with her publisher. The letter, in fluent English, informed her that her beloved husband had had an affair with a woman named Sophie whom he'd met in France during the war. And he had never told her. And now here was a Marguerite Vernier – her married name – a translator living in Dijon, purporting to be Philip's daughter. Marguerite supplied details that only her mother, Sophie – still living – could have told her and Maddie had been forced to believe the story.

It had been so hard for them all to come to terms with. For a long time Grace hated the woman. Why had she ruined their memories of their father? Couldn't she have kept quiet? But as letters and photographs had passed between them over a period of six months she'd begun to like the sound of her new half-sister. It had been Marguerite who'd suggested that they all meet. She'd always wanted to visit London. Grace cautiously agreed, but Maddie did not feel ready and Sarah adamantly refused to have anything to do with it.

Marguerite was lovely, Grace thought now as they drank their tea and talked. Close up she saw there were white threads in the auburn, but her hair was still luxuriant and beautifully cut, not in a trendy style, but something more timeless. Her clothes were classic as well – designer label probably, well-tailored. Grace, slim in her flared skirt and gypsy blouse felt unsophisticated in comparison, but she sensed that Marguerite didn't mind about such things. Instead the woman spoke of growing up after the Nazis had left, the continuing shortage of food, the vicious reprisals on collaborators. Her uncle, Sophie's brother, had returned from forced labour in a German factory in the Ruhr and taken over the farm. When Marguerite was seven Sophie married a government official from Dijon, where in due course Marguerite had studied English at the university and met her husband, Gilbert, an architect. She and Gilbert were happily married with two teenage sons.

'They, too, had always wanted to visit London.' Marguerite's eyes sparkled. 'They love the pop music.'

'You brought the boys with you?' Grace asked, grinning.

'Yes. Gilbert has taken them straight to the hotel, but . . .' Here Marguerite blushed. 'I hope you will not mind, but they will come here to the café soon. They want to meet their aunt!'

'Of course,' stammered Grace, overwhelmed. 'I don't mind at all.'

'Are you certain?'

'Very.' Things were progressing so quickly, but she was curious to meet them, this side of the family that had appeared out of the blue.

'I wish we could meet Sarah. I always wanted a sister and now I have two!'

'Maybe one day,' Grace said gently. 'It's different for her. She remembers our father from before the war and when he was away I think she missed him the most. I resented it when he came back. In 1946, he was finally demobbed. Apart from a few months in 1941 I had no memory of him, you see, but when he returned for good everything changed. We'd been living at Knyghton – Uncle Lyle's house in Norfolk – but Dad made us move back to London for his job. I missed Nadya and Milo, Aunt Anna's children – she'd been married before – and our new baby cousin, Johnny. I missed my school and the animals, our Great-Aunt Gussie, who died soon after, and the dear Fleggs who looked after us. Sarah minded leaving too, but not as much as me. She remembered London and I didn't.'

'Yet you live in London now?'

'Oh, yes, I came to love it.'

'And your mother, Maddie? In one of your letters you wrote that Philip never told her about his affair with my mother.'

Grace offered Marguerite the cake plate, which was politely refused, but it bought time to think about her reply. She said carefully, 'That's why my mother was so surprised to hear from you. She said something about her and Dad having agreed a long time ago to have "no more secrets" between them, whatever she meant by that. The worst thing is that Dad's dead so she can't confront him about it. She feels betrayed, I suppose.'

Marguerite looked gravely back at her and she nodded. 'And do you feel that, too? That our father betrayed you?'

Grace shrugged. 'A little.' Then she smiled. 'But it's hardly your *fault, is it, what our parents did? And I'm glad that I've met you and sorry that you didn't have a chance to know Dad.'*

'That's my fault for leaving it so late. Maman wouldn't have minded if I had tried to find him, but I never wanted to. He'd never been a part of my life. But she's getting old and my stepfather is dead. She often speaks of Philip now – I believe that she loved him very much – so I told myself that it was time. Grace, if ever you or Sarah visit France I hope you'll come to Dijon. It would mean the world to her.'

Grace smiled. 'I'd like to do that,' she said.

It was at that moment that the door shot open and three tall figures jostled their way inside. A rangy, smiley man in a trim suit and two surly-looking teenage boys, both with their mother's gorgeous colour hair, and Philip's narrow face. The women rose from their chairs and everyone was introduced – Gilbert, Jean-Marie and François. The boys' expressions turned to friendly curiosity as they shook hands with their Aunt Grace.

Jean-Marie, the elder, spoke in French to his mother and she laughed and explained to Grace, 'The boys want to know if your mother really is Madeleine Anderson, the famous children's writer?'

'Yes,' said Grace, 'she is. Have they read her books?'

'All,' François said and grinned.

'When they were younger, of course. She is very well known in France.'

'I think that will help us in our cause,' Grace said, her eyes sparkling. 'Mum always loves meeting her readers.'

She knew her mother would come round eventually for she was such a generous and loving person, so positive and brave. She'd supported their father in the dark days after the war when the German

Kommandant had been tried for the murder of Philip's comrades and Philip's testimony had helped secure the man's conviction. As for Grace, she wanted one day to retrace her father's footsteps through France, and it was wonderful to think that Sophie, Marguerite and their family would be there to help her. Maybe she would even write a book about it.

Author's Note and Acknowledgements

Philip Anderson's story is fictional, but it is inspired by historical events. Most of us are familiar with the events at Dunkirk in May 1940, when in Operation Dynamo, a great flotilla of boats great and small arrived to rescue 300,000 stranded Allied soldiers from the beach where they'd been cornered by the victorious German forces. Less well known is what happened to those left behind. Many were captured and marched to prisoner-of-war camps in Germany, but many hundreds also escaped and tried to make their own way to safety down through France and neutral Spain. It wasn't long before a number of undercover resistance networks sprang up to assist them and Reverend Donald Caskie in Marseilles was a key figure in one of these. It was incredibly dangerous work and impossible to know whom to trust in that city full of spies. Every kind of adventure imaginable is told about the Allied evaders and those who helped them in *Home Run: Escape from Nazi Europe* by John

Nichol and Tony Rennell and in Caskie's own memoir, *The Tartan Pimpernel*.

There really were atrocities after Dunkirk such as the one Philip survived. The most notorious is the massacre at Le Paradis in the Pas-de-Calais region, a war crime committed on 27 May 1940 by members of the 14th Company, SS Division Totenkopf, under the command of Hauptsturmführer Fritz Knöchlein.

Soldiers mainly of the 2nd Battalion, the Royal Norfolk Regiment had become separated from their unit. They occupied and defended a farmhouse against an attack by Waffen-SS forces in the village of Le Paradis. After running out of ammunition, the British troops surrendered to the Germans, who led them across the road to a wall where they were mowed down by machine-gun fire and finished off with bayonets and pistols. Ninety-seven British soldiers were killed. Two survived, with injuries, and hid until they were captured by German forces several days later.

After the war, Knöchlein was convicted by a war crimes court, with the two survivors acting as witnesses against him. He was executed in 1949.

There are memorials in the locality of Le Paradis and in Norwich Cathedral Close to the ninety-seven soldiers who died.

I am grateful as ever to my wonderful agent, Sheila Crowley, and to Sabhbh Curran and their colleagues at Curtis Brown Literary Agency for all their hard work on my behalf. At Simon & Schuster I wish to thank my marvellous editor

Suzanne Baboneau, Ian Chapman, Louise Davies, Sophie Morgan, Sara-Jade Virtue, Rhiannon Carroll, Amy Fulwood, Gill Richardson, Dominic Brendon, Sian Wilson and all their colleagues as well as Sally Partington for her excellent copy-editing and Anne O'Brien for proofreading.

My thanks and love as ever to David, Felix, Benjy and Leo, who help me more than they know.